WAITING FOR LOVE

GANSETT ISLAND SERIES, BOOK 8

MARIE FORCE

Waiting for Love
Gansett Island Series, Book 8

By: Marie Force
Published by HTJB, Inc.
Copyright 2013. HTJB, Inc.
Cover Design by Diane Luger
Print Layout Isabel Sullivan
E-book Formatting Fairies
ISBN: 978-1-942295-23-5

marieforce.com

View the McCarthy Family Tree here. marieforce.com/gansett/familytree/

View the list of Who's Who on Gansett Island here. marieforce.com/whoswhogansett/

View a map of Gansett Island. marieforce.com/mapofgansett/

The Gansett Island Series

Book 1: Maid for Love *(Mac & Maddie)*
Book 2: Fool for Love *(Joe & Janey)*
Book 3: Ready for Love *(Luke & Sydney)*
Book 4: Falling for Love *(Grant & Stephanie)*
Book 5: Hoping for Love *(Evan & Grace)*
Book 6: Season for Love *(Owen & Laura)*
Book 7: Longing for Love *(Blaine & Tiffany)*
Book 8: Waiting for Love *(Adam & Abby)*
Book 9: Time for Love *(David & Daisy)*
Book 10: Meant for Love *(Jenny & Alex)*
Book 10.5: Chance for Love, *A Gansett Island Novella (Jared & Lizzie)*
Book 11: Gansett After Dark *(Owen & Laura)*
Book 12: Kisses After Dark *(Shane & Katie)*
Book 13: Love After Dark *(Paul & Hope)*
Book 14: Celebration After Dark *(Big Mac & Linda)*
Book 15: Desire After Dark *(Slim & Erin)*
Book 16: Light After Dark *(Mallory & Quinn)*
Book 17: Victoria & Shannon (Episode 1)
Book 18: Kevin & Chelsea (Episode 2)
A Gansett Island Christmas Novella
Book 19: Mine After Dark *(Riley & Nikki)*
Book 20: Yours After Dark *(Finn McCarthy)*
Book 21: Trouble After Dark *(Deacon & Julia)*

More new books are alway in the works. For the most up-to-date list of what's available from the Gansett Island Series as well as series extras, go to marieforce.com/gansett.

For Julie and the eight-year job interview—we did it! We really did it!

CHAPTER 1

"*I*'m absolutely, positively, totally and *completely* done with men," the woman sitting behind Adam McCarthy announced—loudly—to everyone on the noon ferry to Gansett Island. "Done, done, *done*."

The voice was familiar, so Adam sat up taller, hoping to overhear enough to figure out who she was without having to get involved.

"I've followed two men to the ends of the earth and regretted it both times. From now on, I'm off men. You heard it here first."

A slight slur to her words had him wondering if she'd been drinking. *Who cares? What business is it of yours? Ignore her.*

"Did I mention I'm *done* with men?"

Adam had no idea who she was talking to, and figuring that out would require him to turn around. And there was no way he was turning around. He had his own problems and no desire to take on someone else's, even if it was possible that he knew her. He knew a lot of people. That didn't mean he had to jump to their rescue when they were on the verge of making fools of themselves.

With the day stormy and the seas rough, the woman played to a captive audience inside the crowded cabin. Adam was used to rough rides. He'd been taking the ferry all his life. Others weren't so fortunate, and the distinctive sound of barfing soon filled the airless cabin.

Rough seas and rocking boats had never made him sick. The smell of vomit, however... No one was immune to that. He got up and told himself to get out of there. Walk to the door and the fresh air... But curiosity got the better of him, and he made the huge mistake of turning around.

His mouth fell open when he saw his brother Grant's ex-girlfriend Abby Callahan scrambling for the garbage can.

While she was violently ill, Adam stood paralyzed with indecision. She hadn't seen him, so he could still get out of there unscathed. And then, as if Adam had conjured him from a dream, Big Mac McCarthy's voice sounded in his conscience, warning of dire consequences if Adam walked away from a family friend in her time of need.

Not for the first time in his adult life, Adam cursed the values his father had hammered into him and his brothers from the time they were young boys.

He took a deep breath he instantly regretted due to the pervasive smell of vomit filling the cabin, choked back a wave of nausea, walked toward her, took her by the arm and escorted her outside.

Naturally, she fought him off. "What do you think you're doing?" Her words were garbled and slurred, and she smelled as if she'd spilled an entire bottle of eighty-proof something or other on her clothes.

"Did you sleep in a bar last night?" he asked when they were outside and both taking deep, gulping breaths of cold, damp, fresh air.

"Adam," she gasped when she realized who he was. "No, I did *not* sleep in a bar. I had two drinks on the plane this morning, and the man in the next seat spilled his tequila all over me."

Adam cringed at the thought of tequila for breakfast. Those days were a distant memory. "As I recall, you don't drink."

She wobbled when the boat pitched violently to the side, and he steadied her with a hand to her arm. "I had an occasional glass of wine," she said as she pushed him away. "I'm all done being a nice girl who does what everyone expects of her. I'm going to drink and party

2

and curse like a sailor and have sex with strangers and…" Her chin began to quiver.

"Don't you dare cry."

"I'll cry if I want to. I'll do any damned thing I want."

"Since you're new to swearing, you might consider adding a 'god' in there." She seemed to have no idea what he meant, so he elaborated. "*God*damned is a lot more hard-core than plain old damned."

Her eyes were big and brown and shiny with unshed tears. "Are you making fun of me?" she asked, incredulous. "Feel free. My day can't get any worse. My *life* can't get any worse, so do *your* worst."

"What're you even doing here? Don't you live in Texas now?"

"Not anymore." Her chin trembled violently, and tears spilled from her eyes as if someone had turned on a faucet.

Adam was instantly sorry he'd asked. Mascara ran down her blotchy face as she sniffed and sobbed. Because he was too much of a gentleman not to, he patted her shoulder and muttered a soothing word or two, all the while wishing the deck would open up and swallow him.

He'd had a hellish few days of his own and didn't need to take on anyone else's problems. In the midst of a professional implosion the likes of which he'd never imagined possible, he'd received word from home that his brothers were missing in a boating accident. Thankfully, they'd all been found safe, but Adam wouldn't be completely at ease until he saw them with his own eyes.

As for Abby, the last he'd heard, she was engaged to the island's former doctor, Cal Maitland, and living with him in his home state of Texas. Adam took a surreptitious glance at her left hand and didn't see a ring. Uh-oh. Even as he wondered what'd happened between her and her fiancé, he didn't dare risk more tears by asking.

"I'm homeless at the moment," she said after a long period of silence as the boat bobbed and weaved through the surf.

Retching noises from the deck above had Adam pulling Abby back from the rail, just in time to avoid a direct hit.

The momentum propelled her into his arms. She pressed her face into his shirt and broke down into sobs.

for God's sake! Why had he turned around back in the cabin?

ad he allowed himself to get sucked into this situation? None or ...t mattered now that he was firmly *in* the situation. Because he'd known her all his life, because she'd very nearly married his brother, he put his arms around her and patted her back. "It'll be okay."

"No, it won't." She sniffed and seemed to be using his shirt as a tissue. Lovely. "It's never going to be okay again."

"That's not true," Adam said, though he tended to agree with her. He'd had the same feeling repeatedly in the forty-eight hours since his world blew up in his face.

"It is true. All I ever wanted was to fall in love with a wonderful man, get married, have a family and maybe a career that satisfied me. Now I have nothing. I gave up my business for him! Do you *know* how successful Abby's Attic was?"

"I heard it was very popular."

"I made a quarter of a million bucks there last year, and I walked away from it like it meant nothing to me. All for a man who wasn't worth my time."

While Adam knew he should at least attempt to defend mankind, he was stuck on the money. "You made a *quarter million* dollars selling T-shirts?"

"And toys. There's big money in toys, especially when you're the only toy store on the island," she said, hiccupping loudly. Her hand covered her mouth. "Oh my. Excuse me." This was followed by another hiccup, louder than the first, and more tears. "My life is a mess."

He shouldn't ask. It was none of his business. And yet… "What happened with Cal?"

She used her own sleeve—thankfully—to wipe her nose and eyes, which smeared the mascara into dark smudges under her eyes. "His ex-girlfriend happened. Apparently, he's not completely over her, or some such baloney."

"You mean bullshit."

"What?"

4

"If you're going to swear now, you want to say bullshit rather than baloney."

"Oh, right. Yes, it's a big pile of bullshit."

"Much better."

That drew a tentative smile from her.

"So what's the deal with the ex?"

"She comes sashaying up to him every time she sees him and makes sure to flip her fake blonde hair and bat her fake eyelashes and rest her fake boobs on his arm, and he acts like it's no big deal that she's *totally* flirting with him. This goes on for weeks. She's over at the house every day, supposedly to check on his sick mother because they're *so very close*, you see, but really it's all about more chances to hang all over Cal. I finally got sick of it and confronted him about it. That's when..." Her chin quivered anew, but she managed to blink back the tears this time. "That's when he admitted he still thinks about her. *Candy*. Her name is *Candy*! Can you stand that? She makes me sick. It's all so...so..."

Nearly breathless with anticipation, Adam raised his brows.

"Screwed up," she said.

He shook his head. "You can do better."

"I can't."

"Yes, you can. You're a whole new woman now, remember?"

Her face turned bright red, and in that moment, he discovered she was rather adorable, raccoon eyes and all. "Fucked up," she whispered, turning a deeper shade of scarlet as the curse passed her lips.

Adam rewarded her with a big smile. "Now we're getting some-where." The ferry passed the buoy that marked the island's northern coast, but the mist was so thick he could barely make out the bluffs. "So you really think you can have sex with strangers?"

The question clearly caught her off guard. "Of course I can."

"I don't think you can. You're not that kind of girl."

"How do you know what kind of girl I am?" she asked, indignant.

"Um, you dated my brother for ten years. I think I have a slight idea."

"You don't know me at all. He never knew me either. No one does."

"Abby... Come on, that's not true. You and Grant were the real deal for a long time."

She shook her head. "No, we weren't. I thought we were—I thought Cal and I were, too, but I've never had the real deal." Turning her big eyes up at him, she said, "Have you?"

The question hit him like an arrow to the heart. "I thought so until recently, but no, I haven't either."

"What happened to you?"

Adam smiled and shook his head. "Not worth talking about."

"I told you all my bad stuff," she said between persistent hiccups. "It seems only fair that you tell me yours."

Adam hadn't intended to tell anyone at home about what'd happened in New York. He'd planned to see his brothers, make sure they were okay, check on his parents and get back to the city to resurrect his career before the damage became irreparable. But here was Abby looking up at him with her liquid brown eyes, and suddenly the whole sordid tale was pouring out of him. When he was done, she stared at him, openmouthed, until a hiccup lurched her out of the trance.

"That's... It's... It's *horrible.*"

He tilted his head, urging her silently to try again.

"Seriously fucked up." This was said with no hint of whisper or blush, which made Adam want to cheer. "How long had you been seeing her outside of work?"

"Seeing her for three years, living with her for two of them."

"And no one at work knew?"

"Nope. My own company policy of no fraternizing at work had come back to bite me in the ass, so we went way out of our way to keep it quiet. From what I can gather, one of the employees saw us somewhere, and we were...we were kissing...and reported us to the board. The funniest part, if you can consider any of this funny, is that it all came down to a dentist appointment."

"How do you mean?"

"The chairman of the board called both of us. I was at the dentist. She was at the office and took the call. Before I was out of the chair, she'd accepted a deal to force me out of the company I founded. I'd lost my company and my girlfriend in the time it took to get my teeth cleaned. Hilarious, huh?"

"No," she said, her tone hushed and the hiccups gone. "It's not funny at all."

"It's kinda funny." He hated to think what he might do if he didn't laugh.

"I'm sorry that happened to you, Adam." Her hand on his arm was strangely comforting. He'd felt very alone during the last few unbelievable days. "You've worked so hard to build that company."

"Fourteen years, and the only mistake I made was taking on a partner four years ago." He leaned against the rail as the breakwater for South Harbor came into view. "You know what the best part is?"

"What's that?"

"I'm the only one with the first clue about the actual work we do. She runs the business side. I oversee the technical end. She and the board have no idea what they're in for without me there to take care of the technical stuff. I'd love to be a fly on the wall."

"They'll be begging you to come back in no time at all."

"Probably."

"Will you go?"

He shook his head. "I gave that company everything I had, and this is the thanks I get? They can kiss my ass."

"I don't blame you for being bitter. You got royally screwed—in more ways than one."

"Yep."

"So what'll you do now?"

"I'm not sure exactly. After the accident, I wanted to come home and see my brothers—"

Her eyes went wide. "What accident?"

"You didn't hear about the sailboat in Race Week that got hit by the freighter? All three of my brothers and Grant's friend Dan were on the boat."

"Oh my God! Are they all right?"

7

"They will be. Grant and Dan got the worst of it, but Mac and Evan were fine."

Abby looked like she might be sick again, so he nudged her closer to the rail. "Take some deep breaths."

She did as he directed while blinking rapidly. "It's been over between Grant and me for a while now, but to hear he could've died..." The hand she rested over her heart said it all.

"Believe me, I've had some rough moments of my own since I got that news from my parents. It was a very close call. All three of my brothers." He shuddered just thinking about what could've happened.

The next thing he knew, she was hugging him, tightly, and it felt really good to have the arms of an old friend around him. And then he felt her breasts pressed against his chest, and his mind went blank. She was no longer an old friend—or his brother's ex-girlfriend— offering comfort. Rather, she was a sexy, curvy woman who fit perfectly in his arms and had awfully nice breasts, too. Had he ever noticed that before? Not that he could recall. She'd always been Grant's girl, so he hadn't looked too closely.

Adam released her and stepped back, noticing how shiny her dark hair was. He wondered if it was as soft and silky as it looked.

Surprised by his abrupt retreat, Abby stumbled, forcing him to reach out and steady her. With his hands on her shoulders and her gaze once again focused on him, Adam had to remind himself that this was *Abby*. She'd nearly been his brother's *wife*. He withdrew his hands from her shoulders and was thankful when the ferry passed through the breakwater into South Harbor.

They stood side by side at the rail as the ferry backed up to the pier and the cars began to drive onto the island.

"You won't tell anyone, will you?" she asked in a small voice after a long period of awkward silence.

"Of course not. You won't either, right?"

She shook her head. "If you need to talk to someone who knows what's going on, I'll be at the Beachcomber."

"Not at your folks' place?"

"No way. My mother told me I was a fool to give up a successful business to chase after yet another man. The last thing I need right now is her reminding me every day that I can't trust my own judgment when it comes to men."

"Well, I'll be at my parents' place for a day or two while I figure out what's next if you need someone to talk to."

"That's nice of you. Thanks, Adam. Thanks for everything. You've been really...nice."

"I know everything seems awful right now—for both of us—but this has got to be the worst of it, right?"

"If you say so," she said with a weary sigh as they took the stairs single file to the lower deck.

Since he had only a backpack, he helped her with two of her three suitcases, dragging them up the hill from the ferry landing and across the street to the Beachcomber Hotel. A bellman came down the stairs to assist with her luggage.

"You'll be okay?" Adam asked.

"Sure. I'm a survivor. It's how I roll."

If only she didn't look so devastated, he might've bought that line. He cuffed her chin playfully. "Hang in there."

"You, too."

Adam walked away, heading in the direction of his parents' North Harbor home. At the corner, he glanced back to find Abby exactly where he'd left her, looking up the steep staircase to the Beachcomber, as if seeking the fortitude to move forward.

CHAPTER 2

*O*n the way through town, Adam noted the Sand & Surf Hotel was back open for business with flags flying and the deck full of guests enjoying rocking chairs that overlooked South Harbor. The sight of the iconic hotel open again made him smile. He couldn't wait to see his cousin Laura and hear all about the renovations his brother Mac had overseen with his business partner, Luke Harris.

A second sign announced Stephanie's Bistro, which was also now open inside the hotel. Adam had heard rave reviews about the grand opening of Grant's fiancée's restaurant and looked forward to eating there while he was home.

He took a small detour to his sister Janey's house to see if she was around. He knocked on the door, waited a long time and was about to move on when he heard feet shuffling inside.

His hugely pregnant younger sister let out a squeal of delight when she saw him on her front porch. "What're you doing here? Come in!"

Adam dropped his backpack on the porch and pulled open the screen door. "I'd give you a hug, brat, but I don't think I could get my arms around you."

"Please try," she said, her eyes filling as she reached for him.

As he'd already had more than his share of emotional women for one day, he did his best to hug his sister around the enormously pregnant belly. Her menagerie of special-needs dogs and cats circled around their feet, sniffing him thoroughly. Over Janey's shoulder, he noticed her German shepherd, Riley, who sat apart from the others, eyeing him suspiciously—as usual. "No one told me you were having quadruplets," he said, glancing at her extremely swollen abdomen.

"Shut up. It's not funny."

"Yes, it is."

"Maybe a little funny," she conceded. "So what're you doing home?"

"I needed to see the boys, and you and Mom and Dad. Is everyone okay?"

"They will be, but what an awful day that was. I can't even tell you…"

He put his arm around her and planted a kiss on the top of her blonde head. "I know what you mean. That was one of the worst phone calls of my entire life."

"What would we have done—"

"Don't, Janey. Please. Don't even go there."

"You're right. Nothing good will come of that." She subtly swept away a tear. "Sorry, I'm an emotional disaster area lately."

"Carrying quads will do that to a girl."

She play punched him in the belly, putting a little more muscle behind it than usual.

"Um, ow. That hurt."

"Good. It was supposed to. I can't believe you're here right now when I was just about to call you." She took him by the hand and dragged him to her desk where her laptop was open. "I'm trying to register for fall classes, and it's not working. I don't know what I'm doing wrong. Maybe it's a sign."

"Of what?" Adam asked as he let her push him into the desk chair.

"That I'm not meant to go back to school."

"What the heck are you talking about?"

"Do you promise not to tell anyone? That means *anyone*."

"Yes, I promise."

11

She nibbled on her thumbnail. "I don't want to go back to school."

"Janey—"

"I want to be a mom. I want to take care of my baby. Joe has the business, so we don't need the money."

Adam took her hand and squeezed it. "Janey, stop. *Stop.*" He waited until he was sure he had her attention. "Do you remember the conversation we had after 9-11 when I told you I didn't want to live in the city anymore?"

"Vaguely."

"I remember it like it was yesterday. You told me I'd just been through a traumatic thing, and it wasn't a good idea to make big decisions after something like that. Do you remember?"

"It's starting to come back to me now."

"What you said made a lot of sense, and it kept me from making an impulsive move based solely on emotion."

"I'm glad I was able to help you, but what's that got to do with me?"

He rested a hand on her huge belly and received a kick from his niece or nephew. "From what I'm told, this is a pretty traumatic thing for a woman. It wreaks havoc on you physically and emotionally. This might not be the ideal time to be making big decisions."

"Every time I think about leaving the baby for long days at school followed by longer nights of studying, I feel physically ill."

"Who will take care of your baby while you're doing all that?"

"Joe."

"So he or she will have one parent available to him or her all the time, right?"

"I suppose so."

"And what do babies remember about the first year or two of their lives?"

"Not much."

"Don't do anything rash, Janey. You've wanted to be a vet for so long, and you're *so* close. Don't quit now. At least wait until after the baby arrives and see how you feel then."

She released a deep sigh that had Riley nudging at her hand.

Patting his head, she said, "All right. You win. I'll wait to decide anything."

"I don't want you to have regrets later."

"The stupid website won't let me do anything."

Adam put fingers to keyboard to do what he did best. "Ah," he said a couple of minutes later. "Here's your problem. You need an s after the http because it's a secure site."

"A single letter cost me an hour of my life?"

"Welcome to my world." With a few more keystrokes, he had her logged into the course selection area. "There you go."

"You're the best. Thank you. For this and the words of wisdom."

"That's what big brothers are for."

"In my world, they're usually good for little more than four huge pains in my ass."

The comment made him laugh for the first time in days. "It's good to see you, brat."

"You, too. Mom and Dad will be thrilled to have you home. Oh, and I'm sure Mom will throw a welcome-home dinner, which means I won't have to cook tonight. Yay."

"Glad I could help you out. Hey, so guess who I saw on the ferry?"

"Who?"

"Abby."

Janey's eyes widened at the mention of her close friend. "Are she and Cal here for a visit? She never said a word to me about coming home."

"Not exactly. Apparently, things with Cal are kaput."

"Are you *shitting* me?"

"Nope. She was tipsy on the ferry and telling everyone she is done with men—permanently."

"Oh my goodness! She hardly drinks at all, so things must be really bad if she'd drinking during the day. Where's she staying?"

"At the Beachcomber until she finds a place."

"I'd better get over there and check on her."

"Might be a good idea. She's in pretty rough shape." Adam took a minute to scratch the ears of each of Janey's pets, which he knew his

13

sister would appreciate. "So where are Grant and Stephanie living these days?"

"On Shore Point Road. Number twenty-two. They bought the place from Ned. You might want to stop and see Grant on the way to Mom and Dad's. We're all a little worried about him. He's not bouncing back as fast as the others from the accident."

"What's going on?"

"No one knows, not even Stephanie. He won't talk about it."

"I'll go by there." He kissed her forehead. "And I'll see you later at dinner."

She hugged him tightly. "I'm so happy you're here."

As Adam left his sister's house, he realized he was happy to be home where everyone in his life was exactly what they appeared to be —loving, comical, often exasperating and, most important of all, loyal. He'd discovered in the past week there was a lot to be said for loyalty.

Grant's new place was between Janey's and their parents' house but required a slight detour down Shore Point Road. The two-story saltbox sat at the end of a crushed-shell driveway that crunched beneath Adam's feet. With no cars in the driveway, it was hard to tell if anyone was home, but Adam knocked on the door anyway. When no one answered, Adam tried the door and found it unlocked. He ducked his head inside. "Hey, Grant! Are you home?"

Still no answer.

Figuring to see his second-oldest brother at dinner, Adam pulled the door closed and headed back to the road.

"Adam?"

Halfway down the driveway, Adam turned to find Grant standing on the front porch. Even from a distance, Adam could see that his brother looked like hell. His hair was standing on end, he hadn't shaved in days, and, most alarming of all, his blue eyes seemed sunken into the face his brothers had always teasingly called pretty-boy handsome.

Filled with trepidation, Adam returned to the house and dropped his backpack at the foot of the stairs.

"What're you doing here?" Grant asked, scrubbing a hand over his sleepy-looking face.

It was after one o'clock, and he'd still been sleeping? Adam thought.

"This," Adam said as he took the stairs and hugged his brother. "It's really good to see you."

"Ah, yeah, you, too," Grant said as he made a halfhearted effort to return Adam's hug.

Adam was strangely unable to let go. "You guys scared the shit out of us."

"We're okay." Grant hugged him tighter for a moment and then released him. "Come on in."

Despite what Grant said, Adam could see that his brother was not okay. He looked anything but okay. "Where's Stephanie?"

"At the restaurant, I guess. She was gone when I woke up."

If Adam was guessing correctly, Grant had woken up about two minutes ago. "Nice place." Adam took a look around the cozy living room that flowed into a decent-sized kitchen. Boxes were scattered about, some open and others taped closed.

"Thanks. We're still getting unpacked." He opened a cabinet and pulled out a can of coffee, dropping a bag of filters onto the floor, which he bent to retrieve. "Want some coffee?"

"No, thanks. I had the daily allotment hours ago."

"Hmm, is that right? What time is it?"

"After one."

Grant seemed genuinely surprised to hear that. "Really? Wow, that's weird."

"It's not like you to sleep the day away," Adam said tentatively.

Grant shrugged as he scooped coffee, dumped in water and turned on the coffeemaker. "Sleep has been hard to come by the past few days. I'm still trying to catch up."

"It must've been pretty scary. The accident..."

"Yeah."

The one-word answer was alarming to Adam, who knew how much his screenwriter brother loved to tell a good story. "Do you want to talk about it?"

15

"No."

That, too, was odd. The Grant he knew and loved talked about everything—he talked everything to death, in fact.

"How long are you here?" Grant asked, leaning against the counter.

"Couple of days."

"Does Mom know you're home?"

"Not yet."

"You'll make her day. I suppose the rest of us will be required to attend your welcome-home dinner."

"You don't have to if you have other stuff to do."

Grant shrugged again, filling Adam with uneasiness. Under normal circumstances, Grant would've had an insulting zinger waiting on the tip of his tongue. Adam debated whether he should mention that he'd seen Abby and decided not to say anything for now. If something was troubling his brother, he didn't want to pile on by telling him his ex-girlfriend was back on the island—and single again.

"I guess I'd better get to Mom before someone else tells her I'm home."

"Probably a good idea."

"You're sure you're okay?"

"Never better."

Grant said what he thought Adam wanted to hear, but there was something about his eyes, Adam decided. He was not fine, and one way or the other, Adam was determined to figure out what was troubling his older brother.

ABBY STRETCHED out on the bed in the third-floor room she'd managed to secure at the Beachcomber, only because someone had canceled their Race Week reservation at the last minute. She'd been so determined to get home that she hadn't even thought of Race Week, which was the unofficial start of the summer season on Gansett Island.

In her old life running Abby's Attic, this would've been one of the busiest weeks of the year. Thinking about her adorable store and all the hard work she'd put into it had new tears running down her face. Right when she thought she'd run out of tears, she discovered there could be more.

She hated that she'd cried all over Adam McCarthy on the ferry. Mortifying! What he must think of her. What would everyone think of her now that she'd chased after two men only to end up alone?

Why had she come back here of all places? Everyone knew she'd failed to bring Grant McCarthy up to scratch—after *ten* years together, five of them in Los Angeles so he could pursue his screen-writing dream. Now she'd also failed to get Cal Maitland to the altar, despite following him home to Texas after his mother had a stroke. They'd postponed the wedding they'd planned to have on the island last fall and had never again talked about setting a new date. That was one of many reasons why she was back on the island.

She hadn't known where else to go. For better or worse, Gansett Island was home, and if she was going to rebuild her life—again— she'd rather be surrounded by friends, even if some of them were nosy busybodies who'd take far too much pleasure in gossiping about her latest romantic failure.

"Oh, Cal, how did this happen?" she whispered, gazing up at the ceiling. They'd been so happy here on the island, but the minute they relocated to his hometown in Texas, it had fallen apart. Nothing was the same. Their easy relationship had become more complicated by the day until Abby had realized her choice was either to get out of there or spend the rest of her life playing second fiddle to all the other people in his life who got top billing. After years of taking a backseat to Grant's illustrious career, she was unwilling to do that again.

Somewhere out there was a man who'd put her first, who'd treat her the way she deserved to be treated. And if that man didn't exist, then so be it. She'd rather be alone than be treated like a piece of furniture by the man she loved, thus her decision to forgo men completely. That had to be easier than this.

A sob erupted from her chest, reminding her that she'd expected to be married by now—a long time ago, if she were being honest. She'd hoped to be a young mother, and now here she was at thirty-two with nothing more to show for those years than yet another failed relationship.

A knock on the door had her rising, wiping her face on a sleeve already ruined by mascara, and running her fingers through her long dark hair, hoping to bring some order to it.

"Who is it?"

"Janey."

Abby disengaged the lock on the door and opened it to admit her dear friend, Janey McCarthy Cantrell, who was hugely pregnant, and out of breath after climbing three flights of stairs. Seeing her friend pregnant triggered Abby's emotions, and suddenly she was crying her heart out while Janey did her best to provide comfort. The gigantic belly made it impossible for Janey to give hugs, so she did the next best thing by sliding one arm around Abby and easing her into the room, shutting the door behind them.

"There, now, it can't be as bad as all that," Janey said when they were seated side by side on the bed. "Cal is crazy about you. We all saw that."

Unable to speak over the torrent of tears, Abby shook her head.

Janey patted her knee. "Take your time, honey. I'm not going anywhere. I'll stay as long as you need me."

This, Abby realized, was why she'd come home to Gansett. For every vicious gossip, there were five true friends who would prop her up and get her through this latest setback. She took the tissues Janey produced from her purse, wiped her face and blew her nose.

"What happened?" Janey asked gently.

"He… He was different there. *We* were different there. It didn't work."

"I'm so sorry, Abby. I know how happy you were with him."

"We *were* happy—here. The minute we moved off this island, the whole thing fell apart. His ex-girlfriend was hanging around all the time. She's probably thrilled that I left. That's what she was hoping for."

"What did he have to say about it?"

"She's an old family friend. She's worried about his mom. Yada

18

yada. He's so obtuse and refuses to see she was angling for exactly what she got—to get rid of me."

"Why would you give her the satisfaction of leaving him to her?"

"Because it's what he wants, too. I could tell he was having second thoughts about us shortly after I got there. I've been down that road before with your brother, and I had no desire to wait it out again and watch something that was once beautiful end ugly."

"What did Cal say when you told him you were leaving?"

Abby looked down at her hands and realized she'd been shredding the tissue. "I didn't tell him."

"So wait... You just *left*? Without a word to him?"

"I couldn't bear the idea of a big, ugly confrontation. And besides, what did it matter? He's made his choice, so I made mine."

"Abby..."

"I've been gone since early this morning, and he hasn't even called. What does that tell you?"

"I'm sure there's a perfectly good reason—"

"I don't want to talk about him anymore. It's finished, and I'm left to start all over—again."

"Will you reopen the store?"

"I don't know." The very idea of the work that would be involved in getting her store open before the season began was so over-whelming she couldn't even think about it. "Tiffany's store is in my old spot."

"I heard Laura is looking for someone to take on the gift shop in the Sand & Surf. Maybe you could do that this summer and then see what's what next year."

The idea sparked a beat of interest in Abby. She'd have to do something to stay busy. "I'll talk to her about it."

"Good!" Always the eternal optimist, Janey beamed with pleasure at having come up with a plan.

"How're you feeling?" Abby rested her palm on Janey's extended belly and felt a flutter of movement within that had her eyes filling again.

"I'm feeling huge and unwieldy."

"You look beautiful."

"Joe says the same thing, but he sort of has to."

"You're so lucky to have him."

"And I know that. You're going to find your true love, too. I know you are."

Abby shrugged off Janey's certainty. "I don't care about that anymore. I'm going to focus on me for once. I'm going to let loose and do all the things I've never done because I was too busy trying to be the perfect girlfriend, the perfect lady. Enough of that."

Janey eyed her with trepidation. "What's that supposed to mean?"

"I'm not quite sure yet, but this is going to be my summer of rebellion, so look out."

"You're totally freaking me out right now."

"Maybe it's time I freaked everyone out. I spent my twenties waiting for your brother to decide to marry me, and I've spent the first part of my thirties working like a dog and waiting for Cal to marry me. I'd say it's high time I busted loose and let off some steam."

"What does 'letting off some steam' entail, if you don't mind me asking?"

"For one thing, I'm going to start swearing. I plan to do some partying, probably some drinking, and if all goes well, perhaps some sex just for the sake of having sex. No relationship required."

Janey's mouth fell open. "I can't see you doing any of that."

"Because I'm too good to be true. Enough of that…bullshit. It hasn't gotten me any of the things I truly want, so maybe if I'm bad for a while, I'll find what I'm looking for."

"Abby—"

"Don't. Please don't. You can't possibly understand how frustrated I am. You have a husband who absolutely adores you and a baby on the way, a career in the works that's perfect for you. It's all fallen into place for you, Janey."

"It's not all perfect."

"It's pretty damned close."

"Yes, I suppose it is, but still—"

"Don't worry about me. It's high time I shook things up a bit, wouldn't you say?"

"I, um, well... Will you promise me you'll be careful? I'll be so worried about you getting hurt."

"I've already been hurt plenty, and I've survived. I think I can survive one wild summer."

"If you say so," Janey said, but she didn't seem convinced.

The more Abby thought about it, the more certain she became that busting loose for a few months was exactly what she needed to get past this latest setback in her life plan. At the end of the summer, she'd reevaluate where things stood, and maybe then she'd have an idea of what her next step ought to be. Until then, it was high time she had some fun.

WALKING from Grant's house toward North Harbor, Adam nodded to a few people he recognized from around town but didn't stop to talk to anyone. Rather, he stewed over the fact that his brother had seemed so detached and exhausted, as if he hadn't slept properly in days.

Something was terribly wrong, a realization that filled Adam with anxiety. While he didn't see his siblings as often as he'd like to, he talked to them all frequently and knew them as well as he knew anyone. To see one of them deeply troubled over something and working so hard to hide it from everyone was upsetting.

Of course, Grant had just been through a major trauma and was no doubt still reeling from the close call. From what he'd been able to piece together, his brothers had been asked to fill in as crew members on a Race Week boat captained by a guy named Steve Jacobson when the rest of Jacobson's crew had been felled by the stomach flu. The sailboat had been on its way back to the island in deep fog when a freighter hit it. Steve had been killed.

Adam's brothers had spent enough time in the cold Atlantic to suffer from hypothermia. Grant had been hailed for saving the life of his good friend Dan Torrington, who'd been the most seriously injured with broken ribs and a broken arm. Maybe something else had happened that Grant wasn't able to talk about yet.

He'd keep trying, Adam decided, until he wore down his brother and got him to talk about what was troubling him. With no job to return to in New York, he had nothing but time to give one of the most important people in his life. He'd make a nuisance out of himself until it became easier for Grant to talk to him than to put up with him.

Adam smiled. He liked that plan.

"Mac! Hey, Mac, is that you?"

Adam bit back a groan. All his life he'd been mistaken for his oldest brother. Though Mac was three inches taller than him, Adam couldn't deny the striking resemblance between them. He turned to see who had made the mistake this time and saw his Aunt Joan chasing after him. You'd think their own aunt would be able to tell them apart!

"Oh, Adam! I'm so sorry! I didn't hear you were home."

He hugged his aunt and kissed her cheek. Like his mother, her sister was petite and blonde and still pretty well into her sixties. "Nice to see you, Auntie."

"You, too, honey. Your mom will be thrilled to have you home, especially after recent events." Joan shook her head with dismay. "What an awful thing."

"I can't even think about it. How's everyone in your family?"

"Oh, good, you know. Busy with all the little ones. You must be excited about a new niece or nephew coming soon."

"I can't wait. I love being an uncle."

Joan smiled affectionately. "I'm sure they adore you. How long are you here?"

"Not sure yet."

"Well, I won't keep you, but it was lovely to see you."

"You, too." He hugged her again. "Tell my cousins I said hello."

"I'll do that."

Adam walked more swiftly as he covered the last half mile to North Harbor, forgoing a stop at the pharmacy to see Evan and Grace.

With his mother's sister in the know that he was home, he needed to see his mom before Joan called to gloat that she'd seen him first.

The McCarthy's "White House," as the islanders called it, came into view, and Adam accelerated to a jog. He burst through the front door just as the phone rang.

"Of course I knew he was coming," Linda said testily as Adam slid to a stop in the kitchen. She scowled playfully at him and held out a hand to him. "Is that the only reason you called?" Linda paused before she said, "Thank you, Joan. I appreciate that. I'll talk to you soon."

"Sorry," Adam said with a grin as he squeezed her hand. "I ran as fast as I could after I saw her in town."

"No one is faster at spreading island gossip than my dear, darling sister."

"I wanted to surprise you."

Linda hugged him. "And you did. What a wonderful surprise."

Adam returned her embrace, comforted by the scent of home, his mother's familiar perfume and the warmth of her affection. He hadn't realized how badly he needed all of that until he was in her arms. He held on much longer than he normally did now that he was all grown up. He'd been through hell in the last couple of days, thinking about what could've happened to his family if even one of his brothers had been killed in the accident, let alone all three. Not to mention the work calamity at the same time.

When his mother pulled back from him, he was surprised to see tears in the eyes of the normally indomitable Linda McCarthy.

"Sorry," she said, dabbing at her eyes. "I've been a wreck the last few days. I suspect I'm driving your brothers crazy hovering over them."

"You? Drive us crazy? Never."

"Oh, hush up. I promised Dad I wouldn't check on them today, but I'm not sure I can keep that promise."

"How about I do it for you?"

"Oh, Adam! Would you?"

"Sure I will. That's why I'm here. I wanted to do some hovering of my own. Reassure myself they're really okay."

"That'd be such a big help. They're sick of me, but they'll be thrilled to see you."

"Grant didn't seem too thrilled."

"So you saw him already?"

Adam nodded. "On the way over here. He'd just gotten up and looked all disheveled. That's not like him."

Linda frowned at that news. "I've been most concerned about him. Mac and Evan seem fine, but Grant… Something's not right."

Adam took an apple from a bowl on the counter and took a bite. "Did you talk to Stephanie about it?"

"Uh-huh. She agrees he seems off but chalked it up to the long day in the water. Did you know he saved Dan's life?"

"I heard that. Maybe it was more traumatic than he led us to believe."

"How could it not be traumatic? A whole day in freezing water trying to keep one of your best friends alive?" Linda shuddered. "I can't even imagine. Dad has had nightmares about it, not that he admits to them, but he wakes up in a cold sweat just about every night."

Adam hated to hear that but wasn't surprised his softhearted father was suffering from the aftereffects of nearly losing three of his sons. "It's going to take some time, but they'll all be fine. I know it."

"I hope you're right, honey." She hugged him again, even tighter than before. "It's so good to have you here. Thank you for coming. I know how busy you are."

At some point, he'd have to tell them about the business, but one telling of that story was enough for today. "I wouldn't be anywhere else."

Linda released him and checked her watch. "Damn, it's later than I thought. I'm meeting Carolina for lunch in town. Do you want to use my car while you're here?"

"Ah, thanks for that kind offer, but I'll pass."

"I don't know why you boys disparage my little yellow bug the way you do," she said, grabbing her purse as she clucked with dismay.

"Because it's a chick car that none of us would be caught dead in.

I'll borrow Dad's truck." He pushed out his chest and flexed his biceps. "Much more manly."

"Suit yourself. When you see you brothers, invite everyone to dinner. We'll put some steaks on the grill."

"With baked potatoes?" he asked with his most charming grin.

"Naturally," she said, rolling her eyes at him as she kissed his cheek. "All your favorites."

"Have you rented out my old room, or is it okay if I crash up there?"

"It's more than okay. Make yourself comfortable. I'll be back in a little while."

"See you then."

She stopped at the door and turned to him. "I love you so much, Adam, and I'm thrilled you're home."

"Right back atcha, Mom." He was, he realized, indeed thrilled to be home where he was loved and respected and appreciated. After the week he'd had, that was exactly what he needed.

CHAPTER 3

Fortified by her visit with Adam, Linda rushed into town to meet her dear friend, Carolina Cantrell. Since Caro's son Joe had married Janey, the two women had been closer than ever, especially now that they were expecting their first shared grandchild.

Linda arrived at the South Harbor Diner only five minutes late, which wasn't bad, considering she should've left ten minutes earlier than she did. "Sorry, sorry," she said, dropping a kiss on Caro's cheek and sliding in across from her. "Adam was on the noon boat, and he came home just as I was leaving."

"You must've been happy to see him."

"Extremely. He's here to see his brothers after the accident."

Caro shook her head with dismay. "It's all I think about. How close we came to utter catastrophe."

"I can't even let myself go there. When I think about poor Steve's family and what they must be going through..."

"He was so young."

"The same age as Evan. It's unbearable. I've been thinking about reaching out to his mother, but I don't know what to say. My boys made it, and hers didn't."

Caro reached across the table to cover Linda's hand with her own. "Mother to mother, I'm sure she'd love to hear from you."

"Maybe." Linda shook off the sadness. "Anyway, this isn't why you wanted to get together."

"No, it isn't." Caro withdrew her hand and crossed her arms, seeming nervous all of a sudden.

"What is it? Is something wrong?"

"No. Everything is actually quite right for once."

Linda raised an eyebrow. "What does that mean?"

Caro released a deep sigh and leaned forward to rest her elbows on the table. "Do you remember last fall when I told you I'd met a man?"

Nodding, Linda said, "A much younger man who you wouldn't name, if I recall correctly." Caro's face flushed with color that made Linda laugh. "Are you *blushing*?"

"Perhaps. A little…"

"Spill it, sister. You've had me wondering for months who this younger man is."

"Seamus," she whispered so softly that Linda almost didn't hear her.

"*Seamus O'Grady?* As in the Seamus who runs the ferry company for Joe?"

"Shhh, keep your voice down. No one knows, well, except for Joe and Janey. They know now."

"Well, well, *well*… Girlfriend gets herself a boyfriend and what do you know? She gets the cutest, sexiest, most eligible guy in town now that most of my sons are off the market."

"He's not my *boyfriend*," Caro said, seeming mortified by the word.

"My apologies. I should've said *lover*."

Caro cringed. "Oh God, that's even worse."

"What would you call him?"

"He defies description."

Linda howled with laughter. "You have to tell me everything. Leave no detail unshared—especially the part about how you told Joe and Janey. How did he take it?"

"Better than expected, to be honest. He was extremely shocked, but he handled it quite well, all things considered."

Over salads and iced tea, Caro related the story of how Janey had helped her to find the courage to tell Joe the truth. "So Joe went down to the ferry landing to confront Seamus. Janey and I were worried that Joe might punch him the way he did David that one time, so we went running after him. Joe wasn't happy that we suspected he might get violent until Janey reminded him that he does have a bit of a track record."

Linda shook with laughter. "It sounds hilarious, even though I suspect it wasn't all that funny to you."

"It was excruciating, but your daughter was amazing. She really smoothed things over with Joe, and I think he took it better than he would have without her help."

"That's very nice to hear about Janey, but Joe wants you to be happy, Caro. You know that."

"I do know, but..."

"But what?"

Carolina met her gaze, seeming tortured and uncertain. "Seamus wants to get married."

"Oh wow! How exciting!" As Linda said the words, she realized Carolina didn't seem excited. "Isn't it?"

"It's so *complicated*."

"What's complicated? Does he love you?"

"Apparently."

"And you love him?"

"It seems so."

"Then what's the problem?"

"Do I really have to spell it out for you? He's almost *twenty years* younger than me, for one thing. For another, he says he doesn't care about having children and a family of his own, but what if someday he regrets that? And what will people say?"

"If I have to guess, I'd bet a lot of the women will be jealous and the men will be looking at you with all-new interest."

"Ugh, that's gross! I don't want their interest."

"Carolina," Linda said with a laugh, reaching across the table for her friend's hands, "do you love him? Do you want to be with him?"

"Yes," she said on a moan. "I want him, I love him, I was miserable without him."

"Then what's the problem?"

"Just because I love him and love being with him doesn't mean I have to marry him, does it?"

"It seems rather important to him."

Carolina sagged into her seat. "He's very old-fashioned sometimes."

"Probably the way he was raised."

Caro let go of Linda's hands and flipped a spoon between her fingers. "Speaking of how he was raised... You know what I spend an inordinate amount of time thinking about?"

"What's that?"

"His mother."

"His *mother*?" Linda said with a laugh. "What about her?"

"I'm thinking about it from her point of view. How would we feel if our sons told us they wanted to marry a fifty-six-year-old woman? How would we feel if our sons were in love with a woman who could never give them children or a family? I can't help but put myself in her shoes and hate me on her behalf."

Linda thought about that for a moment and had to admit Caro made a good point. It would be upsetting to learn that one of her sons would never be a father, but nearly losing three of her four boys gave her a different perspective than she would've had before. "After what happened last week, it's safe to say that all I care about is my boys are healthy and happy and loved. That's all that matters in this life, Caro. What else is there?"

"Children. There are children, and he'd be such a wonderful father."

"Yes, he would, and if that's meant to be, then somehow he'll be a father."

Carolina recoiled in horror. "There's no way I'm having a baby at this age!"

29

"Relax," Linda said laughing. "As you well know, there are plenty of other ways to become parents."

"So you don't think it would be a big fat Gansett Island scandal if Carolina Cantrell the cougar married sexy, *young* Seamus O'Grady, the dashing Irishman?"

"It'll be a huge scandal for a week, maybe two, and then people will get over it and go on with their lives. Look at Tiffany. Her store was all people were talking about until the town council meeting when Blaine basically told them to get a life. Now the store is accepted, it's busy, and some of the same people who spoke out against the store have been seen patronizing it. Scandals come and go. Love is forever."

"I hate when you make sense. It drives me crazy."

"My children would completely agree with you."

Moaning, Carolina dropped her head into her hands. "I can't believe I'm even considering this madness. Marrying a thirty-nine-year-old! I'd be securing my place in hell, that's for sure."

"As Mac and I like to say, we'll be in good company down there."

That drew a reluctant laugh from Carolina.

"And I'll tell you something else, I won't stand for anyone speaking poorly of you around me. You've spent thirty years completely alone. No one deserves to be happy more than you do."

Caro blinked back tears. "Thank you, Lin. I was never completely alone with Joe and you and Mac and your brood to prop me up."

"If you love this man, we'll love him, too. I promise."

The man in question came through the door to the diner and lit up with pleasure when he saw Carolina sitting with Linda.

"Oh *God*," Carolina muttered, making Linda laugh again. Glancing up at Seamus, Carolina said, "What're you doing here?"

"Looking for you, love."

Linda didn't think she was capable of swooning, but the heated look the sexy Irishman gave her friend was positively swoon-worthy.

He nodded to her. "Mrs. McCarthy. Nice to see you again."

"Since you and my friend are apparently an item, you should probably call me Linda to keep me from feeling too ancient."

The comment was met with a scowl from Carolina and a wide grin from Seamus, who slid into the booth next to Carolina, forcing her to move over to let him in. Carolina's face was bright red, and she radiated discomfort, whereas Seamus seemed relaxed and at ease with taking their relationship public.

"So she's been talking about me, aye?"

"That she has."

He leaned forward, green eyes twinkling. "What'd she say? Anything good?"

Linda couldn't help but laugh, even though she knew Carolina wouldn't appreciate it. "I'll never tell."

"Darn." He slipped an arm around Caro, oblivious to the attention they were attracting from nearby tables, kissed the top of her head and drew her in close to him. "I missed you last night." To Linda, he said, "Had to spend the night on the mainland because of a meeting this morning. I couldn't talk her into coming with me."

Caro nudged his ribs with her elbow.

"What? Did I or did I not try to convince you to come with me so we wouldn't have to sleep apart?"

"And that is my cue to leave," Linda said, putting a twenty on the table as she stood.

"You don't have to go," Carolina said desperately as it seemed to dawn on her that without Linda there to block the prying eyes of the other diners, the word would be all over town about her and Seamus before the hour was up.

"I have to get to the grocery store. Adam is home, and the family is coming for dinner. Got to run, but you think about what I said, do you hear me?"

Carolina grumbled something in reply that Linda couldn't make out.

"You know," Linda said, as a deliciously evil idea came to her. "You two should join us for dinner tonight. Joe and Janey will be there, along with the rest of the family."

As Carolina's eyes went wide with dismay, Seamus said, "We'd love to. What time?"

"Six thirty," Linda said, avoiding Carolina's glare on her way to the door. "See you then!"

"I HOPE she didn't leave on my account," Seamus said when they were alone.

"Of course she did. If you're going to start prattling on about our sleeping arrangements, she's not going to hang around for that."

"Seemed like you might've already mentioned our sleeping arrangements before I got here."

"That's not the point! And stop laughing at me. Go sit over there before the whole town is talking about us."

"Sit over where?"

"On the other side of the booth," Carolina said between gritted teeth. Sometimes she wondered if he was intentionally obtuse or just trying to aggravate her. She suspected it was far more of the latter than the former.

"But you're over here, and I missed you so much last night. I could hardly sleep without you."

"I'm sure you slept just fine."

He shook his head. "I'm exhausted. In fact, I need you to take me home to your place and put me down for a nap."

"It's two o'clock!"

"So?"

Ned Saunders came through the door with his fiancée Francine Chester. They stopped short at the sight of Seamus sitting close to Carolina with his arm around her. Ned and Francine waved to them and slid into another booth, leaning in to whisper to each other.

Carolina burned with embarrassment, knowing they were talking about her and Seamus. "Can we please leave?"

"Are you ashamed to be seen with me, Caro?"

He seemed so wounded that Carolina instantly regretted her reaction to Ned and Francine seeing them together. "No."

"Really? Sort of seems that you are."

"It's not that."

"Then what is it?"

"Let's go. We'll talk about it at home."

Reluctantly, Seamus slid out of the booth and held out a hand to help her.

Carolina let him guide her from the booth and then dropped his hand. As she paid the check and exchanged a few words with Rebecca, who owned the diner, she felt the eyes of Seamus and the other patrons on her. The minute they walked out the door, the news about them would spread through the island like an out-of-control wildfire.

Her stomach began to ache when she imagined Joe hearing the gossip and how he might react to it.

When they were outside, Seamus followed her to her car.

Carolina turned to him and looked up to find him studying her intently. "What?"

"I could ask you the same thing."

"I, um, are you coming over?"

"Do you want me to?"

"You know I do."

He smiled, but it didn't reach his eyes, and he seemed more sad than amused. She hated herself for doing that to him.

"Aren't you working today?"

"I'm off until tomorrow morning."

Her entire body tingled at the idea of having him to herself for that many hours. "Oh."

"Is that a good 'oh' or a bad 'oh'?"

"Good," she said, suddenly aching for him as his grin stretched across his handsome face. He was so very, very gorgeous and so incredibly sexy and apparently all hers. That part she still couldn't believe. "Very good."

"Go. I'll be right behind you."

Carolina wasn't sure how exactly she managed to drive home, knowing he was following her, knowing what would happen as soon as they reached her house. Even though she'd once been married—happily married—it all felt new to her because it had been so long since she'd been involved with anyone. And she'd never been with such an intensely focused man.

Her heart beat erratically as she went into the house and went through the motions of putting a kettle on to boil. Tea, she thought, would calm her. But then his hands were on her hips, drawing her back against him, and all thoughts of tea and calm were forgotten. His lips were soft and smooth against her neck as he pressed his erection into the cleft of her bottom.

"I missed you so much last night. I can't stand being away from you."

They'd spent seven straight nights together, and Carolina had thought one night apart would be good for them. "I hated it, too."

Her words seemed to do something to him, and his hands moved over her with an urgency that reminded her of the first night they'd spent together last fall.

Feeling shameless and needy, Carolina bit back a moan. How did he do this to her with just a few well-placed caresses? How did he make her forget entirely about her concerns and reservations? When he touched her this way, there was no room for thoughts of anything other than more of him. Part of her suspected he knew she was powerless to resist him and used it to his advantage.

From behind her, he unbuttoned her jeans and pushed them and her panties down to right above her knees.

"Seamus, wait! Someone could walk in—"

"We'll hear them." His breath was hot against her ear as he slid his erection between her cheeks, arousing and stirring her. When had he freed himself? How did he do this to her every time?

Reaching around her, he shut off the stove and then turned them around. He shocked the hell out of her when he bent her over the kitchen table.

Carolina knew she should put a stop to this, but then his hands were under her top, squeezing her nipples, and it was all she could do to breathe as he entered her from behind.

"Ah, Christ," he muttered. "If there's anything better than this, I haven't found it yet."

Since she completely agreed, Carolina had no choice but to hold on to the table and go along for the ride, helpless to resist him as always.

"Mmm," he said against her ear, sending goose bumps down her spine. "So hot, so wet, so tight."

He loved to tell her exactly what he was feeling when they made love, which was at times embarrassing and at other times hugely arousing.

"You like hearing that, huh?"

"How can you tell?"

"You just got even wetter."

Carolina wanted to die on the spot. She was so far out of her league with this man who wasn't afraid to lay it all on the line, to say what he thought and how he felt. Nothing had prepared her for him or the way he made her feel by taking her hard and fast on the kitchen table in the middle of the day.

His fingers kneaded her bottom as he drove into her, making her cry out from the impact and the overwhelming sensations he drew from her body every time they were together.

"*Yes*, love, tell me you love it as much as I do." He flexed his hips. "Tell me."

"Yes, yes, I love it."

He reached around to stroke the hard bundle of nerves that throbbed for him as he continued to pump into her. "Tell me you love me."

"I love you, Seamus. I love you." The words were no sooner out of her mouth then she was coming hard and crying out from the sheer joy of being loved by him.

"I love you, too," he said, as he pushed into her one last time and let go with a cry of completion. After a long pause, he added, "More than anything." He rested on top of her, breathing hard and pulsing with aftershocks. Keeping his arms around her, he was careful not to rest too heavily upon her.

"I'm sorry," she whispered.

"For what, love?"

"For making you feel like I was ashamed to be seen with you in town. I'm not ashamed. It's… It's all so new. I need some time to get used to it."

He withdrew from her and helped her to stand, steadying her when her legs wobbled under her. "You take all the time you need. I'm not going anywhere."

"Promise?"

With his arms around her, he touched his lips to her forehead. "Ah, love, where would I go when everything I want is right here?"

Carolina relaxed against him and closed her eyes, filled with the certainty that while others might not understand what she was doing with him, she could no longer picture a life without him.

Now if she could just get through dinner with the McCarthys, she'd be well on her way to starting that five-alarm Gansett scandal that Linda predicted. May as well get it over with, because she had no plans to let him go.

CHAPTER 4

*a*dam stashed his stuff in his old room and then left the house to walk down the hill to the marina in search of his dad and Mac. The first one he saw, though, was Luke Harris, co-owner of the marina and a longtime friend.

"Look at what the cat drug in from the big city," Luke joked as he hugged Adam. "Good to see you, man."

"You, too. How's everything going around here?" The marina seemed completely full and hopping with people, dogs, bikes, scooters and other forms of chaos occurring on and around the main pier. Adam was relieved to see business as usual.

"Not bad. How about you?"

"I'll be better when I see the boys. How do they seem to you?"

"Mac acts like nothing happened. From what I hear, Evan is working around the clock to get the music studio open. Your dad is a bit more sentimental than usual."

"*More* sentimental?"

Luke laughed at that. "You heard me right. He was profoundly affected by what happened." Luke sighed and shook his head. "It was a very long day for all of us, but somehow it was worse for him because he couldn't go out and look for them. The fog was so thick…"

"He must've been beside himself." Adam ached for his sweet dad, who would've been tortured by having to wait hours for word about his boys.

"That's putting it mildly. I had to get between him and the Chris Craft a couple of times that day." Luke referred to the classic boat he'd restored for Big Mac years ago. "He's been pissed at me ever since."

"I know it's hard, but try not to take it personally."

"I'm trying."

The way he said the two words told Adam a lot about how difficult it had been for Luke, who viewed Big Mac as the father he'd never had. "How's Syd?"

Luke's entire demeanor softened. "She's great."

Adam gave him a nudge as they walked toward the restaurant. "Marriage seems to agree with you, old man."

"I rather like it."

Adam stopped abruptly and turned to Luke. "You didn't mention anything about Grant."

Luke glanced down at the parking lot. "He's not doing too well. Something's not right, but he's all locked up. We've all tried to get through to him, but he's not talking."

"I saw him earlier, and I have to agree."

"Maybe having you around will get him talking. You two have always been close."

"When we were younger, but not as much now," Adam said, filled with regret to realize it was true. He'd been so focused on his work that he'd let a lot of important relationships slide while he focused on others that turned out to be less important than he'd thought.

They stepped into the marina restaurant where Grant's fiancée, Stephanie, appeared to be doing battle with the cash register.

"*Adam!* Is that really you? You're just the man we need right now! Come. Quickly."

Luke sent him a sympathetic smile and gestured for Adam to proceed to the counter.

"Hello to you, too, Steph." He returned the quick hug she gave him. "What seems to be the problem?"

"This stupid thing keeps rebooting itself right in the middle of transactions. Tell me there's something you can do."

"If you give me a minute to look at it, I should be able to tell you." He reached into the pocket of his cargo shorts and withdrew the glasses that had become necessary for twelve-hour days in front of computers and slid them on.

"Very sexy in a nerdy sort of way," Stephanie said after careful assessment.

"Gee, thanks. You still want my help?"

"Sorry. I just have no time for this. I need to get back to my restaurant, but I can't leave them in the lurch. And I need to check on Grant."

As Adam clicked around behind the scenes on the computer's hard drive, he said, "I saw him a little while ago."

"Was he up?"

"Just."

Her deep sigh said it all.

"What gives?"

"Hell if I know. He's not talking. He tosses and turns all night. When he does sleep, usually during the day, he wakes up sweating and breathing hard like he's been running a marathon or something. He's not working or writing or getting anything done. It's all very unlike him."

"So you're worried?"

"I'm very worried, but I don't know what to do. Everyone says to give him time, but it's been a week, and he's still a mess. Physically he seems fine, so I don't think it's that."

"My mom thinks something happened out there that he can't bring himself to talk about."

"Like what?"

"I don't know, but it had to be pretty traumatic. Too bad there isn't a shrink on this island. Seems like we might need one."

"If he won't talk to me, what makes you think he'd talk to a shrink?"

"Maybe it's something he doesn't want to tell you or any of us because he doesn't want us to know about it." With a few more keystrokes, he had cleared the cache on the register's computer and freed up enough memory to get it running again. "There you go."

Stephanie's eyes bugged. "What did you do?"

Amused by her reaction, he tugged off his glasses. "Do you honestly care?"

"No, I absolutely don't care. I only care that it's working again. Thank you so much!"

"My pleasure. Hey, so before you run off, let me know what I can do to help with Grant. I'll keep trying to get him to talk to me, but if there's something else I can do, call me, will you?"

"I will. Thanks, Adam. I'll take whatever help I can get at this point. Mac and Evan don't want to talk about it either, so they aren't much help, and Dan is in pretty rough shape. The ribs are giving him a lot of grief. Janey is *so* pregnant and hormonal, your mom drives him crazy, and your dad can't talk about any of it without weeping, which makes it harder on Grant." She threw her hands into the air. "You might be exactly what we need."

"I won't leave until he's better. I promise."

She surprised him when she hugged him again. "Sorry to be so blunt about your family."

Adam laughed and patted her back. "You're not telling me anything I don't already know, and I'm happy to do what I can to help."

"I have to go, but let me give you my cell number so we can keep in touch."

They programmed numbers into each other's phones and were swapping them back when Mac and Big Mac came into the restaurant, both of them grinning widely.

"What's this we hear about a visitor?" Mac asked.

Their father made a beeline for Adam, enveloping him in a bear hug that brought tears to Adam's eyes. His father had worn the same aftershave all of Adam's life, and it was one of the many familiar scents of home.

"So nice to see you, son," Big Mac said, stepping back to take a close look at Adam. "You look tired. Have you been sleeping?"

"Not so well in the last week."

"Me either."

Big Mac looked a little haggard around the edges, but with his usual aviator sunglasses in place over his eyes, Adam couldn't gauge the true extent of his father's exhaustion.

Mac playfully nudged their father out of the way so he could hug Adam. "Hey, little brother." Mac messed up his hair the way he always did, and as usual, it aggravated Adam. "Good of you to come check on us."

"I've got to run," Stephanie said to them. "See you all later."

"Bye, Steph."

"Buy you some chowder, son?" Big Mac asked, gesturing to a free table.

"I won't say no to that. I haven't eaten in hours. The boat was kinda barfy today."

"Imagine it would be with the wind whipping the way it is," Big Mac said as he signaled to one of the young women behind the counter to bring them three bowls of chowder.

"Coming right up, Mr. McCarthy."

"Thank you, sweetheart." Big Mac removed his shades and propped them on the top of his wiry gray hair.

Adam bit back a gasp when he got a good look at his dad's eyes, which were red and ravaged.

"Don't look at me like that," Big Mac growled. "I can't help that I've been a freaking wreck over this whole thing."

Mac got up from the table and pushed his chair in. "I'm going home to have lunch with Maddie and the kids. I'll be back in an hour."

"What's up with him?" Adam asked his dad when they were alone.

"He can't stand to see me like this, and I can't seem to make it stop." Blinking back tears, Big Mac stared at something over Adam's shoulder. "It was a very long day. I can't get past it, no matter how hard I try. All I think about is what could've happened."

Undone by his father's tears, Adam rested his hand on Big Mac's forearm, which was already as tan in May as some people would be in August. "Everyone's safe, Dad. Don't drive yourself crazy with what-ifs."

"You're right, and so is your mother and Janey and Mac. Easier said than done, though." He shrugged. "Anyway, here's our chowder. Tell me what's new in New York."

"Ah, well," Adam said with a short laugh. "There's a story that'll give you something else to think about." For his dear old dad's sake, he gladly told the ugly tale one more time.

STEPHANIE LEFT the marina and drove a little too fast on the way into town. Lately she was perpetually rushed, jetting from one job to the other with hardly any time for anything other than work. She'd known it would be chaotic opening her own restaurant while continuing to work for the McCarthys, but the boat accident had added a layer of stress she hadn't planned on.

While she wanted to put Grant first, her schedule would be beastly until Race Week concluded and the crowds subsided a bit until Memorial Day weekend, when the season began in earnest. If she could just get through the next few days, she'd be able to focus on Grant and trying to get him to talk to her about whatever was troubling him.

Rather than stop at home, she placed a call to him from the car.

"Hey, babe," he said as he always did.

She could tell he was making an effort to keep things normal between them, but nothing had been normal since that horrible day last week when she'd spent eight hours thinking about how she'd ever live without him. "Hi, there. How're you feeling today?"

"Fine."

"I woke up in the middle of the night and couldn't find you."

"Oh, sorry. I was awake, so I took a walk. I didn't mean to worry you."

"I seem to be worried about you all the time."

"Don't be. I'm fine. Really."

"Grant—"

"Everything okay at the restaurant?"

Frustrated that he refused to talk to her about what was bothering him, she gripped the wheel a little tighter. "Yes."

"Will you be home for dinner?"

"By eight or so. I need to make sure we get through the rush, and then I'll be home. Want me to bring something from the restaurant?"

"Sure, that sounds good. My folks are doing a dinner for Adam, so I might stop by there for a bit, but I'll be home by eight. See you then."

As the phone line went dead, Stephanie tried to tell herself that it didn't matter that he hadn't said he loved her, the way he usually did. She was still thinking about that when she rushed into the Sand & Surf and nearly ran right into Grant's cousin, Laura McCarthy.

"Whoa, what's on fire?" Laura asked, steadying Stephanie.

"Sorry. I'm always in a rush these days."

"How long can you continue to manage McCarthy's and run your own place, too?"

"I love working at the marina. Mr. and Mrs. McCarthy have been so good to me, and now they're going to be my in-laws. I can't leave them in the lurch right as the season is starting."

"I'm sure they'd understand that you've got your own business to run."

"My goal is to get through this year and then see where things stand."

"See if you can do it without running yourself ragged, huh?"

"I'll try."

As they were about to part company, the main door to the Surf opened, and in walked Grant's ex-girlfriend, Abby Callahan. This day got better and better.

"Abby!" Laura said. "What're you doing here?"

Abby eyed Stephanie with trepidation that added to Stephanie's anxiety. "It seems I'm going to be living here again."

Stephanie bit back a gasp. *Living here?*

"Is that good news or bad news?" Laura asked.

"Some of both," Abby said grimly. "Cal and I have broken it off.

Janey mentioned you might be looking for someone to manage the gift shop, so I figured I'd check to see if I could help you out."

"Oh, that would be awesome," Laura said, shooting Stephanie a glance.

For her part, Stephanie felt like she'd been electrocuted. Grant's ex was back on the island, single again and possibly going to work thirty feet from her in the same hotel? *Shoot me now, please.* "It's, ah, nice to see you home, Abby, but I'm sorry to hear about Cal. I have to get to work." Stephanie gestured to the restaurant. "I'm sure I'll see you soon."

"Congratulations on the engagement and the restaurant," Abby said with a sweet, genuine smile. "I'm so happy for you—and for Grant."

"Thank you." All at once, it was urgent Stephanie get out of there. "See you later." She walked slowly and calmly into the restaurant. Once she cleared the doorway, she headed for her office and closed the door behind her. With her palms flat against the desktop, she focused on taking a series of deep breaths that were supposed to calm her nerves. Too bad it didn't work.

Abby is home. She and Cal have broken up. Grant's first love is free again. He's refusing to talk about what happened to him in the accident. Stephanie's mind raced through all the scenarios and implications, each more grim than the one before. Would Grant take one look at his old love and want her back?

"No." Stephanie ran trembling fingers through her hair. "That won't happen." But what if it did? What would she do?

Why did it feel like everything was spinning out of control, and there was nothing she could do to stop it?

"I'm so sorry to hear about Cal," Laura said to Abby.

"I'm sorry, too. What worked so well here didn't work as well in Texas, unfortunately."

"That's too bad. Are you okay?"

Abby shrugged, refusing to cry anymore. Enough already. "I suppose I will be. Eventually."

"Well, I can certainly keep you busy if you're up for a bit of a challenge. We're waiting for Mac and Luke to finish the trim work in the store, but I can show you the space so you can get an idea of what's available."

"Lead the way."

MADDIE WAS CURLED up on the sofa feeding Hailey when Mac came in through the sliding door from the deck. With one look at his handsome face, she could tell something wasn't right. But then again, nothing had been right since the accident. At first he'd been belligerent about being forced to stay quiet for a couple of days. Now that he was back to work, though, he was quiet, moody and withdrawn.

She was hesitant to broach the subject with him. Rather, she'd chosen to wait him out, hoping he'd eventually confide in her.

"What're you doing home?"

"I live here," he joked as he came over to kiss her and Hailey. "Is she asleep?"

"I think so."

"Want me to put her down?"

"That'd be great. Thanks."

Watching his big hands scoop up the tiny bundle with infinite gentleness nearly brought tears to Maddie's eyes. She loved him more than life and hated that he was hurting and wouldn't—or couldn't—share his burden with her.

He took the baby upstairs for her nap.

Maddie thought about waiting for him to come back down but decided instead to follow him. She fastened the nursing bra and straightened her top before going upstairs, running her fingers through her disorderly curls on the way up. Neither of them had been sleeping well in the last week, and the fatigue was wearing on her. She could only imagine how he felt.

Mac emerged from Hailey's room and seemed surprised to find her waiting for him. "Where's Thomas?" he asked of their son.

"Spending the afternoon with Tiffany and Ashleigh."

"That'll be fun for him."

"Uh-huh." Maddie reached for his hand and led him to their room.

Though he came willingly, she sensed a hint of hesitation. "Where're we going?"

"In here." Without releasing his hand, she stretched out on the bed and compelled him to join her.

He lay down next to her. Though he was close, he seemed a million miles from her, which made her ache with longing. The unusual distance between them was unsettling.

She reached for his hand. "What brought you home in the middle of the day?" she asked after a long moment of silence.

He turned his head to look at her. "I wanted to see you and Hailey."

"We're glad you came. Everything all right at the marina?"

Nodding, he said, "Adam's home."

"Oh, really? Did you know he was coming?"

"No."

"You must've been glad to see him."

"Yeah."

The Mac she knew and loved was always thrilled to see his siblings, so his lackluster reaction to Adam's unexpected visit was yet another reason for worry. "How long is he home?"

"He didn't say. He's having lunch with Dad. Maybe he told him."

"You didn't want to have lunch with them?" That, too, was unusual.

"I told you. I wanted to have lunch with you."

"Are you hungry?"

"Not particularly." His appetite, like his sleep, had been off. That they hadn't made love since the accident was further evidence that something was amiss.

"Mac..."

"Hmm?"

"I wish you'd talk to me."

"I *am* talking to you."

"That's not what I mean, and you know it."

He released her hand and sat up abruptly.

"I'm sorry," she said, regretting that she'd pushed him. "I don't want you to go. Please. You don't have to talk if you're not ready to. But don't go."

A muscle pulsed in his cheek as he seemed to weigh his options. Then he sagged a bit and lay down again.

Maddie was relieved that he'd stayed, but she tried not to show it.

"I'm sorry," he said. "I don't mean to be so touchy."

"You don't have to apologize. I want to help you. Will you let me?"

"I don't know what I need."

"Maybe if you talk about whatever is on your mind, you'd feel better."

He stared up at the ceiling. "I can't talk about what it was like to not know where my brothers were for hours or how it felt to be almost certain they were dead. I can't talk about that, because if I do..."

Maddie blinked back tears, determined to be as strong for him as he always was for her. "What, Mac? Tell me."

"I'm afraid if I do... I might... I might break into a million pieces that can't ever be put back together again the way they were before."

She placed her hand over his fast-beating heart. "I won't let you break. I won't let you. Hold on to me. Let me help."

He wrapped his arms around her and buried his face in her hair as a sob erupted from his chest.

Maddie clung to him, rubbing his back and combing her fingers through his hair. "It's okay, baby. I've got you. Let it out. Everything is okay. Your brothers are safe. Everyone is safe."

He was utterly silent in his despair, but his tears wet her face and neck.

"It had to be awful for you. You're the big brother, and you couldn't help them. You had to be so scared and worried about me and the kids and your parents and Janey."

He didn't speak, but his arms tightened around her.

She turned her head so she could kiss his face. "Everything is okay now." Maddie had no idea how long they stayed like that, wrapped up in each other, his body shaking with sobs he suffered through in silence to spare her. Even in his time of need, he always thought of her.

"I'm sorry," he said, breaking the long silence.

"Don't be sorry. Please don't."

He drew back from her so he could see her.

The sight of his face, ravaged and streaked with tears, broke her heart, but she didn't let him see that. Rather, she brushed away his tears and traced the outline of his mouth. "I love you so much," she said. "I had a very long day to think about what my life might be like without you, and I hope I never feel that way again. Ever."

"I don't mean to make it all about me. I know it was awful for you, too."

"My awful was nowhere near as awful as yours. You don't always have to be strong for me and everyone else, you know?"

"I don't?" he asked with a small, teasing smile that was far more in keeping with her Mac than the grim countenance he'd sported in the last week.

"No, you don't. Sometimes you can let me carry the burden for you."

"You just did, baby." He kissed her softly and sweetly. "Thank you."

Maddie gathered him in close again, bringing his head to rest on her chest. "Close your eyes and try to rest for a while."

"I have to go back to work."

She reached for his belt where he clipped his cell phone so it wouldn't fall into the water when he was working.

"What're you doing?" he asked when she placed a call.

"Hi, Luke, it's Maddie. Mac is taking the afternoon off. I wanted to let you know."

Her husband pinched her rear, making her smile.

"Everything okay?" Luke asked.

"It's going to be."

"Right. Well, tell him not to worry. I've got it covered here."

"Thanks, Luke. He'll see you in the morning." She ended the call and tossed the phone onto the bed behind Mac. "He said to tell you he's got it covered. Not to worry."

"You're being very bossy, sweetheart."

"I know. Now close your eyes and rest. I've got you."

A sigh shuddered through his big frame as he relaxed into her embrace.

Relieved to have taken the first step in what would probably be a long healing process, Maddie closed her eyes, too. They were both exhausted and overwrought. The sleep would do them good.

CHAPTER 5

*A*fter lunch, Adam borrowed his dad's truck and set out to find
Evan's new studio. Following his father's directions, he drove
past the Southeast Light to a parcel of land that their friend Ned
Saunders owned. Adam nearly drove by the driveway that was hidden
by an overgrowth of brush.

On the way down the dirt driveway, he wondered if the brush was
scratching the shit out of his dad's truck and how much grief he'd get
from Big Mac if it was. Oh well, he thought. He could blame it on
Evan's crappy landscaping. Getting Evan into trouble had once been
Adam's primary goal in life. Some things never changed.

At the end of the driveway sat an enormous cedar-shingled barn. A
beat-up truck and the old motorcycle he'd recognize anywhere as his
brother Mac's were parked outside. Adam followed the music inside
to a large room that smelled of freshly cut wood and new paint.
Microphone stands, amplifiers, cords galore and other equipment was
scattered about the space.

Through a pane of glass, Adam could see Evan. He was sitting
down while another guy leaned over him, pointing and talking with
his hands as loud music pounded through the space.

Though he hated to interrupt them, Adam had come a long way to see his brothers. Adam waited until Evan looked up and waved at him through the window.

Evan's eyes widened with what might've been pleasure. He said something to the other man and then removed a headset from around his neck as he stood. He came bounding down a small set of stairs to the main studio where he hugged Adam.

"What're you doing here?" he said, speaking loudly over the music.

"Came to see you and your brothers. Heard you got into a bit of a scrape and wanted to see for myself that you're doing okay."

"I'm fine, Mac's fine. Grant's being weird, but he's always weird." Evan said what he thought Adam wanted to hear, but his eyes told a different story. He was exhausted, wired, disheveled, but doing his damndest to sell the all's-well theme. "How are you?"

"Better now that I've seen you."

"Awww, don't tell me you care."

Adam shrugged. "Not about you. Just about Mac and Grant."

"Oh good. I was worried for a minute there."

He and Evan had fought like tomcats growing up and continued to enjoy a vicious wrestling match whenever possible, but there was nothing they wouldn't do for each other, including lie to each other's faces when necessary.

"Got a minute to show me around?"

"Just. We've got a ton of work to do before our first artists begin to arrive next week."

"I won't keep you long."

"Come and meet Josh, my sound engineer. I talked him into moving here from Nashville to work with me. He's showing me the basics on the board."

Adam followed Evan up the stairs to the sound booth where he met Josh Harrelson, another victim of the Starlight Records bankruptcy that had taken Evan's debut album down with it.

"Josh, my brother, Adam, here from the Big Apple."

Josh shook Adam's hand. "How many brothers do you have, man?"

"He's the last one," Evan said, laughing. "Lots of cousins, though. I'm going to give Adam a quick tour. I'll be right back."

"Take your time," Josh said. "I've got plenty to do."

Evan walked Adam through three studios on the first floor. "We've got soundproofed walls so we can run three sessions simultaneously. Back here is my office, not that I'm ever in here. Oh, hey, check out the logos we came up with." He held up a board with three different renditions of the Island Breeze Records logo. "Any preferences?"

"I like the one that has the island in the backdrop and the surfboard."

"I do, too. I think we're going to go with that one."

"I meant to tell you—you need to cut back the brush on the drive-way. This place is hard to find."

"I've got Alex Martinez coming to do that this week. Remember AM?"

"Sure, his brother PM was in my class."

Adam recalled that the brothers' nicknames had come from one being a morning person and the other a night owl. "I thought Alex had moved off-island to work at the U.S. Botanic Garden."

"He did, but he came home when his mom got sick."

"What's wrong with his mom?"

"Alzheimer's."

Adam followed Evan up the stairs. "Oh, shit. That sucks."

"Big-time. I guess Paul needed help running the business and taking care of her, so Alex quit his job and moved home."

Adam felt for the guy. It must've been a bitter pill to go from working at the U.S. Botanic Garden to cutting grass again for his family's landscaping business. He knew a little bit about bitter pills himself these days.

"Is Mom having a big dinner for you tonight?"

"So I'm told."

"I may not make it, but I'm sure Grace will be there."

"How are things with you guys?"

"Couldn't be better."

Evan showed him the four bedrooms and two bathrooms they'd installed upstairs for the artists who'd be coming to the island to record at the studio. "We're booked through the summer and into October."

"That's great, Ev. Congratulations. It looks amazing."

"Thanks." Evan gave a not-so-subtle glance at his watch. "I hate to say it, but I've got to get back to work."

"No problem. Hope we can hang out while I'm home."

"Yeah, sure, I'd love to. Good to see you, bro," Evan said as he jogged up the stairs to rejoin Josh.

Adam left feeling like Evan was working awfully hard to act like everything was fine. He knew Evan almost as well as he knew himself, and all his instincts told him his little brother was anything but fine.

HER CELL PHONE began ringing around five, and Abby ignored the first call from Cal as well as the second. By now he'd found the note she left him and might be upset that she'd left. Or maybe he was relieved. Probably the latter. After the second call, though, she became curious and checked her voice mail.

"Hey, babe. I'm just home from my mom's and wondering where you are and what you want to do for dinner. Give me a call."

Abby let out a groan. He hadn't found the note she'd left in plain sight on the kitchen table. Knowing him, he'd gone directly to the fridge for a beer and was now sprawled on the sofa watching ESPN. The familiar image gave her a pang of longing for him that she quickly pushed to the back of her mind. She'd made her decision, and now she had to live with it.

She listened to his second, more urgent message with a growing sense of dismay. Was she going to have to *tell* him she'd left him? God, she hoped not. It'd been hard enough to write the note. She couldn't imagine having to say the words, which was why she went with a text.

I left you a note on the table.

Oh, sorry, missed that. BRB.

Knowing full well what the note said, her heart beat fast and her hands got sweaty while she waited for him to read it. When the phone rang a third time, she took the call. She owed him that much after the year they'd spent happily together before it all went wrong.

"Are you *serious*?" The anger in his voice came right through the phone.

"Are you really surprised?"

"Hell, yes, I'm surprised!" His Texas drawl became more pronounced when he was upset. "You never said a word about leaving until you were gone. What the hell, Abby?"

"Nothing has been right between us since I got there. You know that."

"I'm dealing with a crisis! I'm sorry if I wasn't able to give you enough attention."

"You think that's it? Proves how totally clueless you are."

"Will you please stop talking in code and tell me what the hell that means."

"You have unresolved feelings for Candy." Saying the other woman's name made Abby feel a bit sick. "I'm not willing to compete with that."

After a long stretch of silence in which Abby wondered if he was still there, he said, "Feelings for Candy. Right. That's why I asked *you* to marry me, because I still have feelings for her."

"You admitted you still think about her! I have eyes, Cal. I can see the way you respond to her. You never look at me the way you look at her, and I got tired of being the other woman in my relationship."

"I can*not* believe you didn't talk to me about this."

"I did talk to you. You said I shouldn't worry about your feelings for her. I don't agree. What's there to say?"

"A lot! You left without even giving me a chance!"

"I've given you lots of chances. I got tired of being ignored."

"And we're back to that. My mom is sick. She needs me. I'm sorry if you felt ignored."

"Your mom isn't the only one who needs you. Candy does, too. You should be with her. The two of you have all kinds of history, and your mom loves her."

"*I* don't love her! I love *you*."

"You do love her. You're lying to yourself—and to me—if you deny it."

"Oh my God, I can't believe you're telling me who I love!" Abby wiped away tears. "I left the ring in your top dresser drawer."

"So that's it? Over and done with?"

"I'm sorry, Cal. But I've done this once before—"

"*You're really going to compare me to Grant McCarthy?*"

"The situation is similar. That's the only comparison I'm making."

"It's not similar. I love you, and I made a commitment to you, which he never did. But if you don't feel the same way, I can't do anything about that."

"I do feel the same way. I did..."

"Past tense?"

"It's been very hard for me to watch the way you react to her, and to realize it wasn't going to work out between us after all. It was very...hard."

"I never meant to give you the impression anything was happening with her. I swear to you that's been over for years."

"I'm sure you'd like to believe that."

He released a frustrated sigh that she heard quite clearly through the phone. "Where are you?"

"Where else? Gansett."

"You should've talked to me before you left."

"Maybe so, but I knew you'd try to talk me out of doing what was best for me."

"This isn't what's best for you or for me."

"I'm sorry it didn't work out for us, and I hope your mom continues to improve."

"This is not over."

"Bye, Cal." Abby ended the call and turned her face into her pillow to muffle the sounds of her sobs. Not that anyone could hear her, but she was ashamed to once again be crying her heart out over a man who'd chosen something else—or some*one* else—over her. How many times in one lifetime was a woman supposed to get her heart broken?

Despite what he'd said, Abby had seen him with Candy enough to know the truth. Even if he wasn't ready to admit it yet, she knew and wasn't willing to waste any more of her life waiting around for him to figure it out. It was better to get out now before things got really ugly.

Disgusted with herself over the pity party, she wiped her face and went into the bathroom to splash cold water on her eyes. When she caught a glimpse of herself in the mirror, she grimaced at the red eyes and nose that looked back at her.

A knock on her door had her drying her face and running her fingers through her hair. Whoever it was would be able to tell she'd been crying. She opened the door to her mother. Could this day get any better?

"Oh Lord," Constance said as she brushed by Abby on her way into the room. As always, every hair on her mother's gray head was perfectly in place, and her outfit coordinated down to the pink espadrilles that matched the pink collar of the shirt that peeked out from under a designer sweater.

And as usual, Abby felt like a schlump next to her mother. She'd spent most of her life trying to measure up to her mother's idea of perfection and had fallen short more often than not.

"By all means, come in. Please."

"What happened?"

"A lot of things. None of it I wish to talk about."

"You've been crying."

"Really? I didn't know that."

"Save your sarcasm, Abigail."

"How did you hear I was home? How did you know what room I was in?"

"It's a small island. Word gets around. What're you doing here when you could be with us?"

Abby raised her brows and let the expression speak for itself.

"Whether you believe me or not, I liked Cal. I wanted it to work out for you two. I was worried when you postponed the wedding—"

"Because his mother had a *stroke*, Mom. What would you have me do? Drag him to the altar when he'd rather be with his mother?"

"I never said that. I only wish you'd learned from the past and gotten married before you went after him."

"Clearly, I haven't learned a thing, but thanks for pointing that out to me. I hadn't been thinking that myself or anything."

"You're in a mood."

"Do ya think?"

"Maybe you two will work things out. Some time and space—"

"We're not going to work things out. It's over."

Constance blew out a deep breath and sat on Abby's bed. "What's your plan?"

"I don't have much of a plan. I'm going to find an apartment and run the gift shop at the Surf this summer. After the summer, I'll reevaluate."

"I so wish you hadn't given up your business."

Abby wanted to scream, but she held her tongue. "Anything else you'd like to get off your chest?"

"I'm not your enemy."

"I never said you were. But stating the obvious doesn't help."

Constance stood and hooked her pink-patterned purse over her shoulder. "Your father and I would do anything for you. I hope you know that."

"I do," Abby said, blinking back new tears. Her parents' intentions were always good, even if their standards were a little too high for her liking. "Thank you."

Constance gave her a quick hug and a kiss on the cheek. "I've missed you. It's good to have you home, even if the circumstances aren't ideal."

"Thanks, Mom."

"Come see us."

"I will."

At the door, Constance paused and turned to Abby. "I'm sorry this has happened to you, but you're a strong person and you'll get through it."

Her mother left before Abby could form a reply to the unprecedented compliment. She'd always felt like a failure in the eyes of her exacting parents. Sure, she'd always known they loved her, but they had been disappointed when she moved to LA with Grant without the benefit of marriage and even more so when she went to Texas to be with Cal.

"Enough of dwelling on the past," she said to herself as she went into the bathroom and got out her makeup to repair the damage to her face. "This is my summer, and it's time to start having some fun. Damn it." Smiling at her reflection, she whispered, "Fuckin' A," and dissolved into giggles at the sound of a word she'd rarely used before today.

Rome wasn't built in a day, and it was going to take a while before words like that rolled off her tongue naturally. But she'd get there. Starting tonight, everything was going to be different.

DINNER WAS the usual McCarthy family fiasco, and Adam loved every minute of the noise, the kids, the food, the love. Being surrounded by those who loved him best brought home once again how completely taken in he'd been by someone who hadn't deserved his love.

He volunteered for grill duty so he could have a minute to get himself ready for some lighthearted family fun. After the trauma of the accident, his parents and siblings had enough on their minds without taking on his crap, too. Adam was determined to keep his problems to himself for as long as he could. He was, however, glad he'd told his dad. It was nice to have one person firmly in his corner. Well, Abby, too. She'd been very supportive, which he appreciated.

If only he could stop thinking about Sasha and trying to figure out when things had gone so wrong between them that she could sell him out for money without blinking an eye. Whatever had happened, he'd been completely oblivious.

He'd pictured her here, planned to bring her home sometime this summer. Up until now, he'd kept her a secret from his family because he knew how his mother got her hopes up at the first sign of a girl-friend. His siblings falling in love one after the other had bought him some time to keep his relationship private for that much longer.

Sasha... Adam hated himself for missing her, for wondering if she missed him or had regrets about what she'd done. He hated himself for thinking about the apartment they'd shared or what would become of all the things they'd bought together, back when they still planned a life together. Three whole days ago.

Who cared about wineglasses or sofas? He'd cared about *her* and had thought she felt the same. That was the part that truly galled him —how he could've lived with, slept with, made love with and worked with a woman who cared so little in the end that she could slide a knife in his back without a thought about all they'd shared.

"You cooking that steak or killing the cow all over again?"

Big Mac's voice brought Adam back to the present, where he discovered he was jabbing the barbeque fork methodically into the steak.

"I can't stop thinking about what you told me earlier," Big Mac said. "I'm sorry you're hurting, son."

His dad had promised to keep the story to himself until Adam was ready to share his news with the rest of the family. "Shit happens."

"Shit like this doesn't happen. You got screwed, and what I've been wanting to know since you told me is what you're planning to do about it."

Adam flipped the steaks and stepped back from the smoke. "Nothing."

"You're just going to let go of the company you founded from the ground up?"

"That's exactly what I'm going to do."

Big Mac leaned against the rail, arms crossed, beer in hand. "Why?"

Back in the day, Adam would've wilted under the intensity of that stare. "Because I don't care enough to fight for it."

"You don't care enough about the business you gave fourteen years of blood and sweat and tears to?"

"Nope."

"I refer to my original question. Why?"

"I told you."

"Stop the bullshit and tell me the truth."

"It was a sign."

"Of?"

"That it's time for a change. In more ways than one."

"And what will this change entail?"

"I don't know yet."

"If you need a job, you can work at the marina."

Adam smiled at his dad. "I appreciate the offer, but the good news in all of this is they owe me a shit ton of money that they have sixty days to pay me. After that, I can do whatever I want."

"Which is?"

"Don't know yet. I'm assuming I'll figure that out." Adam looked at his dad. "Don't tell, Mom, okay? She's upset enough about the accident. I don't want to give her more to worry about."

"I told you I wouldn't tell anyone, and I won't."

"I'm already sorry I told you because I can tell you're fretting over it."

"Fretting is part of my job description as your dear old dad." Big Mac wrapped a tree-trunk arm around Adam's neck and hugged him. "We'll get you through this, buddy."

Adam didn't dare say a word, so he nodded and held on tight to the man who'd been his rock. "Thanks, Dad." When his dad released him, Adam looked inside and saw Carolina Cantrell come into the kitchen with Seamus O'Grady's arm around her. "Dad?"

"Yeah?"

"Is Carolina...*dating* him?"

"Who?"

"Seamus?"

Big Mac looked and then looked closer. "Well, I'll be damned."

"Nothing this awesome ever happens in New York," Adam said, laughing. "Carolina looks like she's being tortured."

"He seems pretty pleased with himself, doesn't he?"

"Seriously. I saw Janey earlier, and she never mentioned this." Adam stacked the cooked steaks on a platter that he handed to his dad.

"Apparently, your mother has been holding out on me," Big Mac said. "What do you say we go inside and get the dirt?"

"I'll be there in a minute."

"You didn't ask for my advice, but I'm going to give it to you anyway."

"I'd be disappointed if you didn't."

Big Mac smiled. "You've been away from home a long time. A few weeks here might be just what you need to get your legs under you again and to figure out what's next."

"Why do you think I'm here?"

"Don't stay out here by yourself too long. There's a whole houseful of people in there who love you and would do anything for you."

"Thanks, Dad."

When he was alone, Adam grabbed a beer from the cooler and cracked it open, taking it with him as he wandered to the rail that surrounded the big deck. The sun was setting over the Salt Pond as he looked down upon the hotel and marina, filled with memories of summers spent on the docks or rolling down the hill at the hotel with his siblings.

Those had been good times. The best of times. Like his brothers, he'd yearned for a life away from the confines of the island where they'd been raised. However, like them, he'd learned the real world could be a cold, hard place. There was nothing cold or hard about Gansett Island. Rather, it was a soft place to land while he figured out what he planned to do with the rest of his life now that he no longer had to consider the business that had defined him for most of his adult life or the woman he'd hoped to spend the rest of that life with.

Just as he had the thought, his phone chimed with a text message. Used to being chained to his phone around the clock, he thought about ignoring it. But curiosity got the better of him, and he withdrew it from the pocket of his shorts. He couldn't believe it when he saw it was from Sasha.

I'm so sorry, Adam. I made a mistake. Can we talk? I miss you and I love you. Please?

Adam wished he'd gone with his first instinct to ignore the text.

61

She *loved* him? She sure had a strange way of showing it. He wanted to write back and say that, but he refrained. Let her suffer the way she'd made him suffer for days now. It had probably only registered with her that she was royally screwed without him to handle the technical end of the business, so naturally she was trying to make amends.

Too little, too late, he decided as he deleted the text and her name from his list of contacts. He had nothing left to say to her. If only it was that easy to erase the memory of her from his heart and mind.

"Son?" his dad said from inside. "Are you coming in to eat?"

Adam realized he was starving—for dinner and the company of his loving, if often exasperating, family. "Yeah, I'm coming."

CHAPTER 6

Sitting at the McCarthy's dining room table with Seamus's chair far too close to hers, Carolina had trouble swallowing her food. Taking her relationship public was one thing. Doing it here was another thing altogether. She'd helped to raise Janey and her siblings, and the shock on the faces of Mac, Adam and Big Mac had been mortifying. Thankful for small favors, she was glad Evan and Grant hadn't made it to dinner, but she was certain they'd hear her news before the day was out.

Apparently, Linda had refrained from telling anyone—even her husband—the news Carolina had shared earlier in the day. Thus Carolina's inability to eat or breathe or make eye contact with the young people who'd been a part of her life since her son Joe befriended Mac McCarthy in second grade. What would they think of her now? The woman who'd stayed with them when their parents went on vacation, who'd shared holidays, birthdays, graduations and other milestones with them? Now she was sleeping with a man their age.

Her skin felt hot and tight, and her throat closed, making it impossible to eat anything. She put down her fork and dabbed at her lips with her napkin.

"Carolina?" Maddie said from across the table. "Are you all right?"

Immediately, Seamus turned to her, and his eyes widened. "What is it, love?

Carolina couldn't seem to speak or get enough air to her lungs.

"She's having an allergic reaction," Janey said, getting up as quickly as she could.

"Linda," Grace said, "get some allergy medicine. Hurry."

"Carolina!" Seamus said. "Say something, love. You're scaring me."

"Mom!" Joe cried as he rushed around the table to her.

Janey came around the table where everyone but Caro was now standing. "Give her some room." She pushed through the group, dipped a napkin into a glass of ice water and ran it over Carolina's face.

The cold water on her heated skin felt heavenly.

"You're okay, Caro. Try to breathe."

Carolina focused on her daughter-in-law's blue eyes and drew shallow breaths into her lungs.

"That's it."

Linda returned with the medication. "I only have the liquid kind."

"That's better," Grace said. "She'll be able to get it down easier."

Carolina continued to focus on Janey as she swallowed the liquid that brought immediate relief to the tightness in her throat.

"What are those red splotches on her face and neck?" Seamus asked.

"Hives," Janey said.

Mortified to be the center of attention, Carolina cleared her throat and took a couple of greedy breaths. "I'm fine, everyone. Sorry about that."

"What do you think caused it, Caro?" Linda asked, hovering close by.

"I have no idea. I've never had hives before." By now her skin was beginning to itch. "I think I'd like to go home, if that's all right."

"Of course, honey," Linda said. "Take the medicine with you in case you need more during the night."

"I have some at home."

"Do you want us to come with you?" Joe asked.

"No, honey. I'm all right."

"Are you sure you shouldn't be seen by David?" Joe asked.

"No need. I'm really fine."

Joe nodded and kissed her cheek. "Okay, then. I'll call you in the morning to check on you."

"I'm so sorry about this," Carolina said. She turned to Adam. "Sorry to ruin your welcome-home dinner."

"You didn't," he said, giving her a hug. "No worries. We're just glad you're okay."

Carolina received hugs from Joe, Janey, Big Mac and Linda on the way out the door. Seamus held the car door for her and waited until she was settled to get into the driver's side.

"You scared the life out of me in there, love."

"I'm sorry. I don't know what happened."

"I have a few thoughts about what happened."

Caro looked over at him, surprised to realize he was angry. "Like what?"

"I think you were so freaked out about being there with me that you broke out in hives." This was said as he pulled the car away from the curb in front of the McCarthy's house.

She had no idea how to respond to that. "It was something I ate."

"No, it wasn't. It was Mac and Adam and Maddie and Grace seeing us as a couple for the first time and you stewing over what they had to be thinking of you cavorting with a much younger man. That's what caused it."

"How can you say that? Since when has acute embarrassment ever caused hives?"

"So you admit you were acutely embarrassed. That's great."

"I didn't say that!"

"Yes, you did. Have you ever gotten the hives from eating steak or potatoes or salad before? Yeah, I didn't think so."

"I can't believe you're blaming *me* for getting hives!"

"I can't believe you're denying that you worked yourself into a nervous frenzy that resulted in hives."

Since Caro couldn't deny that she'd done exactly that, she didn't try. Rather, she kept quiet on the rest of the ride. She was too itchy and uncomfortable to fight with him anyway. When they arrived at her house, he went directly to the bathroom and turned on the tub.

"Do you have any oatmeal?" he asked when he returned to the kitchen.

"I think so. Why?"

"It'll help with the itching. Put it in the bathwater." He stood rigidly in the middle of her kitchen, seemingly making an effort to avoid looking at her.

As Caro retrieved the container of oats from the cabinet, she noticed her hands were trembling. She wasn't sure if it was residual shock from the attack or worries of a different kind.

"I'm going to go," he said.

She spun around to face him. "Where?"

"I don't know. Somewhere else. When you work this stuff out in your head, love, call me. Until then, I don't want to cause you any more distress."

"I don't want you to go. Please don't go."

"It means a lot that you want me to stay, but I can't do this. I can't convince you to come to grips with this situation with the force of my personality or charm you into wanting what I want. You have to figure that out for yourself." He rested a hand on her shoulder and kissed her forehead. "When you do, if you do, call me."

"You're not being fair to me."

"Maybe not, but I'm being fair to me. And right now that's what I need to do. If you feel sick again, call Joe." He turned and headed for the door.

"Seamus! Wait! Can't we talk about this?"

The screen door slammed shut behind him as he walked out, the gravel driveway crunching under his feet as he made his way to the company truck he used on the island. After he drove away, Caro stared out the window for a long time before she remembered the bath and went to turn off the water.

She sprinkled the oatmeal on top of the water and then stripped off her clothes and slid into the tub. The cool water soothed her burning, itching skin but didn't do much for the ache in her heart.

Maybe she'd finally succeeded in driving him away for good. As that thought registered, the dam broke and her sobs echoed off the bathroom walls.

GRANT SAT in the waiting room, hoping to see David Lawrence before he left for the day. His leg bounced up and down, and he couldn't stop biting his nails. The childhood habit he'd long ago kicked had resurfaced as a source of comfort in the last week. At this point, he'd take any comfort he could get. He also needed sleep, which was why he'd come to the clinic after regular hours, hoping to catch David before he left for the day.

He couldn't go through another night like last night. The racing of his brain, the images he'd never forget, the fear, the horror, the shock… It tormented his waking and sleeping hours, and he'd give anything for some relief.

The doors that led to the examination rooms swung open, and Victoria Stevens, the nurse practitioner who worked with David, came through on her way out. She had her purse and car keys in hand, but she stopped short when she saw him in the waiting room.

"Grant? What're you doing here?"

"I'd like to see David, if he's got a minute."

"He's done seeing patients today. Could you come back in the morning? I'm sure he'd sneak you in—"

"I need to see him today. Now."

Victoria took a measuring look at him. "Let me check with him. I'll be right back."

While he waited, Grant paced the small room, worried about what he'd do if David refused to see him or worse yet, refused to give him something that would knock him out for a few hours. He needed to be knocked out, and nothing he'd tried on his own had worked.

Victoria returned. "Grant? Come on back."

He held back a whimper of relief as he followed her down the hallway to David's office.

"Hey, Grant," David said, gesturing to his visitor chair. A stack of folders and paper littered the desk. "Come in and have a seat."

"Do you want me to stay?" Victoria asked.

"That's okay," David said.

"I'll see you in the morning. Bye, Grant."

"See you."

David sat back in his chair. "What's up?"

Grant stared at the man who would've been his brother-in-law had he not cheated on Janey a year before they were supposed to be married. Grant had known him a long time, and if there'd been any choice of seeing another doctor, he would've chosen anonymity over this. But on Gansett Island, there was no other choice. David was the only doctor.

"Grant? Is everything all right?"

"I need something to help me sleep."

"Tell me what's going on."

"I'm not sleeping, and even when I'm technically sleeping, I'm still aware and half-awake, and I'm tired all the time. If I could just get some sleep, some real sleep, I'd be a lot better."

"What's keeping you awake?"

"How the hell do I know? I feel like I'm amped up or something, like I've had a whole pot of coffee when I haven't had any."

David stood up and signaled for Grant to follow him into an exam room.

"Can't you just give me something and call it a day?"

"I need to check your heart and blood pressure as well as your other vital signs."

Grant sighed—deeply—as he sat on the exam table, forcing himself to remain still while David listened to his heart and checked his blood pressure and pulse.

"Your pulse is a little fast, but otherwise, you're good."

"So you'll give me the stuff to sleep?"

David sat on a stool. "Tell me why your mind is racing. What do you see when you close your eyes?"

It was the one question Grant couldn't answer. He simply couldn't put words to the horror. So he shook his head. "Nothing, really. But I can't seem to shut down and sleep. I really need to sleep."

"You look awful."

"So I hear."

"I'll give you a script for seven days of sleep medication. After that, though, you're going to have to talk about what happened if you want to stop reliving it every minute you're awake or asleep."

David's words struck at Grant's deepest fear. That someday he might have to tell people... He might have to tell his family what really happened out there.

"Grant? What is it?"

"Nothing." He shook off the unsettling thoughts.

"I'll give you one of our samples for tonight since the pharmacy is already closed. You can fill the script in the morning. I want to see you back here a week from today. I'll have the secretary call you in the morning to make an appointment."

Grant extended a hand that David shook. "Thank you for this. I know things have been weird between you and our family since... Well, anyway. I appreciate it."

"Happy to help. Do yourself a favor and unload on someone before it eats you alive."

Startled by David's insight, Grant nodded and left the room, clutching the sample box David had given him like the lifeline it was. Tonight, he would sleep. Tonight, he would finally get some peace. Tonight, he could forget for a little while anyway. If he got some sleep, maybe tomorrow wouldn't be so agonizing.

THE MCCARTHYS WERE LINGERING over dessert when Stephanie came in, looking flustered and frazzled. "Grant isn't here?" she asked after taking a quick visual inventory of the family gathered around the dining room table.

"No, honey," Linda said. "We assumed he was with you."

"I haven't seen him since this morning. I tried to call him to see if he was here, but he didn't answer his phone. I don't know where he is."

Grace got up and went to Stephanie, putting an arm around her and bringing her to sit at the table. "I'm sure he's fine," she said.

"He's not fine. He'd never miss being with you guys if he was fine."

"Neither would Evan," Grace said. "But at least he called to say he was tied up at the studio."

"What's Grant's excuse?" Stephanie said. "He hasn't worked since the accident."

Adam watched the goings-on with an increasing sense of dismay. He glanced across the table to catch Maddie reaching for Mac's hand.

All eyes seemed to land on Mac, as if the rest of the family was silently asking him what they should do.

Maddie squeezed his hand.

Mac stared at their joined hands, seeming to draw strength from his wife. "It was tough out there," he said so softly it was almost a whisper. "We all went through our own personal hell, but we also had hours to wonder what'd become of each other. It's going to take some time. That's all I can say."

Linda nodded and brushed away a tear.

"We have to let them do this their own way, as hard as it may be for us," Mac said.

"You're not running away or burying yourself in work, and you went through the same thing they did," Janey said.

"That doesn't mean it hasn't been hard on me, too."

Janey seemed taken aback by her brother's unusually sharp tone. "I didn't mean to imply otherwise."

"Sorry, brat," Mac said. "I shouldn't snap at you, but it doesn't help to have everyone watching our every move, waiting for us to need you. If we need you, we'll tell you."

"So I'm supposed to be fine with not knowing where he is?" Stephanie asked.

"I'll go see if I can find him," Adam said.

"Thanks, Adam," Stephanie said.

"How about some dinner?" Linda asked Stephanie.

She shook her head. "Thanks, but I'm not hungry."

"Try not to worry," Grace said. "He probably forgot about dinner and went for a walk or something."

"Yeah," Steph said, "I'm sure that's all it is."

She said what she thought the family wanted to hear, but Adam could tell she didn't believe it. He wondered if his parents could tell, too.

The others left a short time later, and Adam helped his mom clean up while his dad went down to check on the marina. Adam couldn't help but notice she was unusually quiet.

"He's fine, Mom."

"No, he isn't. And neither is Evan. Mac is trying to be strong for everyone else, but he's not himself either. It's difficult to pretend like everything is fine when it isn't."

"It's like Mac said. It'll take some time."

"I'm wondering if we need to get a shrink over here to talk to them."

"I'm sure they'd be all for that," Adam said with a laugh.

"I called Uncle Kevin," she said of Big Mac's younger brother.

"Mom!"

"What? He's gotten a lot of attention for his work with posttraumatic stress. I wanted his advice."

Adam leaned against the counter and crossed his arms. "What did he say?"

"Why should I tell you? You think it's a stupid idea."

"I didn't say that."

"I had to do something! I can't sit idly by and watch my kids suffer while they go on pretending nothing is wrong."

"Tell me what he said."

She seemed to sag as she, too, leaned against the counter. "Some of the same stuff Mac did. That we need to give them time and space to come to terms with what happened and how they feel about it. We need to let them go through it in their own way."

71

"At what point do we intervene?"

"That was my question, too. He said to give it a few weeks, and if they don't seem better, he'll come out for a visit."

"Did you tell Dad you called him?"

"It was his idea. He asked me to make the call because he can't talk about it without crying."

"He might need Kevin, too."

"I thought the same thing."

Adam reached for his mom and hugged her. "I know it's very upsetting, but they're strong guys with tons of support around them. I have to believe they'll be okay. Eventually."

"I hope you're right. I'm worried about all of them, but Grant in particular."

"I'm going to see if I can find him."

"Thank you, honey. It would make me feel so much better to know where he is."

"That's why I'm here, Mom." It wasn't the only reason, but with all her other concerns, it was the only reason he was sharing with her. "Try not to worry, and don't wait up."

"Okay."

He kissed her forehead and went to grab a jacket.

LONG AFTER GRANT left the clinic, David hoped he'd done the right thing by giving him sleeping meds. Clearly something big was on Grant's mind, and adding sleep deprivation to the mix wasn't helping. He made a note to follow up with Grant in a few days to see if the medication had helped. Maybe by then he'd be looking for someone impartial to talk to about whatever was keeping him up at night.

Victoria appeared at his office door. "Your not-so-secret admirer is here, bearing gifts." This was said *sotto voce* with a teasing smile and a wink.

David would never admit to anyone, especially Victoria, who loved to tease him about it, that he'd begun to look forward to Daisy's end-of-the-day visits to the clinic. Ever since he'd tended to her after her ex-boyfriend beat her up, she'd been extremely devoted to him. "I thought you left."

"I met up with your *friend* in the parking lot and waited with her until you were done with Grant."

"That was nice of you. Thanks."

"You're not leading her on, are you?" Victoria whispered.

"Of course not. We're friends."

"*Just* friends?"

Her questions were annoying him. "Yes."

"Does she know that?" Victoria asked with an eyebrow raised in inquiry.

"Send her in."

"Yes, sir."

"Send her in, *please*."

"Don't do anything I wouldn't do in the exam rooms."

David felt his face heat like an embarrassed schoolboy. "*Victoria!*" he said in a low growl.

"I'm going, I'm going!"

Rattled by Victoria's insinuations—and how close to home they struck—he ran his fingers through his hair to straighten it after the long day at the clinic and stood to tuck in his shirttail. Why was he primping for her?

She came around the corner a minute later, her sweet smile leading the way as she proceeded hesitantly. Her long blonde hair was pulled back from her face, and her big blue eyes were luminous and bright with excitement. Even though her face still bore the yellowing bruises from Truck's assault, she looked a little better every day.

He'd enjoyed watching her become less timid and more confident as she recovered from her injuries. After a few days of checking on her at home after work, David had stopped himself from going back again. She was on the mend and didn't need to be checked every day.

Once he'd stopped going to her, however, she'd started coming to him. He told himself it didn't mean anything. They'd struck up an unlikely friendship after the incident with her ex. That's all it was. Except that he'd come to look forward to talking with her, to hearing her opinions and insightful thoughts on whatever was on his mind.

"David? Are you okay?"

He realized he was staring at her and blinked—twice—to clear his muddled brain. "Yes, sorry. Come in. Have a seat." It had taken some doing to get her to call him by his first name, and he was pleased she'd taken that step.

"Am I bothering you?"

He sat in the chair behind his desk. "Not at all. I was just catching up on some paperwork." Gesturing to the stack of charts on his desk, he said, "It never ends."

"I brought you some of the pot roast one of my friends made for me."

David's mouth watered as the smell reached him at the same moment the words *pot roast* registered in his brain. "You didn't have to do that."

"If you keep forgetting to eat, you won't be much good to your patients."

"You sound like my mother."

Her soft peal of laughter made David feel ten feet tall. "Something tells me that's not a compliment."

"She likes to fuss over me, too."

"Is that what I'm doing? Fussing over you?"

"I'm not sure. Are you?"

"I...I probably shouldn't have come." She looked uncertain again, and David hated himself for messing with her hard-won confidence.

"Why did you come, Daisy?"

Her bottom lip disappeared between her teeth.

David fixated on her mouth, which was almost too lush for her small-boned face. It occurred to him that he'd thought about that mouth and those lips far more often than he should have over the last few days. What was wrong with him? She was a patient, a woman who'd been battered by the man she thought she loved. She didn't need him thinking about her mouth, for crying out loud.

"David?"

"I'm sorry, what did you say?"

She stood. "I should go."

He rushed to his feet. "No, don't."

"I, um…"

"Please stay. Tell me why you came."

"Are you listening this time?"

Smiling, David went around the desk and leaned against it so he was closer to her as she settled back into the chair. "Yes."

"I was saying that I enjoyed talking to you when you came to see me. I thought maybe you might've enjoyed it, too."

"I did." He glanced at the container she held. "That smells really good."

She tipped her head and studied him, seeming amused. "Tell me the truth—did you forget to eat again?"

"Maybe. We've been slammed with the stomach flu that's led to lots of dehydrated patients. I admitted several of them, in fact, so I'll be staying here tonight." He stopped himself when he realized he was rambling. "But you don't care about that."

"Yes, I do. I'm interested in your work."

"Oh. You are?"

She nodded and handed him the container. "It needs about two minutes in the microwave."

"Thanks. I really appreciate this."

"It's nothing," she said with a shrug.

"It's not nothing. It's very thoughtful."

Her smile lit up her sweet face, and David was astonished by the wave of tenderness and longing he experienced when he made her smile. "Are you in a rush?"

"Nope. Nowhere to be until next week when I go back to work."

"In that case, maybe you could stick around to keep me company while I eat?"

"I'd love to."

.   .   .

ADAM LEFT HIS PARENTS' house and walked into town, checking all the usual haunts he and his brothers preferred along the way, but no one had seen Grant all day. In town, he thought about walking to the end of the breakwater to see if Grant had been foolish enough to venture out there alone—in the dark—but thought better of it. If he was out there, he was on his own. Adam didn't see the point in risking his own safety on what was probably a fool's errand anyway.

At the Sand & Surf, he ducked inside to see if Grant had turned up there. His cousin Laura was working the front desk and let out a happy squeal when she saw him. She got up fast and then sat back down just as quickly.

"What's wrong?" he asked as he went around the reception desk to hug her.

"Bouncing back slowly from the stomach bug," she said, grimacing. "Too slowly."

On closer inspection, he discovered her face was unusually pale and drawn. "I heard it whipped through the island."

She nodded. "I was one of the unlucky ones who got it, but I can't seem to shake it off. It lasted twenty-four hours for everyone else. Figures, right? But you're not here to listen to me complain. I was sorry I couldn't make your dinner. Our front-desk person called in sick, so I'm covering for her."

"You missed the grand unveiling of Gansett's newest couple."

"Who's that?"

"Seamus O'Grady and Carolina Cantrell."

Laura's eyes widened, and her mouth fell open. "Get outta here. Really?"

"Yep. Although I think he's a lot more relaxed about it than she is. She broke out in hives in the middle of dinner."

"Holy cow! This is huge! Janey has been holding out on me."

"On everyone, apparently. Besides Joe and Janey, who only recently found out, no one knew except for my mom, and she only heard about it today."

"Very interesting. I'll have to get the scoop from Janey. So what're you doing home?"

"Came to check on the boys and see my folks. Crazy doings around here lately."

"You know it," Laura said, shaking her head and making her blonde ponytail swing side to side. Her blue eyes filled with tears. "That was one long-ass awful day."

Adam hugged the cousin who'd been like a second sister to him.

"I cry every time I think about it," Laura said, wiping her eyes with the back of her hand.

"You haven't seen Grant tonight, have you?"

"No, he hasn't been in."

"Does he usually come by?"

"If Steph is working, he stops in for a drink or dinner. I haven't seen her tonight, though."

Laura's fiancé Owen Lawry came in from the porch, carrying his guitar like a backpack. "I finished my set, babe. Want to get something to eat? Oh, hey, Adam. What's up, man?"

Adam greeted his old friend with a hug. "Just looking for my wayward brother."

"Which one?"

"Grant."

"Haven't seen him today. Did you look at Sam's? Or Celtica?"

Adam nodded. "Checked all the usual places. No one's seen him, and he's not answering his phone."

Owen and Laura exchanged glances.

"What?" Adam asked, as a sinking feeling attacked his stomach.

"He's been...kinda off since the accident," Owen said. "Definitely not himself."

"So I've heard and seen for myself. If you see him, give me a call, will you?"

"Sure," Owen said. "Will do."

"You don't think he's with Abby, do you?" Laura asked softly.

Thunderstruck, Adam stared at his cousin. The thought had never occurred to him. "As far as I know, he doesn't even know she's home."

"Still," Laura said, "might be worth checking."

"I'll do that."

"While you're home," Laura said, "I could use your expertise with our reservation system. It's giving us fits."

"I'd be happy to take a look."

"Thanks." Laura covered her mouth and braced a hand on her desk.

Owen stepped closer to her, gripping her shoulder. "Babe? What's wrong?"

"Nauseous. Again."

"Ugh, that damned flu is hanging on. Let's get you upstairs. I'll get Holden from my mom, and she can come down to cover for you here."

"She's got a date with Charlie tonight." For Adam's benefit, she added, "She's been seeing Stephanie's stepdad."

"Sounds like an outbreak of romance around here. Good for them."

"We think so, too," Owen said, as he held out a hand to Laura.

"I'll watch the desk until Sarah comes down," Adam said.

"Thank you." Laura gave him another quick hug. "So nice to have you home, cousin."

"Good to be here. Feel better." As Adam watched Laura and Owen go up the stairs arm in arm, he experienced a pang of yearning. He'd had that—or so he'd thought. Watching his cousin and friend together, so obviously in love, made Adam long for what they had, to have what each of his siblings had found with their partners in the last few years.

Growing up in a family of five kids, surrounded by cousins and friends, there hadn't been much opportunity to be lonely, and he'd been too damned busy building his business over the last fourteen years to have time for loneliness. But now, leaning against the reception desk at the Sand & Surf, Adam felt more alone than he had in a long time.

"Here I come, Adam!" Sarah Lawry called a few minutes later as she came down the stairs.

Adam snapped out of his funk as she approached the registration desk, out of breath from the sprint through the hotel.

Sarah gave Adam a peck on the cheek. "So nice to have you home, and thank you for covering the desk."

"You must not have had much faith in my abilities if you ran from wherever you were to get down here to relieve me."

Sarah laughed and patted his arm. "We had full confidence, but Laura said she was certain you had better things to do than watch our desk."

"I was happy to do it."

Stephanie's stepfather, Charlie Grandchamp, came into the hotel. His gray hair was cut into a severe-looking buzz cut, but his entire demeanor softened at the sight of Sarah at the desk, and his blue eyes positively twinkled. There was no other word for it.

Sarah's face turned bright red, which Adam thought was adorable. "You know Grant's brother Adam, right?" she said to Charlie.

"Sure." Charlie shook hands with Adam. "Good to see you."

"Likewise." Watching the way Charlie and Sarah looked at each other, Adam experienced yet another craving to be part of something so sweet and sincere. He hadn't found it yet. Sasha had never turned red at the sight of him. That was for sure.

"I can stay if you guys have plans," Adam said.

"It's nothing that won't keep," Charlie said.

"The overnight girl gets here in half an hour," Sarah said.

Charlie plopped down in one of the overstuffed chairs in the lobby reception area. "I can wait."

Adam was about to say his good-byes and continue the search for Grant when Stephanie came in.

"Oh, hey, guys," she said, bending to kiss her dad. "What's going on?"

"Just waiting for Sarah to be done with work," Charlie said.

"Any sign of Grant?" Adam asked.

As Stephanie shook her head, her lips set with displeasure. "I went home to see if he was there. He wasn't, but his phone was, which is why he's not answering. I can't imagine where he is. I was going to check on the restaurant and then head over to the Beachcomber to see if he might be there."

"I'll do that," Adam said.

"Thanks, Adam. Send me a text if you find him."

"You do the same."

"I will."

"I'm sure he's fine, honey," Charlie said to his daughter. "Probably went for a walk or something and lost track of time."

"Yeah," Stephanie said. "I'm sure that's all it is."

Adam could tell by the tension he saw around her eyes and mouth that she was downplaying her concerns, which made him even more determined to find his brother.

CHAPTER 7

*W*ith the sun heading for the horizon, Kara Ballard brought her launch to a smooth landing at the floating dock next to McCarthy's Gansett Island Marina and helped her passengers disembark. After an endless day on the water, she was ready for some dinner and some peace. She would get the former, but the latter was hardly assured.

Her routine over the last week had been to work all day, pick up something for dinner and then head over to Dan Torrington's place, where she helped him by typing up the notes he'd made during the day for the memoir he'd been working on before the accident. Fortunately, he was left-handed so he could still write longhand, but the bulky cast on his broken right arm made it impossible for him to type.

They'd talked about getting software that could type for him, but Kara was helping him edit as they went along, so this system was working for him. With his book deadline looming, he needed all the help he could get.

Kara had willingly volunteered to type for him, but he'd been grumpy and out of sorts since the accident. Not that she blamed him. He'd been through a traumatic thing, but sometimes she wanted to remind him that his injuries and limitations weren't her fault. She was trying to help him, not that he seemed to appreciate that very much.

For a brief period this afternoon, she'd considered taking a night off from going to Dan's, but her worries over what he'd eat for dinner as well as her concerns about his deadline had her turning over the launch to her relief driver and heading up the main dock at McCarthy's.

She stopped at home to shower off the sunscreen and salt spray, changed into shorts and a tank top, grabbed a sweatshirt and called in a takeout order to Mario's. By now she knew that Dan was extremely fond of Mario's fettuccine alfredo. Despite her efforts to get him to try something else, he asked for the same thing every day and always insisted on paying for the food.

So they'd slipped into this odd routine without a mention of the night they'd spent together or the awkward parting the morning after when he left to join his friend Grant and Grant's brothers on the ill-fated sailboat. It was like the night of amazing sex had never happened.

Kara tried to tell herself that was because he was recovering from painful injuries, but she couldn't help but wonder if or when the Dan she'd known before the accident would ever reappear. That Dan had been positively besotted with her—or so it had seemed. He'd pursued her relentlessly until she finally broke down and went out with him— and slept with him on the first date, breaking her own personal rules about such things.

Their uncomfortable exchange the next morning had haunted her during the long day of waiting to hear if he'd survived the horrific accident. Over and over again she'd regretted telling him that despite the best sex of her life, she wasn't interested in a relationship with him. She'd told him nothing was going to happen, and he'd accused her of using him to get laid.

Kara had been a mixed-up jumble of emotions after he left to go sailing. The night with him had been her first sexual encounter since her longtime boyfriend dumped her two years earlier for her sister. With the hindsight of a week and a horrible day of not knowing whether Dan was alive or dead, Kara now knew that she'd been frightened by the powerful connection she'd found with him.

She'd never experienced that, even with the man she'd once planned to marry. Dan had rocked her in every possible way, first with his relentless determination to get her to go out with him and then in bed with lovemaking unlike anything she'd known before. Now she could see that she'd been frightened, which was why she'd pushed him away.

He was too damned much for her and had been from the start. But then the accident happened, and he'd been the most severely injured. He'd asked for her that night, and she'd been with him ever since, except for the hours she spent at work. She even slept most nights on his sofa after working long hours to type his manuscript for him.

After seven days of this routine, Kara was running on fumes but determined to help him make his deadline. Perhaps when the book was done they would talk about the mess they'd made of their fledgling relationship. A big part of her didn't want to talk about it. He was still too much for her, and always would be. The drama of the accident and its aftermath hadn't changed that fact.

She picked up the order at Mario's and arrived at the house Dan was renting from Ned Saunders, the island's resident land baron and cab driver. The small house was nestled in a wooded area near the island's south coast. In the distance, the sound of waves crashing against the rocks reminded Kara of how close they were to the shore.

Bags in hand, she let herself into the house and followed the sound of Dan's voice to the living room. He was on the sofa with his broken arm resting on a pillow, papers scattered around him, his dark hair standing on end as if he'd been tugging at it, and he wore a look of bemused aggravation on his face. Even with the dishevelment, he was sinfully handsome. Smiling, he waved her in, seeming happy to see her as always.

She was never certain if he was happy to see *her* or if anyone would've done after the long day alone.

"He said the keys you're looking for are in the bedside table drawer next to your pleasure devices." Dan held the phone away from his ear as the person on the other end screamed so loud that Kara could hear her. "Don't shoot the messenger." He grinned at her, flashing the dimples she found irresistible. "Those were his exact words." Dan continued to placate the woman on the other end of the line for another five minutes before he ended the call. "That, right there, is why I hate handling divorces."

"I didn't think you did divorces."

"I don't, usually. But after I helped Tiffany Sturgil with hers, I've been in hot demand around here."

"I thought her ex-husband was the island lawyer."

Dan scratched at the stubble on his jaw. Though he wrote with his left hand, he shaved with his right, which was why Kara had been helping him with that, too. "He is, but since the town council meeting when Blaine told off Jim, his business has been way down. I've been flooded with calls."

"You don't have time to be taking new cases with your book due."

"I know, Mom, but Tiffany asked me to help out her friend, so I did."

This was said with a shrug and the charming grin that Kara had fallen victim to the night he'd taken her out and ended up in her bed. "Are you ready to eat?"

"I'm starving. I thought you'd never get here."

"Sorry to keep you waiting, but I do have a business of my own to run, you know."

He got up off the couch slowly and painfully.

Since she couldn't stand to see him in such agony, she looked away and busied herself with getting dinner on the table.

His hand on her back made Kara freeze with surprise. He hadn't touched her since the morning after their night together.

"I know you have a business to run, and all I meant was that I was looking forward to seeing you."

"Oh." She turned to face him, taking a careful study of the healing cuts and bruises on his stunning face. "You were?"

"Of course I was. Why would you think otherwise? I live for the time with you every day."

Kara stared at him, wondering if she'd heard him correctly.

"Why are you so surprised?"

She hated the way he could see right through her. That had been a source of aggravation from the first time she met him the winter before at Luke and Sydney's house. He'd undone her from the very start. "I don't know. I don't know anything anymore."

Dan took her hand and brought it to his lips. "What don't you know?"

Despite the zing of absolute pleasure that traveled up her arm when his lips brushed over her skin, Kara worked her hand free. "Let's eat and get to work. We've got a lot to do and not much time to do it."

The wounded expression on his face reminded her a lot of the morning she'd told him she wanted nothing more with him. Why was it that his hurt became hers? Why was it that she couldn't find a way to broach the elephant standing in the room between them? They'd gone on like nothing had happened between them, falling into this strange businesslike relationship.

Kara had no idea what it meant or what he wanted from her, other than someone to bring him dinner and type his notes for him. And what did she want from him? That too was a puzzler. She'd thought she wanted nothing to do with him until the long day when she didn't know if he was dead or alive. That day had changed everything.

"Aren't you hungry?" he asked when he was seated at the table.

Kara got him a beer and opened it for him the way she did every night. "Yes, I'm hungry."

"I wish you'd tell me what's bugging you," he said between mouthfuls of pasta.

"Nothing."

He winced, wiped his mouth with a napkin and sat back in his chair. "I hate that word."

Kara regretted using it when she'd vowed never to say it again in his presence. "I'm sorry. I don't mean it that way."

"You mean the way you used it to describe what you wanted from me after we had sex?"

Kara's face got very hot as she put down her fork. Her appetite was suddenly gone. "Why are you doing this? You haven't said a word about what's going on between us since the accident—"

"Because I don't *know* what's going on! And I'm afraid to scare you away by asking."

"You, I… I don't know either. Everything is so different, and I'm not sure…"

He took her hand and wrapped his much warmer hand around it. "What are you not sure of, honey?"

His use of the word "honey" made her belly quiver. "You, us. This. Whatever it is. This is exactly why I told you I didn't want to get involved. I hate all the uncertainty and confusion."

Dan tugged on her hand. "Come here."

"I'm right here."

"Closer."

Though she was still uncertain and confused, she stood and let him guide her onto his lap. "I don't want to hurt you."

"Then don't make any sudden moves."

Kara couldn't help but smile at the amusement she heard in his tone as she sat perfectly still on his lap.

His good arm encircled her. "Kiss me."

"We were having a conversation."

"We still are. Now kiss me."

Exasperated by him—as usual—she leaned in and pressed a chaste kiss to his lips.

"I know you can do better than that." He swept her hair off her neck and set off a riot of sensation with his lips. "But I suppose I haven't exactly earned better in the last week."

"Don't say that. You've been in a lot of pain."

"That doesn't mean I should neglect you."

"You haven't neglected me." Now she felt guilty for thinking about herself in the midst of what he was going through.

"Yes, I have. I've taken advantage of your good nature."

"That's not true. I've been happy to help you."

"That day when I left your place… I was really upset."

Kara cringed, hating that she'd done that to him. When she started to say so, he stopped her with a kiss.

"The thought of never having the chance to be with you that way again was killing me. It was all I was thinking about on the boat. Grant even asked me what the hell was wrong with me. I told him I was hungover, only I was heartsick rather than booze sick."

"I'm sorry. I never meant... I don't know what I meant. I was overwhelmed after spending the night with you. I handled it badly."

"I figured that out about an hour after we left the dock. It occurred to me that it'd been a big deal for you to be with me after what you went through with what's-his-name and your sister. I thought maybe you were dumping me before I could get around to dumping you."

If she wasn't trying so hard to remain still, she might've squirmed because of how accurately he'd pegged feelings she had yet to acknowledge.

"Am I warm?" he asked, gazing up at her.

She nodded.

"The last thing I remember before we got hit was reaching for my phone to call you. I was going to tell you that no matter what you were thinking or feeling after the night we spent together, it was all going to be fine. I was going to tell you that I'd be over after I got in to talk to you. And I would've said that our night together was the best I'd ever spent with anyone."

Kara's mind raced as she tried to process everything he'd said.

"I sure do wish I'd gotten to make that call. Maybe then you wouldn't have spent the last week wondering where you stood with me, and I wouldn't have been tiptoeing on eggshells, worrying about driving you away when all I wanted was to keep you close."

Kara moved very carefully to put an arm around him, leaning her head against his. "Well, this is a fine mess we've made of things."

He laughed and then groaned when his ribs protested. "Don't make me laugh."

"Sorry."

"When I woke up at the clinic, all I could think about was you. And when you came, when I saw you there by the bed, I felt better. I felt like I could breathe again."

"I couldn't believe it when Blaine came to my house and said you were asking for me. I thought you'd never want to see me again."

"No such luck."

"I was so scared that day," she whispered. "When I heard about the accident and that you were missing… It was like someone had pulled the chair out from under me and sent me reeling. All I could think about was how we'd left things and whether I'd get a chance to tell you how sorry I was for what I said."

"Don't be sorry. I get it." His hand slid over her hair in a soothing pattern that made her sigh with pleasure. "So how would you feel about going steady?"

Kara laughed. "Are you sure you want to take on an emotional basket case like me?"

"Very sure."

"All right, then. But don't say I didn't try to warn you."

"I've been warned, and I still want you. I've wanted you from the first time I saw you last winter at Luke's. And I want you even more after the night we spent together. As soon as these damned ribs heal, and I can move without feeling like I've been stabbed, we'll pick right up where we left off."

"Thanks for the warning."

"No problem."

"You have a book to finish."

"I know."

"We should get to it."

He held her even tighter. "Uh-huh."

"Dan…"

"Hmmm?"

"Dinner? Work?"

"Kiss me."

"I did kiss you."

"Do it right this time."

He was positively incorrigible, and she adored him. The realization shocked her. Where had that come from? When had she begun to adore him? If she were being honest, probably when he brought her diet Mountain Dew and talked her into going out with him.

"What's wrong now?" he asked, his brows furrowing with concern.

"Nothing," she said, running her fingers through his unruly hair, attempting to bring order to it.

"For once, I don't hate that word," he said with that smile—and the dimples—that made her melt.

She tipped her head and kissed him as softly and as sweetly as she possibly could, mindful of his injuries and the need to stay still.

His hand in her hair anchored her to him as his lips parted and his tongue teased her lips.

Kara tightened her hold on him, falling into the kiss with a kind of abandon she'd never experienced before him. But he had battered his way through her defenses with his easy charm and cutting wit, wiping all thoughts of what's-his-name and what he'd done to her from her heart and mind.

"Whoa," Dan said when they came up for air many minutes later. "You're making me forget I'm injured."

As her lips tingled, she leaned her forehead against his. "If you try to do anything more than that, you'll remember."

"Can we do some more of that later?"

"Only if you get all your work done."

"Let's get busy!"

BIG MAC TOOK a walk down the main pier of the marina, checking to make sure the boats were secured, the power cords were on the docks and not in the water where they didn't belong, the hoses had been turned off and everyone was tucked in for the night.

At the far end of the dock, a forty-two-foot powerboat full of young people enjoyed a Race Week party. Why was it that every year Race "Week" lasted longer and longer? The sailboat races attracted all sorts of people and boats, even powerboats like this one that came to the island for the parties rather than the races.

"Evening," Big Mac said to one of the men on the boat's aft deck. "Is the captain around?" He'd seen the guy earlier in the day but didn't see him among the crowd.

"Hey, Tony! The marina guy is looking for you."

"Marina guy" was damned proud of the business he'd built over the last forty years from a collection of rickety buildings and falling-down docks.

The captain emerged from the cabin, wearing a dopey smile to match his glassy eyes. "Hi there, Mr. McCarthy. What's going on?"

His regulars called him Big Mac, but he appreciated the show of respect from the young man, even if the words were slurred. "I want to remind you we have an eleven p.m. quiet time here. Have your fun, but wrap it up by eleven."

"Oh, we will, don't worry."

"My good friend the police chief makes sure to send someone by every night to make sure no one is disturbing the peace."

"I hear ya. We'll behave."

"Thanks very much. Have a nice evening."

"You, too, sir."

The "sir" was a bit much, Big Mac thought with a chuckle as he wandered to the end of the pier and looked out at the pond, where deck lights on hundreds of boats sparkled like stars in the darkness. He'd been standing right here talking to his son Mac when Steve Jacobson had approached them about recruiting some guys to fill in for a crew that had been stricken with the stomach bug.

Big Mac had urged his hardworking son to take a day off and go with Steve. Mac had recruited Evan, Grant and Dan to go, too. They'd set off in high spirits, looking forward to the day on the water that had ended so tragically.

Alone on the dark pier, Big Mac rested his elbows on the top of a piling and used the his palms to mop up the tears that kept coming and coming and coming, no matter what he did. He wondered if they would ever stop. He'd always known he probably loved his kids a little too much. Just as he'd always know that his effusive love drove them crazy, especially when they were younger and more easily embarrassed.

Unfortunately for them, he didn't know any other way to love but all the way. An entire day spent pondering what it would be like to lose even one of them, let alone three at once, had broken something in him that wouldn't be easily mended.

"Oh, hey," Luke said. "Didn't realize you were out here."

Big Mac wiped his face and turned to the young man who'd been a son to him in every way that mattered. "What're you doing here so late?"

"I suspect the same thing you are—checking on our friends at 11 D."

"I had a little talk with them. I think we understand each other."

"Oh good. I'm sure you were more diplomatic than I would've been."

"You would've done fine."

"See you in the morning?"

"Bright and early."

Luke nodded and started to walk away, but then he turned back. Hands on hips, he leveled a steady look at Big Mac.

"Something on your mind, son?"

"I'm sorry… I wanted to say that because I know you're pissed at me and with good reason—"

"Pissed at you? What're you talking about? I've never been pissed with you a minute of my life."

Under the lights on the main pier, he saw Luke's cheek twitch, and his jaw was set with unusual tension that told Big Mac a lot about how upset Luke was over their supposed rift. "You're going to deny you've been pissed since last week when I stopped you from taking the boat out?"

They'd nearly come to blows when Luke physically restrained him to keep him from going out on his own to look for his boys.

Big Mac rubbed at the stubble on his jaw, trying to think of what he should say to fix this. "It's true I wasn't pleased that you stopped me, but with hindsight, I can see you did the right thing. The Coasties didn't need another missing boater on their hands."

"It was bad enough that the others were missing. I couldn't let something happen to you, too. And the fog was so thick. So thick."

Big Mac stepped forward, put a hand on Luke's shoulder and squeezed. "I'm glad one of us was thinking clearly, and I'm sorry if I've given you the impression I was pissed. I might've been in the moment, but I'm not now. Okay?"

Luke nodded, the relief showing in his expression.

"You're one of my kids, Luke Harris. I could never be truly pissed at you. Never."

"Shit... You gotta put it that way, huh?"

Big Mac hugged him. "'Fraid so."

Luke returned the embrace and patted him on the back. "Thank God they're all right."

"Yes. Thank God. And thank you. You did the right thing, but then again, you always do. You're a good man, and I'm proud to call you one of my own."

When Luke stepped back from him, Big Mac thought he saw a tear or two in the younger man's eyes. They'd all done their share of weeping lately. "You can't possibly know how much that means to me," Luke said.

"Go on home to your wife, son. Everything's okay here." And it was, Big Mac thought as he watched Luke walk up the pier to the parking lot. Everything was okay. He just had to keep telling himself that in the hope that someday soon he'd believe it.

Linda was enjoying a glass of wine at the kitchen table when Big Mac returned from the marina. "Everything all right down the hill?"

"Yep. Got a couple of party boats still in from Race Week, so I wanted to make sure they aren't going to keep everyone else up all night."

"Remember when that would've been us? Up all night with our friends, partying till the sun came up?"

"That was a very long time ago."

"Those were fun times."

He popped open a beer and joined her at the table. "Yes, they were. Before five kids came along and ruined everything."

Linda shared a smile with him. They'd never done anything more fun than raise those five kids and their assortment of cousins and friends.

"I ran into Luke down there. The poor kid thought I was pissed with him for stopping me from going out after the boys."

"Oh, no. All this time he was thinking that? What did he say?"

Big Mac relayed the essence of their conversation. "I told him I could never be truly pissed at him."

"He loves you so much."

"I know. And the feeling is entirely mutual. What a good kid he is to be down at the docks checking on things so late. I sure got lucky when I hired that eager fourteen-year-old."

Linda covered his hand with hers. "He got lucky, too. He got a job *and* a dad out of it."

They shared a warm smile.

"I'm worried about Grant," she said. "Really worried."

"I am, too."

"Something happened to him out there. Something big."

"I'm afraid you might be right."

"Adam has gone to find him."

"Oh, good," he said with a sigh of relief. "That's good. I thought about going to look for him, but I figured he wouldn't want to be found by me. I can tell I've been irritating them since..." As his eyes filled, he took a deep breath and blew it out. "Since it happened. I'm trying not to think about it. I'm trying to remember to count my blessings. Trying to remember everyone is safe. Other than that..."

"I think about poor Steve and his family and how easily it could've been ours."

He nodded in agreement. "You don't think I should go looking for Grant, do you?"

"Adam said he'd call when he found him."

Big Mac nodded. "Hard for me not to go after them the way I would've back in the day. Gotta remind myself they're not little kids anymore."

"I know, love." Not being able to go after them had been the worst part of an awful day for him. Old habits were hard to break. "You know what would make you feel better?"

"What's that?"

"We need to go to bed early and watch a movie. I'll even let you pick. Some James Bond will get your mind off it."

"I don't need a movie."

Linda eyed him. "What, then?"

"I need you." He stood and tugged on her hand to urge her to her feet. "You can get my mind off it a lot better than James Bond can."

Ridiculously complimented by his words as well as the raw hunger she saw on his face, she let him tug her up. She was no sooner on her feet than he was kissing her, his arms wrapped tight around her. His kisses had always had the power to take her breath away, and tonight was no different.

Reason finally had her pulling back from him. "Mac, wait. We need to go upstairs. Adam is home. He could come back any time. We'd scar him for life."

"Hurry," he said, swatting her on the rear as he directed her toward the stairs.

Laughing, Linda scurried out of his reach on the way upstairs. "Do you still have that doohickey you got at Tiffany's store?"

"Um, yeah. You don't exactly use and return such things."

"We're going to need that."

Her heart raced and the breath got caught in her throat as he bypassed the buttons on her blouse and pulled it over her head.

His eyes widened when he got a look at the sheer bra she wore that left nothing to the imagination. "Where'd you get *that*?"

"Also at Tiffany's store," Linda said with a saucy smile. "I thought you might like it."

"I *love* it. I love that store. I need to see if she's in need of some investors. We've got to keep her in business."

Linda laughed, feeling more carefree and lighthearted than she had since the moment the island's police chief, Blaine Taylor, found her at the hair salon with the news that her sons were missing. Tugging at the faded T-shirt her husband had worn to work, Linda helped him take it off, giggling as she did every summer at the "farmer's tan" that encompassed his face, neck and lower arms, leaving the rest of his torso white.

He scowled playfully. "Don't make fun of my tan."

"Why break tradition?"

Waggling his brows, he said, "How about you show me your tan lines."

Linda made a big production out of removing the dress pants she'd worn to work at the hotel, revealing an equally sheer pair of panties that matched the bra.

He let out a low whistle as he reached for her.

"Not so fast, sailor." She tugged at the button to his shorts and made quick work of them and the boxers he wore underneath.

They fell on the bed in a tangle of arms and legs. His kisses were ravenous, desperate and so, so hot. The older he got, the sexier he became to her. Her fingers sifted through the thick gray hair that had once been as dark as their sons'. The gray only added to his incredible appeal.

Tonight he seemed inclined to take rather than give, which was fine with her. He was always a generous lover, and she was happy to return the favor. She'd give him whatever he needed, whenever he needed it.

He broke the kiss, gasping as he cupped her breasts through the bra. "Lin…"

"What, honey?"

"I love you so much."

"I know." She wrapped her arms around him, holding his head against her chest. He was so much bigger than her that she often felt delicate and fragile next to him. Now, however, he was fragile, and she was determined to support him. "I love you, too. I love how much you love all of us."

"I love you all too much."

She released her tight hold so she could see him. "No such thing."

His smile softened his expression as he framed her face with his big hands. "Prettiest girl I ever met," he said. When he kissed her, he kept his eyes open.

Moved by his words as much as the gentle slide of his lips, Linda looped her arms around his neck and let him take them both away from it all. So much for her plans to care for him. He took over, removing the bra and panties with practiced skill.

As he kissed his way down the front of her, he said, "You know what I think about all the time?"

"What?" Linda said, gasping from the tug of his lips on her nipple.

"What would've become of me if you hadn't given up your fancy life in the city to come to my island to be with me?"

She fisted a handful of his hair, arching her back to get closer to him. "What choice did I have? I was head over heels in love. Still am."

"With me?" he asked, looking at her with blue eyes that danced with mischief. The relief at seeing his vivacity returning after the terrible fright they'd sustained made her want to weep. Instead of tears, though, she went with humor.

"With your island."

He let out a grunt of protest and dug his fingers into her sides, tickling her as he drew hard on her nipple.

The combination had Linda tightening her hold on his hair, torn between laughter and screaming from the pleasure. "Mac! Stop! I can't take that."

He tugged again on her nipple, gentler but still insistent. "Tell me who you were in love with."

"You, God, only you. I was in love with you from the first second I ever laid eyes on you."

He scooped her up effortlessly, drawing her in tight against him as he thrust into her.

His strength had always been a huge turn-on for her, never more so than right now when he held her so tightly, controlling their every move.

She loved the way he dominated her in bed but let her dominate him the rest of the time. The dynamic had worked well for them for nearly forty years, and as Linda gave herself over to the pleasure, she could only hope they had many more years to spend together.

"God, Lin," he said, shuddering. "That's so good. So good."

It had always been so good, she thought, as she peppered his face with kisses.

He turned his head slightly, enough to join their lips. "So glad you picked me, babe."

"As if there was any choice."

"You could've had anyone."

"I only ever wanted you."

"Luckiest guy who ever lived."

And then there were no more words as he let his body speak for him, loving her so completely and so thoroughly that Linda was left spent and gasping when it was over.

"Whoa," he said after a long period of breathy silence. "We still got it, huh?"

Linda released a shaky laugh. "Sure do."

He reached for her hand and brought it to his lips. "We've been so lucky, you and me. Great kids, great business, great friends, great home, great life. Last week I thought our luck had finally run out."

Linda turned on her side to face him. "It hasn't run out, and it isn't all luck. A lot of it was hard work and good parenting."

"True, but still... How lucky do any two people have a right to be?"

"You have to stop thinking about it, Mac. You have to find a way to put it behind you. We all do."

"I'm trying, babe. Believe me. It's the last freaking thing I want to be thinking about, and yet there it is, all day every day, taunting me with the reminder of how very close we came to losing so much."

Determined to keep him distracted, she crawled on top of him and reached over to the bedside table drawer where she'd stashed the vibrating "doohickey" she'd bought at Tiffany's store.

Her husband's eyes lit up when he saw what she had in her hand.

"What're you about, my love?"

"I remember a time," Linda said, sprinkling his chest with kisses, "when partying wasn't the only thing that kept us up all night. Remember that first summer we were married, before Mac was born?"

He massaged her shoulders, working his way down her back to cup her bottom. "Oh, yeah. That was the best summer ever."

"It sure was." She pressed a soft kiss to his lips. "What do you say we make *this* the best summer ever?"

"Would this best summer ever include that thing in your hand and whatever else Tiffany thinks we shouldn't live without?"

Linda howled with laughter. And she'd thought he'd be resistant to toys in their bedroom. How wrong she'd been about that. "Whatever you want."

His strong arms came around her, crushing her to him. "I like the sound of that."

"Everything is going to be okay, Mac."

"It will be as long as I have you."

Linda took a moment to enjoy the sweet warmth of his embrace before she wriggled free and set out to take his mind off his worries for a little while longer.

CHAPTER 8

*A*dam left the Surf and crossed the street to the Beachcomber, the iconic white hotel that anchored Gansett's picturesque downtown. He cut through the lobby to the bar, where he took a quick look around but didn't see Grant.

"Hi, Adam," the bartender, Chelsea, said. "I hadn't heard you were home."

"How's it going, Chelsea?"

"Race Week madness. We'll all be glad when it's over."

As she said the words, a roar went up from the other end of the bar. "What's going on down there?"

"Some of the sailors are teaching Abby Callahan how to do tequila shots. Pretty entertaining. I don't think she's ever done one before."

Chelsea was still talking as Adam launched off his barstool and stalked to the far end of the bar where he found Abby in the middle of a circle of men. They were cheering her on as she sprinkled salt between her thumb and index finger. She wore a low-cut black top that showed off some rather significant curves, as well as deep red lipstick that highlighted her full mouth. With her dark hair loose around her shoulders, she was like a living, breathing wet dream.

In all the years that Abby had dated Grant, Adam had never

thought of her as anything other than pretty, probably because she was his brother's girlfriend. As he stared at her now, though, he realized she was hot. Smoking hot and about to take another shot of high-test liquor. That snapped him out of his stupor to take action.

He pushed through the crowd of guys and grabbed the hand that held the shot glass, sloshing tequila all over her audience.

One of the guys fought back. "Hey, dude, what the hell are ya doin'?"

"Party's over," Adam said as he yanked on Abby's arm and pushed the protestor back.

She resisted his effort to extricate her. "Cut it out!"

"No wife of mine is going to behave this way in public," Adam said, full of righteous indignation.

"*Whoa*," the mouthy guy said, hands in the air. "She never said anything about being married."

"She tends to go a little crazy when we're on vacation away from the kids," Adam said with a good-natured grin. "But you can't blame her. Six kids in six years would make anyone crazy."

"*Six* kids? Shit, man. Do *you* need a drink?"

"I'm good. Come on, *honey*. Time to call it a night. Say good night to your new friends."

Abby muttered her good-byes and stared daggers at him as he half walked, half dragged her toward the lobby.

Out of the corner of his eye, he caught Chelsea watching in amusement as he marched Abby out of the bar.

"What the heck do you think you're doing?" Abby fought against the grip he had on her arm. The slight slur to her words told him she'd gotten in a few shots before he arrived.

"So the drinking is going better, but the swearing still has room for improvement, huh?"

"I can't believe you ruined everything! I was having *fun*! Now they all think I'm married, so none of them will sleep with me. Thanks a lot!" She pushed him away and swayed erratically.

Adam put his arm around her and guided her to the stairs. "You don't want to sleep with one of them."

"*Yes, I do!* Why can't you get that through your thick skull?"

"Because I know you, Abby. You're not like that."

"You don't know anything about me, and I want to *be* like that. I can't do that with you ruining everything." They had reached the first landing, between the first and second floors, when she stopped short, her eyes big and glassy.

"Are you going to be sick?"

She took a couple of deep breaths and shook her head. "I don't think so."

"Which room is yours?"

"I'm not telling you that. Go home, Adam. I don't need you to save me from myself."

"You need someone to save you before you make a huge mistake that you'll instantly regret."

Her eyes flashed with anger. "I don't know where you get off thinking you know me better than I know myself," she said, loud enough for everyone in the lobby to hear her. "If I want to drink and swear and have meaningless sex, it's *my* business!"

"I'll have meaningless sex with you, baby," a male voice called up the stairs.

"Get your eyes off my wife," Adam growled. He thought he heard the other man mutter, "Sorry" under his breath, but he wasn't sure.

"I'm not his wife!"

"Move it," Adam said to her. "I'm not leaving until you're locked in your room."

"How do you know I'll stay there when you leave?"

"Who said I was leaving?"

"No one invited you to stay."

"We're making a scene. Let's have this argument in your room."

Scowling at him, she wrenched her arm free of his hold and marched unsteadily up the stairs. Adam followed a step or two behind, ready to catch her if she stumbled. On the third floor, she stopped outside Room 323.

"I'm here. You can go now."

Not wanting to leave her upset and alone, Adam scrambled to

think of some way to continue their "conversation." But before he could come up with a plan, his phone dinged with a text that he only checked because he was concerned about his brother.

From Stephanie: *Grant came into the restaurant. Went for a walk, forgot his phone. Crisis averted. Thx for the help.*

No problem. Glad he's okay.

"Well, that's a relief," Adam said to himself as much as to Abby. He fired off a quick text to his parents to let them know Grant was okay.

"What is?"

"Grant showed up at Stephanie's restaurant. We couldn't find him for a couple of hours."

"Where was he?"

"Went for a walk and forgot his phone."

Abby's snort was most unladylike. "*Grant?* Walk for hours without his phone? That'll be the day. He might miss a call from Hollywood, and the world will end."

Adam laughed at her spot-on assessment of his brother. "Very true." It was also yet another reminder of how out of character Grant's recent behavior had been.

Abby leaned on the door jamb. "You're worried about him."

"We all are."

"If there's anything I can do…"

"That's nice of you, thanks." Once again the conversation stalled, but Adam didn't feel comfortable leaving her to her own devices in her current mood. Why he'd decided her own devices were his problem was something he could figure out later, after he'd seen her safely into her room. "I heard from Sasha."

Abby gasped, and her full lips pursed fetchingly. "Really? What did she say?"

Adam was so focused on her sexy mouth that it took a second for the question to permeate the fog in his brain. "Um, she's sorry. Wants to talk to me. Loves me, etc."

"What did you say?"

"Nothing," he said with a shrug. "She texted. I haven't replied."

"Are you going to?"

A door opened down the corridor, and a sleep-mussed head poked out. "Do you mind? People are sleeping."

"Oh," Abby said. "Sorry." Before Adam's dazzled eyes, she reached into her top and pulled a room key card out of her bra. When she caught him watching her, she blushed madly. "What? I didn't want to take a purse with me."

"I hope you've got ID stashed in the other cup."

Over her shoulder, she stuck her tongue out at him. "It's in my back pocket, if you must know."

The movement of her tongue detonated his stockpile of lust, sending it all to his groin in a rush of heat that had him removing his jacket to hide the effect she'd had on him. What the hell was that all about? Adam found himself once again trying to remember that this was *Abby*, who had nearly *married* his brother—the same brother who was going through some sort of private ordeal and probably wouldn't appreciate Adam lusting after his ex.

A huge bed dominated the small hotel room. Since there was nowhere else to sit, Adam lowered himself to the corner of the bed, keeping his jacket strategically placed over his lap. "Hot in here," he muttered.

"No such thing as air-conditioning in the hotels on this island." She opened a window, sending a cool breeze billowing through the small space.

Abby sat next to him on the bed, kicked off her extremely high heels and crawled up to the pillows. "Are you going to write back to Sasha?"

"No."

"Won't you have to deal with her eventually? You live together, right?"

"Lived. Past tense."

"What about all your stuff?"

"I've got my computers. That's all I care about. I'll send movers to get the rest."

"And the business?"

"It's all hers. They have to buy me out, which they're in the process of doing, but beyond that, it's a done deal. I don't expect to ever see her again."

"Since you insist on forcing your company on me, I'd much rather talk to your face than your back."

"Sorry." Adam turned to find her resting on her side, head propped on an upturned hand. The position did wondrous things for her cleavage. He forced his gaze off her chest and found her watching him with amusement and confusion mixed into her expression.

"Are you sad at the idea of never seeing her again?"

While Adam didn't want to discuss Sasha, he was anxious to keep Abby talking so she wouldn't kick him out and head back to the bar in search of trouble. "It's funny. A week ago, the idea of never seeing her again would've been unimaginable. Now... Not so much. "

"I know what you mean."

"Do you think you'll see Cal again?"

"He says it isn't over, but for me it is."

"So you talked to him?" Adam stretched out facedown on the bed but kept about six feet between them. All at once, that space seemed critical. The last thing either of them needed was an explosives-laden rebound with an old friend.

"He called earlier. Apparently, he didn't see the note I left him. He wanted to know what we were doing for dinner."

"Did you tell him about the note?"

She nodded, and her chin wobbled ever so slightly. "He was... He was more upset than I'd expected him to be. I didn't think he'd care."

"And he did."

"Yes."

"Are you sorry you left?"

"No! He might want to deny what's going on with Candy, but I know what I saw, and I'm not playing second fiddle to her. *Candy...* Makes me gag just thinking about her."

"Can I play devil's advocate for a second here?"

She eyed him cautiously. "If you must."

"Are you mad at her or at him?"

"Both of them. Her for coming on to him—obviously—when she knows he's engaged, and him for acting oblivious to the whole thing."

"Is it possible that he *is* oblivious?"

"Maybe," she conceded, "but if he is, I don't want to be married to that, you know?"

"Makes sense." Adam paused for a long moment. "Neither of us did anything to deserve what happened to us. We both tried our best to have healthy relationships that were screwed up by the actions of others."

"That's so true!" Her dark eyes sparkled with righteous indignation that was undone when she burped. Loudly. And then they both lost it, laughing so hard that the people in the next room pounded on the wall and yelled for them to shut up. That set off another round of quieter laughter.

When it was over, they lay on their backs, looking up at the ceiling, breathing hard.

Abby reached across the expanse of snowy-white linen and took his hand. "Thank you."

He looked over at her, noting that her eyes sparkled now from laughter tears. "For what?"

"Making sure I didn't do something I'd regret."

"No problem. Sorry if I was a little heavy-handed about it."

"That's okay. But really, Adam, *six* kids? Are you out of your freaking mind?"

"Is that the best you've got?"

She bit back a smile. "You're out of your fucking mind. Clearly."

"There it is!" he said, ridiculously proud of her. "I didn't mean to presume that I know you so well. I know you well enough, if that makes sense. You just broke up with the man you once planned to marry. I can't see you jumping into bed with someone else the same day you left Cal."

"And yet here we are," she said with a smile that drew one from him, too.

"You know what I mean."

"Yes, I do, and you're right. As much as I want to be that kind of girl, I need to take at least a day or two to recover from what happened with Cal before I start shopping for his replacement."

The idea of her shopping for Cal's replacement disturbed Adam for reasons he didn't dare explore further. "What do you think you've been missing out on? What's been so wrong that you want to become someone else entirely? There's nothing wrong with who you are now."

"That's very sweet of you to say, but there's lots of stuff wrong with me. I can't keep making the same mistakes over and over and not try to learn *something* from them. You know?"

Adam's heart beat fast as it dawned on him that she was still holding his hand, and he rather liked the way her soft hand felt wrapped around his. Neither of them seemed inclined to break the connection. He licked lips that had suddenly gone dry. "And you think jumping into bed with guys you don't know will fix whatever's wrong?"

"Maybe not, but at least I'll have some fun while trying to figure out what's next."

"You never said what it is you think you've been missing out on."

"I can't tell you that. It's too personal."

"Maybe if you told someone and you talked it out a bit, you wouldn't feel so determined to do something crazy and out of character."

She surprised him when she jerked her hand free and sat up. "What is so wrong with going a little crazy? While you were off being crazy in the big city, I was playing house with your brother, who was so fixated on his precious career that he barely gave me a thought. While you were off sleeping with every woman in New York City, I was rebuilding my life and falling in love *again* with a man who I thought was all about me until I realized he's actually all about someone else! *And you want to know what I've been missing out on?*"

Adam stared at her, completely bowled over by how drop-dead gorgeous she was when pissed off.

"*What* are you staring at?"

"You. You're quite something when you're stirred up."

"Fine, make fun of me. Whatever. Like this day hasn't already sucked." She flopped back down on the bed, defeat radiating from her.

Adam moved closer to her, drawn to her despite the many, *many* reasons why it was a very bad idea to be drawn to her, of all people. "I'm not making fun of you, Abby." He brushed the hair back from her face. "Rather, I'm having seriously inappropriate thoughts about how gorgeous you must be when you're turned on."

A flush of color crept from her breasts to her face, settling in her cheeks. "Stop it," she whispered. "You don't think about me that way. Don't act like you do."

"I never have before," Adam conceded. "You were my brother's girl. Off limits."

She ventured a tentative glance at him. "And now?"

"Now I find myself having inappropriate thoughts about you."

"You feel sorry for me."

"I only feel sorry that you've been disappointed. I don't pity you, if that's what you mean."

"You don't?"

Adam shook his head. "Do you pity me? I wouldn't blame you if you did. What kind of man allows his girlfriend to steal his company right out from under him?"

"I don't pity you either. And if I had to guess, I'd say the kind of man who lets that happen has stopped caring about her and the company if he's here rather than there, fighting for what's his."

Her insight astounded him. That was it—exactly. It was what he'd failed to adequately convey to his father earlier. He just didn't give a shit anymore. He still had all the talent and know-how that enabled him to build the company in the first place. No one could take that away from him. The company was replaceable, and so was Sasha. "You're right," he said, meeting her gaze. "You're absolutely right. I couldn't care less about the company or her. Not anymore."

Abby's smile lit up her face and warmed the places inside him that had gone cold after Sasha's betrayal. "I feel better than I did," she said. "Thanks."

"Me, too. Thank *you*. And for the record, I didn't sleep with *every* woman in New York City."

Her sleepy eyes closed, and her lips formed a sweet smile. "Half of them, then."

"I'll give you that."

Abby's eyes flew open in shock that softened when she saw his teasing grin. "You McCarthy boys are too handsome for your own good. I bet you've had your share."

"I guess," he said with a shrug, pleased by the backhanded compliment.

"You probably know what you're doing." Her hand swooped up to cover her mouth. "I didn't mean to say that out loud."

Adam studied her, trying to decide whether he dared to pursue it. His better judgment told him to let it go. Curiosity, however, won out over better judgment. "Do you mean in bed?"

Her complexion went from pleasingly peachy to blazing in the fraction of an instant as she looked away from him and nodded.

Adam's mind raced as he pondered the implications of what she was saying. Had she been with men who didn't know their way around in bed? Including his brother? He scrubbed that thought from his brain as soon as he had it. Not going there...

"I shouldn't have said that," she whispered.

"Tell me what you mean."

She shook her head.

"Abby..."

"You wouldn't understand."

"Try me."

Moaning, she placed her hands over her face. "This is why I shouldn't drink. *Ever*. My mouth gets ahead of my brain, and I say things that should never be uttered out loud."

Adam was still stuck on the idea of her mouth getting ahead of her brain. It put some seriously salacious ideas in his head. With her hands over her eyes, he took advantage of the opportunity to stare at that sexy mouth without her knowing he was staring. "Come on... No judgment. I promise."

"I can't believe we're having this conversation."

"It's the new you."

That drew a reluctant smile from her even as she kept her hands over her eyes. "I...I have trouble, you know..."

"Coming?"

"Cripes," she sputtered. "Put it right out there, why don't you?"

"We're both adults, aren't we?"

"If you say so."

Adam laughed and pulled one of her hands clear of her face. Without releasing her hand, he said, "Why do you suppose that's a problem for you?"

"I have my theories."

"You have my full attention."

She dropped her other hand and turned her head to look at him, her expression arrestingly lovely. "That's it. That's the issue. I never had their full attention. And without it..."

"It can't happen for you."

"Yes." She got a faraway look in her eyes as she fixated on something over his shoulder. "Even when things were good with Cal, he was always getting called away or waiting for a baby to be born or dealing with a crisis at the clinic. In Texas, he was working and tending to his mother. We had to hurry and take advantage of whatever time we had, and hurrying doesn't work for me."

"Did they know?" Adam told himself not to think about the fact that one of the men she was talking about was his brother.

She shook her head. "I got very good at faking it."

"Aw, shit, Abby."

"Screwed up, huh? You have to swear you'll never tell anyone, Adam. Promise me."

"I promise."

"Not even Grant."

"*Especially* not Grant."

They shared a smile that made Adam a tiny bit grateful for Sasha's betrayal. Without it, he wouldn't be having this unexpectedly special moment with this adorably sweet and surprisingly sexy woman. "I was always so concerned about hurting their feelings that I faked it rather than let them think they weren't satisfying me."

"Have you ever, you know, by yourself?"

"Ugh, I think I just *died* of embarrassment."

"Have you?"

"Yes!"

"So you know you can."

"*Yes.*"

"Interesting."

"What does *that* mean?"

"At least I get now why you've got meaningless sex on your bucket list."

"Exactly."

"Except..."

"What?"

"You had genuine feelings for Grant and Cal, but couldn't get there. What makes you think it'll be better with someone you don't care about?"

Her big brown eyes flooded with tears that made Adam feel like an ass for asking the question.

"Sorry. I shouldn't have said that."

"I have to *try*. Don't you see that? If I don't try, how will I find something better?"

Since Adam didn't have a good answer to that question, he didn't say anything. He stared up at the ceiling for a long time, and when he looked over at her again, he saw that she'd dozed off with tears staining her cheeks. Those tear streaks made him sad.

The cell phone peeking out of her hip pocket caught his attention.

Moving slowly and carefully—and without taking the time to change his mind or consider the ethical consequences of what he was about to do—he withdrew the phone without waking her. Luckily it wasn't password protected, which he'd have to talk to her about at some point. He accessed the settings and programmed it so he could check her location at any given time.

Even though his conscience strongly objected, he'd made a decision during the enlightening hour he'd spent with her. If anyone was going to help her go a little crazy this summer—in bed and out—it was going to be him. Now he just had to convince her to let him while making sure his brother never, ever found out about it.

OWEN GOT HOLDEN CHANGED, fed and settled in his crib. The little guy looked up at him with big, trusting eyes that made Owen weak in the knees with love. After helping to raise his six younger siblings, he'd never pictured himself acting like a dad to someone else's kid. But now he couldn't imagine life without the little guy.

Except for the one day every month when Holden's biological father came to the island to visit him, the baby belonged to Owen and Laura, and Owen couldn't imagine loving a child of his own any more than he loved Holden. He loved the way the baby snuggled into his embrace and squeezed his finger or gnawed on his thumb while teething. He loved how Holden stared up at him as Owen fed him a bottle, and he loved that he was just as good as Laura was at getting him to burp.

He'd even mastered diaper changes and could do them now in the dark when necessary. Since Holden came into his life, Owen had thought more about his own childhood than he had in years, wondering mostly how anyone could harm an innocent child. Soon he would have to testify about his miserable upbringing at his father's trial.

The thought of seeing Mark Lawry again—for the first time in more than a decade—made Owen feel sick and anxious, so he tried not to think about it. But there was nothing he wouldn't do to support his mom and her domestic violence case against his dad. His siblings felt the same way. They were willing to walk through fire, literally, to make sure their father could never again hurt anyone else the way he'd hurt them.

Lying on his back in the crib, Holden looked up at him, his chubby legs bicycling the blanket right off. Laughing, Owen put it back over him. "Playtime is over, buddy. Time for some sleep." He turned on the musical mobile and smoothed a hand over the baby's soft hair. "See you bright and early."

Owen's days of sleeping until noon after working a late gig were long over. Getting up with the baby was now one of his two favorite ways to start the day. His other favorite way involved the baby's mother. With Holden settled for the night, Owen wandered into the bedroom to check on her.

Laura lay on the bed staring up at the ceiling. Her face was unusually pale, which it had been since the stomach flu hit her the week before. Most of the other islanders who'd had the bug had bounced back a day or two later. After a week, Laura was still flattened, even though she'd insisted on working and taking care of the baby.

"Is he asleep?" she asked.

"On his way." Owen lay next to her and reached for her hand. After seven months together, it still stopped his heart to realize he could hold her and touch her and make love to her any time he wanted. She was his to keep, and nothing in his life had ever been more precious to him than her and the baby they both loved. "How're you feeling?"

"Like crap. I feel like I've been sick the whole time I've known you."

Smiling, he kissed her hand and then leaned over to kiss her lips. "You have not been sick the whole time. You were pregnant, which doesn't count as sick, and you had the flu."

"Why is everyone else over it, but I'm still feeling so bad?"

Owen didn't let on that he'd asked himself that same question. "You..." He forgot what he was going to say as another thought struck him, one he hadn't had before.

"What?"

He forced himself to meet her gaze. "Is it... Is it possible you might be pregnant again?"

Her face lost all remaining color, which wasn't much to begin with. "No! I can't be pregnant! Holden is only three months old!"

"Um, I hate to tell you that you can, in fact, be pregnant. Whether or not you are is something for Victoria to confirm, but don't tell me it's not possible. We haven't exactly been careful."

Tears filled her eyes and spilled down her cheeks. "I can't be," she whispered.

Touched by her dismay, he turned on his side and put his arms around her. "If you are, it certainly wouldn't be the end of the world. We're getting married in August, long before the baby would arrive. It's all good, honey."

"No, it isn't. I can't be throwing up all day every day in the midst of our busy season."

Owen smiled into soft blonde hair "Maybe it won't be as bad this time as it was with Holden."

"It would certainly explain why I feel like death warmed over. Oh God, Owen! How could this have happened?"

"I can tell you if you really don't know."

"Don't be funny," she said between sobs. "There's nothing funny about this."

"Yes, there is."

She punched his shoulder. "Easy for you to say. You're not the one who pukes your guts up for months when you're pregnant."

Choking back a laugh he knew she wouldn't appreciate, he tightened his arms around her. "I'm the one who scoops you up off the floor."

"I'm not ready for another baby! I can barely handle the one I have."

"You're an awesome mom, and there's nothing you can't handle."

"You have to say that. You did this to me."

He drew back from her so he could see her pretty face, which was now puffy and red from crying. At least she had some color in her cheeks. "And it was the most fun I ever had doing anything to anyone."

"Stop making jokes."

He kissed the pout off her lips. "Stop acting like the world has ended."

"I don't want to be sick all summer," she said with a moan. "It's so awful."

"I know, honey, but I'll be right there with you, just like I was last time, and we'll get through it together. And in a few months, we'll have another baby to love as much as we love Holden."

"Don't get too excited before we know for sure."

She was right, yet he had a sneaking suspicion that he was right, too. It would explain a lot about why she'd been feeling so poorly. "Hmm, let's examine the evidence, shall we? Exhibit A: feeling crappy for more than a week." He rested a hand on her flat belly, where there was no sign of a new life growing inside her—yet. She'd bounced right back to her pre-baby figure after giving birth to Holden in February. His hand moved from her belly to her chest, cupping a full breast.

"Don't. They hurt."

"Ah-ha! Exhibit B: sore boobs, and, might I add, a bit bigger than usual. Not that I'm complaining."

She sniffled as new tears flooded her eyes. "*Owen.*"

He cupped her face, forcing her to look at him. "I love you. I love everything about you. I even love you when you're puking. If you're pregnant, I'll take very good care of you and Holden, so don't worry about anything."

She banged her head against his chest repeatedly until he laughed and stopped her by holding her tight against him.

"When can we find out for sure?" he asked.

"Tomorrow," she said, her voice muffled by his shirt.

"I want to come."

"You already did. That's what got me into this mess."

Owen roared with laughter, thrilled by her, by them, by their amazing life together. And now, maybe, another child… For a guy who'd grown up in the midst of violence and fear, life didn't get any sweeter than this.

CHAPTER 9

Stephanie kept a watchful eye on Grant as he sat at the bar in her restaurant, pushing food around on his plate and nursing a beer. Under normal circumstances, he would've cleaned his plate and been on his second beer by now. He'd be shooting the shit with the other people at the bar, doing what he did best—telling stories. But tonight he kept his head down and didn't engage with anyone, even the bartender Cissy, who'd become a friend to both of them.

Cissy caught Stephanie's glance and sent her a questioning look.

Stephanie shrugged. She wished she knew what had him so withdrawn, but he wasn't talking about it, at least not to her. She also wanted to know where he'd really been earlier. Had he heard that Abby was home and gone to see her?

That thought made Stephanie's stomach hurt. Would he want Abby back now that she was single again? *No. Of course not. He loves you, you ninny. He's engaged to you.* But what if— *Stop it. Just stop.*

"Hey, hon." Her stepfather's voice jarred her out of the disturbing thoughts. "Got a table for your dear old dad?"

"I thought you guys were cheating on me by going to Domenic's tonight."

Charlie chuckled. "Sarah had to work late, so we missed our reservation."

"I feel so bad about that," Sarah said as she joined them.

"I told you I don't care where we go, as long as we go together." Charlie raised his arm to put it around Sarah, and she flinched away from him.

When she realized what she'd done, she seemed horrified. "Sorry," she muttered, her face flushing with embarrassment.

"Let's try this again," Charlie said, slowly raising his arm and looping it around her shoulders. "Better?"

Sarah nodded, and Stephanie led them to their table. She loved them together, two wounded souls finding comfort in each other. Speaking of wounded souls... She seated Charlie and Sarah and went over to the bar to try—again—to talk to Grant.

She slid onto the barstool next to him. "Do I need to be concerned about my chef?"

"What?"

She nodded to his plate, which was mostly untouched.

"Oh no. It's amazing, as always. I'm just not very hungry."

"We missed you at your mom's for dinner."

"Oh shit. I totally forgot about Adam's welcome-home thing."

"Everyone was worried when we couldn't reach you."

"Sorry. I was... I forgot."

Stephanie didn't mention how wildly out of character it was for Grant to miss an opportunity to spend time with his family, especially when most of them were there. She didn't think he'd want to hear that right now. "You ready to go home?"

"Are you?"

"I could be."

"Sure. Whenever you're ready."

He looked so tired that her heart ached for him. Whatever was keeping him awake at night was doing a number on him. She'd give anything to share his burden, but he wasn't sharing, and she'd stopped asking to keep the peace. "Give me five minutes."

Stephanie went to talk to her manager and hostess, putting them in charge for the rest of the evening with orders to call her if anything came up that they couldn't handle. While she normally wouldn't leave so early, she needed to spend some time with Grant.

She collected him from the bar, where he'd left a generous tip for Cissy.

"Have a good night, you guys," Cissy said.

"You, too."

As Stephanie drove them home, he didn't say anything, and she left him alone, even though she churned with questions and worries she didn't dare share with him.

At home, they dodged the boxes scattered throughout the living room and kitchen, a reminder of how much work still needed to be done at their new place. If only she could find some time to deal with it.

Grant went into the kitchen for a glass of water.

Stephanie followed and saw him pop a pill that he chased with the water. "What're you taking?"

"Sleeping pill." He turned to her, weariness clinging to him like a heavy blanket. "Desperate times…"

"Where'd you get it?"

"David."

"So that's where you were earlier?"

"Yeah. Sorry to have worried you."

"Oh," she said, blowing out a sigh of relief. At least he hadn't been with Abby. "I thought…" She shook her head. "Never mind."

"What did you think?"

She shook her head again. "Doesn't matter."

"Where did you think I was, Steph?"

"I didn't know. No one knew. We were worried. We've *been* worried."

"You didn't think I was with someone else, did you?"

"I hoped not."

He let out a huff of indignation. "Really? I'm off your radar for a couple of hours, and you have me with another woman?"

"Not just any other woman."

117

His brows knitted with confusion. "Who?"

"Abby's home."

His genuine surprise at that news was further comfort to Stephanie. "She is? With Cal?"

"Apparently, that's over."

"Huh. That's surprising." He met her gaze, his blue eyes dull and flat. "So you thought I might be with her."

"It crossed my mind."

He shook his head in disbelief. "Unbelievable."

Stephanie's stomach hurt, and her heart beat fast and erratic. "What am I supposed to think? You've been completely out of it since the accident, brooding in silence, not sleeping, not writing, not talking to me or anyone. And then you go missing the same day your ex-girlfriend returns to the island, suddenly single again. What would you think if you were me?"

"I wouldn't think that! We're *engaged*. I made a commitment to you. I'm not going to cheat on you the first chance I get. Give me some credit, will you?"

Stephanie wanted to scream and yell and pound her fists on his chest. Whatever it took to get him to tell her what had him so wound up in knots. For now, she was grateful he was talking to her about something. "I'm sorry. You're right. I shouldn't have gone there."

"No, you shouldn't have."

Her insecurities had caused them trouble in the past, and the last thing they needed now was more of that kind of trouble. "You know my weak spots. I can't help that I go right to worst case."

"Don't go there. I'm not interested in her. I'm interested in you."

Deciding to take a chance, Stephanie went to him and slid her hands over his chest and linked them behind his neck. "You're interested in me?" she asked with her best teasing smile.

His lips formed the closest thing to a smile she'd seen since the accident. "You know I am. I love you."

As his arms came around her, she wanted to sing hallelujah. "I love you, too. And I hate to see you hurting. I wish you'd talk to me, Grant. Tell me what happened out there. Let me help."

His smile faded, and the remote expression returned. "I can't. I just can't."

"The offer is on the table. I'm here, and I'm not going anywhere. Whatever you need, whenever you need it, you know where I am."

He hugged her tightly as a deep sigh shuddered through him. "That helps, babe. Thank you."

"Hold on to me."

"I don't want anyone but you, Steph. No matter what else may be going on, don't worry about that, okay?"

"Okay." She closed her eyes tight against the rush of emotion. It felt so good to be held by him, to be close to him, to breathe in the scent that was his and his alone. "Let's go to bed."

They got ready in silence, Stephanie watching him out of the corner of her eye as she brushed her teeth. At least her heart had stopped racing and her stomachache had let up at his words of love and reassurance. She'd take the partial victory.

Since the accident, they'd abandoned their usual sleep-naked-and-make-love-as-often-as-humanly-possible philosophy, but when she saw him get into bed unclothed, her heart skipped a happy, hopeful beat. She pulled her T-shirt over her head and dropped it into the hamper.

She slid in next to him, shivering from the chill of the sheets.

Grant reached for her and she snuggled into his embrace, sighing with pleasure as his warmth chased away the chill that had taken up residence in her bones during the long day he'd been missing—and stayed there during the long week since.

"Feels good," she said.

"Mmm."

"Do you want to, you know..." She didn't know how to phrase it, because she'd never had to ask before.

"Tired."

"Oh, okay."

He squeezed her shoulder. "Sorry."

"It's fine." She kissed his chest. "Everything is fine." As she spoke, she ran her hand over his chest and belly, hoping to soothe him. "Grant?"

A big snore answered for him.

While Stephanie was relieved that he would finally get some rest, she was left feeling unsettled and lonely for him.

ABBY WANTED TO DIE. Not because her head pounded from the tequila or because her mouth was drier than the Sahara Desert. No, she wanted to die because she remembered, in excruciating detail, telling Adam McCarthy about her orgasm issues.

Moaning, she rolled her face into the pillow. Maybe if she held her breath long enough, she could expire before she ever had to face him again. What in the world had led her to tell him *that* of all things?

And one of the men she'd been complaining about had been his *brother*, for God's sake. "Oh, please… Take me. Take me right now. It's been a good life, but I need to be put out of my own misery."

She said the prayer and then waited for action. When nothing happened, she let out another moan and tried to remember how their conversation had gone from mutual sharing about what had gone wrong in their respective relationships to her telling him *that*.

It was his fault. He'd been far too sweet and willing to listen. He'd made it way too easy for her to spill her guts to him.

Taking one of the extra pillows from the bed, she placed it over her face and hugged it tightly with both arms. Was it even possible to suffocate oneself? She'd like to find out.

"What the hell are you doing?"

Adam. *No.* Please, God, make him go away! Where had he come from?

He yanked the pillow off her face. "What're you doing?"

"Hiding from the sunlight." She couldn't look at him. She just couldn't. He knew…things…about her that no one else knew. She'd told him her deepest, darkest secret. "What're you doing here? How'd you get in?" As she said the words, the scent of coffee permeated her hangover and made her mouth water, which was a welcome relief from the dryness.

"I never left."

"Oh. So...you..."

"Fell asleep."

"Where'd the coffee come from?"

"Downstairs."

"How did you get back in?"

"I took your key. Hid it in my boxer shorts."

She couldn't help the laugh the comment drew from her, even if she still wanted to die from the embarrassment of oversharing.

He held out a cup to her. "Since I don't know how you like it, I took a chance with cream and sugar. Want some?"

Desperately. "Yes, please. Thanks." Since she probably had Godzilla breath from the tequila, the coffee couldn't make it worse, could it? And was it at all fair that he was drop-dead gorgeous in the morning? His hair was sexily mussed, while hers was plastered to her skull. The whiskers on his jaw only made him more ridiculously handsome than he was when freshly shaven. The DNA gods had blessed him and his brothers with far more than their fair share of sexiness. That was for sure.

Coffee in hand, he sat on the bed next to her, pillows at his back, and stretched out his legs.

Abby would never, ever admit to anyone that she'd always thought he was the most handsome of the four McCarthy boys. She'd thought so even when she'd been dating his brother and had often felt guilty for her scandalous thoughts. As gorgeous as Grant was, there was something about Adam that had always gotten to her, which was another of her deep, dark secrets—one she planned to keep to herself forever. Not that she'd planned to share the other one... Speaking of that, she felt the need to explain herself to him.

Don't. You'll only make it worse.

But I have to say something! How can I leave that hanging out there without at least an apology for oversharing?

You'll only make it worse.

121

How? How is that possible?

"Adam."

She caught him mid-sip. "Hmm?"

"What I said last night—"

"I've been thinking about that all morning."

Abby sucked a mouthful of coffee into her windpipe, which was promptly expelled all over the white comforter. Coughing and gagging, she tried to recover the oxygen that had been expelled from her lungs along with the coffee.

Adam dutifully patted her back until she stopped coughing and could breathe again.

"That was embarrassing."

"Housekeeping isn't going to be happy with you," he said, surveying the disaster on the comforter.

"It's your fault! How could you just say *that* like it was no big deal that you'd been thinking about what I told you?"

"Because it isn't a big deal."

"Maybe not to you, but did it occur to you that I wish I'd never told you?"

"I'm glad you did. How can I help you get to the bottom of it if I don't know about it?"

"Wait... Help me?" A dazzling array of erotic images cycled through her addled brain as the words "get to the bottom of it" registered. "It's none of your business!"

"I've decided to make it my business," he said with a smug smile that made her want to punch that handsome face.

"Really. Well, as much as I appreciate your offer—"

"Don't you want to *hear* my offer before you blow it off?"

"No! I most definitely *do not* want to hear your offer!"

"You disappoint me," he said with a cluck of dismay. "And here I thought you were all Ballsy McBalls-A-Lot, ready for a big adventure."

"Ballsy McWho? And for your information, I *am* ready, but I don't see what it has to do with you."

"That's what I'm trying to tell you. Are you ready to listen?"

"Do I have a choice?"

"Always."

The earnest way he said the single word intrigued her. No matter what he might have in mind, the choice was hers. He'd never force himself on her. While she'd known that about him, the reminder was welcome in light of what she'd told him the night before. "Fine. What's your big idea?"

Adam put his coffee on the bedside table and reached for her hand. "I think we both know you need to shake things up a bit. We also know there are certain things you're not willing to do, even if they sound good on paper. Sleeping around is one of them. If you think you feel sick today after a few drinks and spilling some secrets to me, imagine how you'd feel waking up next to a guy you barely know after sharing your body with him."

The thought turned Abby's stomach, but it didn't take much to do that this morning.

"So I'd like to volunteer to be your partner in crime. We'll do anything you want—in bed or out. Skinny-dipping, motorcycle rides, tattoos, tequila shots, all-nighters and as many orgasms as you can handle. Whatever you want, whenever you want it."

Abby stared at him, incredulous—and intrigued. "You'd get a tattoo for me?"

Adam tossed his head back and laughed—hard. "That's the part you're fixating on? Did you hear anything else I said?"

"I heard it."

"And?"

"What's in it for you?"

"Seriously? You're really asking me that?"

"Yes!"

"I don't know if you've looked in a mirror lately, but you're a very sexy woman who's looking to bust loose and have some fun. What red-blooded guy wouldn't want to be a part of that? Besides, I could go for some lighthearted fun after what I've just been through with Sasha and the company."

"And the fact that I dated your brother doesn't factor into this at all?"

"It does. In fact, it's one of my two conditions."

She shifted onto her side to face him, and that was when she realized she was braless. When had that happened? "This I've got to hear."

"Condition one is we keep our arrangement between us. No sharing the dirty deets with Janey or Laura or anyone else. I don't want Grant to know we're seeing each other until I'm ready to tell him, but only because it might upset him, and I don't want to do that when there's something else on his mind."

"This is a small island. If we're seen together, it might get back to him."

"It might, and if it does, I'll deal with it when and if it happens. In the meantime, I'd prefer to keep it between us."

"Fair enough. What's the second condition?"

His expression became very serious. "I don't share with anyone. If you're seeing me, you're not seeing—or sleeping with—anyone else."

Abby withered under his intense scrutiny. She couldn't begin to imagine how hideous she must look. Since she hadn't gotten around to removing her mascara the night before, she probably had raccoon eyes, too. But he'd said she was sexy and gorgeous. Did he mean that, or was he only looking for some easy sex with a woman who'd declared her intention to sleep around more than once in his presence?

"Are you making this offer because you think I'm easy?" The words popped out of her mouth before her conscience could warn her they might be a bad idea.

His eyes darkened with what might've been anger. "It's not because I think you're easy. I never thought that for a second. You're the one who thinks that. Not me."

Abby closed her eyes and tried to think through the tequila fog. It wasn't a *bad* idea to have a partner in crime she could trust to be upstanding. If there was one thing she knew about Adam and his family after all the years she spent with Grant, it was that Big Mac McCarthy had raised some damned fine men.

What might it be like to be on the receiving end of Adam McCarthy's full attention? He had no job at the moment and nothing to do but spend time with his family and with her, if she desired. *If she desired...* That thought sent a tingle to the juncture of her legs and made her nipples pop up for a look around.

Had he noticed that? Abby opened her eyes to find his gaze trained on her chest. Yep, he'd noticed and was apparently pleased by her reaction if the bulge in his shorts was any indication. Was she actually considering his idea? It seemed so. She liked that he didn't pressure her. He'd laid out his case and let her think about it. But she noticed then that he hadn't let go of her hand while she did her thinking.

She turned her head to meet his gaze. "Can we get the tattoos first?"

His smile lit up his face and made his blue eyes dance with delight. "We can do whatever you want. Does this mean we have a deal?"

"Yes. We have a deal."

He kissed the back of her hand. "Good, now let's have some fun."

HOLY FUCKING SHIT, Adam thought as the needle cut into his bicep, creating the outline of Gansett Island he'd decided on after much debate. He bit his lip to keep from crying out in pain. He'd had no idea it would hurt this much. Thank God he hadn't gone with the bigger version of the island that the tattoo artist had suggested. This one would be plenty big enough.

Focusing on breathing in through his mouth and out through his nose—and not crying like a baby in front of the woman he was trying to impress—Adam focused on Abby in the chair next to him having a red rose inked onto her lower back. Her eyes were closed and her lips formed a small contented smile. How could she *smile* while a *needle* was piercing her skin?

"Doing okay?" her guy, Duke, asked as he rested a soothing hand on her bare back. Duke. What kind of name was that? The guy had muscles on top of his muscles, and his arms were covered with "sleeve" tattoos that Abby had asked him all about before choosing her image.

Adam wanted to tell *Duke* to keep his hands to himself, but that would require removing his lip from between his teeth. So he watched and seethed and held back the need to whimper. When had he become so proprietary where she was concerned?

"Hanging in there, Adam?" his guy, Jeff, asked.

"Uh-huh."

"People are often surprised by how much it hurts, so don't be afraid to make some noise."

"It's not as bad as I thought it would be," Abby said, smiling at Adam.

While he felt clammy and shocked from the pain, she was glowing and happy as could be. She must have a really high threshold for pain. He used to think he did, too. Now he knew better.

"Unfortunately, no one will be able to see it," Adam said, rehashing their earlier argument in which he'd tried to convince her to put the tattoo where it would be easily seen.

"I'll know it's there. That's enough. For now, anyway."

Adam hoped she wouldn't expect him to go through this hell again. Once was more than enough for him.

"Almost got the outline done," Jeff said. "Then we'll just have to fill it in. That's going to take some time, so get comfortable."

Awesome, Adam thought, trying to focus on more pleasant things such as the sex he might get to have with Abby. But as the needle once again penetrated his skin, all thoughts of sex fled from his brain, and Adam couldn't think of anything other than getting the fuck out of that chair.

"THAT WAS SO MUCH FUN!" Abby said, as they walked along Ocean Avenue, enjoying ice-cream cones after the tattoos were finally finished.

Adam was forcing down ice cream he didn't really want. He'd much prefer an ice pack and a couple of ibuprofen.

She practically skipped along next to him. "Did you *love* it?"

He was far more pleased by her excitement in doing something wildly out of character than he'd been by the tattoo. "More than anything I've ever done."

"Are you being sarcastic?"

"Maybe a little." He eyed her through his sunglasses. "Yours didn't hurt?"

"Oh yeah, it hurt a lot, but I was so excited to be doing it that I was almost high off the pain. Does that make sense?"

"Ah, yeah, I guess."

"You think I'm crazy, don't you?"

"I never said that." He tossed the rest of his ice cream into a trash can while trying not to watch too closely as she licked hers. "What's next on our agenda?"

"You said something about a motorcycle?"

"That I did. I can either go get Mac's from Evan, or I can rent one. Any preference?"

"Whatever you want."

"Renting would be more immediate."

"Then let's rent. You paid for the tattoos, so let me pay for the bike."

"Not happening. I got it."

She stopped walking and turned to him. "Why can't I pay for something?"

"Because. I don't roll that way. When I take a lady out, I pay."

"You do know the Stone Age is over, right?"

"I've heard that news, and yet, I'm still paying." Ignoring her scowl, he took her hand and tugged her along as he headed to the rental place that shared the parking lot with the Gansett Island Ferry Company. Once there, Adam said to the attendant, "I'm looking for the biggest, baddest, fastest motorcycle you've got available."

"You're in luck," the young man said. "I've got one good one left."

"Yay!" Abby said. "Does it go really fast?"

"Yes, but I don't recommend going too fast on island roads."

"We'll take it easy," Adam assured him. He signed the paperwork, handed over his credit card and took possession of the bike and two helmets a few minutes later. "Go put on some jeans, and I'll pick you up at the Beachcomber."

"It's too hot for jeans."

"Trust me, babe, if we crash, you'll be very glad you wore jeans."

"I thought you knew what you were doing."

"I do, but that doesn't mean everyone we'll be sharing the road with knows what *they're* doing." He tweaked her nose. "Jeans or no ride."

"You're kinda bossy sometimes."

Adam straddled the bike and strapped on his helmet. "I've heard that a few times in my life. It's the curse of being a middle child."

"How do you figure?"

"Someone was always telling me what to do, so now that I'm all grown up, I like to call the shots." He crooked his finger to bring her in closer. "Especially in bed." Adam smiled at her flustered reaction to the outrageous comment. "Pick you up in ten."

When he glanced in the rearview mirror and saw her fuming, he laughed. And then he decided to use his ten minutes to stop by Grace's pharmacy to get some pain medication before his arm literally fell off his body.

ABBY STOMPED BACK to the Beachcomber, irritated with herself as much as him. His high-handedness drove her crazy, but what drove her even crazier was that she was turned on by it. Who knew she liked a man who took command and got things done? Thirty minutes after she suggested they get tattoos, he'd had her at the island's only tattoo studio.

She'd managed to resist his suggestion that she put the tattoo somewhere people could see it. She hadn't completely lost her mind, but she'd enjoyed the pleasurable pain of being inked. Next time, she might put the tattoo where it could be seen. Why not? What did she care if people saw it?

By the time she'd stomped up the stairs to her third-floor room, she was breathing hard and mad at herself. *Why* hadn't she listened to

Adam and put the tattoo somewhere visible? What good was it if no one knew she had it? She rifled through her suitcases until she found a pair of faded jeans and pulled them on.

So much for her new, go-wild philosophy… She now had a tattoo no one would ever know she had unless she got down and dirty with them, and since she made her deal with Adam, she wouldn't be getting down or dirty with anyone but him. Not that the idea of getting busy with him didn't cause her girl parts to tingle with interest, but she wanted other people to know she was different now. Not just Adam.

The first chance she got, she was going back for a second tattoo, and this one would be somewhere more visible. Pleased with her decision, she grabbed a sweater and headed downstairs to meet Adam, who was waiting for her in the street outside the hotel.

He smiled when he saw her coming, and Abby felt her earlier irritation yield to the excitement of another adventure with him. Halfway down the stairs, it occurred to her that she was probably too excited to be going out with him. She had to remind herself to keep her emotions out of it. They were having fun, not a relationship.

When she joined him at the curb, he plopped the helmet onto her head and adjusted it for her. "Ready?"

"Uh-huh."

"Slide on and put your arms around me. Hold on tight."

"Where do I put my feet?"

Adam pointed out the passenger footrests.

As she put her arms around him, Abby was hit with a sudden bout of shyness.

He must've sensed her hesitation, because he turned to her. "What's wrong?"

"I…I was thinking…"

"About?"

"The one thing we didn't talk about earlier."

"Which is?"

"Boundaries."

"What kind of boundaries are we talking about?"

"The relationship kind." Abby forced herself to look at him. "We talked about exclusivity when it comes to sex, but we didn't talk about not letting this get serious or anything. I don't want that. I thought I should make sure you knew that."

"I don't want it either, so don't sweat it. We're both right out of serious relationships that went bad. We've got no business doing anything other than having fun."

"Good," she said, pleased that he understood. "That's a relief."

"We're on the same page, Abs. Don't worry."

The nickname seemed to take them both by surprise. No one had ever called her that before, and she discovered she liked it coming from him.

"Shall we?" he said.

"Yes, please."

He fired up the bike and pulled away from the curb, navigating through the traffic that clogged downtown on the way to the less congested roads that circled the island.

As Abby giggled with the sheer joy and freedom, she tightened her grip on Adam's waist. When her hands connected with his abdomen, she realized he was all muscle. She had to stop herself from exploring further, if for no other reason than she didn't want to distract him.

They made two full loops around the island before Adam pulled into the parking lot at the bluffs and cut the engine. He got off the bike and removed his helmet.

Abby fumbled with the strap to her helmet, so Adam helped her. "That was amazing. I loved it."

"I'm glad."

"But it's not really a true adventure if I don't get to drive."

"Have you ever driven a motorcycle?"

"Nope."

"Well you don't start with one like this. I can give you some lessons on Mac's old bike, if I can wrestle it away from Evan."

"I'd like to learn."

He held out his hand to her, and they headed for the stairs that led to the beach below. "Looks like we've got the place to ourselves today. Another week, and the tourists will invade."

"When I was in business, I used to live for the invasion. Now I kind of like the peace and quiet."

Adam stopped her from going all the way to the beach and tugged her hand to invite her to sit next to him on the stairs. "Have you given any thought to what you'll do for work?"

"I'm going to run the gift shop at the Surf for Laura this summer. After that, we'll see. I may reopen the Attic next season, but it's getting late for that this year."

"It might be nice to have a summer where you don't have all the responsibility of running your own business."

"My thoughts exactly. Have you made any plans, yet?"

"Not really. I've had a few people ask me to help them with some things here. It's enough to keep me busy for a couple of weeks. After that, we'll see," he said, using her words.

His phone chimed with a text. "Crap."

"What's wrong?" Abby asked.

"Forgot to tell my mom I wasn't coming home last night."

"That wasn't very nice."

"I know. It's been a long time since I had to tell her where I was. I've fallen out of the habit."

"Doesn't mean she won't worry about you."

"I've been duly chastised by both of you. Won't happen again."

While Adam exchanged texts with his mother, Abby kicked off her shoes and wandered down to the water, dipping her toes into the chilly surf. By the time he joined her, she'd rolled up the cuffs of her jeans and wandered in farther. The sand between her toes was a welcome reminder of summer days at the beach, one of her favorite places to be.

"We used to come down here to skinny-dip when we were kids," Adam said when he joined her.

"I've never done that."

"*Never?* You grew up on an island, and you've never skinny-dipped?"

"Nope."

"You really did miss out, didn't you?"

"I was too busy being a good girl. They don't have as much fun as the bad girls."

His lips quivered with amusement. "So now you've gone to the dark side."

"You know it, and I'm never going back. It's all about me now. It's all about what *I* want."

"Good for you." He bumped against her playfully. "You should have everything you want."

"I couldn't agree more." She thought of something else she wanted to say, but hesitated.

"What?"

"I don't want you to get the wrong idea if I ask about Grant, but I can't help being concerned about him after what you told me yesterday."

"I understand. My mom said he slept better last night and seems to be more like his old self today, according to Stephanie."

"I'm glad to hear that." She glanced up at him. "You don't think it's weird that I asked about him, do you?"

"Not at all. You were with him a long time, and you still care about him. I get it." He took her hand. "Let's walk." They wandered along the shore, enjoying the view of the sandy cliffs and ocean. "You ever miss him?"

"I did for a long time. The first year was a nightmare. I missed him so much. Every day I questioned whether I'd done the right thing leaving him in LA."

"Why did you leave?"

"He didn't have any time for me. He was always working, and I felt like a distraction rather than a girlfriend. My mom was hassling me about whether he was ever going to marry me. After a while, I got tired of telling her we were getting married and then having it never happen."

"Did you guys ever talk about getting married?"

"Occasionally, but it never went anywhere, so I decided to leave. Part of me thought he'd come after me," she said with a bitter laugh. "But he didn't. That told me a lot about where I stood with him. The next time he came home, before Mac's wedding, I was already seeing Cal. Of course, once he heard I had someone else, Grant was all about trying to get me back, but it was too late."

"Were you still in love with him?"

She shook her head. "It took me a long time to realize that died long before I left him. I used to think Grant couldn't love anyone as much as he loves his career, but then he met Stephanie. They seem really good together."

He dropped her hand and bent to pick up a rock that he sent skimming over the waves. "Does that bother you? That he has with her what he never had with you?"

"Not really. We weren't meant to be. I accepted that years ago. I'm sure he knows that by now, too." She glanced at him. "Your brother never told you any of this?"

"My brothers and I have long-standing, unwritten rules on not grilling each other about our girlfriends. We have all we can do to handle our mom's questions. We don't pile on."

"Why am I not surprised?"

"What can I say? We McCarthy boys stick together."

"I'm concerned about causing a rift between you and Grant with this deal of ours. I'd hate that."

"Maybe I'll talk to him about it."

"Really? You'd do that?"

"If it would make you more comfortable with it, then yeah, I'd do it."

"What would you tell him?"

"That we're hanging out, having some fun, helping each other through a rough time. Something like that."

"How do you think he'll react?"

"Truthfully, I think it'll be the least of his concerns. He's got something else weighing on him."

Abby wasn't sure how she felt about the idea of Grant not caring— at all—that his brother was seeing her. "You know, girls have a secret girlfriend code."

"Which is?"

"No dating my exes."

"Guys aren't usually as territorial, especially years after they've moved on with someone else."

"So you'd be fine with one of your brothers dating Sasha?" she asked with a smile.

"I'd probably warn them to lock up their valuables, but otherwise, I don't suppose I'd care."

Abby laughed at the valuables comment. "And you just broke up with her a few days ago."

"So Grant ought to be fine with it, right?"

"If you say so. It's not like this is a relationship or anything. That would probably be different."

"Exactly."

"So when can we skinny-dip?"

Adam stopped walking and turned to her. "That's usually done under the cover of darkness."

Abby took a long look around the deserted stretch of beach. "Who would know?"

"You're serious."

She forced herself to look at him, wishing he wasn't wearing sunglasses so she could see his eyes. "Dead serious."

"I've never done it during the day."

"So we'd both be doing something new."

"I don't know, Abby. We might get caught. Would you be okay with that?"

"Would we get arrested? Fingerprinted and all that?"

He laughed. "Why do I get the feeling you might enjoy that?"

"Another thing I've never done. Have you?"

"I'll never tell."

"You have! What'd you do?"

Adam laughed and shook his head. "No way are you getting that out of me."

"Come on! After what I told you last night, you have to tell me."

"Nope," he said as he took off down the beach, jogging away from her and her questions.

Abby gave chase, and when she got close to him, she leaped onto his back, expecting him to keep moving. Instead, he went down like a fallen oak, landing with an *oof* in the wet sand. Somehow she ended up on top of him. Shocked by the turn of events, Abby burst into laughter. That hadn't gone as planned.

"Shit, girl," he said when he could talk again, "are you trying to kill me?"

Abby was crippled with laughter.

"Glad you think it's so funny. I may never walk again."

That only made her laugh harder. And then she realized their bodies were perfectly aligned and one part of him was letting her know it approved of her proximity. She pushed up his sunglasses so they rested on his forehead. "That's better," she said.

His arms encircled her, keeping her pressed to him. "Now that you have me where you want me, what do you plan to do with me?"

The old Abby would've apologized for tackling him, for getting his clothes wet, for acting less than ladylike. The new Abby stared into his eyes and took the wordless dare he issued. She bent her head and kissed him, keeping her eyes open and fixed on his as their lips met tentatively at first.

"Tell me about being arrested."

"Make me."

Abby had no idea how to make him do anything, so she gently pressed her lips to his again, hoping to cajole him into talking.

"That's the best you can do?"

"Are you enjoying this?" she asked testily. Did he have any idea how much courage it had taken for her to kiss him in the first place?

"Oh yeah. Very much so. The seep of cold, wet sand at my back and warm, soft woman at my front... What's not to enjoy?"

"Do you want me to get off you?"

"Absolutely not."

His smile was contagious. "Are you going to tell me what I want to know?"

"Are you going to kiss me like you mean it?"

"Will that get me the information I want?"

"You'll have to do it to find out."

"You drive a hard bargain, Mr. McCarthy."

He tilted his hips suggestively, pressing his erection against her belly. "Very hard."

Knowing he was turned on and that she'd done that to him filled her with confidence as she tipped her head and brought her lips down on his again, this time keeping her mouth slightly open. She slid her lips over his, back and forth several times until his arms tightened around her. On the next pass, she dabbed her tongue lightly over his bottom lip, drawing a groan from him.

"Abby," he gasped. "Stop teasing me."

"Is that what I'm doing?"

"You know you are."

She smiled at him, enjoying the teasing. Had kissing ever been so fun? Not that she could recall. There was something to be said for playful fun that had nothing to do with building something that might —or might not—last forever. This was about right now, right here, and it felt pretty damned good.

Abby decided to show him some mercy, kissing him again like she meant it this time, sending her tongue into his mouth to tease and flirt. For the longest time, she wondered if he was going to respond in kind. And then his hand was in her hair, anchoring her to him as he rolled them over, taking control of the kiss.

Her world was reduced to the cocoon of his body sheltering hers from the sunlight. It didn't matter that they were making out in the middle of the day in a place where they might be seen by anyone. It didn't matter that he was Grant's brother or that they were nursing broken hearts. All of that faded away as he took possession of her mouth in sweeping, passionate kisses that had her pressing against him intimately, asking for more.

Their tongues met and mated in an erotic dance that made her nipples tighten, wishing he would notice them.

He pulled back from her abruptly, staring down at her with a dazed look on his face. "Wow."

She couldn't seem to look at anything other than his sexy mouth. "Yeah, wow."

"Can we do that again?"

"I don't have anywhere to be today." Until Mac and Luke finished their work on the gift shop at the Surf, she was free and clear. "Do you?"

He shook his head and came back for more, kissing her until her lips were numb and her body aching for fulfillment. As if he knew that, he shifted ever so slightly, pressing his erection into the V of her legs.

She cursed the jeans he'd made her wear for putting a barrier between them. Since she couldn't have what she really wanted, she sent her hands on an exploration of his muscular body. Reaching the hem of his jacket, she delved underneath, seeking skin as his tongue explored her mouth in great detail.

When her fingers made contact with his back, Adam gasped and flexed his hips, letting her know what her touch did to him.

He broke the kiss and turned his focus to her neck. "God, Abby... I want to kiss you everywhere. I never expected..."

"What didn't you expect?"

"This. You. Us."

"It's pretty hot, huh?"

"Ah yeah, you could say that." He combed his fingers through her hair, making her scalp tingle.

"We could go for a swim to cool off."

"You're not letting that go, are you?"

"You're not afraid, are you?" she asked with a challenging smile.

"Maybe a little."

"Of what?"

"Of what might happen if we get naked together. I'd prefer a little privacy when that happens the first time. After those kisses, I can't be responsible for my actions."

It was, Abby discovered, a huge turn-on to realize he was wrestling with his attraction to her and trying to do the right thing. "If you tell me about being arrested, I'll let you kiss me again when we're back at my room."

His eyes heated with desire that fueled hers. "In that case, I might tell you there once was a college spring-break trip to Florida that might've resulted in a night in jail that my parents still don't know about because I was over eighteen at the time."

"Ooooh, blackmail! I love it!"

"You wouldn't..."

"Don't give me reason to."

"I've been warned. You'd kill my reputation and make Mac's life complete. As far as my family knows, he's the only one who's ever been arrested."

"For flattening mailboxes with Joe. That story is McCarthy family legend."

"So you see how important it is that they never find out about me."

She snuggled into his embrace. "You'd better be nice to me."

"I have a feeling that being nice to you is going to be very easy to do."

Abby smiled, pleased with him, with their day so far, and filled with anticipation about what else might happen before the sun went down.

CHAPTER 10

$\mathcal{E}$very day Ned Saunders went home after the eleven o'clock ferry arrived to check the mail—and to have lunch with Francine. Lately, the mail was the more important item on his agenda. Surely any time now the letter they were waiting for would arrive, and he and Francine could get busy planning the rest of their lives.

As he drove his cab toward home, Ned grappled with growing frustration. It'd been almost two weeks since Bobby Chester had agreed to file for divorce from his ex-wife Francine, who also happened to be the love of Ned's life.

When was Bobby going to come through with the papers? Ned had personally seen to it that Bobby had Francine's new address, and he'd hired Dan Torrington before the boat accident to make sure Bobby kept up his side of the deal they'd made when he insisted on spending time with Maddie and Tiffany before he would file. That had happened two weeks ago, so what was the delay?

Since Dan was down with his injuries, Ned didn't want to bug the guy, but the waiting was making him crazy. Francine, on the other hand, was matter-of-fact about it, telling him every day that it would happen when it was meant to. Whatever that meant. If the papers didn't arrive soon, Ned was going to the mainland to have yet another conversation with Bobby. Enough was enough already.

Francine said they had everything they needed. A piece of paper, she claimed, wouldn't change anything. They rarely disagreed, but he didn't agree with her this time. That piece of paper would change *everything*. It would make her his *wife*. It would make her and her girls and their children his *family*. He wanted that more than he'd let on to her or anyone. He wanted it more than he'd ever wanted anything.

With his heart pounding, he slowed the cab and approached the mailbox at the end of the long driveway leading to the home he shared with Francine. He pulled open the mailbox and saw a large brown envelope that filled him with excitement. Was this it? At long last...

When he saw the return address from a lawyer's office in Providence, he let out a happy shout. *"Halle-freaking-lujah!"* Mail in hand, he hit the gas and flew down the dirt road, skidding to a stop in the yard where Francine was on her knees planting impatiens in gardens that had suffered from years of neglect before she moved in with him.

"What in the devil has gotten into you, old man?" she asked as she stood and rubbed her hands together to rid them of dirt. She missed the streak of mud on her cheek, which only made her more adorable to him.

He bounded out of the car, waving the envelope over his head. *"Deeeeevorce* papers, baby doll!"

Her mouth fell open, and she gasped. "Really?"

"Would I lie to ya? Open 'em up! Let's get 'em signed and back on the afternoon boat!" He took her hand and tugged her inside. "I'm hearin' wedding bells a'ringin'! Want me ta open it?"

Her hands were clutched in a nervous pose that tugged at his heart. The poor gal had been through the wringer with Bobby Chester, especially lately when he insisted on spending time with their girls before he'd initiate the divorce. Francine had hated asking that of her daughters, but they'd done it for her. "Please," she said. "Go ahead."

Ned tore open the envelope and scanned the letter from the

lawyer. Divorce papers and something else, too. "Well, I'll be goddamned."

"What? What is it?"

"The bastard set up college funds for the grandkids. Twenty-five thousand bucks each."

"You're kidding me."

Ned handed her the letter and the paperwork detailing the trust funds that had been established in the names of Thomas and Hailey McCarthy as well as Ashleigh Sturgil. The lawyer had noted that funds would also be established for any future grandchildren. Envelopes addressed to Maddie and Tiffany had been enclosed.

Francine shook her head as tears filled her eyes. "Finally," she whispered. "He finally came through for them."

"Aww, honey, don't cry. You know I can't stand it when ya cry." He put his arms around her and patted her back awkwardly. He never had any idea what to do when she cried. Luckily, it didn't happen very often. She was tough as nails, his gal, and it took a lot to break her.

"I'm sorry," she said, sniffling and wiping her face, which made mud of the dirt on her face.

"Come 'ere, doll." He took her over to the sink, wet a paper towel and wiped her face, showing her the results when he was done.

She laughed through her tears. "God, I'm a mess."

"Yer my mess, and I love ya."

"I can't believe he did this."

"About time, doncha think?"

"Yes, for sure."

"Ya gotta tell the girls."

She nodded.

"Invite 'em for dinner. I'll stop at the pier and get some lobstas. We'll make a night outta it."

"You don't have to do that, Ned."

He tipped her chin up and kissed her. "I want ta. We still got some a them chicken nuggets that Thomas likes?" He pulled open the freezer door and rooted around, looking for the chicken the boy loved. "All gone. I'll get some a that, too, and them apple juice box thingies for Ashleigh." Turning to her, he stopped short when he found her watching him with a smile on her pretty face. "Whatcha looking at, doll?"

"You."

"What'd I do now?"

She came over to him and rested her hands on his chest, looking up at him with that soft, sweet expression that turned his insides to pudding. Whenever she looked at him that way, the thirty-plus years he'd spent without her melted away, and he was right back in the throes of first love. "You're a wonderful father and grandfather, and we're all so very lucky to have you."

"Oh, well…" Ned couldn't believe the tears that filled his eyes, "That's mighty nice a ya to say, doll."

"I mean it, and I love you, too." She kissed him, her hands framing his face in a tender caress. "What do you say I sign those papers so you can send them back on the boat this afternoon and we can get busy planning our wedding?"

"I think that sounds like the best idea ya ever had." He kissed her again, lingering a bit this time. Her sweet kisses made him as crazy for her now as they had when they first met. "Do ya think it would be okay if we put them papers on the late boat?"

"I'm sure it'd be fine. Why?"

He waggled his brows at her. "I got celebratin' on my mind."

"Is that right," she said with a grin. "Anything in particular?"

"Come with me, and I'll show ya."

CAROLINA SPENT the morning trying to work on some new designs for her jewelry, but ended up staring out the window at the bird feeder while her pencil dangled between her fingers. At times like this, she wanted to go back to the peaceful days before she met Seamus, before she discovered he had feelings for her that he'd gone out of his way to keep to himself for a long time after they first met.

She wanted to go back to last fall, to the night they'd spent together at Joe's house on the mainland, before she'd known what it was like to be held by him, to be loved by him. Surely she'd been better off not knowing. This, she decided, was a form of purgatory she never could've imagined. Knowing he was out there, just a few miles from her, wanting all the things she'd tried to tell herself she didn't need anymore...

She'd been alone a long time after her husband, Pete, died in an accident when Joe was only seven. After the initial shock of losing her husband so suddenly had faded somewhat, she'd settled into a life that was short on excitement but fulfilling nonetheless. She'd had her son, her work, her friends, a home she loved here on the island and another she'd kept for years in Connecticut until she decided to move back to the island permanently.

Everything was fine until *he* came along and turned her well-ordered life upside down, tempting her with a taste of what might be possible if only she had the courage to take a chance. Instead, she'd freaked out over what people might think and driven him away, probably for good this time.

How many times was he supposed to keep coming back for more of her special brand of punishment? How many times could she hurt him before he stopped wanting her? Before he stopped loving her.

That last thought finally broke her. Tears ran down her face, landing in a puddle on the paper that had been intended for new designs. The pencil landed on the desk as she dropped her face into her hands, letting the despair wash over her.

This whole thing was her fault. She never should have let him tempt her. She'd known from the very beginning that he was too young for her, but that hadn't stopped her from walking straight into the flame of his love, knowing all the while she would surely get burned. And now that she knew what it was like to be with him, to be loved by him, to be consumed by him, how could she resist the life he offered? How could her mouth continue to say *no* when her heart and soul said yes, yes, *yes*?

She couldn't continue to say no, because living without him now would be impossible. She'd learned to live without Pete because she hadn't had a choice. Living without Seamus would be her choice, and she couldn't do it. She couldn't make that choice and go on with her life as it had been before. That was no longer possible. He'd seen to that with every word, every smile, every gesture, every time he called her "love" and stopped her heart.

Before the thoughts had been fully processed, she was up and moving, reaching for keys like a blind woman in the dark and rushing from the house without her purse or a care to what she must look like after the sleepless night.

Somehow she managed to drive into town without killing herself or anyone else, arriving at the ferry landing and parking outside the office building where he worked when he was on the island. It hadn't occurred to her that he might not be there, that he might be on the mainland, working in his other office. It hadn't occurred to her that he might be captaining one of the boats or off getting something to eat. If he wasn't there, she'd wait for him. He'd come back eventually, and she'd be waiting.

She rushed into his office, stopping short when she saw that he was there but not alone.

When she burst into the room, her son stood—tall, blond, handsome and concerned. "Mom? What is it? What's wrong? Are you feeling okay?"

Carolina, who'd put her son at the center of her life for more than thirty years, looked past him now to the man behind the desk whose small smile told her he knew exactly why she'd come. "I'm fine, honey," she said haltingly. "I...I need to see Seamus, if that's all right." She tore her gaze off Seamus and looked up at Joe. "I'm sorry to interrupt."

Joe looked at her quizzically. "It's no problem. We were done. Call me later?"

Nodding absently, Carolina returned her focus to Seamus, who waited patiently, as if he had all the time in the world to hear whatever she'd come to say.

Kissing her on the cheek, Joe stepped around her and left the office, closing the door behind him.

"You're giving your poor son fits, love."

That lovely Irish brogue made her heart sing with joy. "I know. I'm a terrible mother."

Laughing, Seamus came around the desk to embrace her, encouraging her to rest her head on his shoulder. "You're one of the best mums I know."

Carolina expelled a great sigh of relief when she realized he wasn't going to send her away. He wasn't going to tell her that she'd finally succeeded in changing his mind about her. Rather, he ran a soothing hand up and down her back.

"How're the hives?"

"Itchy, but the oatmeal helped."

"I'm a first-class arse for leaving you when you were feeling poorly."

She looked up at him, her determination fueled by the beauty of his face, the lyrical lilt of his brogue and the love he'd shown her from the start. "And I'm a first-class fool for letting you think I give a rat's *arse* about what anyone thinks of us." His eyes widened at her unusually forceful statement. "I don't care, Seamus. I don't care anymore about anything other than being with you. If people don't get it, I don't care."

She had barely finished the statement when he was kissing her madly, deeply, holding her so tightly she could barely breathe.

"Ah, love, Joe's not the only one you've given the fits to," he whispered against her lips before he went back for more.

"I'm so sorry," she said, clinging to him. "I never meant to make you wonder if I felt the same way you do."

"I never wondered about that, love. Not for one second. I worried that you weren't going to give yourself permission to take what you want, but I never wondered if you loved me as much as I love you."

"I do. I love you just as much."

"I know." He brushed the hair off her face, studying her intently, seeming to take inventory.

Carolina tried not to think about how scary she must look.

"Did you sleep at all?"

She shook her head. "Can't you tell? You?"

"Not a wink."

"And strangely you look as good as ever while I'm—"

"Beautiful."

She snorted with disbelief. "You must be in love."

"Completely, totally, absolutely and forever in love."

Was it possible for a grown woman to actually swoon? "Seamus," she said with a sigh.

He gathered her in close to him, and when she rested her head on his chest, she could hear the steady beat of his heart. "Yes, love?"

"Are you almost done working?"

"I can be."

"Will you come home with me to stay?"

"There's nothing I'd rather do."

Relieved and overwhelmed to have made a decision once and for all, she held on tight to him for a long time before she took his hand and led him from the office.

JOE WALKED AWAY from the ferry landing, unsettled by the sight of his mother so broken up. Wondering what was transpiring between her and the man Joe had hired to run the ferry business while he was in Ohio, he walked aimlessly without a destination in mind.

It had taken a few days to wrap his head around the idea of his mom with a guy who was only a couple of years older than him. At first, he'd been shocked and slightly outraged to think that maybe Seamus had taken advantage of Carolina's loneliness to forward his own agenda.

Almost as soon as Joe had that thought, however, he'd been ashamed of it. Seamus had never been anything but upstanding and reliable. He'd made it possible for Joe to be with Janey while she was in vet school without having to worry incessantly about the business his mother's late parents had left to both of them.

Hands in pockets, head down, Joe nearly collided with someone on the sidewalk. He was muttering an apology when he looked up and realized it was Mac. Joe let out a laugh. "Sorry, man. Not paying attention to where I'm going. What're you doing in town?"

"Finishing up the gift shop at the Sand & Surf and in need of coffee. Want to join me?"

"I could definitely use more coffee."

"It's on me. Let's go." On the way through town, Mac said, "Not working today?"

"I had the early run to the mainland. Got another round-tripper at the end of the day."

They wandered into the South Harbor Diner, landing in their usual booth that overlooked the ferry landing and busy downtown. Rebecca, the owner of the diner, greeted them with steaming mugs.

"Nice to see you guys," she said. "Been a while."

"Too long," Mac said with a smile for Joe.

Before Mac and Maddie moved out of her apartment in town, Mac and Joe had met for coffee most mornings when Joe was on the island. But things changed. Time passed. Life got in the way.

"So why were you walking through town with the weight of the world on your shoulders?"

"This thing with my mom and Seamus..."

"Ah, I see. I wondered what you thought of it, but I couldn't exactly ask you last night in front of them. So you don't approve?"

"It's not that. He's a good guy. He's been a lifesaver for me since we moved to Ohio. I couldn't be there without him taking care of things here."

"But?"

His oldest and best friend knew him as well as anyone, except for maybe Janey. "I worry about her getting hurt."

"A reasonable concern."

"She was alone a long time." Joe took a drink of his coffee, savoring the taste and the aroma as well as the comfort of a lifelong friend who was also now his brother-in-law.

"And she belonged only to you all that time," Mac said, raising a brow.

"It's not that."

"Not even a little bit?"

Joe stared down at his mug. "Maybe a little."

"You're not losing her, Joe. You know that."

"I know, but it's… It's weird, I guess, to see her getting involved with someone after all this time. And that he's basically our age. It's weird."

"Probably will be for a while and then, like you being married to my baby sister, you get used to it and it doesn't seem so weird anymore—well, until my baby sister gets knocked up, and then it's all kinds of weird again."

Joe laughed his ass off. Mac had such a way with words. "Let's hope my fifty-six-year-old mother doesn't get knocked up."

"Now that, my friend, would be weird."

Joe held up his coffee cup in agreement. "I don't know if I've said this out loud or only thought it, but I'm so damned glad you didn't die last week."

"Aww, thanks." Mac blinked back mock tears. "I'm touched. Really."

"All kidding aside, I have no idea what we would've done without one of you, let alone all of you."

"Believe me, I had a lot of hours in the water to think about where my brothers were and whether they were okay. And to think about Maddie and my kids…" Mac shook his head as if he couldn't bear to go there.

"Are you okay, Mac?" Joe held up a hand to stop his friend from replying. "I heard what you said last night at dinner, but this is me. You'd tell me if you weren't really okay, wouldn't you?"

"Sure, I'd spill my guts all over the table, because that's how I roll."

The humor gave Joe hope. The Mac he knew and loved was nothing if not funny. "Fine, be that way. You know where I am if you need me. Let's leave it at that."

"Likewise."

"What're you guys up to tonight?" Joe asked.

"I'm told there's a dinner at Ned and Francine's. With lobsters."

"Lucky dog."

"I am lucky. I think about that a lot. What happened last week was a good reminder of how great my life is. I'm trying to stay focused on that and not sweat the small stuff. You might want to try it."

"That's not the worst advice you've ever given me."

"On that note," Mac said, laughing as he tossed a five and a couple of one-dollar bills on the table and got up, "I gotta get back to the hotel before Laura sends out a search party. And I gotta finish this job for her before things get really busy at the marina."

"Thanks for the coffee."

"Any time."

Mac left with a wave for Rebecca and headed back to the Surf. Watching him go, Joe pondered what Mac had said about being lucky and not sweating the small stuff. He thought about calling his mom to make sure she was all right, but Joe felt pretty confident that she was in good hands with Seamus, even if he wasn't entirely sure what he thought of the two of them together.

Since there wasn't anything he could do about his mom at the moment, Joe's thoughts turned to his lovely wife, who was working today at the vet clinic. He got up, intending to head over there to see how her day was going, when his cell phone rang. Surprised to see the vet clinic number on the caller ID when he'd just been thinking about the place, Joe took the call.

"This is Joe."

"Hi, Joe, it's Doc Potter. Have I caught you at a bad time?"

When he heard the doctor's casual tone, Joe released the breath he'd been holding, waiting to hear something was wrong with Janey. "Not at all. What's up?" He stepped outside, heading in the direction of the clinic.

"It's about Janey."

Joe stopped walking. "What about her?"

"Has she seemed a tad bit...down...lately?" When Joe didn't imme-diately answer, Doc Potter continued. "She doesn't seem herself, and I thought perhaps the job might be too much for her, and she doesn't want to hurt my feelings, so she hasn't said so. I didn't want to upset her by asking, so I figured I'd call you."

"She hasn't said anything to me about not feeling up to working. In fact, she was excited to get back to work at the clinic, even though I suggested she might want to take it easy this summer."

"Huh," Doc said thoughtfully. "She's definitely not got her usual sparkle."

Joe felt like a jerk for having to be told that by her boss. "I'll come by and see if she's up for a lunch break with her husband."

"I'm sure she'd enjoy that. I hope I haven't overstepped by calling you. It's just that I care for her very much."

"I know that, Doc, and so does she. I appreciate the call."

"Take her to lunch, and tell her I gave her the afternoon off. She works too hard."

"Thanks. I'm on my way." He moved a little quicker now, passing the Sand & Surf on his way to the clinic on the outskirts of town.

"Hey, Joe," the receptionist, Lisa, said when he arrived. "Janey's in the back doing inventory. Want me to tell her you're here?"

"If it's okay, I'd rather surprise her."

Lisa smiled. "Of course. Go on back."

With a wave for Doc as he passed his office, Joe found his wife in the supply closet, clipboard in hand, glasses perched on her nose, her hair in a messy bun with a second pen pushed through it. The big baby belly protruded from a white lab coat, making him smile at how she managed to look studious and serious and sexy as hell all at the same time. Sometimes Joe still couldn't believe that he'd finally gotten the girl he'd always wanted but never thought he'd have.

"Hey, baby," he said.

Her eyes lit up with delight at the sight of him. "Where'd you come from?"

"The usual places—the ferry landing and the diner with your brother."

"Which one?"

"The bossy pain-in-the-ass one."

"What's my darling Mac up to?"

"Working at the Surf today, finishing up the gift shop for Laura."

"He and Luke and Shane did such a great job there. It looks so good."

As she spoke, Joe studied her, looking for signs of the funk that Doc had mentioned but didn't see anything out of the ordinary. Was she keeping something from him? That wouldn't be like her—

"Joe? Are you all right?"

"Oh, sorry. What did you say?"

"I was blathering about the hotel. Nothing important. What were you thinking about?"

He stepped into the small storage room, closing the door behind him. "You." With his hands on her face, he leaned in for a kiss. "That and this, too." He stole a second kiss.

She smiled mischievously. "I'm at *work*, Joseph."

"I hear you're going to own the place someday. They probably won't mind."

At that, her smile faded a bit. "Probably not."

Determined to get to the bottom of whatever was troubling her, he said, "How about some lunch?"

"It's only eleven."

"And you're probably already starving."

"I could eat," she conceded. "But that's hardly news. I'm a bottomless pit lately. Let me check with Doc to see if he can spare me."

"I already talked to him, and he said it's fine."

"Are you guys talking about me behind my back?"

Joe led her from the storage room. "Of course we are."

Janey laughed, which he'd hoped she would. Come to think of it, he couldn't recall the last time he'd heard her laugh. It pained him to realize she'd been troubled about something and he hadn't noticed. "I probably shouldn't be surprised." She ducked her head into Doc's office. "Thanks for giving Joe permission to take me for an early lunch. I'll be back in an hour."

"Have a nice time," Doc said with a wink for Joe.

Holding hands, they left the clinic.

"Where to?" Janey asked.

"Let's go home and make some sandwiches. You can put your feet up and relax while I wait on you."

"Ohhh, I like the sound of that."

Because he couldn't resist, Joe dropped her hand and put his arm around her, drawing her in close to him as they walked the short distance to the little house she'd bought when she was still single. They were going to need a bigger place on the island after the baby arrived, but for now they were enjoying their final months in the cozy cottage.

At home, they spent a good ten minutes greeting her menagerie of pets, who swarmed them with enthusiastic kisses. Janey laughed at the way Pixie tried to leap into her arms, wanting Janey's full attention as always.

After she took them outside and brought them back in again, Janey said, "Let me sit down, guys. I'll scratch every one of your ears while Joe finishes making lunch."

She snuggled into the sofa with the dogs while Joe prepared grilled cheese sandwiches in the kitchen. He cracked open a cola for himself, poured a tall glass of milk for Janey and carried everything into the living room. The dogs knew their rules and scattered from the sofa to allow them to eat in peace.

When they were first together, Joe had been blown away by how well behaved her pets were, but now he was used to them and expected nothing less. All of them had been abused or neglected before Janey came into their lives and showed them true love and devotion.

They did whatever she told them to do when she told them to do it. Joe called her his little dog whisperer. There was no question she had a special touch with animals, which was why he was thrilled to see her finally pursuing her lifelong dream of becoming a veterinarian.

"This is so good," she said between bites. "Thanks for pampering me."

"Any time, baby."

"I'll probably need a second lunch around two."

"I'll get it for you."

"You've got better things to do than bring me food at work."

"I'll get it for you right here. Doc gave you the afternoon off."

Her eyes widened with surprise. "He did? Why?"

Joe finished the soda and put the can on the coffee table before he reached for her hand and linked their fingers. "Because he's worried about you. He says you seem down about something."

Frowning, she looked away from him, gazing at her German shepherd, Riley, who stood watch over her, as always. "So you guys really were talking about me."

"Not in a bad way. He called me because he was worried, and he didn't want to upset you by bringing it up. You know he loves you as much as anyone, except for me, of course. I love you best of all, which is why I'm hoping you'd tell me if something was worrying you or upsetting you or causing you to lose your sparkle."

"Is that what he said?"

Joe brought her hand to his lips, kissing her softly. "Uh-huh, which led me to wonder why I haven't noticed your missing sparkle. Are you keeping something from me, hon?"

"No! I don't do that. You know I don't."

"I know you don't usually, but since he's seeing something I'm not, I can't help but wonder. That's all."

"We've had a lot going on. With the pregnancy and the accident and my brothers and your mom and Seamus… It's been…a lot." Her chin quivered ever so slightly, but he saw it.

"What is it, honey? Talk to me. The accident was so upsetting, but the boys are fine—or they will be. In time. You know that, right?"

She nodded, her eyes glistening with unshed tears that broke his heart.

"Come here." He released her hand, raised his arm and waited for her to get comfortable against him before he put his arm around her and pressed his lips to the top of her head. "What's wrong?"

"You won't want to hear it."

"What does that mean? Of course I want to hear it."

"I tried to tell you once before. I tried to tell Adam, too, but he said the same thing you did—"

"About what, Janey?" Joe asked, becoming more alarmed by the second.

"About the baby and school and how I might've changed my mind about some things."

"We talked about this—"

"*You* talked about it. You told me I'd be making a big mistake to give up on vet school when I'm so close to being done."

"I still think that's true."

"But what about what *I* want? Does that matter at all?"

Flabbergasted, Joe pulled back so he could see her face and was stunned to find tears rolling down her cheeks. "Of course that matters. Where's this coming from, Janey?"

"It's coming from me and the baby." She rested her hand on her belly. "We didn't plan to get pregnant yet, but we did, and now... Everything is different. I don't want what I wanted a year ago. I want different things."

"What things?"

"I want to be a mom. I want to be here with my family and your mom. I want our baby to be with his or her cousins every day, not just in the summer. I don't want to miss *anything*." A sob hiccupped through her as the floodgates opened. "And if I go back to school, I'll be gone all day, and I'll have to study all night. I'll miss *everything*."

Joe wiped the flood of tears from her face as he tried to process what she'd said. How had he missed this? How had he not seen she was this torn up?

"I'm sorry," she whispered. "You've given up so much so we could spend the last two years in Ohio—"

"I didn't give up anything. I got to be with you, which was the only thing I wanted. There was hardly any sacrifice involved in that."

"Still, you know what I mean. You went to so much trouble, and it might be for nothing."

"It hasn't been for nothing, Janey. You've got two years of school done now that you didn't have before. You're halfway there."

"But still a long way from the finish line. The baby will be running around and talking back to us by the time I'm done. I can't spend two years being less than half a mother to this child, Joe. That's not what I want. That's not what he or she deserves."

He ran his fingers through her soft blonde hair, thinking about what he should say and how he should say it. "I'm so sorry I didn't pick up on this sooner. I hate that you've been this upset and I didn't know."

"It's not your fault. I've been an emotional disaster area for months now. Victoria says it's the hormones."

They were quiet for a long time, each taking comfort from the closeness of the other. Joe's mind raced with plans and implications and thoughts of the painting class he taught to freshman art students. None of that mattered when stacked up against what his beloved wife wanted and needed.

"What'll we do, Joe?" she asked in a small voice that made him ache.

"To me, it seems rather simple."

"It does?"

Nodding, he said, "You'll take this year off from school, spend it with the baby, and then next summer, we'll see how you feel about going back to finish. With your perfect grades, they'll probably let you do whatever you want."

"And you'd be okay with dragging out our time in Ohio even more than we already are?"

"If it means you'll be happy, I'm fine with it. So what if it takes one more year than we'd planned. I would, however, really like to see you finish, but only because I suspect you might regret it someday if you don't."

"I probably would," she said with a sigh.

"So we'll take this year off from school and let you settle into being a mom?"

"I'd like that more than anything."

"Then that's what we'll do."

She let out a happy squeal and hugged him as tightly as she could with the big belly in the way.

After a minute, Joe realized she was crying again. "What? I thought you'd feel better now that we figured out a plan."

"I do."

"Then why are you crying?"

"I'm happy," she said with a laugh. "I'm so happy."

She killed him when she looked at him that way. "That's all that matters."

"You need to be happy, too."

"If you are, then I am. That's all it takes."

Her hand on his face took his breath away. "I love you so much. I have to be the luckiest person in the whole world."

"Nope. That'd be me." He brushed away the last of her tears and kissed her.

She smiled at him as her hand moved from his face to the back of his neck. "Do we really have all afternoon free?"

"Mmm-hmm," he said against her lips, reluctant to end the sweet kiss.

"You know what I could really use?"

"What's that?"

"A nap."

Intrigued, he said, "What kind of nap?"

She let loose with her sexiest grin. "The really good kind."

"I could be talked into that."

Her laughter warmed his heart as it always did. "You're so easy, Captain."

"Only with you. Put your arms around my neck and hold on tight."

When she did as he directed, he slid his arms under her, scooping her up with a grunt and groan for effect that had her pinching him. "Not funny."

"Yes, it was." He stole another kiss as he carried her to the bedroom, where he was more than happy to help her out of her clothes and into bed.

When he joined her, she snuggled up to him as best she could.

Wanting to get in on their embrace, the baby thumped around between them, making them laugh.

"Joe?"

His hands and eyes were on her belly, watching the baby move around inside her and marveling at the miracle of it all. "What, honey?"

"Thank you—for this love, this life, for understanding what I need. All of it. Thank you."

"God, Janey," he whispered, overwhelmed by her. "It's my pleasure. Every second of it. Thank *you*." He kissed her then, and for a long time, he thought of nothing else but *her* pleasure.

CHAPTER 11

*A*dam left Abby at the Beachcomber with a promise to call her in a couple of hours. They both had things they needed to do, and in his case, he had someone he needed to see. At first he'd thought the best thing would be to keep his growing friendship with Abby a secret from Grant.

Now that he'd had time to rethink that plan, he could see it would be the worst way to proceed. He enjoyed a harmonious relationship with his siblings because they didn't play games with each other. When Grant had so many other things on his mind at the moment, surely this wasn't the time to make things worse by being less than honest with him.

With that in mind, Adam left the Beachcomber and stopped at the Surf, hoping first to see Laura about the work she wanted him to do on the reservation system.

"She's at a doctor's appointment," Sarah told him when he found her at the reception desk. "The poor thing can't seem to kick the flu."

"I hope she's okay."

"I'm sure she will be. I'll tell her you stopped by."

"She can call my cell whenever she's ready to talk about the reservation system."

Sarah's eyes lit up with delight. "Oh, are you going fix that for us?"

"That's the plan."

"Thank goodness."

"Maybe you can tell me what the problems are, so I can be thinking about what needs to happen."

"Well, one of the biggest challenges we have is that families have been coming to the Surf for several generations now, and they have traditions tied up with the place. Take the Morton family, for example. They come every summer and have since I was a kid growing up here and my parents were running the place. They ask for the same rooms every year with several amenities and upgrades. My mom used to keep track of all that in a notebook she carried with her everywhere she went, but she also has a photographic memory that I don't have—and neither does Laura. We need to be able to better manage those requests now that we're fully computerized. Does that make sense?"

"It does," Adam said, his mind already racing with custom programming ideas that might fit their needs. "Let me think about that and talk some more with you and Laura."

"That'd be great. We'll take whatever help you can give us. I'll tell her to call you."

"Thanks, Sarah. Have a good day."

"You, too. It's so nice to have our own computer whiz back in town."

Adam smiled at the compliment. "That's nice of you to say. See you." He left the Surf buoyed by Sarah's confidence in him as well as the project she'd outlined. He'd always enjoyed the challenge of finding creative solutions to his clients' vexing issues. There was nothing more satisfying than hearing that something he'd done had helped a business to achieve new efficiencies or economies.

As the adrenaline pumped through his veins, he remembered all at once that he no longer had clients or a booming business or a host of daily challenges to work through. The loss of his company seemed to finally hit him right in that moment, stealing the breath from his lungs and sending him reeling. The pain of it was physical, gripping his chest in a fierce hold that had him dropping onto the stoop of the building next to the Surf, which was, thankfully, abandoned at the moment.

Adam had no idea how long he sat there waiting for his heart rate and respiration to return to normal as the whole thing came crashing down on him. Computronic Solutions Incorporated, or "the Other CSI," as they had called it, was gone. The company he'd built from scratch—at first from the living room of the loft he'd rented in Lower Manhattan—was no longer his.

With his elbows propped on his knees, Adam dropped his head to his hands, combing his fingers through his hair absently as he thought about the long struggle that had led to CSI becoming one of the top computer consulting companies in the city. He thought about what his dad had said about fighting for what was his, and what Abby had said about how he must not care anymore if he didn't put up a fight.

As days of numbness and shock finally wore off, Adam discovered that he did care, and he was very, very angry. Not just at Sasha. That was only part of it. He was equally furious with the board of directors he'd hand-chosen who'd turned on him in favor of his so-called partner, who'd apparently sold them a bill of goods.

All at once, it became clear to him that he was a fool not to fight for what was his. Even if he never got back what he'd lost, he could, at the very least, make life difficult for the people who'd screwed him over.

He drew his phone from his pocket, wincing when his tattooed bicep protested the movement, and found his lawyer's number on his list of contacts.

"Adam," Rick Levinson said when he came on the line, sounding relieved to receive Adam's call. "I was wondering when I'd hear from you. Where've you been?"

"Licking my wounds," Adam said with a laugh.

"Dude, you got royally screwed. I couldn't even believe it when I heard the news. I've been waiting for you to call."

"I needed a couple of days. It wasn't only the company that screwed me over."

"I heard that, too. I didn't know that you and Sasha were a couple."

"No one did. We kept it quiet for obvious reasons."

"I have to say, though, I wondered a few times when I saw you two together. There was definitely something..."

Whatever it had been was definitely over now. Adam thought about the morning he'd spent with Abby. Now that was *something*— something sweet and fun and sexy—and yet pure, too. He already knew with one-hundred-percent certainty that she'd never treat him the way Sasha had.

"Adam? Still there?"

He realized he'd punched out on Rick. "Yeah, I'm here."

"What do you want to do?"

"I want to fight for what's mine."

"Right there with you. Since I had a feeling you might say that at some point, we've been all over it for a couple of days now. I think you've got a very solid case, and with your approval, we'll move forward with filings." Rick outlined the strategy his team had put together to fight Adam's ouster from the company. They had come to the conclusion that discrediting Sasha was the first step in what might be a long battle.

It would get ugly, Adam thought. Someone he'd once cared deeply about would become his enemy. If he succeeded in regaining control of the company, he'd have a mountain to climb in restoring CSI's reputation in the business community while also repairing the damage done to the morale of their workforce. The question became —how could he *not* pursue it?

"Do it," he said to Rick. However it turned out, he'd figure out the way forward the same way he always had—one step at a time.

"I'll keep you posted."

Adam ended the call and took a few minutes to regain his equilibrium and then got up and continued on to Grant's house. He pounded on the door for several minutes before Grant appeared with a towel wrapped around his waist, his hair dripping.

"What the hell?" he asked Adam as he pushed open the door to let him in.

"Thought you were sleeping the day away again."

"Sorry to disappoint you, but I've been up since eight and actually getting some work done, which is a welcome relief." He went into the bedroom to put on basketball shorts and a T-shirt.

It was a welcome relief to Adam, too, to hear that Grant was having a better day. "That's good news."

"You know it," Grant said when he returned to the kitchen. "Want something to drink?"

"I could use a drink drink, if you've got anything."

Grant stopped and gave Adam an inquisitive look. "What's that all about?"

"I just agreed to file suit to get back the company my now ex-partner and ex-girlfriend stole from me."

"I'd say that warrants a midday drink." Grant rooted around in a kitchen cabinet and produced a bottle of whiskey. "Will this do the trick?"

"Bring it, brother."

Grant poured several fingers worth in a short glass and handed it to Adam.

"Join me so I'm not drinking alone?"

"Not today. Not when I'm finally getting back to work."

"Fine. Be that way." Adam downed the shot in one big gulp, feeling it burn its way through his insides.

"More?"

"In a minute maybe."

"So what gives with the company?"

Even though he hadn't come here to talk to Grant about that, he told him anyway. And when he was done, Grant reached for Adam's glass, poured him another shot and pushed it toward him on the counter.

Adam tipped his head back and downed it.

"Feel better?"

"Surprisingly, yes, I do. Sorry to unload on you when you've got enough of your own shit going on."

"Trust me, I'd much rather focus on your shit than mine."

162

"You know… The McCarthy brother bartending skills work both ways. Whenever you're ready to talk about it."

"I'll keep that in mind."

Adam nodded as his stomach tightened with the realization that it was now or never on the subject of Abby. "There was something else I wanted to talk to you about if you have another minute," Adam said, diving in before he could rethink his way out of having this conversation in the first place.

"What's that?"

"Abby."

Grant's brows furrowed with confusion. "What about her?"

"We ran into each other on the ferry yesterday and unloaded on each other about our ugly breakups. Then I ran into her again last night when I was out looking for you." Adam didn't bother to mention that he'd dragged her out of a bar and spent the night in her hotel room. Some details were better left unmentioned.

"So?"

"So I kind of like her. I like talking to her, and she gets what I'm dealing with. I was wondering if you'd have a problem if I hang out with her."

This time Grant's brows narrowed in obvious annoyance. "Define 'hang out.'"

"Do I really have to?"

"Yeah, I think you do."

"You know, hang out… and stuff."

"That clears it right up. Are you asking me if I mind if you have a fling or whatever it's called with my ex-girlfriend?"

"Ah, sort of. Yeah."

"Hell, yes, I mind! She's not like that. She doesn't fool around with random guys and then move on to the next one."

Adam decided it wouldn't be wise to mention Abby's recent changes in philosophy on those matters. "I'm not a random guy, Grant. It's me. You know I'd be straight up with her. We're both raw after what we've been through and looking to have some lighthearted fun. I like her. I think she likes me. That's all it is."

163

"Did you *like* her that way when I was dating her?"

"Get real. I never gave her a second look when she was your girl-friend, and you know it. Bottom line—she's not your girlfriend anymore. You're happy with Stephanie. Why should you care if I hang out with Abby?"

"I don't want you to hurt her, Adam. I did enough damage where she's concerned. That's why I'd rather you found someone else to hang out with."

"But I like *her*. She gets what I'm dealing with. She's not looking for anything more than something fun—same as me. Is that really such a threat to you?"

Stephanie stepped through the back door, startling them both. "Why are you threatening him?" she asked with a teasing smile as she went up on tiptoes to kiss Grant's cheek.

He put an arm around her, giving Adam a warning glare over her head.

"I'm not threatening anyone," Adam said, looking directly at his brother as he said the words.

"Good," Steph said. "No bickering allowed in our house."

"That's right," Grant said.

"Then I'd better get out of here," Adam said. "I'll see you guys later."

Grant followed him to the door. He grabbed Adam's arm. "Adam..."

"*Aah!*" Adam pulled back his recently tattooed arm.

"What?"

"Sore arm. Long story." He put a hand on his brother's chest to stop the conversation. "I heard you, Grant."

"So what're you going to do?"

"Have some fun and do no harm. I promise."

Grant nodded but still looked annoyed as Adam walked down the stairs to the driveway.

The crushed shells crunched under his feet as Adam made his way out to the road that led back to town. All the way, he could feel his brother watching him.

. . .

"WHAT WAS THAT ALL ABOUT?" Stephanie asked after Adam left.

Grant turned to her, and she could see that he was angry. "Nothing."

"You're getting awfully good at keeping things from me. Should I be worried?"

His shoulders seemed to lose some of their stiffness. "No." He came back into the kitchen and put the cover on the bottle of whiskey. That had been the first thing she'd noticed when she came in, after, of course, the visible—and unusual—tension between the brothers.

"Kind of early for whiskey, isn't it?" Stephanie asked the question casually, mindful of his fragile state and not wanting to make anything worse.

"It was for him. Not me."

"What's up with him?"

"He's had some issues with his company. He's working it out, but it's been tough."

"Oh. So why did you seem pissed with him when I came in?"

Grant leaned against the counter and folded his arms, his gaze fixed on her as if he was trying to decide what he should say.

The longer the silence stretched between them, the more anxious Stephanie became. She wished she didn't automatically go to worst-case scenario every time the slightest thing went wrong, but her tumultuous life before she met Grant had given her ample reason to do so. "Never mind," she said, unable to bear the tension for another second.

"Wait." He paused, his jaw pulsing with tension, which was never a good sign. "I want to tell you what we were talking about, but there's almost no way to tell you without making you think I want something that I don't."

"Oh, well, if that's all it is..."

He shook his head and blew out a deep breath. "He wants to date Abby."

Stephanie hadn't seen that one coming, and suddenly she couldn't seem to breathe as she recalled what Adam had been saying as she came into the kitchen. She sucked in a breath and fought to maintain her composure. "Why would he think you'd be threatened by that?"

"I'm not threatened by it. Not at all. I want you to hear me on that. Do you?"

As she nodded, her mind raced and her palms were suddenly damp.

"Say it. Tell me you heard me."

"I did," she said haltingly. "I heard you."

"Come here."

Because she couldn't stay away, Stephanie crossed the room to him, stopping in front of him. "I'm here."

"Closer."

She moved another inch forward.

"Closer," he said with the sexy grin she hadn't seen since before the accident.

A happy gasp escaped from her tightly clenched jaw, releasing all the pent-up tension with it.

He put his arms around her and looked into her eyes. "I love you. I don't care if my brother dates her. I will care if he hurts my friend, however. I don't want to see her hurt again. She's had enough already. Okay?"

"You…"

"What, Steph?"

She forced herself to look up and meet his gaze. She forced herself to ask the question. "You don't think it would be weird to see him with her?"

"Maybe the first time. And the second. After that, it might seem less weird. But it's no threat to me—or to us. I promise." He dipped his head and kissed her, softly at first and with more intent when she responded with greedy enthusiasm. It had been a very long week.

Her hands coasted over his chest and up to link around his neck. She couldn't get close enough to him.

Judging by the way his arms tightened around her and the thrusts of his tongue, he felt the same way. "Missed you," he said between kisses.

"Me, too. I've missed you so much."

"I don't like that furrow between your brows," Grant said, placing a kiss on the area in question. "I don't like that you think what we have isn't going to last."

"I wish I wasn't like that. You don't know how badly I want to believe that everything is going to work out perfectly. I'm just not wired that way. I have visions of you seeing your brother with Abby and wanting her for yourself again."

"That's not going to happen. I wish he'd chosen to 'hang out' with someone else, but not for the reasons you think. It's because she's been through a lot. I don't want anyone, especially my own brother, trifling with her. She deserves better."

"Adam is a good guy. Your father didn't raise any other kind. Any woman would be in good hands with you or one of your brothers."

"That wasn't always true for me. I didn't treat her the way she deserved to be treated." He kissed her forehead and nose on the way to her lips. "I'm trying hard not to make the same mistake with you. Don't let me, okay?"

"I won't."

He nuzzled her neck, placing kisses in places he knew made her crazy. "I'd be lost without you, Steph. You were the one thing that kept me going out there. Thinking about you, getting back to you…"

It was the most he'd said about the long day in the water, and she had to refrain from urging him to keep talking. Judging from the press of his erection against her belly, he wasn't in the mood to talk.

"I was so scared," she said, choosing to focus on how she'd felt rather than pushing him to share more about what'd happened to him. "We've had so little time together, and all I could think about while we waited to hear something was whether that would be all we'd get."

"We're going to get so much more," he assured her. "We're going to get everything."

She wanted so badly to believe him.

"Do you have to go right back to work?"

Looking up to gauge his meaning, she found his eyes blazing with heat she hadn't seen since before the accident. She had a million and one things to do at both restaurants, but none of that was as important as him. "Not necessarily. What's on your mind?"

He smiled as his hands moved over her back in a gentle caress, working downward until he cupped her bottom and lifted her.

Stephanie curled her legs around his waist and held on tight as he walked them into the bedroom, stopping in the hallway to press her against the wall and kiss her senseless. God, she had missed him and this. It'd only been a week, but it felt like a lifetime.

Without breaking the kiss, he came down over her on the bed and made fast work of pushing clothes out of the way.

"Hurry, Grant," she whispered urgently as she squirmed under him. "I can't wait." He had her on the verge of exploding with only the press of his body against hers and the hot, intense kisses.

He pulled back from her only long enough to free himself from his clothes, surging into her with a quick thrust that had her arching her back to get him deeper.

Stephanie reached the first peak seconds after he entered her, crying out with the thrill of it.

"Ah, Christ, that's good," he groaned, pushing hard into her to ride the wave of her climax.

She opened her eyes and saw him watching her, still hard and moving slowly inside her.

"That was quite something," he said, brushing his lips against hers and sending a riot of sensation rippling through her that started the climb toward a second release.

"I was pent up."

He laughed and gathered her in tight against him. "Take this off," he said, tugging her shirt up and over her head and releasing the front clasp on her bra. "Much better," he said as his chest hair rubbed against her nipples.

Stephanie tightened her arms around him, closed her eyes and focused on enjoying every second of their reunion. For so many hours she'd feared never seeing him again, never holding him, never making love with him, never talking to him or waking to his gorgeous face on the pillow next to hers.

As he dug his fingers into her hips and picked up the pace, it became clear to her that she never would've survived losing him. Her life, too, would've been over—at least the life that she'd come to love almost as much as she loved him.

"Grant..."

"What, honey?"

"Love you. More than anything."

"Me, too. Me, too." He pushed hard into her, tipping her over the edge again. His muffled cry against her shoulder and the surge of heat within her only made the ride sweeter. Everything was sweeter when they did it together.

For a long time afterward, she held him tight and gave thanks for all they had. The rest faded away, unimportant. She had everything she needed as long as she had him.

LAURA AND OWEN emerged from the clinic into afternoon sunshine. Her legs were rubbery beneath her, making her tighten her grip on his arm to remain standing. "I...I need to sit," she said. Her hands were trembling, and her skin felt clammy.

Owen steered her to a bench in the middle of a small garden outside the clinic's main door and sat next to her, seeming equally shell-shocked.

"Say something," she said after a long period of stunned silence.

"I have no idea what to say."

"Did that really just happen?"

"I think it did."

Lightheaded and nauseated, Laura bent at the waist, forcing fresh air into her lungs.

He rubbed comforting circles on her back. "Are you going to be sick?"

"I don't know. Maybe. Are you?"

Owen laughed, relieving some of the tension. "Not sure yet."

Laura sat up straight, moving slowly in deference to the lightheadedness, and turned to him. "*How* are we going to do this? Can you tell me that? *Three babies* in one year *and* a hotel to run?"

She knew she sounded slightly hysterical, but who wouldn't be after Victoria confirmed that the stomach flu wasn't the flu after all but indeed another pregnancy—and this time she was expecting *twins?* Apparently, she was six weeks along. A transvaginal ultrasound had revealed two strong heartbeats.

Owen massaged her shoulders. "First, take a deep breath."

Gazing into his familiar gray eyes, she did as he directed.

"Now take another." After she inhaled and exhaled a second time, he said, "Keep breathing, Princess. No matter what happens, we'll deal with it."

Laura hated the hysterical tension that gripped her chest, the tears that pooled in her eyes and the overwhelming need to cry that came with them. "A year ago, you were footloose and fancy free, living the good life. It was a big enough deal for you to take on Holden—and me. But this... It's just too much. You'll be running for your old life—"

He kissed the words off her lips. "Stop. I'm not going anywhere. And for your information, I never lived the good life until I lived with you—and Holden. It's not too much. It's everything I've ever wanted."

"That's not true! You never wanted any of it!"

"I had no idea how much I wanted it until I had it. Don't you see?" With his hand on her face, he compelled her to look at him. "I didn't know what I was missing. How could I know, growing up the way I did? I love you, I love Holden, and I'll love our babies, too. I promise."

"It's too much," she said, shaking her head as tears spilled down her face.

"It's just enough, honey." He cupped her cheeks and swept up the tears with his thumbs. "How lucky are we? How blessed?"

"I'll tell you one thing, mister, you'd better get all the sex you can while I'm pregnant, because after these two are born, I'm never going near you again if you can get me pregnant this easily—and *two* of them to boot!"

Laughing, Owen dragged her up and tossed an arm around her. "Yes, you will. You can't resist me."

Because she couldn't exactly deny that, she elbowed his ribs. "Watch me." A new thought made her nauseated again. "Oh my God, what'll I tell my dad?"

"Tell him he's going to be a grandpa again, just a little sooner than we'd planned."

"Since this is all your fault, why don't *you* tell him?"

He made a distressed face that made her laugh. "Do I hafta?"

"I'd say that's the least you can do after you knocked me up so thoroughly."

Puffing out his chest, he said, "I did do a pretty good job, didn't I?"

Even though she was amused by his pleasure in the earth-shattering news, she couldn't let him see that, so she scowled at him. After this extremely unexpected development, she figured she had the right to be a bit grouchy until she wrapped her head around it.

At the car, he turned her to face him and eased her back against the sun-warmed metal. "I'll be glad to tell your dad this awesome news," he said, nuzzling her neck, "and I'll make sure to tell him again how very much I love his beautiful daughter who has made me so happy. So damned happy."

"Keep talking," she said, bending her neck to give him better access. "Maybe I'll forgive you before the wedding."

Chuckling, he held the passenger door for her. "Let's go tell our little boy that he's going to be a big brother."

Laura was glad—and relieved—that Owen was so excited about the new babies. But all she could think about was nine months of nausea, three babies in one year and a hotel to run. It might take her a while to match his excitement, but she'd get there. Eventually. Or at least she hoped so.

ABBY SHOWERED, blow-dried her hair and treated the site of the tattoo with antibiotic ointment. She bent and twisted to get a look at it in the mirror, frustrated all over again with herself for taking the safe route with a small tattoo on her back that no one would see unless she wanted them to.

"You're doing a heck of a job shaking things up, girlfriend," she whispered to her reflection. "You're doing a *hell* of a job, I should say." She shook her head in disgust. "You're such a bad *ass*. Unable to hold your liquor, unable to swear respectably, unable to get a tattoo that people will actually *see*, unable to get off during sex. No wonder things didn't work out with Grant or Cal. I bore *myself*. Why wouldn't they be bored, too?"

She was sick to death of wanting to be different. She was fed up with wishing for something else but not knowing how to make it happen. She'd thought she found what she wanted with Cal, but that hadn't worked either. And now here she was, right back where she started with nothing much to show for the last ten years of her life.

"Well, that's not entirely true," she said, thinking of the nest egg she still had from Abby's Attic. Thinking about her adorable little store made her heart ache even more over what she'd given up for a man, so she chose not to go there. Rather, she relived the kiss on the beach with Adam for probably the hundredth time since it happened an hour ago.

That was some kiss. It was unlike any kiss she'd ever had. Maybe it was because they'd been on the beach, outside where anyone might see them, that it had been more exciting than other kisses. Maybe it was the slightly scandalous notion of taking up with her ex-boyfriend's brother that had set her hormones abuzz.

No, she thought. It wasn't any of those things. It had been Adam and the way he'd looked at her as if she was something—or someone—special to him. While they'd always been friendly after knowing each other all their lives, something different had clicked between them on the ferry ride home the other day. Sitting behind him on the motorcycle had been thrilling. Walking the beach with him had been thrilling. Kissing him had been incredibly thrilling.

She ran her fingers over her lips and couldn't wait to kiss him again. Maybe later when he came over… For a brief instant, she wondered what Grant would have to say about Adam dating his ex.

Would Grant's objections put a damper on whatever was happening between her and Adam? They'd better not, or she'd be having some words with Grant McCarthy. After his years of indifference toward her, he had absolutely no right to interfere with anything she did, even if she did it with his brother—a thought that made her laugh nervously.

Doing *it* with Adam McCarthy was something she'd never even considered before yesterday, and now it was all she could think about. Grant had better not get in the way of what was turning out to be the most fun she'd had with a guy in ages... Since she first got together with Cal, back when things had still been fun between them rather than strained.

Even though Adam had been awesome about helping her to bust out of her shell, Abby was well aware that he couldn't do it for her. She had to do it herself, or it wouldn't mean as much.

Before she could spend any more time thinking, she grabbed her purse and phone and headed for the door. Not wanting to lose her nerve, she kept her head down as she walked through town. On the way, she passed Tiffany's new store, Naughty & Nice, housed in the former home of Abby's Attic. She experienced a profound wave of regret at seeing another store where hers had done so well. However, she loved Tiffany and wished her all the best with her new store.

"Abby?"

Speaking of Tiffany, she approached Abby on the sidewalk, holding a coffee in one hand and a bank deposit pouch tucked under her other arm. As always, Tiffany looked stylish and amazing in an eye-popping orange print dress that made Abby feel like a dowdy frump next to her.

"I thought that was you! I didn't hear you were home."

Abby gave her a quick hug. "The store looks great, Tiffany. I hear you've made a tremendous success of it."

"After a few bumpy weeks, it seems to be catching on."

"Congratulations. I never had a doubt that you'd be great at it."

"I'm glad you didn't. I was filled with doubts. So how's Cal?"

"That's...um...over."

"Oh, I'm sorry. I hadn't heard that either."

Abby shrugged off the pain and disappointment. It'd been over months ago, if she were being truthful, so every day seemed to get a little easier.

"Do you have time to come in and take a look at the store?"

Even though she was anxious to get to the tattoo place, she was curious about what had become of her store. "I'd love to."

Abby followed Tiffany into a space that in no way resembled Abby's Attic. Where her store had been sweetness personified, Tiffany's was all about sex—and in some cases, raunchy sex. Abby's senses were overwhelmed by the scents, the textures, the sheer volume of choices. "It's incredible, Tiff. Truly."

"You really think so?"

"I do. I love it." Abby didn't say what she really thought—that the store brought home all the many ways she felt inadequate as a woman. She'd have no idea where to begin among the many choices Tiffany had provided for her customers. She was lost in a sea of femininity.

"Why do you look so sad?"

Startled by Tiffany's astute assessment, Abby forced herself to make eye contact with the other woman. "I feel out of my league in here."

"How so?"

Abby ran her fingers over a lacy garter belt and nodded. "I've never been one for sexing things up."

"Well, isn't that too bad? A body like yours ought to be shown off."

Abby uttered a most unladylike snort of laughter. "Sure."

"You don't think so?" Tiffany put down her coffee and came over to open one of the oversized dressing rooms. She gestured for Abby to step inside. "Face the mirror."

Abby did as directed and tried to look anywhere but at herself, anywhere but at the woman who so desperately wanted to be different but didn't know where to begin.

"Is it okay if I get personal?"

"Ah, sure. I guess so."

Tiffany unbuttoned Abby's blouse and pushed it off her shoulders, revealing the utilitarian white bra that Abby had worn since she was old enough to wear bras. "Hmm," Tiffany said. "Nice tattoo. Just got it?"

"Today."

"Good for you. I'm guessing a D cup?"

Abby's face flushed with color. She'd always been sensitive about breasts that had gotten too big too fast when she was a teenager. "Yes."

"Stay put. I'll be right back."

Over the next thirty minutes, Tiffany Sturgil changed Abby Callahan's entire perspective about lingerie and how important it could be to feeling sexy. Once she got a load of what her too-big breasts looked like in a lacy midnight-blue bra, it hadn't taken much encouragement for Tiffany to talk her into enough underwear for two weeks' worth of sexy, not to mention several new dresses designed to show off her assets.

"You're going to need a thong for that dress," Tiffany said, taking a close look at Abby's posterior in a slinky black number that hugged her curves. All thoughts of shyness had disappeared the first time she bared her breasts to try on the bra that Tiffany insisted would do wonders for her cleavage. She'd been right about that and about every other choice she'd made for Abby.

"I've never worn a thong before. I can't get past the feeling of having a nonstop wedgie."

Tiffany laughed. "I hear that all the time from first-timers, but trust me, once you go thong, you never go back." She held up a scrap of midnight-blue lace, dangling it in front of Abby like a metaphor for the life she wanted so badly but hadn't known how to find.

Abby took hold of it, stepped into the dressing room and closed the door, not wanting Tiffany to see the basic cotton panties that matched her equally boring bra. She slid the thong into position, grimacing at the sensation of having fabric wedged where it didn't belong. "How long does it take before you don't notice that you've got something jammed up there?"

"A couple of days max."

"If you say so."

"Check out what it does for the dress," Tiffany said.

Abby turned, putting her back end to the mirror and looking over her shoulder. She had to admit the dress flowed better with the thong than it had without it. "Okay. I'm sold."

"Well, you kinda had to take the thong either way after you tried it on."

The dry comment made Abby laugh. She opened the door to share the laugh with Tiffany. "You're too much."

"I hear that almost every day."

"You're also crazy good at this." Abby hugged Tiffany. "Ring it up. I'll take it all. Thank you so much. This was exactly what I needed."

"My pleasure. You've done wonders for my coffers today."

"And you've done wonders for my self-confidence."

"You're a beautiful woman, Abby. Any guy would be lucky to spend time with you. Don't let a few setbacks keep you from taking new chances. I'm living proof that even the most unhappy person can find true love and happiness."

"Are we talking about Blaine?"

Tiffany smiled and nodded.

"Oh, I'm so glad to hear that! The last time you and I were together right in this store, he came in, and the two of you nearly burned the place down just by looking at each other."

The soft look of love on Tiffany's face told the full story. "He's amazing and everything I never thought I'd have."

"I'm so happy for you. You deserve it."

"So do you. It's going to happen for you, too. I know it will."

Abby wanted so badly to believe Tiffany, but she'd learned to be pragmatic about these things. Some people didn't meet the person they were meant to spend forever with and were just fine on their own. If that happened to her, she'd find a way to make a worthwhile life for herself. But the time she'd spent with Tiffany had filled her with a new sense of optimism. Maybe, just maybe there might still be hope for her and romance after all.

Tiffany offered to have her assistant, Patty, run Abby's purchases back to the Beachcomber for her.

"That'd be great. I've got another stop to make while I'm out."

"Go on ahead, and come back soon, okay?"

"I will. Thanks again, Tiffany."

"My pleasure."

Trying to ignore the unnatural feel of the thong between her cheeks, Abby hustled through town, arriving at the tattoo studio ten minutes later.

"Back again so soon?" Duke asked when she walked in. He was sitting in one of the chairs, reading the latest issue of the *Gansett Gazette*. "Everything all right with your ink?"

"I want another one."

Duke glanced at Jeff and then at Abby. "You sure about that?"

Abby's heart pounded as she nodded. She walked over to the book she'd looked through earlier when she'd been seeking something safe. At the time, another design had called to her, but she'd dismissed it as too much. "This one," she said when she found it. "On my ankle." The dark purple morning glory came with a winding vine that would curl twice around the back of her leg.

Duke came over to look at what she'd chosen. "That'll take a couple of hours."

"I've got the time if you do," she said, feeling defiant and elated.

"Right this way, madam."

Abby all but skipped to the chair, delighted with herself and her decision to do something unexpected. "Do you mind if I make a few calls while you're working?"

"As long as you hold still, have at it."

She pulled a notebook from her purse and prepared to spend the time reconnecting with the former suppliers she'd worked with at Abby's Attic. Laura had given her carte blanche to set up the gift shop at the Sand & Surf any way she saw fit, and it was time to get to work.

CHAPTER 12

hree hours later, Abby emerged from the tattoo parlor, sore but still elated. Because of the location, this one had hurt a lot more than the other one, but she had no regrets. It was gorgeous! Purple was her favorite color, and the flower had come out magnificently.

She checked the messages on her phone—again. She'd expected to hear from Adam by now, but he hadn't called or texted. The sun had set during her hours in the chair, and the first stars twinkled in the night sky. Without much thought to her destination, she walked in the opposite direction of the hotel, drawn to the beach where placid water rolled gently onto the sand.

Abby kicked off her shoes and waded into the water, gasping at the first contact of cool water on inflamed skin. Her mother had always extolled the healing properties of salt water, so Abby kept her lower leg in the water. A half-moon sat just above the horizon, where the hulking outline of a ship was visible in the waning daylight.

The beach was completely deserted. Anywhere else, Abby might feel anxious about being there alone. But this was Gansett Island, and she'd never felt anything but safe here. That sense of safety sparked a reckless desire for yet another new experience. She waited until twilight faded and darkness set in before she walked up to the cooling sand and tucked her phone into her purse and set it on her sandals.

Before she could lose her nerve, she quickly added her denim jacket, T-shirt and jeans to the growing pile. Down to her new underwear, she hesitated. That was close enough, right?

"No, it isn't. If you're going to do this, do it right." Her hands trembled with excitement and fear of being caught as she unclipped her bra and slid off the thong, nearly groaning with the relief of tugging it from where it didn't belong. Standing completely naked in the great outdoors for the first time, she extended her arms and spun around, overcome by the sheer naughty joy of doing something so far outside her comfort zone. As she dashed into the cold water, she let out a squeal of delight, even as her mother's voice in her head warned against ever swimming alone.

Growing up on an island, the litany of dangers had been hammered home from a young age. Perhaps that was why she'd never taken any chances. Perhaps that was why she was just now, at the age of thirty-two, first experiencing the sublime delight of swimming naked. And it was sublime and delightful. The sluice of the cool water over her skin sent shock waves to all her most sensitive areas. Her nipples tightened from the cold as much as the excitement of doing something new.

She stayed close to the shore in waist-deep water, floating on her back as the half-moon worked its way higher in the sky, casting a glow over the water. A million stars dotted the night sky, and she picked out some of her favorite constellations. As she floated in peaceful serenity, she couldn't help but wonder why she'd never done this before. She already couldn't wait to do it again.

ADAM COULDN'T FIGURE out where Abby might be. He'd told her he'd be by to see her after dinner with Joe and Janey, but here it was almost eight, and there was no sign of her at the Beachcomber. He tried her cell phone again, but, like the last three times he'd called her, it went straight to voice mail.

When he thought about where he'd found her the night before, his gut clenched at the idea that she might've gone looking for trouble without him. Why did that thought make him so damned mad? They had a deal, after all. She'd agreed to let him be her partner in crime, so if she was out looking for some other guy to fool around with...

Storming through the Beachcomber lobby, he stopped short when he realized he was jealous. How ridiculous was that? He was jealous of some nameless, faceless guy that she might or might not be messing around with. What business was it of his? If she wanted to call off their deal, that was her prerogative, but damn it, she ought to at least tell him.

"You're out of your mind, man," he muttered as he took the back stairs from the Beachcomber and crossed the street to the Sand & Surf to see if she might be working in the gift shop.

Laura was at the desk when he came in. "Hey, cuz," she said. "What's up?"

"Have you seen Abby, by any chance?"

"Not tonight, why?"

"No reason." Adam decided to go with evasive so his entire family wouldn't be buzzing about him and Abby before anything significant had even happened between them. "I had a question for her and couldn't find her. She's not answering her phone."

"She's probably out going wild," Laura said with a laugh. "That's her goal for this summer."

"So I've heard," Adam said, not at all comforted by Laura's offhand comment. "How are you? Feeling better?" She still seemed paler than usual.

"A little. Turns out I'm not sick—exactly."

"Oh no?"

"Can you keep a secret?"

"I'm insulted you would ask."

Smiling, Laura crooked her finger for him to come closer. "I'm pregnant."

"Oh my God, that's awesome!" When she seemed to grimace, he said, "Isn't it?"

"It's unexpected, as is the fact that there are two of them in there."

"Two."

"That's what I said."

"Holy shit. Twins."

"Three kids in one year. Holy shit is right."

"Well, um, congratulations?"

"Thank you, and if you say better me than you, I'll smack you."

"I didn't actually say it."

Smiling, Laura gave him a play smack to the arm that connected with the tattoo.

The flash of pain took his breath away. "New tattoo," he said through gritted teeth. "Why does everyone have to hit me there?"

"You got a tattoo? Let me see!"

Adam took off his jacket and rolled up the sleeve of his shirt, exposing angry red skin that would someday resemble Gansett Island. At the moment, it looked like burnt pizza.

"Ouch. That looks like it hurts."

"Just a little."

"Sorry about the smack. What brought this on?"

"An impulse, I guess you could say."

"So, Sarah said she gave you the overview of our reservation system challenge?"

"She did, and I've already given it some thought. I'll be by to work on it in the morning."

"That's great, Adam. Thanks."

"I'm going to press on. If you see Abby, tell her to call me."

Laura eyed him as if she was intrigued and wanted to ask more. But thankfully, all she said was, "I will."

"Congrats again, and tell Owen for me, too."

"I will."

Back on the sidewalk, Adam considered his options for a minute before he withdrew his phone, ignored the resounding objections of his conscience and pinpointed her location using the coordinates of her phone. "What the hell is she doing at the beach at this hour?" He walked to the far side of town, cutting through the ferry-landing parking lot to get there quicker. Would he find her alone, or had she gone there with a guy?

The thought of that had Adam jogging the last quarter mile, cresting the dunes in time to see Abby float into a moonbeam. When he realized she was naked, every thought drained from his head and all the blood in his body rushed to his groin. "Good God," he whispered, gripped by the erotic scene and relieved to find her alone, even if he was dismayed at the idea of her swimming by herself at a deserted beach.

And then the devil took hold of him as he realized another opportunity that had him holding back a laugh at the thought of it. Moving stealthily and using the faint light of the moon to guide him, he found her pile of clothes in the sand and gathered them, her shoes and purse, retreating toward the dunes about a hundred feet from where she'd left her stuff. He sat to wait, holding back the need to laugh so he wouldn't alert her to his presence.

Maybe it wasn't very nice to play a practical joke on her, but it wasn't nice of her to disappear for hours without a word to him when they'd made tentative plans. It served her right, or so he told himself. His conscience was being a real pain in the ass where she was concerned.

He didn't have to wait long for her to emerge from the water and venture up the beach looking for her stuff. He'd bet everything he had that she was now regretting her impulsive swim when it dawned on her that she didn't have a towel or any way to dry off before getting dressed. She had bigger problems than that, not that she'd realized it yet.

Adam could just barely see her from where he sat, but he could tell she was looking for her stuff and becoming increasingly nervous, which made him feel extra guilty. Time to make his presence known.

"Looking for something?" he called out to her.

She let out a squawk of surprise. "*Adam?* What're you doing here?"

"I could ask you the same thing."

"Did you take my clothes?"

"Maybe."

"Oh my God! What are you, *twelve?*"

"Apparently."

"Give them back. This instant!"

Smiling, Adam held back a laugh that would get him into even more trouble. "Come get them."

"I am not doing that."

"Since you need what I've got, I think you'd better do what you're told."

"This is not funny." She might be getting madder, but she was also getting closer.

"Yes, it is." His eyes adjusted to the dark and feasted on the sight of creamy white skin, sweet nipples and a thatch of dark hair at the juncture of her thighs. His mouth went dry as she stopped a foot from him and held out her hand.

"Give me my clothes."

"Make me."

"Adam!"

Leaving her clothes in a neat pile on the sand, he got up, brushed the sand from his hands and stepped closer to her. "You're lucky it was me who found you here and not some creep."

"I'm not entirely sure you aren't a creep."

"I'm not," he said as his hands landed on her shoulders to draw her into his embrace.

"Don't touch me. I'm mad at you." Her words and actions didn't jibe as she snuggled against him.

It was all he could do not to caress every inch of bare skin. "Cold?"

"What do you think? How did you find me anyway?"

"Someone told me they saw you heading this way." He bent his head and nuzzled her neck, pushing her heavy, wet hair out of his way.

She shivered, and her arms encircled his waist as she looked up at him.

"You're so beautiful," he said, his voice husky and rough. He couldn't fight the need to kiss her for another second, capturing her cold lips in a kiss designed to warm her up from the inside out.

To his amazement and delight, she kissed him back, matching his hunger with plenty of her own. Her tongue met his every thrust, twirling and dancing in an erotic dance that made his head spin. This kiss put the earlier one to shame, he decided as his hands moved from her shoulders to her breasts.

When his palms covered her hardened nipples, Abby gasped and broke the kiss. "Adam…"

"What, sweetheart?"

With her hand on the back of his head she guided him to her breast, telling him what she wanted. He was happy to oblige, drawing her nipple into his mouth and running his tongue back and forth over it. When he added a bit of suction, she cried out, and her grip on his hair became painful—not that it stopped him from doing it again.

Only when he realized she was shivering from the cold rather than his attention did he pull back from her. "Let's go back to your room and get you warmed up."

"How do you plan to do that?"

"You'll have to come with me to find out."

"I'm still mad at you for stealing my clothes."

"You can punish me to your heart's content."

"Is that right? I'll have to give that some rather significant thought."

As Adam doled out each article of clothing—stopping to take a good long look at the bra and lacy thong—all he could think about was how soon he could help her take them off again.

"I CAN'T EAT ANOTHER BITE," Mac announced as he pushed back from a table full of lobster shells. "Even if I beg, don't let me have any more."

"Right there with you," Blaine said. "Uncle."

Ned chortled with delight at their pleasure in the meal he'd planned down to the last potato. They'd fed the kids earlier, and now Thomas and Ashleigh were watching their latest favorite movie, *The Little Mermaid*.

Baby Hailey was snoozing in her mama's arms. Maddie had quit eating long before her husband finished.

"It was a wonderful treat, Ned," Tiffany said. "Thank you."

The others chimed in with their thanks as Francine handed out wet wipes.

Mac and Blaine each took a side of the table and rolled up the newspapers they'd put down on the table, scooping up the discarded lobster shells.

"You can take that right out to the can in the driveway," Francine said, holding the screen door for them.

When she came back to the table carrying a plate of brownies, Ned caught her eye and nodded, encouraging her to get on with the reason for the dinner party. He opened new beers for himself, Mac and Blaine and refilled the ladies' wineglasses.

Mac and Blaine came back in and took turns washing their hands at the kitchen sink before returning to the table. Groaning, Mac dropped into his chair. "That was some kinda good."

"Glad ya enjoyed it," Ned said, delighted to be presiding over a family dinner in the home where he'd lived alone for decades. He loved everything about being part of his new family—the kids running around and making a racket, the playful bickering between Maddie and Tiffany, the razzing he and Francine withstood any time the kids caught them kissing or hugging each other. He'd never been happier in his life, and he wanted nothing more for those he loved than to see them happy, too.

Under the table, Ned patted Francine's knee, hoping to prop her up for the conversation she needed to have with her girls.

Glancing at him once more, Francine said, "There was another reason we wanted to have you over tonight—other than the lobster."

"The brownies?" Tiffany took one of the chocolate treats, broke one in half and fed part of it to Blaine, who watched her every move like a man who was madly in love.

Those two kids were crazy about each other, and it warmed Ned's heart to see Tiffany so happy after all she'd been through with her ex-husband.

"I received the divorce papers from your father."

"Finally," Maddie said.

"No kidding," Mac added. "About time."

"That wasn't all he sent," Francine said, handing an envelope to each of her daughters.

"What's this?" Tiffany asked.

"He's established college funds for the kids," Francine said.

Over the sleeping form of her baby daughter, Maddie stared at her mother. "You're kidding me."

"No."

Tiffany opened her envelope and quickly read the note inside. Maddie left hers on the table, apparently not as curious as her sister.

"What does it say, hon?" Blaine asked Tiffany.

"That he was glad to have the chance to see me, and he wanted to do something for my daughter because he owes me for all the years I had to do without. He says he knows it's not much in light of what I deserve, but it was the best he could do. He said he'd be happy to see Ashleigh and me any time we'd like to see him. All I have to do is call, and he'll come. And he said he loves me. Always has." Her voice broke, and she shook her head.

Blaine put his arm around her, and she rested her head on his shoulder.

"Do you want me to open yours for you, babe?" Mac asked Maddie.

Her lips were set firmly as she shook her head. "I'll look at it later."

"Want me to take Hailey?"

"No, thank you." She held on tighter to the baby.

Ned met Mac's worried gaze.

"When will the divorce be final?" Tiffany asked.

"I signed the papers and sent them back this afternoon," Francine said. "The note from your father's lawyer said six months."

"You need your own lawyer," Maddie said. "He owes you a small fortune in back child support, not to mention emotional pain and suffering. College funds for your grandchildren are a nice gesture, but they don't come close to what he owes you."

Ned reached for Francine's hand. "We've talked to Dan, and yer mom and I have talked about it, too. There ain't nothing she wants or needs from him, 'cept a divorce. We got everything we need."

"Still, it's not fair, Mom," Tiffany said. "You should get some sort of settlement."

"Ned is right," Francine said. "The only settlement I want is the piece of paper that says I'm no longer married to Bobby Chester. I'll never regret marrying him, because I got you girls out of it. But it's time now to move on with my life, and by signing the papers and not asking for anything more, that'll happen a lot sooner."

The girls were quiet as they thought it over.

Ned cleared his throat and worked up his courage. "I wanta say somethin' else. None a you kids will ever want for nothin'. I made a lotta money buyin' and sellin' houses over the years, and never spent much of it on anythin'. Mac and his siblings are my heirs, but you girls have been added inta my will as well. And yer kids won't hafta wait for me ta kick it to have their college paid fer. If ya don't want the money from yer daddy, send it back to him. Yer kids won't suffer any if ya do. I waited a long, long time to have a family of my own, and there ain't a one a ya that's gonna want for nothin'. That's all. That's what I wanted to say."

Francine and the girls stared at him.

"What?" he asked, squirming after a long minute of silence.

Maddie transferred Hailey to Mac and got up. She went over to Ned. "Stand up."

Glancing at Francine, who shrugged, Ned did as Maddie asked. When the girl hugged the stuffing out of him, he nearly cried like an old fool.

"We've waited a long time to have a dad who took care of us. Thank you." She kissed his cheek and made him blush.

"It tain't nothin'."

Tiffany got up and hugged him, too. "It's more than we've ever had."

"We should get the kids home to bed," Maddie said to Mac.

"Sure, hon, whatever you want."

"Thanks again for the lovely dinner, Ned—and Mom," Maddie said.

"Our pleasure, honey," Ned said, glad to know both girls were in loving relationships with good men who would support them through this latest development in their complicated relationship with their father.

He and Francine saw them off a few minutes later, helping to buckle toddlers into car seats and waving as they drove away.

"You didn't tell me you'd added the girls to your will," Francine said as they walked inside to finish cleaning up. The house would smell like lobster for days. "You continue to amaze me, Ned Saunders."

Embarrassed by her effusiveness, he said, "I did it a long time ago. Added you, too."

"That's very kind of you."

"It tain't about kindness, doll. It's about makin' sure yer set if I kick the bucket."

"Don't talk like that. I don't like it. I plan to make your life complicated for many years to come."

"I'll look forward ta that." Smiling at her sauciness, he squirted liquid soap into the big pan they'd used to boil the lobsters. "Maddie seemed ta take the latest news from Bobby kinda hard."

"It's always been hardest on her. She remembers him living with us and remembers him leaving. Tiffany had no memory of him."

"I'm certainly no fan a his," Ned said in what had to be the understatement of his lifetime. "But he didn't hafta do what he did for the kids. I gotta give him credit for that."

"Yes, I suppose we do, but I don't want to talk about him anymore."

"What would ya rather talk about?"

"Our wedding," she said with a smile for him. "Where would you like to have it?"

"Anywhere you want, doll. Tell me where ta be, and I'll show up with bells on." He couldn't wait to marry her, to put his ring on her finger—finally—and have the rest of his life to spend with the only girl he'd ever loved.

. . .

MADDIE DIDN'T SAY much on the ride home, and Mac decided to leave her be until they got the kids bathed and off to bed. It took three bedtime stories to lull Thomas to sleep. Mac tried to remain patient with the boy, but he was anxious to be with Maddie.

When Thomas finally stopped chattering, Mac moved carefully to get up from the "big boy" bed that his son was so proud of. Clicking on the night-light, he left the door propped so they could hear him if he woke up in the night. Luckily, both their kids were pretty good sleepers, but he still wanted to be able to hear them if they woke up, and he didn't trust those baby monitors Maddie swore by.

At times, Mac still couldn't believe the changes in his life over the last couple of years. He'd gone from being the most happily unencumbered bachelor in the world to the happiest family man any guy could be. He wouldn't trade one second of his new life to go back to the way he used to live.

In the master bedroom, he found Maddie propped up against a big pile of pillows, breastfeeding their daughter. The letter from her father sat on the bedside table, unopened.

"Is she asleep?" Mac asked in a whisper.

"Think so."

"Want me to take her?"

"Sure."

Although they were old hands at this by now, they still moved carefully so as not to wake the sleeping baby. Mac lifted Hailey into his arms, loving the way she snuggled her little face into his neck. He didn't move for a long moment, waiting for her to settle again.

Knowing how much he loved snuggling with Hailey, Maddie smiled at him. That smile turned him to mush every time, reminding him that she'd made his new life possible.

Mac walked the baby into her room and put her down in the crib, tucking blankets in around her.

Hailey's eyes opened for a heartbeat of a second, and Mac froze, waiting to see what she would do. She popped her thumb into her mouth, turned on her side and drifted off.

He released the deep breath he'd been holding and tiptoed from the room after making sure the baby monitor was on.

"All set?" Maddie asked when he returned.

"Yep. Two for two. I got the touch."

"You're a regular baby whisperer."

Mac stretched out next to her on the bed, turning on his side to face her. "Are you going to read it?"

"I don't want to."

"Want me to do it for you?"

Rolling her bottom lip between her teeth, she contemplated his offer. "I suppose one of us has to look at it." She reached for the envelope and handed it to him.

Mac opened it, looked over the paperwork that set up college trust funds for his children and then scanned the letter her father had enclosed. "Do you want me to read it to you?"

"I guess…"

Mac took her hand and held it against his chest. "Dear Maddie, I hope this finds you doing well. It was so good to see you recently and to be able to spend some time with you. While I know it was difficult for you to extend the overture to me, I thank you for having me to your home. I like knowing where you live and that you are happy with your new family."

Mac glanced up and saw that she was staring intently at the wall, her face expressionless as she listened to him.

"I realize it's rather inadequate after all this time to say I'm sorry for what I did. It's inadequate to admit that I probably had no business getting married or fathering children when I was far more concerned with partying and hanging out with my friends than I was with changing diapers. That, of course, is no fault of yours. It's my fault and mine alone. All of you deserved far better than you got from me, and seeing each of you again has brought home to me just how much damage my immature behavior did to people I loved.

"Believe it or not, I did love you. I *do* love you. I always have. I thought of you and your sister all the time. Seeing you again has also brought home just how much I missed with you both. For years after I left, I thought about going back and trying to fix what I'd done, but I lacked the courage to face you—and your mother—and for that I take full responsibility. It's important to me that you know I thought of you every day and will continue to do so for as long as I live."

A small whimper of distress escaped from her tightly clenched lips. "Maddie—"

"Please finish. Please."

Mac forced his attention from her back to the letter, hating the pain it was causing her. "I want you to know the funds for the children were not done to assuage my guilt, which is not insignificant, but rather to perhaps make life a bit easier for my grandchildren than it was for my children. That's all. I promise the money is given with no strings attached.

"I also promise that you'll not hear from me again, unless you wish to. I've enclosed my address and phone number, and my door is always open to you and your sister as well as your families. If I had my life to do over again, I never would've left. I shall always regret that and the pain I caused you. With all my love and best wishes, your dad, Bobby Chester."

Mac folded up the letter and put it back in the envelope. "Are you okay, honey?"

Even though she nodded, tears slid down her cheeks, breaking his heart. "I wasn't expecting him to say all that."

"It must be nice to hear how he feels after all this time, to know he regrets what he did."

"I guess. It doesn't change anything, though."

"Maybe not," Mac said, choosing his words carefully, "but at least he owns it."

"Yeah. There is that."

"Come here, baby." He held out his arms to her and waited for her to settle into his embrace before closing his arms around her. Brushing the hair off her face, he kissed her forehead and then her lips. "What can I do for you?"

She slid an arm around his waist. "This is good. Really good."

"Will you respond to him?"

"I was just thinking about that. I should thank him for the money, I suppose, but how do I address the thank-you note? Do I say, 'Dear Dad' or 'Dear Bobby' or 'Dear Mr. Chester'?"

Mac couldn't imagine what it might be like to not know how to address his own father. "I suppose you could call him whatever feels comfortable for you."

"I don't know what that is."

"You can think about it for a few days and see what seems right."

She shifted in his arms, raising her head to press her lips to his. "I don't want to think about it anymore tonight."

"Oh no? What do you want to think about?"

Her smile lit up her caramel-colored eyes. "What do you think? It's been a while."

"Sorry about that."

"No need to be sorry, but I'm all for you making it up to me."

Mac could tell she was making an effort to be lighthearted when her heart had to be burdened by what her father's note had said. Determined to take her mind off her worries, he moved so he was on top of her. He was never more at home anywhere than he was in her welcoming embrace. Tonight was no different. Her arms came around him, her fingers combed through his hair, and her legs hugged his hips.

After more than a week since he'd last made love to her, it didn't take long for the desperate need she inspired in him to override his plans for a slow seduction.

"Mac," she gasped. "Don't wait. I need you."

That was all he needed to hear. Their coupling was fast and furious and deeply sensual, as always. For a long time after they were married, he'd expected their ardor to cool, but rather, it had only intensified. This time was no different.

Maddie arched her back and dug her fingers into his backside, trying to keep him inside her while she climaxed.

Her orgasm triggered his, and he cried out from the power of it.

"Holy moly," he whispered into her ear, sending a shiver through her.

"Mmm," she said, holding him close. "Just what I needed."

"Happy to be of service, my love. Any time."

Her laughter reassured him that she'd get through this latest trial. They'd get through it together.

TIFFANY READ and reread the letter from her father, absorbing the words she'd waited forever to hear. He loved her. He'd always loved her. He regretting leaving, wished he had it to do over. This changed everything. All her life, she'd been influenced by the bitterness of her mother and sister. Before she met her father as an adult, she'd had no memory of him. It was like he'd never existed to her. She knew that wasn't the case for her mother and Maddie, and had tried to be empathetic toward their feelings even as she yearned for something, anything of the man who'd fathered her.

Now she had that and so much more.

Blaine came into the bedroom and pulled off his shirt, drawing Tiffany's attention to his muscular chest and six-pack abs.

"How many stories did she talk you into?" Tiffany asked.

"Four."

"You are way too easy."

"What can I say? I'm putty in her hands—and yours." He dropped his shirt, pants and boxers into a pile on the floor that would still be there after he left for work in the morning.

No man was perfect, she thought as she held out her arms to him, but hers was as close to perfect as any man got. She'd expected him to lie beside her, but he came down on top of her, making her squeal when he nibbled on her neck.

"What're you up to, Chief Taylor?" Tiffany closed her eyes and sighed with pleasure, as she did every time he was near. She kept waiting for the other shoe to drop, for the whole thing to go bad, but it only got better.

"About nine inches and growing," he said as he always did, making her giggle—like always.

She slapped his rear, drawing a groan from him. "You're so fresh."

"You love me."

"Yes, I do. I love you so much."

"I never get tired of hearing that, baby."

Before she knew what hit her, he was inside her, making tender sweet love to her. How did he do that? How did he walk in the room, strip out of his clothes and rev her up so easily? In the past, it had taken a lot more effort to get her in the mood. "I don't know how you do this to me every time."

"Do what? What am I doing?"

"Making me crazy without lifting a finger."

He withdrew from her suddenly, making her wish she'd kept her mouth shut. "I skipped over all the preliminaries, didn't I?"

"I don't care. Come back."

"In a minute." He set out to kiss her everywhere, or so it seemed to Tiffany. By the time he entered her again, she was hovering on the brink of an explosive release, which detonated the second he pushed into her. "God, that's hot. You make me pretty crazy, too. You know that?"

She looked up at him, so sexy and amazing, so devoted to her and her daughter, and the words tumbled out of her mouth before she took even a second to contemplate what she was saying. "When are you going to move in with us?"

He stopped moving and stared down at her, his expression unreadable. "I...ah... I didn't know you want me to."

Her casual shrug belied the pounding of her heart and the fear that he might say no. "You sleep here every night that you're not working."

"True." Though he kept up the movement of his hips, she could tell she'd taken him out of the moment with her offer.

Determined to keep his mind on the task at hand, she ran her tongue over his nipple and bit down gently, drawing a sharp inhale that regained his attention.

He captured her mouth in a passionate kiss as he gathered her in tight against him and came hard without breaking the kiss. For a long time afterward, he held her close. Steeped in his familiar scent and the scratch of his late-day whiskers against her neck, Tiffany was certain she'd never been happier or more content in her life.

He'd very quickly become essential to her, and she could no longer imagine a day without him in it. Best of all, her daughter was equally smitten with their handsome cop.

"I didn't mean to throw that out there the way I did," she said after a long period of silence.

"You knocked the wind out of me for a second."

She ran her hands over his back and down to cup his lovely rear. "You recovered rather nicely."

He chuckled and raised his head to kiss her. "I did, didn't I?"

Though she was on pins and needles waiting for his answer, she nodded and gave him a playful smile.

"The thing is..."

Tiffany's stomach clenched the way it used to when she was with her ex-husband. His explosive temper was something she'd never gotten used to, and her stomach had been in a constant state of upset. She told herself Blaine was nothing like him, but she wanted it to work with him so badly. Sometimes she wondered if she wanted it too badly.

"I'd sort of hoped we might get married," he said.

It was Tiffany's turn to stare at him in shock. "Married."

"That's what I said." He kissed both cheeks and then her lips. "Not that this counts as an official proposal, but what would you think if I did propose?"

"I...um...I just got divorced."

"So? Are you planning to play the field now that you're free?"

"Of course not. You know I'm not."

"Then why not make it official?"

"I thought we'd take baby steps."

Blaine withdrew from her and turned onto his back, reaching for her hand and bringing it to his lips. "I understand that you've been through a lot, and the last thing I want is to pressure you for something you're not ready for. But you should know I'm all in, Tiff. With you and with Ashleigh."

Her eyes filled with tears that she blinked back because she refused to ruin this special moment by bawling. She'd done enough of that when she was married. "I love you so much. You know that, right?"

"Yes."

"I'm not ready to talk about getting married again. That has nothing at all to do with you, though."

"Okay."

"So what do you think about baby steps?"

He turned on his side and rested his hand on her belly. "I think, besotted bastard that I am, I'll take whatever you're willing to give and be very, very grateful for every minute I can get with you."

Releasing a sigh of relief, Tiffany turned into his embrace and kissed his chest. "This has been a really nice day."

"You've waited a long time for the men in your life to love you the way you deserve to be loved."

"Yes." As much as she didn't want to cry, she couldn't help the tears. These were happy tears, however. They'd been a very long time coming.

CHAPTER 13

*A*fter Abby confessed to feeling self-conscious about walking into the Beachcomber with wet hair and clothes, Adam put his arm around her and kept her engaged in back-and-forth banter about how foolish she'd been to swim alone at night as they cut through the lobby to the stairs. They'd almost made a clean getaway when he heard his name coming from an all-too-familiar voice. His arm immediately dropped from Abby's shoulders.

He turned and let out a gasp of surprise when he saw his parents, dressed up for a night out. They looked at him and then at Abby, seeming shocked to see them together.

"Abby," Linda said, kissing Abby's cheek. "I hadn't heard you were back on the island."

Adam couldn't believe his well-connected mother had missed that tidbit.

"Will Cal be joining you?"

Abby ran a hand over her wet hair. "He… I…"

"Abby and Cal have broken off their engagement," Adam said, trying not to squirm under the heat of his father's steely stare.

His parents took a moment to absorb that piece of information. He could almost hear their wheels turning as they wondered what he was doing in a questionable embrace with his brother's ex-girlfriend.

"How'd you get all wet?" Linda asked.

"We went for a walk on the beach and Abby tripped."

Linda eyed him shrewdly, no doubt picking over his every word and seeing his story for the lie that it was.

"We were about to have a drink in the bar," Big Mac said. "Join us."

When was the last time his father had ordered him to do anything? And when was the last time Adam had refused a direct order from his dad? Um, never?

"I need to grab a quick shower," Abby said, gesturing to her wet hair.

"We'll save you a seat," Big Mac said.

Adam smiled encouragingly at Abby, noting the heated flush of her cheeks. She was clearly mortified and probably dying for a moment alone. "Meet you in the bar?"

"Sure," she said hesitantly. "I'll be fast." She scurried up the stairs and disappeared.

Adam followed his parents into the bar, where they found a table in the back where they were almost certain to be undisturbed. Great...

Chelsea waved to them from the bar. "I'll be right with you."

"What in the world are you doing with Abby?" Linda asked, cutting right to the chase.

"Hanging out. Having some fun. Nursing our broken hearts."

"Broken hearts?"

"Her breakup with Cal was messy, and I... I recently ended something that was equally messy. Maybe even more so."

"Tell her, son," Big Mac said.

The last thing Adam felt like doing was reliving Sasha's betrayal again, but he couldn't exactly refuse to tell his mother what had happened in New York. When he was done, she stared at him agog.

"You never said a word about her. When did you hear about this?" she asked her husband.

"Only last night."

"You were with her for how long?" Linda said to Adam.

"A couple of years."

"A couple of *years*? Why would you keep that from us, Adam?"

"I don't know. It just seemed easier that way."

"And she wasn't at all curious about your family? Your home?"

"She was. We'd talked about coming here together this summer. I'd even thought, fleetingly, about asking her to marry me. But none of that is happening now."

Chelsea arrived with beers for him and his dad and a glass of white wine for his mom. How comforting was it to be in a place where the bartender knew exactly what they wanted?

"Thanks, sweetheart," Big Mac said to Chelsea. "You can start us a tab. We're going to be here awhile."

Adam bit back a groan when he realized his dad was taking a certain pleasure in watching him squirm.

"Sure thing, Mr. McCarthy. Let me know if you need anything."

"What about your company?" Linda continued when they were alone. "Surely, you're not going to let her *steal* it from you?"

"No, I'm not."

"Is that right?" Big Mac said. "You've changed your tune since last night."

"I did some thinking, talked to my lawyer and made a plan. It's all in the works as we speak."

"Good," Big Mac said. "You've saved me from having a big, fat come-to-Jesus conversation with you about that."

"Thank you, Jesus, for small favors," Adam said, drawing a grunt of laughter from his dad.

"So let's have a come-to-Jesus conversation about what you're doing hanging all over your brother's ex-girlfriend," Linda said.

"I told you. We're hanging out. Having fun. Helping each other through a rough time."

"Have you given any thought at all to what Grant will think of this? He's fragile enough right now after the accident—"

"I talked to Grant about it earlier today."

"You…you talked to him about dating his ex-girlfriend?" Linda said.

"Yes."

"And?"

"What can he say, exactly, Mother? It's been over between them for a very long time. He's engaged to Stephanie now. What's it to him?"

"Adam… My goodness! I've always thought of you as positively brilliant, but can't you see the potential for real trouble with your brother over this?"

"No, I can't. He's happy with Stephanie. Things between him and Abby were over years ago because he treated her like a piece of furniture in his life. He'd tell you that himself. I like her. She likes me. We make each other laugh. How is that wrong?"

"One of the things I'm most proud of," Big Mac said, "is how close the five of you are to each other. I'm going to tell you right now that I won't stand for you doing anything to risk a falling-out with your brother. Especially now when things with him are so unsettled. You'll find me right smack in the middle of that."

"So I'm supposed to put my life on hold while he works out his shit? He won't tell anyone what's bothering him. How are we supposed to help him if we don't know what's wrong?"

"We wait and we remain patient and we don't do anything to make it worse," Big Mac said.

"There're a lot of single women on this island," Linda said. "Take Chelsea, for example. You've always been friends. And then there's our friend Jenny, the lighthouse keeper. She lived in New York for years. You two probably have a lot in common. And then—"

"Mom! Stop. Don't even think about playing matchmaker for me. I'm enjoying the time I'm spending with Abby. Being with her makes me feel better after what happened with Sasha. I'm not giving that up just because it might give Grant a few minutes of disquiet. He had his chance with her, and he totally blew it. He's said as much himself."

"Is this where you were last night when you didn't come home? With her?"

"We were talking and fell asleep. Nothing to get wound up about."

"You're playing with fire, son," Big Mac said, his expression grave.

"I'm thirty-five years old, Dad. You know I love you both, and I love Grant, too. But this really has nothing at all to do with him—or with you. I'm sorry if that sounds disrespectful, because I don't mean it that way. I'm asking you not to make it into something it isn't. We're hanging out together. That's all it is so far. She's not looking for anything serious, and neither am I."

"If that's the case, you'd be a fool to let it come between you and your brother," Linda said. "I can see risking your relationship with him if it were serious between the two of you, but to just 'hang out,' it doesn't seem worth the risk."

"Let me decide that. I'm asking you to stay out of it and let me figure this out for myself. And please, give me a little credit where Grant is concerned. I'd never do anything to intentionally hurt him, and I'd never let anything come between us. Ever."

A flash of red caught his eye, and Adam turned to see Abby come into the bar in a formfitting red dress with a neckline that left very little to the imagination. Her dark hair was shiny under the lights, her lips glossy and red, her smile wide as she recognized one of the men she'd flirted with the night before and accepted a hug from him.

Adam gripped the back of his chair tighter to keep from getting up and making another scene that she wouldn't appreciate. He knew a tiny bit of relief when she pointed at the table where he sat with his parents and disentangled from the octopus.

"I still can't believe you've got six kids," the guy said in a booming voice that could be heard throughout the crowded bar. "You're one smoking-hot mama!"

On that, he and Adam agreed.

Only when she started toward their corner table was Adam able to tear his gaze off her and close his mouth, which had fallen open when she made her entrance. He glanced over to find his parents watching him very closely.

"Just hanging out, my ass," his dad muttered the second before Abby arrived at their table.

· · ·

THE DRESS WAS WAY TOO much for drinks with the McCarthys. Abby had come to this conclusion about halfway down the stairs to the lobby. She'd known a moment of hesitation when she put it on, but after the time she'd spent with Tiffany today, she was determined to be a newer, better version of her old self. Even though the dress was too much, Adam's reaction to it had been absolutely perfect and worth every cent she'd spent at Naughty & Nice.

"Self-confidence is the key," Tiffany had said. "If you feel confident, you'll project that to others."

The red dress made Abby feel confident about walking into that bar to meet Adam and his parents, who must be wondering what they were doing together. Would they disapprove? And if they did? Would she care? Would he?

Stop it. That's not helping your confidence.

What did wonders for her self-confidence was the greeting she received from Les—or was it Len?—one of the guys she'd met the night before who made a big deal out of her when she walked into the bar. He greeted her with a hug and a suggestive smile.

"You look amazing, baby. Are you sure you're married?"

"Afraid so," Abby said, relieved to rely on the cover story Adam had concocted for her. "My husband is right over there with his parents, and he's the jealous sort."

"If I had a wife who looked like you, I'd be the jealous sort, too."

"That's kind of you to say. It was nice to see you again, but I'd better go join my family." Thinking of the McCarthys as her family reminded Abby that she'd once expected to be a McCarthy, but that hadn't happened.

As she walked away, Les—or Len—called after her. "Still can't believe you've got six kids. You're one smoking-hot mama!"

When she realized the McCarthys had heard what he said, her face got very warm as Adam stood and held a chair for her. Big Mac also stood in a show of respect that Abby found charming. She'd always had a great big crush on him.

"You look gorgeous," Adam said when he returned to his own chair.

"Thank you. I went shopping today. Time for something new."

"I saw something just like that dress in Tiffany's store," Linda said.

"That's where I got it. She's done a wonderful job with the store, and she's exceptionally good at getting her customers to part with their money."

"That she is," Linda agreed.

"What the heck have you bought there, Mom?"

"None of your business, honey."

"Oh my God," Adam muttered.

"Just because there's snow on the roof doesn't mean the fire's out, son," Big Mac said with a wide grin, making Adam groan.

Abby couldn't help but laugh at his distress.

"So you've got six kids now?" Linda asked, winking at Abby. "You work fast."

Abby glanced at Adam, uncertain how she should respond.

"That guy was hassling her last night," he said, "so we made up a little story."

"Is that right?" Big Mac said, eyebrow raised in inquiry as he studied his son.

Chelsea came over to take Abby's order.

"Saved by the bartender," Adam said. "I've never been so happy to see you, Chelsea."

"Well, that's nice to hear. What can I get you, Abby?"

"White wine, please." She'd learned her lesson with tequila. While it supposedly made some women take their clothes off, apparently it made her confess her deepest darkest secrets. She still couldn't think about the things she'd told Adam last night without wanting to die, so she didn't allow her brain to go there.

"What's your pleasure? Pinot? Chardonnay?"

"I'll try Pinot, please." Truth be told, she had no idea what the difference was between the various types of wine, so she'd have to experiment and find one she liked. She used to drink Chardonnay once in a while, mostly to be sociable when she was with Grant, but she'd never really tried anything else. Well, until she started swilling tequila.

"Coming right up."

"Another round for us, too, please, sweetheart," Big Mac said.

Chelsea seemed to melt a little when Big Mac called her sweetheart, but then again, she was only human.

"It's so nice to see you, Abby," Linda said. "We're sorry to hear things didn't work out with Cal."

"I was sorry, too." She hesitated to say more but could tell from the earnest expressions on the faces of Mr. and Mrs. McCarthy that they were interested in what'd happened. "It was different in Texas. We didn't... It didn't work there."

"That's too bad," Linda said. "But better to find out now than after the 'I dos.'"

"Yes, that's true." Anxious to turn the conversation away from her sorry love life, Abby tried to think of something else they could talk about. "You must be excited about being grandparents again. Congratulations."

"We're thrilled for Janey and Joe," Big Mac said. "Can't wait for August."

"She'll have a lot on her plate with the baby and school," Abby said.

"If anyone can handle it, she sure can," Linda said.

"That is so true," Abby said.

The conversation seemed to lag a bit, making Abby wonder why Adam was being so quiet. Couldn't he contribute something? But no, he sat there fiddling with his beer bottle and sneaking looks at her as she talked to his parents. And why did he keep looking at her? Was there something on her dress? She glanced down to find nothing other than a little more breast than she normally showed, but nothing obscene.

She looked up, met his gaze and tried to challenge him to look elsewhere, but he kept his eyes locked on her, almost daring her to look away.

Chelsea arrived with their drinks, which gave Adam something else to focus on besides her chest.

It wasn't lost on Abby that her entrance had bowled him over. That was ridiculously flattering and did amazing things for her self-confidence. If only his parents weren't watching their every move, she might be able to enjoy his reaction a little more.

As she took a sip of her wine and pondered the deeper meaning of their attraction to each other, his hand landed on her thigh—under her dress. She choked on her wine, which somehow ended up in her windpipe. The coughing fit that followed was almost as embarrassing as telling Adam her sex secrets.

He patted her on the back until she'd coughed the wine out of her windpipe.

"Sorry about that," she croaked, mortified as she dabbed at her eyes.

Linda pushed a glass of ice water toward Abby. "Have a drink."

As she drank from the cool glass of water, she caught Adam giving her a smug smile and wanted to smack him. He knew exactly what he'd done to her—for the second time that day—and wasn't the slightest bit sorry. Between that and stealing her clothes at the beach, he was batting a thousand today.

"They told me I might find you in here, darlin'."

Abby froze at the sound of the familiar voice. This could *not* be happening. She looked up to find Cal gazing down at her, seeming perplexed by the glass of wine sitting in front of her.

His eyes slid over the front of her dress, stopping at her chest and then moving back up to her face. He greeted the McCarthys and shook hands with Big Mac and Adam. "Could you spare me a minute or two?" he said to Abby. "I came all the way from Texas to see you."

She had no idea what to say. Was she on a date with Adam? Would he understand if she left to talk to Cal? "I...um... We're—"

"Go ahead," Adam said. "We'll wait for you."

Only the tight set of his mouth told her he was unhappy with the turn of events. And was it wrong of her to be so glad that he was clearly dismayed by the appearance of her ex-fiancé? "I'll be back in a few minutes," she said to Adam, loud enough for Cal to hear.

"We'll be here."

"Excuse me," she said to Mr. and Mrs. McCarthy, who seemed intrigued by the drama playing out before them. She hated playing the starring role. She hoped they knew that. When had her life turned into such a three-ring circus?

With that question foremost on her mind, Abby got up on trembling legs and let Cal guide her from the bar with a hand on her back. She wanted to tell him not to do that. She wanted to remind him that he no longer had a right to touch her in that proprietary way, but she was more concerned about getting out of there without making another scene.

"Better watch out, pal," Les or Len said. "Her husband won't take kindly to you touching her."

Cal's normally amiable expression turned hostile in an instant. "Her *husband* won't, will he?"

"Come on, Cal," Abby said, pushing him from the bar into the lobby. She headed toward a somewhat secluded arrangement of chairs in front of the fireplace and took a seat. Her stomach ached as Cal's reappearance reminded her of all the hopes she'd once pinned on him —hopes that had been dashed when she saw him with his ex-girlfriend and discovered they still had significant feelings for one another. *Don't forget that.*

Rather than sit in the chair next to hers as she'd expected him to, he stood, hands on hips, fuming. "What the hell is going on here, Abby? What was that guy talking about? What husband?"

"It's something I told him to get him to leave me alone."

"Why're you all cozy with the McCarthys?"

Grant had been a sore subject between them from day one. "They're my friends." She glanced around the lobby, worried about the formidable Gansett Island gossip machine. As Cal had once been the island's only doctor, everyone knew him—and her. "Would you please sit down?"

"I don't want to sit. I've been sitting all day trying to get here on three different airplanes."

"People are looking at us, Cal. I'm asking you to please sit and have a civilized conversation with me."

"Let's go to your room."

"No."

"I don't understand what's happened to you." He ran his fingers through his blond hair in a frustrated gesture that further ramped up her anxiety. "That dress… It's not you, and were you *drinking?* You don't drink."

"I do now, and this dress *is* me. It's the new me."

He took a second closer look at the dress, his gaze lowering to fixate on the new tattoo on her ankle. "Are you kidding me? You're gone one day and now you have a *tattoo?* You're hanging out with your ex-boyfriend's family, drinking and wearing low-cut dresses?"

Abby had to remind herself they were in public, that people were watching. She kept her voice low. "I have two tattoos." That wasn't what she'd planned to say, but the words came out of their own volition.

His eyes bugged. "Are you having some sort of crisis or something? I wasn't paying enough attention to you, so you come home and go nuts?"

"I'm not saying another word until you sit down and be quiet."

He flopped into a chair. "There. Happy now?"

"For the first time in a really long time, I am happy. Thanks for asking." As the words came out of her mouth, she realized they were true. The months of indecision over what to do about another relationship that wasn't working were over. She'd made her decision, and now she intended to stick to it. "I'm happy to be home."

"Your home is in Austin with me."

She shook her head. "No, it isn't. I'm sorry, but this is where I belong, and I'm not leaving again. I've done that twice now, and it hasn't worked for me either time. Lesson learned."

Mentioning her past with Grant was never a good idea where Cal was concerned, but history couldn't be rewritten. "It doesn't matter at all to you that I love you? That I want to marry you?"

Abby took a moment, choosing her words carefully. "I don't believe you love me as much as you think you do. I believe you love the idea of me, waiting patiently at home for you to fit me into your busy schedule. I believe you actually love Candy. You're *in love* with her."

He stared at her, incredulous. "I can't believe you're still telling me who I love! I came all this way to see *you*. I love *you*. I want to marry *you*."

As he repeated the words, the same words he'd said over and over and over again to her, Abby knew she didn't love him anymore. Not the way she once had. Not like she had before she saw him with the other woman he loved, whether he wanted to admit it or not. He was very good at saying what he thought she needed to hear, but his words and actions were in sharp contrast. She wanted more out of love than what she'd found with him.

"How many nights did I make dinner for someone who never came home? Who never even bothered to call? How many nights did I go over to your mom's, hoping for a few minutes with you, only to find you hanging out with Candy? Fifteen? Twenty? When was the last time we made love? Do you even know? I do. It was in December. It's May now. Does that sound like your idea of a loving relationship? It's not mine."

"Abby—"

"My life is here," she said before she could lose her nerve. "Yours is in Texas. We tried, Cal, and for a while it was great, but then it wasn't. I can't go back there again. It wasn't easy for me to leave, but I did what was best for me. For the first time in a very long time—maybe ever—I'm focused on what I want. Our relationship isn't what's best for me. It's not what I want."

"What about me? What about what I want?"

"You need to think about what that is."

"No, I don't."

Abby glanced at the doorway to the lounge, wondering what Adam and his parents were talking about while she was out here with her ex-fiancé. What a mess.

"Somewhere more important to be?" Cal asked.

"I was in the middle of something. I didn't know you were coming."

Elbows on knees, he leaned forward, blond hair falling over his forehead. She'd once found that adorable. "Let me ask you something."

She wanted to say no, but after more than a year together, she owed him some closure at the very least. "Okay..."

"Why'd you leave without talking to me?" he asked in a soft tone that tugged at her emotions. "Didn't I at least deserve the chance to ask you not to go?"

"I was afraid you'd talk me out of leaving, and it was what I needed to do."

"You're giving up on us too easily."

She shook her head. "No, I'm not. I fought long and hard to make this work, but I couldn't do it by myself anymore. I've already been through that once before, and I couldn't do it again. I'm sorry."

"You know I hate when you compare me to Grant McCarthy."

"I know." She refused to apologize for the apt comparison to what had happened between her and Grant.

He reached for her hand. "I admit I didn't handle things well in Texas. I spent more time than I should have with my mom—"

"That wasn't the problem, Cal. That's not what this is about."

Releasing her hand, he rolled his eyes in frustration. "What do you want me to say? I've known Candy all my life. We're *friends* the way you are with the McCarthys. That was over a long time ago."

"I stand by my belief that you have unresolved feelings for her."

"How do I convince you otherwise?"

"You can't."

He shook his head in what seemed to be astonishment. "This is insane. You know that, don't you? I'm right here, Abby. I'm here with you. I'm telling you I love you, and you don't believe me? Why would I be here if I didn't love you? Why would I have come all this way if you weren't the one I want?"

The pain she heard in his voice had her doubting everything, which was what she'd gone out of her way to avoid before leaving Texas. Then she thought of Candy, of all the times she'd seen her and Cal together and how often she'd seen the truth of their relationship, even if he couldn't see it.

"I'm sorry you came all this way, but I've made my decision, and I intend to honor it."

"You're throwing away a good thing."

"It wasn't a good thing for me. I'm sorry if it hurts you to hear that."

He stared at her for a long moment before he got up and walked away. That was when she noticed her hands were shaking. So much for self-confidence.

ADAM SPENT AN EXCRUCIATING fifteen minutes alone with his parents waiting to see if Abby would come back. A staggering array of unsettling possibilities passed through his overactive imagination. All the while he attempted to make small talk with his mind occupied elsewhere.

What if Cal convinced her to give him another chance? And why did that possibility make Adam ache? What the hell was wrong with him? Until a few days ago, he'd barely given Abby a thought since she broke up with his brother. Now she was all he could think about? What was up with that? How did that happen so fast, and what was it about her that was so damned attractive to him?

Everything, if he were being honest. She was a beautiful woman on the inside as well as the outside. It pained him to watch her trying to turn herself into someone new when there wasn't anything wrong with who she already was. He liked that she was sweet and sensitive and maybe a tiny bit naïve when it came to sex. He found her extremely refreshing after being with sleek, sophisticated Sasha the last few years. How could he have thought that was what he wanted in a woman? Now he knew better.

"Adam?"

He looked up to find his parents watching him expectantly. Crap. "Yeah?"

"Did you hear what your mother said?"

"I'm sorry. I didn't."

"I said that it seems to me that you like Abby a lot more than you let on," Linda said, intuitive as always. They didn't call her Voodoo Mama for nothing.

His first impulse was to deny it. That would be the easier path, the path less fraught with peril. "Maybe," he said, bracing himself for the onslaught of parental disapproval.

"She seems to like you, too," Big Mac said.

"Maybe."

"Are you worried about what might be happening with Cal?" his dad asked.

"Maybe."

"Honestly, Adam!" his mother said. "Is that the only word you've got?"

"Perhaps."

His dad let go with a low, rumbling chuckle that drew a smile from Adam. "You've always been the toughest of our five nuts to crack," Big Mac said.

"Thank you. I think."

Big Mac rested his elbows on the table. "I only mean that you've kept to yourself more than your siblings did."

"Middle-child syndrome," Linda added.

Adam chewed on the end of a plastic stirrer. "Is that your official diagnosis, Mom?"

"Perhaps," she said, sticking her tongue out at him.

Adam laughed. How could he not? He adored them, even if he didn't feel the need to tell them everything.

"You know we're on your side, son," Big Mac said. "Even if we don't agree with everything you do, we're always on your side."

That's all it took to put a lump in Adam's throat. "I know that, Dad, and it means a lot to me. It's always been important to me that I make you proud. Both of you."

"There's never been a single day when we weren't proud of you," Big Mac assured him.

His dad was so free with his love that sometimes it overwhelmed Adam to be on the receiving end of it. "I'm not about to do anything to change that track record. I promise you that."

"Here she comes," Linda whispered—loudly.

Adam turned to watch her come toward them. The impact of that dress was no less powerful the second time around. He zeroed in on her face, looking for clues to what might've happened with Cal, but she kept her expression neutral, giving nothing away.

He stood to hold her chair for her and waited until she was settled before he took his own seat. "Everything okay?"

"Yes," she said, smiling at him. "I'm sorry for the interruption."

Adam wanted the full story, and he wanted it now. "Are you..."

Abby reached for his hand under the table. "Later."

At the feel of her fingers closing around his, Adam felt like he could breathe again. Why did it matter so much to him that she'd come back? Why did it mean everything to him that she'd reached for his hand and held on, even though his parents were watching their every move? This situation was getting out of control, he decided as he disentangled his hand from hers. Time to take a small step back, out of self-preservation.

Her puzzled glance made him feel like a jerk.

Big Mac made a production out of stretching and yawning. "I'm zonked, honey. Time to take me home and put me to bed."

"Honestly, Dad. Do you have to put it that way?"

"How else should I put it?" Big Mac asked with a mischievous grin.

Adam and his dad lunged for the check that Chelsea had left on the table. His dad beat him to it.

"My treat," Big Mac said smugly.

He knew better than to argue with his generous father. "Thank you, Dad."

"Yes, thank you, Mr. McCarthy. It was so nice to see you both."

"You, too, honey," Linda said, kissing Adam and then Abby. "Come to dinner sometime soon."

"I'd love to."

Big Mac mussed Adam's hair and kissed Abby. "Don't stay out too late, kids."

"Bye, Dad." Adam was grateful his parents hadn't asked what time he'd be home. He didn't want to have to tell them in front of Abby that he'd see them tomorrow. When they were gone, Adam turned to Abby, thrilled to finally be alone with her. To hell with self-preservation, he thought as he took her hand. "What happened?"

"He said all the usual things—he loves me, wants to marry me, is sorry about what happened in Texas."

"And?"

"And what?"

Adam wanted to scream with frustration. "What did *you* say?"

"What do you think I said? That it didn't matter anymore. We're over."

Relief flooded his veins, making him feel a bit lightheaded. Bringing their joined hands to his lips, he kissed the back of hers while holding her gaze. Had he ever noticed how extravagantly long her lashes were? Or how sparkly her brown eyes could be when she was pleased with herself?

She tipped her head for a closer look at him. "Were you worried?"

Why was it that so much seemed to hinge on his answer? "Very."

Her smile lit up her face and had him zeroing in on her lips as all sorts of erotic images spiraled through his brain, one right after the other.

"Can we please get out of here?" he asked.

"Where would you like to go?"

"Upstairs."

She looked at him for a long time, as if making an important decision. "Come on, then."

Adam didn't have to be told twice. He was up and out of his chair so fast, it tipped over behind him, making her laugh at him. After he righted the chair, he hustled out of the bar in hot pursuit.

"Go get her, dude," their buddy from last night said, raising his beer in tribute to Adam.

He choked back a nasty retort and dashed into the lobby, thrilled to see it deserted for once. Even the front desk was devoid of people, which was rare. That was a lucky break. No one would see him follow Abby upstairs.

She was nearly to the first landing when he caught up to her. "What did your parents say when Cal showed up?" she asked.

"Nothing."

She cast a glance at him over her shoulder. "Not one thing?"

He urged her to keep moving. "I don't remember, and I don't want to talk about my parents."

"They didn't say *anything* about us being together?"

"That's talking about my parents, which we aren't doing."

"Adam!"

"What?" He was so completely fixated on her legs as he followed her that he nearly crashed into her when she stopped and turned to face him. "What's that on your leg?"

She smiled and lifted her leg so he could see the new tattoo.

"You went back."

"And got one where people could see it."

She was so proud of herself that he couldn't help but smile at her. "Good for you. It's gorgeous."

"Thank you. I think so, too, but I want to know what your parents said about us being together."

Adam let out a tortured groan. "Can't we please go to your room and talk about it?"

"Fine, but we *are* going to talk about it."

"Thanks for the warning."

Outside her door, he watched as she once again withdrew her room card from her bra. "What else you got in there?"

"Wouldn't you like to know?" she asked as she opened the door and went in ahead of him.

The door clicked shut behind him. "Yes, I would."

"Talk first."

He spoke as quickly as he ever had in his life, like a spokesperson on speed. "They were surprised to see us together. They mentioned Grant and how he might feel about it. I assured them that I talked to him about it—"

"What did he say?"

"He was primarily concerned with me doing something to hurt you. He said you've had enough of that."

"That's certainly true. So, he didn't seem at all, you know…"

He took a step that brought him closer to her in the small room. "Jealous? Angry? Disappointed in me or you?"

"Any of the above?"

He spoke normally now, because the time for fooling around was over. "All of the above. But as I pointed out to him—and to my parents—he had his chance with you and totally blew it. He'd tell you that himself. He's also very happy with Stephanie and doesn't have a leg to stand on where you and I are concerned, and he also knows that."

"Still…" Her hands landed on his chest in an almost absent gesture that tripped all his circuits. "He wasn't mad at you, was he?"

"Maybe a little. At first. Once he has a chance to get used to the idea, I'm sure he'll be fine with it. He loves us both, right?"

"I suppose." She looked up at him with those guileless brown eyes. "So your brother knows, your parents know, Cal knows that we're really done. Where does all that leave us?"

Because he couldn't live another second without touching her, he put his arms around her and drew her in closer to him.

Her hands slid up his chest to link behind his neck.

Bending his head, he kissed from her throat to her ear, drawing the lobe between his teeth. "It leaves us alone together in a hotel room with only this astonishing red dress between us."

She let out a nervous laugh. "That's not the only thing," she said, tugging on his shirt for emphasis.

"It's the only thing coming off tonight."

"What does that mean?"

"It means," he said, kissing her lightly as he drew her zipper down her back, "tonight is all about me finding out what you like, what makes you sigh, what makes you scream."

"I don't scream."

"We'll see about that."

"Adam…"

"Shhhh. We have all night. I have nowhere to be and nothing on my mind except you."

"Nothing?" she asked with a coy smile.

"Not one thing."

"And there's nothing in this for you?"

With a light brush of his fingers over her shoulders, he sent the dress into a puddle at her feet. His mouth went dry at the sight of the black bra and scrap of panties she'd worn under it. "Not this time. This time is all about you. Leave everything to me."

CHAPTER 14

*F*or the first time in several days, David had no patients spending the night at the clinic. The worst of the stomach flu seemed to be over, thank goodness. It had been quite a siege, the worst he'd experienced since taking over the island's medical practice from Cal Maitland.

Even though every muscle in his body ached from days of nonstop work, he wasn't tired and had no desire to go home alone. Hearing about Laura McCarthy's unplanned pregnancy had reminded David once again of where he should've been in his own life—married to Laura's cousin Janey with a child on the way.

Except Janey was married to Joe Cantrell and expecting his baby, not David's. Lately, David had realized he was tired of thinking about Janey and all the ways he'd screwed things up with her. He was tired of dwelling on what should've been and ready to focus on the future.

And more and more, he found himself thinking of Daisy. He wasn't sure he was ready for another full-blown relationship, but maybe it was time to start dating again. Nowhere was it written that a date had to lead to forever. So if he asked Daisy to dinner—a real dinner at a restaurant—it didn't mean he was making promises to her that he might not be able to keep, did it?

She'd been so nice to him at a time when her own life was in disarray. If he took her to dinner to say thank you, he wouldn't be starting something he couldn't finish, would he? After spending his entire adult life with the same woman, he'd never done the casual-dating thing before, so the rules were somewhat of a mystery to him.

One thing was patently clear, however—he was definitely overthinking this. It was a meal, not a marriage, for crying out loud. Disgusted with himself, he got into his car and headed for Daisy's place in town.

By the time he parked in front of her house, he'd nearly talked himself out of the whole thing. But he soldiered on, took the rickety steps to her porch two at a time and rapped on the door, half hoping she wasn't there. Then he wouldn't have to follow through and could have a stress-free, relaxing night at home.

He was about to give up when the door swung open, and there she was. Her hair was in a ponytail and her clothes were covered in various colors of paint.

She seemed pleased but surprised to see him. "David. I wasn't expecting you, as you can tell," she said with a delicate, sweet laugh. "I'm doing some painting."

"So I can see. I'm sorry to bother you. I was in the neighborhood and thought I'd see if you were interested in dinner, but you're busy."

"Not that busy."

She had a way of making him feel better about himself. He didn't know what she did or how she did it, but he always felt better when he was with her.

"Do you want some help with the painting?"

"You don't feel like doing that after how many days at the clinic?"

"Four or five. I lost count."

"Give me fifteen minutes to clean up, and we'll have dinner." She stepped back from the door and gestured for him to follow her inside where the odor of fresh paint was pervasive. "I was fixing the hole Truck put in the wall, and once I got going, I decided to change the color." She took a measuring look at the dark orange wall. "What do you think?"

"It's not one you see every day."

"I know," she said with a laugh. "You probably think I'm crazy."

"Not at all. I like it."

"You don't have to say that. I'm not sure *I* like it. I'd hoped it would be warm and welcoming, but it's just kinda…orange."

He laughed. "That it is, but you might like it better when you finish."

"Maybe. What do you feel like eating? Pizza?"

Watching her talk about the paint had him oddly captivated, which gave him the courage to take a gamble. "I had something a little nicer in mind. Maybe Stephanie's?"

"Oh."

"That doesn't sound good to you?"

"It sounds expensive. I don't need that if you don't."

"It's not that I *need* it. I thought it would be fun, and you might enjoy it. After all the nights you've fed me lately, I wanted to return the favor."

"Pizza would be fine."

"I've heard such raves about Stephanie's, but I haven't had time to try it yet," he said, hoping to cajole her.

"I don't have anything to wear there."

David wanted to shoot himself for not thinking of that. "No problem. We can go there another time." Great, he thought, commit to a second date when this one was starting off so well.

"I might have one thing that would work."

"We can go wherever you want. It wasn't my intention to make you uncomfortable."

She shocked the hell out of him when she went up on tiptoes to kiss his cheek. "I know, and you didn't. I'll be quick."

After she dashed upstairs to change, he stood rooted to the spot where she'd left him, his cheek still tingling from her impulsive kiss. If she could unman him with a simple kiss to the cheek, what would a real kiss with her be like?

He'd never kissed anyone but Janey. And the woman he'd cheated on her with, of course.

Remembering that incident jarred him out of his thoughts about kissing Daisy, and he wandered over to plop down on the old sofa she'd once delightedly told him she found abandoned by the side of the road outside of town. He recalled her pleasure in telling him about the find.

At some point, if this went anywhere, he'd have to tell her he'd cheated on Janey. After what she'd been through with her abusive ex-boyfriend, she deserved to know the truth about what she'd be getting with him.

"Let's see how dinner goes before you worry about emptying your closet of skeletons," he muttered.

True to her word, fifteen minutes later she came skipping down the stairs wearing a pretty summer dress and carrying a sweater. "I hope this is okay."

He stood to greet her. "You look lovely, as always." Extending his arm to her, he said, "Shall we?"

She looked up at him with big, trusting eyes and curled her hand around his arm. "Yes, please."

GRACE GAVE Evan seven days and seven nights to bury himself in his work before she went to bring him home. Driving to the studio, she was nervous about what she might find there. In all the months she'd spent with Evan, she'd never once been nervous about seeing him.

Until now.

She cringed as the overgrown brush scraped against the side of her car, adding to the scratches from the last time she'd been here a couple of weeks ago, before the accident that had changed everything. He hadn't been the same since then, and she was determined to bring him home for at least one night so they could reconnect.

She hoped he'd be happy to see her.

The old motorcycle of Mac's that Evan had been using was parked in the driveway, if you could call it that. While the building had been fully refurbished and was ready for business, the grounds needed some major work.

Grace stepped inside and gave her eyes a minute to adjust to the near darkness. She followed a light to the back of the studio where she found Evan in his office bent over a laptop. She knew a moment of relief when she realized he was here alone.

"Hey, stranger," she said.

"Grace? What're you doing here?"

His eyes were red and rimmed with fatigue, his hair was standing on end, and it had been days since he last shaved. The poor guy was working himself to death. "Looking for you."

He sat back and gestured for her to come in. Rather than take one of the visitor chairs, however, she went around his desk and slid onto his lap. His arms encircled her waist, and Grace snuggled up to him, breathing in his comforting, familiar scent.

"Missed you," she said.

"I've missed you, too. I'm sorry I've been spending so much time here. There's an endless amount of stuff that has to get done before we officially open next week."

"I know, but I wondered if I might be able to lure you home just for tonight."

"I don't think I can, babe. I've got all these invoices—"

Grace kissed the words right off his lips, going for broke with a kiss designed to remind him of what would be waiting for him at home. "Please?"

"Aww, baby, what am I supposed to say when you ask me like that?"

"How about, 'Yes, Grace, I'd love to go home and sleep with you tonight.'"

He smiled and kissed the end of her nose. "Yes, Grace, I'd love to go home and sleep with you tonight."

"Excellent."

He squeezed her tight before he released her. "You're full of beans tonight."

"I'm lonely for you."

When they were both standing, he embraced her again, kissing the top of her head. "I'm sorry. I didn't mean to neglect you."

"Have you been hiding out here?"

Perplexed by the question, he said, "Hiding from you?"

"Not from me, but from something else maybe?"

"I'm not hiding, Grace. I'm working. I promise."

"Okay."

"Let's get out of here."

She waited while he shut down all the equipment and locked everything up. Outside, she watched him glance at the motorcycle with a bit of trepidation. "How about I drive?" she asked. "I can bring you back in the morning before work."

"Are you sure?"

"You're exhausted, Ev. Let me drive you home."

"I won't say no to that."

"You need to do something about this landscaping."

"I've got my friend Alex Martinez coming tomorrow."

"Is he related to the Martinez Garden people?"

"One of their sons. I went to school with him and his brother Paul. Alex is a master gardener. He worked for a time for the U.S. Botanic Garden in Washington. He came back to the island after his mother got sick, because Paul needed help running the business."

"Is his mom Marion Martinez?"

"Yes, I think that's her name. Do you know her?"

"I haven't met her, but her sons come into the pharmacy. Nice-looking guys."

"So now you're checking out the customers, Ms. Ryan?"

Grace smiled at his proprietary tone. "I might be madly in love with my sexy boyfriend, but I'm not blind or dead."

He leaned across the console to nibble on her neck. "Madly in love, huh? That boyfriend of yours is one lucky bastard."

"I keep telling him that, but sometimes I wonder if he knows it."

"He knows, baby. You don't ever need to wonder about that."

"I was kidding, Evan."

Resting his head on her shoulder, he said, "I know."

At home, Evan took a shower and shaved while Grace brushed her teeth and changed into a nightgown. Listening to him in the shower, she realized how much she'd missed sharing their home in the last week. Nothing was the same without him around.

She got in bed and picked up the book that had been keeping her company during her nights alone, but couldn't seem to concentrate on what she was reading.

Evan emerged from the bathroom in a cloud of steam. Once it cleared, she saw that he was completely naked and heading for the bed.

She licked her lips in anticipation.

"Aaah," he said as he settled in next to her. "Feels good to be in a real bed. That sofa in the office isn't very comfortable."

She rested her hand on his chest. "I'm proud of what you've done with the studio, Evan. It's going to be an awesome success. I know it."

He covered her hand with his own. "I sure hope so."

"Why do you look so worried?"

"I've got a lot riding on that place. A lot."

"You're worried about protecting Ned's investment, but you know he gave you that money free and clear—"

"That's not the part I'm most concerned about."

"Then what?"

"I can't tell you. It'll make you mad."

She tugged lightly on a tuft of chest hair. "Now you have to tell me."

"Only if you swear not to get mad."

"I have a feeling I shouldn't do that before I hear your big secret."

"You have to swear you won't get mad if you want to hear it."

"Fine. I swear. Now tell me."

"I promised your dad I wouldn't propose to you until the studio is making real money." He looked over at her. "And I really want to propose to you."

Grace went cold all over with shock. "You... He... You did *what*? When did this happen?

"A while ago."

"Oh my God! I can't believe him! This is outrageous! You don't have to honor that promise, Evan. I absolve you."

"I do have to honor it, Grace, and you can't absolve me. I gave him my word."

"*Why* would you do that?"

"Because it seemed to matter a lot to him that you not marry a freeloading loser."

Grace had never been more furious in her life. "I'm going to kill him. I'm going to kill them both."

"No, you're not. He has a good point, and if you were my kid, I'd probably feel the same way about my smart, studious daughter shackling herself to a musician who's had more bad luck than good."

"*This* is why you've been working like a madman over there?"

"Not the only reason, but the most important one. I'm determined to show him—"

"Stop," Grace said, blinking back tears as she covered his mouth with her fingers. "Don't say any more. You don't have to show anyone anything, least of all my family or me. You're *everything*. From the first minute you came over to me after that rat bastard Trey abandoned me here without a nickel to my name, you've been my everything. You always will be. I don't care if you're dirt poor and never have another paying job. None of that matters to me, and if you know me at all, you know I've long ago stopped letting my parents' opinions matter to me. If I'd continued to listen to them, I'd still be three hundred pounds and as miserable as any person could possibly be."

"Grace..."

"I love you, Evan. I love you exactly the way you are. The studio could be the most successful in the business, and I wouldn't love you any more than I already do."

"Do you know," he said, leaving a trail of kisses from the crook of her elbow along the tender skin of her inner arm, "that I thank God every day for the rat bastard who abandoned you at our docks?"

"Is that right?"

Nodding, he kissed the palm of her hand and then looked up at her. "Marry me, Grace."

"Of course I'm going to marry you. All you had to do was ask."

"Stay there," he said, bounding out of bed.

"Where're you going?"

"You'll see." He returned a minute later, slid back into bed and tugged her in close to him. "Hold out your left hand and close your eyes."

Smiling, Grace did as he directed, holding back tears as he slid a ring onto her third finger. "Can I look yet?"

"Go ahead."

"Oh, Evan! Oh my God, it's *gorgeous!*" A large, emerald-cut diamond sat surrounded by smaller diamonds in an antique setting. She couldn't stop staring at it. "When did you do this?"

"Remember when I went to the mainland to buy the equipment for the studio?"

"That was a couple of months ago."

"Uh-huh."

"You've had it all this time and never said a word?"

"I told you. I wanted to get the studio off the ground before I asked you."

Grace threw her arms around his neck and held on tight.

"Do you like the ring? If you want something different—"

She kissed the words right off his lips, putting everything she had into a kiss that she hoped would tell him all he needed to know about how much she loved the ring—and him.

"Whoa, Nelly," he said when they resurfaced many minutes later. "I take that to mean you like it?"

"I love it. It's absolutely beautiful."

"I want you to know I paid for it with the money I made on my record deal, not the money Ned gave me for the studio."

It touched her to know that he cared about such things. "You shouldn't have spent so much on me."

"Who else should I spend it on?"

"When I went to fetch you tonight, I didn't think our evening would turn out this way," she said, still gazing at the gorgeous ring. "I can't believe it. I never thought anything like this would happen to me. And then last week, when you were missing all that time... I found out what it feels like to have your heart literally break."

"Aww, baby. I'm so sorry I put you through that. You were all I could think about out there. Thinking about you kept me going."

They held each other for a long time, and then he drew back so he could see her face. "Are you happy?"

"So happy. Happier than I've ever been."

He kissed her softly, holding her gaze. "So am I. No one has ever had so much faith in me or loved me the way you do. Have I ever told you how glad I am that you insisted on trying to pay back the money I loaned you?"

"If I recall correctly, you were annoyed with me for tracking you down."

"That wasn't annoyance. It was relief. Pure and simple. I'd never been so happy to see anyone." As he spoke, he moved them as one so he was on top of her. "I've been happy to see you every day since then, too. There's no one I'd rather be with in this whole world."

Cradling him between her legs, she raised her hips, letting him know what she wanted.

He didn't have to be told twice. "There's nothing like this, Grace. No one like you." He made slow, sweet love to her, driving her crazy the way only he could, her one and only love. "When do you want to get married?"

"As soon as we can."

"We can't upstage Laura and Owen."

Grace wondered how he could think so clearly when he was making a muddled mess out of her brain one stroke at a time. And then he reached down to where they were joined and caressed her in all the right places, clearing every thought from her head that didn't involve the incredible high that came with loving him.

"God," he said, groaning. "I love you. I'm so glad you're gonna marry me."

Laughing and crying, she held him close, soothing him as he reached his own release.

"This winter," he said when he could speak again. "We'll get married this winter."

"Fine by me."

. . .

RECLINING against a huge pile of pillows, Abby couldn't take her eyes off Adam as he unbuttoned his shirt and took it off at her request but left his pants on. "Could I ask you something?"

"Anything you want."

"Is it weird that before yesterday we never thought of each other this way, and now..."

"Now it's all we can think about?"

Biting her lip, she nodded.

"I think," he said, as he crawled from the foot of the bed to join her, "it's a matter of timing. It's a matter of both of us being in this place and this time and finding something in each other that we need right now."

"That's a nice way to put it."

He reached out to run his index finger over her cheek, a soft touch that sent tremors ricocheting through her body. "Are you nervous about doing this with me?"

"A little."

"Why? Because of Grant?"

"No. I'm not thinking about him. I haven't thought about him that way in a very long time."

"Then why?" His finger moved from her face to her neck and down to the valley between her breasts, which were still contained by the bra.

"I'm afraid it'll be like it was before."

"Unsatisfying, you mean."

"Yes."

"If it is, will you tell me?"

"I don't know..."

"I'd want you to. I don't want you to fake anything with me."

Abby tried to focus on the conversation, but that was hard to do with his finger moving slowly over her belly, circling her navel and continuing straight down her middle, over the seam between her legs.

"Does that feel good?"

"Yes." Her heart beat wildly as she waited to see what else he would do.

The tip of his finger moved lightly down her inner thigh to the back of her knee, before taking the same slow, torturous journey back up. This time when he reached the juncture of her legs, Abby gasped.

"Don't think," he whispered. "Close your eyes and just feel."

Although she was hesitant, she did as he asked and gave herself over to the darkness and the tingling trail of sensation he left as his finger slid over her skin. If he could arouse her so fully with the tip of one finger, what else was he capable of?

"You're thinking. I can hear your wheels turning. Let it all go. It's just you and me, and I think you're amazing, beautiful and sexy as all hell. Every guy in the bar was jealous of me tonight because I got to leave with you."

"I doubt that."

"Shhh. You're not thinking. You're feeling."

Abby released an exasperated sigh that turned into another gasp when she felt his lips between her breasts.

"Relax, honey. Let me worship you."

How long had she waited to hear those words? Did he have any idea what a turn-on that was for her?

His tongue was warm against her nipple, arousing her through the lacy bra. When he bit down lightly, she cried out.

"Adam..."

"Hmm?"

"Can I touch you, too?"

"You can do whatever you want as long as you keep your eyes closed and don't think."

"I'll try."

With her hand curled around the back of his neck, she held him to her chest, letting him know she liked what he was doing there.

He found the front clasp of her bra and released it, pushing the cups to the side.

"So beautiful," he whispered, placing soft kisses everywhere but where she yearned for them. "So, so beautiful. I bet you have no idea how sexy you really are. I wish you could see what I see right now." He punctuated his incredibly stirring words with the touch of his tongue on her left nipple. "You taste like heaven." He teased her nipple with only his teeth and tongue, setting off a riot of reaction that settled between her legs in an insistent throb. And then he added suction and more swipes of his tongue.

Abby fisted a handful of his hair, her entire focus drawn to the pull of his warm mouth on her tender nipple. She squirmed under him, trying to get closer.

He responded by aligning the hard column of his erection to her core. And then he turned his attention to her other breast, giving it the same treatment while pressing rhythmically against her.

Her entire body was on fire, straining and yearning for fulfillment.

"Let it happen," he whispered, his breath warm against her breast. "Let go of all your worries and focus on how it feels. Don't think about anything else." He sucked hard on her nipple while pinching the other one, still sensitive from his earlier attention, between his fingers. The combination of his tender words and actions was her undoing.

She came hard, screaming from the pleasure and the full-body orgasm that made her scalp tingle and the soles of her feet burn. Her senses returned slowly, and it occurred to her that if he could do that to her with her panties still on, what might it be like to actually make love with him?

"You're thinking," he whispered.

Abby opened her eyes and met his gaze. "That was amazing."

"It was amazing from my end, too. How about we do it again?"

She was still recovering from the first one. "I don't think I could."

"I'd like to prove otherwise. Will you let me?" He made his case by dragging the tip of his tongue on the same path his finger had taken earlier. Before he reached the waistband of her panties, Abby was already onboard with his effort to prove her wrong.

"Is that a yes?"

"Yes... Yes."

"Close your eyes. No thinking. Only feeling." He moved down on the bed, kissing and licking and nibbling as he went. "Tell me what you like."

He expected her to talk when she could barely breathe? She opened her eyes to find him watching her.

"Abby..." His chin settled on the scrap of silk that covered her as he looked up at her with piercing blue eyes.

"I...I've never been a big fan of...of that."

Adam raised his head and touched his tongue to the heart of her. "This?"

Her entire body heated with acute embarrassment even as her legs parted ever so slightly to make room for him. "Yes."

"Why not?"

Could this be any more mortifying? "I don't know."

"I think you do, but you're too shy to say so. Where has shyness gotten you? Unsatisfied, unfulfilled, unhappy—"

"All right! All right... It makes me self-conscious thinking about..."

"About what?"

She put her hands over her face. "I can't say it!"

"About whether it smells good to your partner? Tastes good? Feels good? Any of those things?"

"Yes, yes and yes," she said, her hands muffling her voice.

"That shouldn't be a problem for us."

"Why?"

"Because you're not thinking, remember? You're only allowed to feel. You're not allowed to think about how it is for me. You're only thinking about *you*."

"I don't know if I can do that."

His hands slid under her, tangling in the string of her thong and tugging it free. "Let's see if you can, shall we?"

As the silky thong slid down over her legs, Abby knew a moment of panic. What if she disappointed him? He'd been so sweet and considerate. "Adam... I don't know about this. I've never been able to, you know... Not like that."

"Do you trust me?"

"As I'm currently spread out naked before you, I'd say it's rather obvious that I trust you."

His wolfish smile made her belly flutter with nerves and desire for something far more than the next orgasm. He was making her want things that only yesterday she'd said she was done with forever.

"Try to relax and let me have my fun. Clear your mind. You did it once before, so let's see if you can do it again."

"Is this fun for you?"

"What do you think?"

"But you're not getting to…"

"Say it."

Looking up at the ceiling, she prayed for deliverance. "Come."

"I've got a hot, sexy woman naked and spread out before me—to use your words. What's not fun about that?"

Abby's thighs trembled as he parted them with broad shoulders and began with kisses and caresses that had nothing to do with the part of her that burned for him. Rather he focused on her lower belly, the place where her leg met her torso, which she discovered was an erogenous zone. After he'd driven her slowly mad with many minutes of teasing and tormenting, he blew a stream of cool air over the hair that covered her.

"No thinking," he whispered as he used his tongue to draw an outline of her sex. "Only feeling." With his hand on her trembling thigh, he urged her to move her legs farther apart. "Open for me, baby."

She let out a whimper as she did what he asked.

"That's it. That's the way." Using his fingers to hold her open, he explored every inch of sensitive, delicate skin with his tongue. He made teasing passes over her clitoris, making her gasp each time. "So sweet, so perfect, so wet." His tongue thrust into her, teasing and retreating while his thumb pressed against the tight bundle of nerves. He kept it up, over and over, until she was thrashing and sweating and completely unconcerned about anything other than finding relief from the sweetest torture she'd ever known.

When he sucked hard on her clit and pushed two fingers into her, she lost it, screaming through the throes of something more powerful than anything she'd experienced before. It took her somewhere outside herself, outside of this room, far, far away from all her notions of what to expect from a lover.

She returned a different person, changed profoundly in the course of a single hour. All those years she'd spent with the wrong brother…

"Adam."

His head rested on her thigh and two of his fingers remained lodged inside her. He flexed them and set off a series of aftershocks that surprised the hell out of her, but then again, he'd already surprised the hell out of her a couple of times. "I'm here, honey."

"Come up here."

Without removing his fingers, he did as she asked, lowering himself on top of her and taking her mouth in a hot, torrid kiss. She tasted herself on his tongue, and for once that didn't bother her. Nothing bothered her. He'd knocked down her walls, stripped her defenses and taught her how to find the pleasure she'd missed out on in the past.

He never stopped kissing her, even as his chest hair abraded her nipples and his fingers continued to move inside her.

Abby simply couldn't believe it when she felt the start of yet another orgasm. "Wait," she said, breaking the kiss.

"What's wrong?"

"I want you."

"I'm right here."

"I want you in me." She reached down to cup an erection that was much more substantial than it had been earlier.

He smiled, seeming pleased by her bluntness. "Not this time. Tonight is your night."

"Can't it be our night?"

His fingers continued the gentle, stimulating glide. "Another time."

"I hope you know I'm apt to turn into a crazy stalker after this."

"Why's that?"

"I'm going to want more. Much, much more."

"Me, too, honey." He took her mouth again, his fingers moving faster as he played her like a virtuoso who'd been born to pleasure her and only her. Somehow, he seemed to know what she needed before she did. "No thinking," he whispered as he coaxed her up and over one more time. "Beautiful, amazing, so sexy. Open your eyes."

When she complied, he said, "The next time you're wondering if I like what you've got going on down there, remember this." He withdrew his hand from between her legs and brought it up to his mouth, licking each finger clean of her essence.

Watching the shockingly erotic sight, Abby realized she was in very big trouble where Adam McCarthy was concerned. Very big trouble indeed.

CHAPTER 15

ith her snuggled into his embrace, Adam was aware of the exact second when Abby drifted off to sleep. She thought he'd undone her. How about what she'd done to him? Watching her let go of her inhibitions and disappear into the moment had been among the most erotically charged experiences of his life.

His dick was so hard he was afraid it might break if it so much as brushed against her. He waited until he was certain he wouldn't disturb her before he disentangled from her and got up from the bed. After pulling a light blanket over her, he went into the bathroom and turned on the shower, hoping the noise wouldn't wake her.

He needed relief, and he needed it right now. Unbuttoning his pants, he worked the zipper down over his raging hard-on, wincing at the near-painful sensation of the teeth sliding over his flesh. Naked, he stepped under the hot water and let it work the knots of tension from his shoulders. At times like this, being selfless was a thankless task.

He'd wanted to show her, to prove to her, that she could step away from her worries and fears and let herself be swept away. While his mission had been successful, it had been at his own expense. With his left hand propped on the shower wall, he wrapped his right hand around the base of his penis and stroked, grimacing at the painful pleasure.

His entire focus was on the slide of his hand, which was why he didn't feel the shower door open until the cool air jarred him out of the trance he'd slipped into.

She stood behind him, her breasts and belly pressed to his back, and she reached around to push his hand away. "Let me."

"Abby…"

"I want to. Let me." She stroked him gently at first, too gently for what he needed. He was about to put his hand over hers and show her what he wanted when she tightened her grip and caressed him harder. In a move he didn't see coming, she cupped his balls with her other hand. He detonated, holding himself up with both hands on the shower wall as she milked him of every drop.

"Christ have mercy," he whispered.

"Did I do it right?"

He uttered a harsh laugh. "If you did it any better, you might've killed me."

As the water rained down upon them, she rested her face on his back as her hands lay flat against his belly. "Right back atcha."

Not entirely trusting his legs to stay beneath him, Adam turned and framed her face with his hands, kissing her gently. "I'm sorry I woke you with the shower."

"I'm not," she said with a meaningful smile.

"Come to think of it, I'm not either."

"What you did…to me, for me… It was amazing. It's never been like that for me before."

"We only needed to get your head out of the equation."

She looked up at him, sweet and guileless. Drops of water clung to her thick lashes. "How is it that you figured that out in two days, but I've been with others for years and they never knew?"

"I guess we just got lucky. A couple of tequila shots, some loose lips, a guy who likes to puzzle through a challenge, and what've we got?"

"Three rather astonishing orgasms."

Adam laughed at the way she blushed when she said that. "Plenty more where those came from."

"And in light of tonight's revelations, you won't think less of me if I pester you for nonstop sex?"

Still laughing, he said, "Pester me, baby." He combed his fingers through the long, wet strands of her hair. "Please pester me."

"Remember you asked for it."

"How could I forget?"

WARM, soft lips on his chest woke Seamus O'Grady from the soundest sleep he'd enjoyed in days. The questions had all been answered to his satisfaction, and he had the woman he loved in his arms to stay. A smile stretched across his face as he opened his eyes to find her watching him.

"Was I snoring or something?"

"No."

"Then what has you awake so early on the one day we can sleep in this weekend?"

"I was waiting to talk to you."

Seamus hated the way those words made his stomach knot with nerves. Had she changed her mind again? He stroked a hand over her hair and touched a finger to the worry line bracketing her mouth. "What about?"

"Your mother."

"If you'd asked me to guess what was weighing on your mind first thing on this fine morning, I never would've guessed that."

"Have you told her about me?"

"I told her I met someone special."

"Did you tell her I'm older than you? A lot older?"

"Are we back to that again? I thought we'd resolved all that and weren't going to make a thing of it anymore."

She twisted his nipple, hard enough to make him wince. "Does she know I'm older than you?"

"I might've forgotten to tell her that part. She was so happy to hear

I've finally met a lass who turned my head that I never got a chance to tell her that part."

"A lass. She thinks you've found someone young, Seamus, and you did nothing to disavow that notion!"

"Are you or are you not a lassie?"

"Lassie is a dog in this country."

Laughing at her indignation, he said, "As opposed to a laddie. My neighbors in Scotland have their lassies and their laddies. You, my love, are most definitely a lassie." He squeezed her bare breast for emphasis, drawing a gasp from her and stirring his recently satisfied libido. Encouraged by her response, he ran his calloused thumb back and forth over the tip, making her tremble.

"Are you sore, love?"

"Kind of."

"I'm sorry. I got a little carried away last night."

"A *little?*"

He smiled sheepishly and went hard as stone as he recalled worshiping her sweet breasts for almost an hour, until she'd begged him for mercy. "Okay, maybe a lot. But that's what you do to me."

"You should invite your mother to come for a visit."

Seamus froze, his interest in her breast forgotten. "My mum? *Here?*"

"That's what I said. Would she come?"

"I don't know. She was here years ago when I first came to America to get a look at the place, but she didn't think too much of it. That was when I was living in Boston, though, and she never has been one for the city. She said it was noisy and dirty."

"Gansett is neither. I want you to invite her to come here. She could stay with us."

"Here. Stay with us. Love… you've never met me mum. You might want to think twice about that."

"Why? What's wrong with her?"

"There's nothing…wrong… It's just that she's, well…"

"You're not afraid of her, are you?"

What had begun as a very nice morning erection shriveled at all this talk of his mother. "Of course I'm not afraid of her. She's me mum. But she's also... Well, you'd have to meet her to see what I mean."

"I'll look forward to meeting her and your father."

"My Da won't come. He hates to travel more than anything."

"You'll call today to invite your mother?"

"Do I have to?"

"If you want a repeat of last night any time soon."

He scowled playfully at her. "Fine, I'll call, but you remember this was your idea."

"I'll remember. She should know that you're never going to be able to make her a grandmother."

"My four oldest sisters have seen to that. She has sixteen grandchildren between them, don't worry about that."

"I thought you had a brother."

"I had two of them and six sisters. Aren't you lucky to be on the receiving end of all that sensitivity training they instilled in me?"

"What happened to your brothers?"

"Sadly, they both died young," he said, amazed by the stab of pain in his breastbone after all this time.

"Oh God. What happened to them?"

"One had cancer. Terrible thing that was. And the other had drug problems. He overdosed about ten years ago."

"I'm so sorry."

"'Twas a long time ago now."

"So it falls to you."

"What does?"

"Continuing the family line." Carolina pulled back from him and sat up in bed, the blankets pooling at her waist. He wondered if she knew how glorious she looked, bare-breasted with her hair rumpled, her face flushed from sleep and her lips red and swollen from his vigorous lovemaking.

"What's wrong?"

"You're the last one."

"The last one of what?"

"The last male in your family. If you don't have a son, your family will die off."

"Did you hear how many sisters I said I have? The family will thrive and prosper for generations to come."

"But none of them will be O'Gradys if you don't have a son. They'll hate me for that."

"I've never felt an ounce of pressure to carry on the family name, and I still don't."

"Your parents might feel differently."

"If they do, they've never told me so. In fact, I think they gave up on seeing me domesticated quite some time ago. Come back down here with me."

Carolina snuggled up to him, albeit somewhat reluctantly.

He rubbed her back until she relaxed a bit. "You need to stop manufacturing reasons that this isn't going to work and start thinking about all the reasons why it will work beautifully."

"Tell me about those reasons."

"Well, we could start with the fact that I'm wildly in love with you, and I think you're wildly in love with me."

"That's one word for it."

Chuckling, he hugged her even closer to him and nuzzled her hair. "For another reason, you've apparently decided you're happier with me than you are without me."

"What else?"

Pleased that she hadn't tried to deny it, "I'm a god in bed. You said so yourself last night."

She groaned loudly. "You caught me in a weak moment. I'd like to retract that statement for fear of it being used against me for the rest of my life."

"No retractions allowed. You only spoke the truth."

"There's absolutely nothing wrong with your ego, is there?"

"I like knowing that I please you. That pleases me."

"Despite your considerable charm and even more considerable blarney, you're still going to call your mother and invite her here to visit, right?"

"All right, love," he said with a deep sigh. "But don't say I didn't warn you."

HER RINGING CELL phone woke Abby. For a moment, she couldn't recall how she'd ended up in bed naked. Then the details of the night before came flooding back in a wave of sensual memories that made her entire body tingle. She found the phone on her bedside table and answered, wondering where Adam was.

"Hey," Janey said. "Did I wake you up?"

"What time is it?"

"Almost ten, sleepyhead. Late night?"

"Yeah."

"Did you do something wild and crazy?"

Abby burned with embarrassment as she thought of what Janey would say about Abby dating another of her brothers. "Maybe."

"Anyone I know?"

"Maybe."

"Who? Tell me right now!"

"I'll tell you when I see you." And she'd hope her close friend wouldn't be mad about her dating Adam.

"You'll see me tonight."

"What's tonight?"

"Girls' night out. I guess Maddie talked to Jenny, and she needs a night out with the girls. It's on for tonight. We're starting at Stephanie's Bistro at seven. See you there?"

"Sure, I'd love to."

"Be prepared to spill the beans."

"Bye, Janey."

Abby rolled over to find a note on the pillow. "Woke up early and went to work on Laura's reservation system. Come over and have breakfast with me when you wake up. Adam."

She read and reread the note, smiling when she remembered the night they'd spent together and the way he'd focused entirely on her pleasure. And then she thought of the shower and how she'd brazenly pushed his hand out of the way and replaced it with her own.

How was it that they'd spent so little time together but he already understood her so well? How was it that she was so willing to do things with him that she wouldn't have dreamed of doing in the past?

He'd probably given up on eating with her a long time ago, so she took her time showering, conditioning her hair, blowing it dry, applying mascara and some lip gloss. She wore one of the summer tops she'd bought at Tiffany's store. The style was demure yet sexy and sheer enough that the light pink bra she wore under it showed through.

Abby smiled at her reflection in the full-length mirror behind the bathroom door. A week ago, it wouldn't have occurred to her to show off her bra. Now she couldn't wait to see what Adam thought of her outfit.

She dashed down the three flights of stairs, out the back door of the Beachcomber and across the street to the Sand & Surf. An older couple was coming out as she approached the main door, so Abby stood aside to let them past. She stepped into the lobby and came to a stop when she saw Adam sitting at the reception desk. He wore dark horn-rimmed glasses and was completely absorbed in what he was doing on the computer.

Abby took advantage of the opportunity to study him when he was in his element. She discovered that his lips moved when he worked, and he talked to himself. And he was absolutely gorgeous. His hair was mussed as if he'd been running his fingers through it repeatedly. His face was freshly shaven, and he wore a polo shirt she hadn't seen on him before, leading her to conclude that he'd been home to shower and change.

Before last night, she'd thought him handsome and intriguing. Now she knew he was sexy as all hell, too. She was about to approach the desk and ring the bell, but he looked up and caught her watching him.

His smile unfolded slowly as he took in her outfit in an equally slow perusal. "I wondered if you were going to sleep all day."

"I was worn out."

He removed the glasses and held them suspended between his index finger and thumb, swinging them back and forth. "Wonder how that happened."

"I have no idea."

"I could refresh your memory later, if you'd like."

Abby leaned on the counter. "I'd like, except it's girls' night out, so it'll have to be late."

"I can do late. Are you hungry?"

"I could eat."

"Let me just call upstairs for someone to come watch the desk. I was multitasking." He made a quick call and then put the phone down. "My cousin Shane is coming down." Adam glanced up the stairs. "Laura is sick again."

"That's too bad. It's got to be miserable with a baby to take care of."

"I know. She's wiped out. Here comes Shane."

Adam's cousin came bounding down the stairs. Like his cousins, he was tall with startling blue eyes, but his hair was much lighter than theirs.

"Do you know Abby Callahan?" Adam asked Shane.

"We met years ago," Abby said, hesitant to mention her connection to Grant in front of Adam.

"She used to date Grant," Adam said, saving her the trouble.

"Oh, right," Shane said. "I remember now. Nice to see you again."

"We're going to grab some breakfast, and then I'll be back," Adam said.

"Take your time." Shane sat in the chair behind the desk. "I've got nowhere to be."

"Thanks." Adam gestured for her to precede him into the restaurant where they waited at the hostess stand to be seated.

"Didn't he get married a couple of years ago?" she asked.

"Yeah. Didn't work out."

"I hadn't heard that."

"It was a bad scene. She was hooked on prescription drugs, and he didn't know it. He's been through a nightmare, the poor guy."

"God, that's awful." And it made what she'd been through seem not so significant.

"He's doing a lot better since he's been here with Laura and the rest of the family." Adam put an arm around Abby and kissed her temple. "I'm starving. I thought you'd never get here."

"You didn't have to wait."

"Yes, I did. I told you I would in the note."

"It was nice of you." Cal wouldn't have waited. He was impatient, always in a hurry and didn't like to be kept waiting.

"What're you thinking?" Adam asked as he held her chair for her.

"That Cal wouldn't have waited for me."

Adam settled in the seat next to her rather than across from her. "That would've been his loss. You look gorgeous this morning. Almost as gorgeous as you looked last night." As he said the last part, his hand landed on her knee and moved up until Abby stopped him from going any farther.

"Will you put the glasses back on?"

He seemed surprised by her request. "You like them?"

"Uh-huh. They make you look smart."

"I am smart," he said with an arrogant, teasing smile as he slid them back on.

His intelligence, Abby thought, was every bit as sexy as what he'd done to her in the hotel room last night. She covered his hand on her leg and wrapped her fingers around his, sharing a smile with him. Neither of them could seem to look away. Abby's insides fluttered with awareness of him and pride in herself for reaching out to take what she wanted.

"Morning, folks," the waitress said. "Coffee?"

She tore her gaze off him and looked up at the young woman. "Please."

"Me, too."

Abby paid attention to every detail as he stirred cream and sugar into his coffee and ordered fried eggs over easy, turkey bacon and rye toast. She'd barely glanced at the menu but asked for an egg-white omelet with vegetables and wheat toast.

"How's the project going?" she asked when they were alone again.

"It's going. I enjoy the challenge of figuring out what the client needs and making the computer give it to them."

"That sounds like a very simplified explanation for complicated work."

"It can be, I suppose, but it's not complicated to me. It's my second language, the only thing I've ever been any good at."

"Not the only thing," Abby said as a blush swept over her.

His ringing laugh and the squeeze of her hand pleased her. She liked making him laugh. When his smile faded a bit, she looked over to see what had caught his attention. His brother Mac and Luke Harris had walked into the restaurant. Mac zeroed right in on them sitting together.

Abby released Adam's hand, and he pulled it back.

"Hey, bro," Mac said as he approached the table with Luke. "Abby. I didn't hear you were home." He leaned in to kiss her cheek. "Nice to see you. Is Cal with you?"

"Nice to see you, too, Mac." She glanced at Adam. "Cal and I broke up."

"I hadn't heard that." Mac's gaze darted between her and Adam. She could almost hear him jumping to conclusions that weren't far from wrong.

"How's the gift shop coming along?" she asked.

Mac forced his eyes off his brother and focused on her. "We should finish it up today."

"That's great. Laura is anxious to get it open by next month. That should give us just enough time."

"So you'll be running the store?"

"That's the plan."

"Adam, could I have a word with you?" Mac asked. "It'll only take a minute."

"Not right now. Later, maybe."

Mac didn't seem pleased to be rebuffed by his younger brother. "Find me before you leave."

"Sure. Luke, good to see you."

"You, too. The girls are getting up a night out tonight, so the guys are coming to my house for some poker. You're welcome to join us."

"I'd love to, thanks. See you then."

Abby watched them walk to the bar where they procured coffee in to-go cups before they left the restaurant. On the way out, Mac took another long look at Adam and Abby.

"He's such a pain in the ass," Adam muttered.

"You love him."

"Of course I love him, but sometimes I want to punch his lights out."

"You two look so much alike it's scary."

"I've been hearing that my whole life. My own aunt mistook me for him the other day." He took a drink of his coffee, his eyes on the door. "You know he's already on the phone with Grant, telling him I'm eating breakfast with you."

"Does that bother you?"

"Not for the reasons you think it might."

"Good thing you already talked to Grant, huh?"

"Yeah, very good thing."

"I don't want to be the cause of trouble in your family."

"Don't worry about that. Grant is happy with Stephanie, and this has nothing to do with him. You two are ancient history. If you'd just broken up with him, that would be different, but it's been over between you guys for a couple of years."

As their breakfast arrived, Abby couldn't help but worry about causing trouble between brothers who'd always been close.

"So YOU ALREADY KNEW HE was seeing her and didn't tell me?" Mac asked Grant. He held the phone in the crook of his neck as he painted the trim in the gift shop.

"I talked to him yesterday, and he mentioned they'd been hanging out. I didn't realize I was required to inform you of this development."

"Very funny. They looked awfully cozy. That doesn't bother you?"

"What do you want me to say? I'm engaged to Stephanie. Why would it bother me?"

"Still… I think it would bug me if one of you guys dated my ex."

"After the way I treated her, Abby certainly deserves to be happy, and if Adam makes her happy, well… Who am I to get in the middle of that?"

"You're very evolved about all of this."

"Don't make a big thing out of it. Leave him alone."

"You're ruining all my fun."

Grant let out a huff of laughter. "You're worse than Mom. You've turned into a regular Gansett Island gossipmonger."

"That hurts me, Grant. Deeply."

"The truth always hurts."

"You sound a little better today," Mac said, feeling as if he was tiptoeing into a minefield.

"I've been sleeping. That makes everything better."

"You know I'm here if you need me, bro. I went through the same thing you did out there—"

"No, you didn't."

Grant's sharp retort caught Mac by surprise.

"I'm sorry," Grant said, instantly contrite. "I didn't mean to snap at you. It's just…"

Mac put down his paintbrush and switched the phone to his other hand. "What, Grant? Say it. Put it out there and get it off your chest. Let us help."

"I…"

Mac waited breathlessly, praying that his brother would finally unburden himself.

"I can't. I'm sorry, but I can't."

Blowing out a deep breath, Mac said, "When you're ready, you know where I am."

"Yes. Thank you."

"Are you coming to Luke's tonight?"

"Yeah."

"I'll see you there."

Mac ended the call, upset and dismayed that his brother was in pain and there was nothing he could do about it.

"What's up?" Luke asked from the other end of the store where he was screwing the plug covers back on now that the paint on the walls was dry.

"Damned if I know. How is it we went through the same thing, and he's so screwed up over it?"

"Something else happened to him. Something so traumatic he can't talk about it."

"If he doesn't talk about it, how will he get past it?"

"Give him some time. Keep doing what you're doing. Let him know you're there for him. That's all you can do."

"It makes me crazy to know he's so upset but keeping it all inside."

"It'll come out eventually. When he's ready."

"Yeah, I suppose you're right."

"Hey, so listen. I'm going to be off-island a couple of days next week. Is that okay?"

"When are you going to stop asking us for time off?" They'd made Luke a partner in their business more than a year ago.

"Old habits die hard," Luke said with a chuckle.

"I hope you're going somewhere fun before the madness begins with the season."

"Not fun, exactly, but a step in the right direction. Syd's having a reversal of her tubal ligation."

Mac grimaced. "What the hell does that mean?"

"It means, you jackass, that we might be able to have kids of our own. If it works."

"Hey, that's cool. Kind of a big step for her, huh?"

"A very big step. It took me a while to convince her that what happened to her kids couldn't possibly happen again." Sydney lost her first husband and young children to a drunk driver. "She's worried she'll be a crazy overprotective mother who never lets the poor kid out of her sight."

"You couldn't blame her for that."

"No, but I told her I'd be there to keep her from going too far overboard. Of course that's if it even happens. There's a chance the surgery won't work, and even if it does, she may not conceive."

"I'll be hoping it goes your way. We all will."

"Thanks. Like I told her, if it doesn't, we'll adopt. There're other options, and we're keeping them all open."

"Good plan. Let me know how it works out, okay?"

"I will. We're keeping it kind of quiet. Syd doesn't want everyone asking questions."

"No one will hear it from me."

Luke crooked a skeptical eyebrow.

"What? I said I won't say anything, and I won't."

Laughing at Mac's indignation, Luke went back to work.

Mac thought about Grant for a long time, wondering what had his brother so upset and wishing there was something he could do about it.

CHAPTER 16

A steady thump, thump, thump woke Laura from a sound sleep. Even though she'd been asleep for hours, her eyes didn't want to open. Exhaustion clung to every inch of her.

"Laura? Princess, are you in there?"

Only two people called her Princess. Was that her dad? What was he doing here? Laura pushed aside covers Owen must've put over her and crossed the room on wobbly legs to open the door.

"Did I wake you?" Frank McCarthy asked. As always, he was impeccably dressed with every one of his silver hairs in place. "I'm sorry. Owen thought you'd be awake by now. He sent me up."

Thrilled to see him, Laura stepped into his embrace and held on for dear life. "What're you doing here, Dad?"

"I talked to Shane yesterday, and he said you were still feeling poorly. Since I have a couple of days free from court, I wanted to come see my kids. I hope that's okay."

"It's more than okay." She released him and took his hand. "Come in. What time is it?"

"Almost four."

"Jeez." She'd been asleep for three hours! "Did you see Holden?"

"I did," he said, beaming with delight over his grandson as he had since the day Holden was born. "Owen has him downstairs. They're 'working' at the registration desk."

"That must be something to see." Owen was doing both her jobs so she could sleep the day away. Laura sighed, furious at herself and her body for betraying her. With the season about to get under way there was so much to be done, and all she wanted to do was sleep—that was, when she wasn't puking.

"He's grown so much in just a couple of weeks. I couldn't get over it."

"A lot happens the first year. He'll be walking before we know it."

"What's wrong, Princess? You're so pale. Are you okay?"

Laura stepped into the tiny kitchen off the sitting room. "Did Owen say anything about what's been going on?"

"Nothing in particular."

"He's a coward," she said with a small smile for her dad as she poured a cola for him and an ice water for herself.

"Why would you say such an awful thing about your wonderful fiancé?"

"Come sit." She carried their drinks to the sofa and curled up in the corner with her legs under her.

Frank settled next to her and rolled up the sleeves of his light blue dress shirt. The color brought out the blue of his eyes. "You really ought to invest in some leisure clothes, Dad."

"What's wrong with my clothes?" he asked with a teasing grin at the old argument.

"Most people wear jeans and polo shirts when they aren't working." She'd bought him plenty of both over the years, to no avail. "You need to learn how to relax a little. I've been telling you that forever."

"I know, I know. I'll have plenty of time to relax after I retire." His expression clouded a bit at that, but he forced a smile for her. "What's got you calling Owen names?"

"We had some interesting news yesterday."

"Nothing bad, I hope?" After losing his wife to cancer when Laura and Shane were still young, her dad had fretted endlessly about their health and safety.

"Depends on your perspective, I suppose. I'm pregnant."

To his credit, Frank's expression never changed. "Well, that's a surprise."

"It was for us, too. Best of all? We're apparently having twins."

"Oh, my goodness, Laura. Congratulations. I think..."

She laughed and squeezed his arm. "Thank you. I think."

"Holy moly, you're going to have your hands full around here, huh?"

"Just a little." She glanced at him. "Are you mad?"

"What? Mad? Why would I be?"

"Owen and I aren't married yet."

"Ah, honey." He put his arm around her and hugged her. "You're a grown woman about to marry a guy I respect tremendously. We're talking about a matter of months."

"I was a little afraid to tell you."

"Don't be afraid to tell me anything. I'm so proud of you and all you've accomplished. You and Owen are wonderful parents to Holden, and you will be to the new babies, too."

Laura rested against his chest, comforted as always by his presence.

Owen came in with Holden on his shoulders a few minutes later. The sight of the two of them took her breath away as it always did. They were awfully cute together, and Owen was so good to both of them.

"There're my guys." Laura held out her arms to take Holden. The baby let out a squeal of delight to see her and snuggled into her arms. "Did Grandpa surprise you, buddy?"

Holden gurgled and held out a spitty fist to Frank.

"Look at him, already shaking hands," Frank said with a smile. He glanced at Owen. "I understand congratulations are in order."

"Oh, thanks," Owen said with visible relief. "I was worried you'd get out the shotgun when you heard the news."

"Not my dad," Laura said. "He's very *mature*."

"That's right," Frank said, making faces that had Holden giggling. "Come see your very mature grandpa."

Laura transferred the baby to her dad.

"Twins, huh?" Frank asked, raising a brow in Owen's direction.

"That's what they tell us." He glanced at Laura. "Feeling better, hon?"

"A little. How are things downstairs?"

"Great. We had a couple of walk-ins this afternoon, and Mac and Luke have the gift shop all finished. Abby was in there for a couple of hours measuring for shelf space and making notes. Speaking of Abby... I've got a little family gossip for you guys."

"Let's hear it," she said, her dad nodding in agreement.

"Apparently, Abby and Adam are seeing each other."

"Seriously?" Laura asked, shocked to hear that. "What does Grant have to say about it?"

"I guess he's being cool about it," Owen said. "I mean, what can he say, really? He's engaged to Stephanie, and it's been over with Abby for a long time."

"Still," Frank said. "Dating your brother's ex. That can be dicey."

"Girls' night out ought to be interesting," Laura said.

"Do you feel up to going?" Owen asked.

"Not really, but since we'll just be downstairs, I can bail out if need be."

"That's true. Luke is having poker night at his house for the guys. I was going to take our little buddy with me, since he's a guy, too."

"I'd be happy to stay with him if you don't want to bring him," Frank offered.

"That's really nice of you, Frank, but I'd think you'd want to go to Luke's and see everyone."

"I would like to see my nephews in light of recent events. How about I lend you a hand over there, then?"

"Sounds good to me."

"Do we have rooms left?" Laura asked Owen. "Dad needs one."

"Don't worry about me, hon. I'm going to stay with Mac and Linda. I already talked to them. I didn't want to put you out when you weren't feeling well."

Laura stuck out her lower lip in a playful pout. "You wouldn't have been putting me out."

"I'll stay here next time, okay?"

"You'd better."

"Twins," Frank said again, making Laura and Owen laugh. "Have you told your mom yet?"

"Last night," Owen said. "She was thrilled."

"So am I," Frank said, removing any doubt that he approved of their unplanned babies.

Laura was greatly relieved that her dad was so happy about the news. As soon as she stopped feeling sick all day, she hoped she would be, too.

FINISHED WITH ALL HER MEASUREMENTS, Abby leaned against the counter Mac and Luke had built to hold the cash register and drew a rough sketch of what she envisioned the store might look like when it was finished. The sketch and the measurements carefully recorded in a notebook reminded her of the early days of Abby's Attic, when she'd had no idea what she was doing or if her store would even catch on.

Now she knew what it took to make a retail venture on Gansett into a success. She only hoped magic would happen a second time. The Sand & Surf gift shop had true potential, located as it was on the front side of the hotel, easily seen by passersby.

She'd toyed with the idea of opening a shop in Austin, but had worried about a small gift shop being lost in the sea of offerings available there. And with everything with Cal unsettled, she'd been reluctant to commit to anything that would keep her tied to Texas if things between them didn't work out. The professional indecision had only added to her discontent.

As she worked and planned, a new idea had come to her that she couldn't wait to run by Laura. The job that had started as a summer diversion had grown into something larger in her mind during the afternoon in the still-empty space. Until she had a chance to talk it over with Laura, though, she wouldn't let herself get too excited about it.

She was so absorbed in her sketches that she didn't hear Adam come in until he was right in front of her, casting a shadow over her notebook.

"Hey," she said, feigning annoyance. "You're blocking my light."

He tipped his head to take a look at what she was doing. "That's really good. I didn't know you could draw like that."

"Anyone can draw a bunch of straight lines, Adam."

"You've got the whole 3-D thing going on. That's amazing. I can picture how the store will look."

Flattered by his praise, she glanced up to find that he was wearing the glasses she found so attractive on him. "Did you finish with the reservation system?"

"Not yet. I need at least another day. Maybe two. I'm rewriting the entire program."

"How do you do that, exactly?"

"You really want to know? You'd probably find it deathly boring."

"Maybe so, but I'm interested in the logic behind it."

"You are? Really?"

"Hasn't anyone ever been interested in how you approach your work?"

"No. Never."

"Well, I am."

That seemed to please him. "I'll tell you all about it sometime. Are you done here?"

"For the most part. I was just doodling."

"We've already established that those are far more than doodles." He glanced at his watch. "We've got a couple of hours before the evening festivities." He stretched dramatically. "I'm sort of worn out after working all day, and I was thinking that you must be, too."

He looked anything but worn out, but she played along because she liked where this was going. "How about we go across the street for a little rest before our big night out?"

"You might be able to talk me into that."

Rolling her eyes and smiling at him, she closed the notebook and stashed it in her purse, shut off the lights and closed the door to the gift shop. In the lobby, Sarah was sitting behind the registration desk.

"I'll see you in the morning," Adam said to her.

"I will, too," Abby said.

"Thanks to both of you for your help around here."

"My pleasure," Adam said.

"Mine, too," Abby added. And it was a pleasure to be back in the business she had loved so much. Mapping out shelving and planning for inventory had filled her with excitement and anticipation. While living in Texas, she'd missed the thrill of running her own business. She'd been bored and often lonely, which had added to her problems with Cal, who'd been so busy he hadn't noticed her discontent.

"What're you thinking about?" Adam asked as they crossed the street to the Beachcomber and scooted in a side door that led to the stairs.

"How much I'm looking forward to having the store open. I missed it while I was away. I hadn't realized how much until today."

"I'm sure you'll make a big success out of it."

"Thank you for the vote of confidence. I was thinking..."

"What?"

"I haven't spoken to Laura about it yet, so it may not happen."

His hand on the small of her back guided her up the stairs in a proprietary way that she enjoyed. "Tell me anyway."

"I'm going to propose that we call it Abby's Attic at The Surf. I was thinking that customers who patronized the Attic might be more likely to check out the gift shop if we give it a name they recognize."

"That's a great idea. I'm sure Laura will think so, too."

"I hope so. She may have something else in mind. I don't want to step on any toes."

"Can't hurt to pitch it to her." They reached the third floor and stopped outside her door. "Where's the key stashed this time?"

She gave him a saucy smile as she reached into her top to retrieve the key card.

"That's so hot. You have no idea how hot." Inside the room, he surprised her when he spun her around to press her back against the closed door. For a long, breathless moment he only stared at her, seeming to take a detailed inventory of her features.

"What?" she asked, unnerved by his intensity. The scent of expensive cologne filled her senses, making her want to get even closer to him.

"You're beautiful. And you've got me thinking about you far more than I should be. Do you know how hard it is to write computer code with a gorgeous, sexy woman occupying so much of my attention?"

Flattered and aroused, she dug her fingers into his hips. "How hard is it?"

"Very, *very* hard."

Before she could make a joke about whether they were still talking about computer code, he removed his glasses, stashed them in his pants pocket, tipped his head and brought his lips down on hers lightly and gently. "All I could think about today was how you looked naked and spread out before me in bed with your silky dark hair fanned out on the pillow. I thought about how sweet you tasted against my tongue—"

"Stop," she whispered, mortified by the image he painted.

"Why?"

"It's embarrassing to think about what I must've looked like."

"How can you be embarrassed when I just told you that thinking about it had me turned on all day?" To make his point, he pressed his erection against her belly.

"All day, huh?"

"All. Day."

"That must get painful after a while."

"You have no idea."

Hearing that he'd thought of her that way and been aroused by the memories of what they'd done together the night before made her feel more brazen than usual. Her hands moved from his hips to the button of his jeans. She tugged on the button, drawing a gasp from him.

"Abby…"

"Yes?"

"What're you doing?"

"This." She unzipped him carefully as he was rock hard, reached inside his boxers and wrapped her hand around the thick column of flesh that seemed to get even harder in her grasp.

His head fell to her shoulder, his breathing became ragged, and his fingers dug into her bottom as he pushed against her.

He was longer and wider than she remembered from last night in the shower. Her sex clenched in anticipation of taking him in as nagging worries took hold that she pushed aside to stroke him. She ran her thumb over the head, rubbing the fluid gathered there over his tender flesh.

He bit down on her shoulder, making her cry out from the unexpected shock of it. And then he was kissing her, his tongue sweeping into her mouth to tangle and tease. Adam made her forget all about what she was doing to him until he surged into her hand, harder than ever.

Breaking the kiss only long enough to whip her shirt up and over her head, he made quick work of unhooking the pink bra and pushing it off her shoulders.

Abby's first impulse was to release her grip on him so she could cover her bare breasts.

"No," he said, seeming to know what she wanted to do before she even finished having the thought. "No." He cupped her breasts, squeezing and caressing, making her crazy with the promise of what was to come. Then he bent his head and used his tongue and lips on her nipple, sucking hard enough to cause her legs to buckle.

"On the bed." He turned them as one and walked her backward until her legs connected with the bed and she fell back, bringing him down on top of her. He began all over again with deep, drugging kisses that sucked every rational thought right out of her head. Her entire world was reduced to his hot mouth, his talented tongue, his hands on her breasts and the press of his desire against her belly.

He left a trail of fire with kisses to her face, neck, throat and between her breasts. Her back arched off the bed, seeking the heat of his mouth on her nipples. With her fingers tangled in his hair, she directed him to where she needed him most.

"Here?" he asked, dabbing her nipple with his tongue.

"Yes. *Please…*"

"So polite." His lips vibrated against her nipple. "Such a lady."

"I was before I met you."

"It's okay to be a little naughty."

"How naughty is a little naughty?"

Laughing, he turned his attention to her other breast. "Let me show you." Licking and sucking and teasing, he set out to destroy her defenses, to make her forget all about being a lady. The noises he coaxed from her were hardly ladylike, but before it registered that she should be embarrassed by her reactions, he would do something else, drawing more sighs and moans and whimpers from her.

And so it went, one sensation on top of another, building and growing until she was desperate for completion.

"Adam…"

He raised his face from the hip bone he'd been investigating with tiny nips of his teeth that ratcheted her desire to unprecedented levels. She hadn't even known that hip bones could be sexy.

"What do you need, honey? Tell me."

"More. I need more."

Displaying the same efficiency he'd shown with her top and bra, he removed her jeans quickly, leaving her only in string-bikini panties that matched the bra.

"Should I be worried at how adept you are at removing a woman's clothing?"

"Not at all. You shouldn't be worried about anything." He pulled his own shirt up and over his head, baring a most excellent chest to her visual perusal. Defined pectorals and rippled abs that made her sigh.

She ran her fingers over each of them. "How does a computer geek get muscles like these?"

"Many, many hours in the gym."

Pressing her lips to the flat disk of his nipple, she said, "Time very well spent."

He cupped her mound through the silky panties, making her strain for more. "I'm glad you think so."

"Adam?"

"Hmm?"

"There's something else I should tell you before this goes any farther."

"That sounds ominous."

"It's more embarrassing than ominous."

"You're not getting embarrassed anymore, remember? You're enjoying a fling with a man who finds you incredibly sexy and desirable."

While she appreciated the reminder, this particular issue had caused her untold problems in the past. As they were down to his unbuttoned jeans and two pairs of underwear standing between them and the next step in the relationship they weren't having, she couldn't postpone this discussion any longer.

"What is it, honey? Put it out there and let's talk about it so you can stop fretting about it."

"The problem I told you about the other night... It's not the only one."

"Okay."

She turned her head, avoiding his gaze as she searched for the words. It was easier to say when she wasn't facing those dazzling blue eyes looking down at her and seeing her in ways she hadn't been seen before. "Sometimes...well, most of the time...I get nervous about... you know..."

"Having sex?"

"Yes." She cleared her throat and forced herself to continue. "When that happens, it's difficult for the guy to... To get it in."

"So...things dry up?"

An infusion of heat took over her face, reminding her of past humiliations. "No, that's not it."

"Then what? It's okay to just say it. I swear I'm not judging you. Not at all."

Encouraged by his kindness, she swallowed hard and looked up at him, forcing herself to look directly into his eyes. "It's like my muscles there seize up and can't relax enough to allow entry."

"I see."

"You do?"

"Uh-huh. All that means is we have to make sure you're as relaxed as we can possibly get you before we try that."

"That's often easier said than done." Cal, in particular, had become frustrated by her inability to accept him, which had put further strain on an already strained relationship. But Abby didn't want to think about him now. Not when she was lying nearly naked in the arms of sexy, thoughtful Adam McCarthy.

He brushed the hair back from her face, his thumbs caressing her cheekbones. "We need to find the off switch for that overactive brain of yours. We need to make it so you're not thinking about anything other than how good it feels when we're together this way."

"I wish I could do that. You don't know how badly I wish I could."

"It's not up to you to do that, honey. It's up to me. If I do my part the way I should, you won't be thinking about anything other than how good it feels."

She had to look away again because she simply couldn't believe how tuned in to her he was after only spending a few days together.

"You're thinking again," he said, kissing her neck and nibbling her ear. "Tell me. Let me in."

"I can't do that."

"Why?"

"Because you'll have me falling for you when we said we weren't going to do that. Because you're already making me wonder how I spent so many years with the wrong men when the right one might've been so close. So very close."

"Abby..."

"Forget I said that. You've got me all discombobulated and saying things I shouldn't be saying."

"I want to hear what you're thinking. Do you want to know why?"

She nodded. God help her, but she wanted to know everything about him.

"Because you've got me thinking the same sort of things. How could we have spent so much time in each other's orbit but never known this was possible?"

Tears filled her eyes, the emotional response infuriating her. "We said we weren't going to do this," she reminded him again.

He peppered her face with kisses, putting particular emphasis on her eyelids, licking the salty moisture from under her eyes.

"We both just got out of big entanglements," she continued, even as his tenderness destroyed her defenses. "We've got no business doing this."

"And yet here we are, thoroughly entangled, all but naked in each other's arms with nowhere else either of us would rather be. Am I right about that?"

Powerfully moved by his assessment, she said, "Yes," the single word barely a whisper.

"Sometimes," he said, kissing her so sweetly, "the most important things happen when you least expect it."

"Is this an important thing?"

"I don't know about you, but it's become very important to me over the last few days."

His admission gave her the courage to offer her own. "Me, too."

"How about we have a little fun now, take the edge off, and later, after we do our girls' night and poker night, we meet back here and take all the time it takes to get you relaxed enough to make love?"

Abby trembled at the promise in his softly spoken words. Because she didn't trust herself to speak, she nodded.

He kissed her, taking it slowly, running his tongue over the seam of her lips until she opened her mouth to let him in. When he sucked lightly on her tongue, Abby nearly died from the pleasure that coursed through her. He coaxed reactions from her that she'd never known possible. He drew her out of her own thoughts and into the moment in a way that no one else had done before.

She clung to him, wanting him closer, close enough that his chest hair abraded her tender nipples and his hard penis pressed against the pulsating tension between her legs.

Desperate to touch and feel all of him, she pushed her hands into the back of his jeans, under the waistband of his boxers, cupping his muscular buttocks as he flexed against her.

He broke the kiss and shifted his attention to her nipple, tugging and biting lightly, but hard enough to make her moan from the pleasure. The tension grew to nearly unbearable heights as he pressed against her and then backed off, and then did it again, over and over until she was lost in the throes of immeasurable bliss, her fingers digging into his backside to keep him right where she needed him until the storm had subsided.

"Abby," he whispered against her breast. "God." The heat of his release on her belly was among the most sensual things she'd ever experienced. Watching him let go, feeling the tension drain from his body and knowing she'd done that to him made her feel powerful and aware of herself as a woman in ways that were all new to her.

"I can't wait to be inside you when that happens," he whispered, his breath against her neck making her shiver.

A twinge of anxiety settled in her belly as she hoped she wouldn't have the problems with him she'd had with past lovers. For some reason, it seemed to matter so much more this time around. Despite her intention to be done forever with men, she was falling hard for Adam McCarthy.

AFTER THE VISIT with Laura and her family, Frank spent an hour with his son Shane, and then decided to walk the short distance from the Sand & Surf to his brother Mac's house in North Harbor. The afternoon sun was warm on his face as he walked past Grace's pharmacy and up the hill that led to Mac and Linda's "White House."

As he walked, he thought of the monumental news Laura and Owen had shared with him. Twins... It was hard to believe that his little girl would soon be the mother of three. But he'd never seen

Laura as happy as she'd been since Owen had come into her life. If anyone deserved to be happy, it was his kids who'd lost their poor mother far too young and had known their share of struggles since then.

He'd done his best to be mother and father to them, and he hurt right along with them when things didn't go their way. Now that Laura seemed happily settled, Frank hoped Shane would find his way before too much longer. His son was still far too withdrawn and quiet after the disaster with his ex-wife Courtney.

In his work as a superior court judge, he saw daily examples of the ravages of drug abuse. He'd never expected to see the same ravages in his own family. Shane had been blindsided to discover his wife had hidden a raging prescription drug addiction for most of the time they'd been together.

It had done Shane good to be here with his sister and cousins as well as his Aunt Linda and Uncle Mac, who'd played such a critical role in the lives of his kids when they were younger. Linda and Mac had opened their doors to Laura and Shane every summer when they were young, and those weeks on Gansett with their cousins had done wonders for his kids.

The island seemed to be having the same impact this time around. Laura was happily settled, delighted with her job managing the Sand & Surf Hotel for Owen's grandparents, who owned it. Shane seemed to enjoy working at the hotel and helping Mac and Luke with their construction business. At least he wasn't sitting in a dark apartment letting life pass him by anymore. That was progress.

Frank approached his brother and sister-in-law's home, noting the blooms in Linda's famous rose garden as he let himself in through the gate of the white picket fence that surrounded the yard. He was almost to the porch when he saw a woman sitting on the top step.

As he approached, she stood, and he saw she was tall and strikingly pretty with curly dark hair that fell to her shoulders. As he drew closer, he could see that she was older than she'd first appeared.

"Mr. McCarthy?"

"I'm one of them, but this is my brother's home. I'm Frank McCarthy."

She shook his outstretched hand. "Betsy Jacobson. I was hoping to see Mr. or Mrs. McCarthy."

"I could give them a call for you, if you'd like."

"I'd appreciate that."

He stepped around her and climbed the stairs. "Come on in."

"Are you sure they won't mind?"

"I'm positive." Frank held the screen door for her and gestured for her to go into the house.

"They don't lock their doors?" Betsy asked.

"No one does around here. Gansett is the safest place in the world."

"Not always," Betsy said.

Frank wasn't sure what to make of her comment, so he went ahead and placed calls to Mac and Linda, who both said they'd be home in a few minutes.

"Can I get you something?" Frank asked while they waited in somewhat awkward silence.

"A glass of water would be great."

"Coming right up." Frank had spent enough time here to know where the glasses were kept and poured ice water for both of them.

Betsy wandered over to the sliding doors that led the expansive deck. "They have quite a view."

"One of the best on the island." Frank joined her at the doors. "That's their marina down there and their hotel." He was surprised to hear a sniffle of what might've been tears from her. "Are you all right?" When he looked over at her, she was staring at the marina.

"My son Steve was killed—"

"Oh God." Frank hadn't made the connection to her last name and the young man who'd been killed in the accident that had nearly claimed three of his nephews. "Your son was the captain."

"Yes."

"I'm so very sorry for your loss."

She wiped away tears. "Thank you. Seeing the marina where he stayed..."

Frank wasn't sure if it was appropriate, but he reached out to pat her shoulder.

"I wanted to meet the McCarthys and to maybe hear more about what happened from their sons, since they were there."

"I'm sure they'll do anything they can for you."

"You're very kind. Thank you."

Linda came rushing in a few minutes later and came right over to Betsy. The two women embraced as if they'd always known each other. Watching them, tears filled Frank's eyes. He didn't even want to imagine what Betsy had been through losing her son so suddenly and tragically.

"I'm so glad you came," Linda said, patting Betsy's back. "I've thought of you constantly."

"I got your message. Thank you so much for your kindness and the invitation to visit." Betsy drew back from her, wiping her face with the graceful pass of fingertips over her cheeks. She moved with the elegance of a dancer. "I'm sorry to come without calling first. I woke up this morning, and before I knew what I was about, I was at the ferry on the way here."

"You didn't need to call," Linda said. "You're welcome here any time."

"That's so kind of you. I was hoping to see your sons, to hear more about what happened. If they're willing, of course."

"I'll call them and ask them to come."

"I'll do it," Frank said.

Linda handed him her phone. "Send a text. Tell them I'd like them to come to the house as soon as possible. That way it comes from their mother."

Frank shared a smile with her. She was the best mother he'd ever known. If she told her kids to come, even her thirty-something kids, they'd come. Frank sent the text to Mac, Grant and Evan on their mother's behalf.

He'd no sooner sent the message when his brother Big Mac came in. His gray hair stood on end, his face was windblown and tanned, and he wore a faded T-shirt and battered shorts with paint-splattered boat shoes. In some ways, the brothers were as different as two men could be. But they shared more similarities than differences. Frank embraced his younger brother, delighted as always to see him.

"That's Steve's mother?" Big Mac asked, his gaze fixed on Betsy.

"Yes."

Big Mac watched his wife speak softly to the other woman, who seemed overwhelmed with emotion.

Frank studied his brother with growing concern. "Are you okay, Mac?"

"It's been really hard, Frankie. I keep thinking about what could've happened to my boys... I can't begin to understand what she's going through."

Frank hadn't heard his childhood nickname in decades. It told him how undone his brother was by what had nearly happened.

"I don't know what to say to her," Big Mac continued. "My boys made it, but hers didn't."

"All you can do is express your condolences and support. That's what she needs. That's why she's here."

Big Mac squeezed Frank's arm. "I'm glad you're here."

"So am I."

CHAPTER 17

*A*n intense ache in her lower leg woke Abby. The tattoo was killing her. Even the light brush of the sheet against her skin was painful. Adam was sleeping next to her, his arm around her in a protective pose that filled her with warmth and pleasure that almost made her forget the pain in her leg.

Watching him sleep, she took in the details of his handsome face. His dark hair was wavy rather than curly, his cheekbones pronounced and his jaw sprinkled with whiskers. He was beautiful to look at and easy to talk to—almost too easy to talk to in light of some of the things she'd shared with him.

To say she hadn't expected this was putting it mildly. She couldn't resist the urge to reach out and run her fingertips over his face.

His eyes opened slowly to find her watching him. A smile tugged at his lips.

"I didn't mean to wake you."

"What time is it?"

"Almost six."

Adam raised his hand from her belly and stretched. Fascinated, Abby watched the flex of muscles.

"Best nap ever," Adam said.

"Except for the pain in my leg that woke me up."

"Is it bad?"

"Pretty bad."

"Let me see."

Abby worked her right leg out from under the sheet and held it up so he could see the angry red outline of the flower and vine.

"Ouch. Would you trust me to put some ointment on it for you?"

"Do you have some?"

"I bought it earlier along with ibuprofen."

"So yours hurts, too?"

"Like a bastard."

Abby dissolved into laughter. "You were so stoic."

"It hurt worse than anything I've ever felt."

"Awww, I'm sorry I talked you into it."

"I'm not. It was fun to share your moment of rebellion. How about that ointment? I'll be gentle."

"Okay," Abby said, filled with trepidation at the thought of anyone touching her sore skin.

Adam got out of bed, which was when Abby realized that he'd shed his jeans and underwear at some point. As she watched him move around the room, her mouth watered with desire for more of him. She feasted her eyes on his muscular backside until he turned around and gave her an even better view.

When he realized she was staring at him, he stopped and seemed to pose for her. "You like?"

Abby bit her lip and nodded.

Smiling at her, he returned to the bed with a tube of ointment in hand. "Ready?"

"I guess."

His touch was exceedingly gentle, so much so she barely felt it as he treated the entire area. "Is that okay?"

"Yes, thank you."

He bent to kiss the inside of her knee. "Remind me I want to spend more time right here later, will you?"

"I'll see if I can remember that."

"I hate to say that I've got to go. I want to run home to change before I go to Luke's."

"I need to get moving, too. I'm meeting the girls across the street in an hour." Abby held out her arms to him, and he crawled up the bed to her, like a big sexy cat on the prowl.

"See you back here later?"

"Yes, you will."

"Text me when you get back."

"I will."

He kissed her slowly, lingering on a thorough exploration of her bottom lip that had her heart pounding in no time at all. "Mmm, so sweet. It's going to be a long night looking forward to later."

"For me, too." She reluctantly released him and he seemed to be equally reluctant to leave her. As she still wore only the thin scrap of underwear, Abby couldn't bring herself to leave the protection of the sheet. The whole new her wasn't quite ready to walk around naked in front of him.

Before he left, he leaned over the bed once more to kiss her. "See you soon."

"Have fun tonight."

"You, too." He was to the door before he turned back to her. "It occurs to me that we need an official date with wine and candles and good food. Tomorrow night. That's what we'll do. All right?"

"All right."

Abby's smile lingered for a long time after he left.

ANNOYED by the summons from his mother, Grant almost ignored it.

"What's wrong?" Dan asked.

Grant had come to visit his injured friend and had been enjoying the relaxing time with Dan when the text had arrived.

"My mom has summoned us to the White House for some unknown reason."

"Are you going?"

"I'd love to pretend like I didn't get the message, but somehow Voodoo Mama would know."

"You're too funny, man. Still worried about getting in trouble with your mommy. How old are you anyway?"

"Thirty-six last time I checked."

Dan grinned and shook his head.

"Until you've encountered Linda McCarthy's wrath, you can't judge me."

"Whatever you say. Mind if I come along? I'm getting sick of looking at my own four walls."

"Isn't Kara coming over?"

"She's working late, covering for one of her people. She'll be here later."

Grant helped Dan up from the sofa, moving carefully so as not to jar Dan's injured ribs. "Things with her are going well?"

"She's amazing. I think I might be in love."

"I never thought I'd hear you say that again." For years after Dan caught his ex-fiancée in bed with his best man the day before his wedding, he'd stayed far, far away from anything that smacked of commitment.

"I never thought I'd say it either. But there's something about Kara that makes me want to take chances again."

Grant helped Dan into a light jacket, which was complicated by the bulky cast on his arm. "I'm glad for you. She seems really great."

"She's been amazing since the accident. I don't know what I would've done without her."

"So get this... My brother Adam is seeing Abby."

"Abby as in your ex-Abby?"

"One and the same."

"I thought she was engaged to that doctor. What was his name?"

Grant closed the door to Dan's house. Outside, he watched Dan cast longing glances at his Porsche, which he'd be unable to drive for quite some time yet. "Cal Maitland. Apparently, that's over. Life in Texas didn't agree with her."

"Is that right?"

Grant held the door to his car for Dan and waited while his friend moved slowly and painfully into the passenger seat. "That's what I heard."

When they were on their way, Dan said, "So what do you think of Adam being with her?"

"It's been over between us for a long time, but it's still kind of weird to think of my own brother dating her, you know?"

"My brother and I dated the same girl once."

Since Dan rarely talked about the brother he'd lost in Afghanistan, Grant was instantly curious. "How did that happen?"

"She was his high school girlfriend. They broke up senior year, and I worked with her a couple of summers later. We went out a few times, but it was making things weird with Dylan, so I broke it off with her. I figured it wasn't going anywhere with her, so why put strain between me and him, you know?"

"Sounds like a good call."

"Will this put strain between you and Adam?"

"If it does, it'll also put strain between me and Steph, because she'll think I'm jealous, which I'm not."

"True," Dan said with a chuckle that came out more like a grimace thanks to his injuries. "Puts you between a rock and a hard place, huh?"

"Seriously."

"So it's just you and me here. How do you really feel about it?"

"I don't know exactly. I guess if I were being completely honest, I'd say I wish he were 'hanging out' with someone else."

"That's fair enough. I can certainly understand why you'd prefer that."

"But the fact is, he's seeing her, and I have to keep my mouth shut about it or cause trouble I don't need with Steph. She's had so many disappointments and catastrophes in her life. I refuse to be one of them, and I don't want to trigger all her insecurities. She's worked so hard to overcome them and to have faith in me—and in us. I can't screw that up. She means too damned much to me to let that happen."

"Aaah, Grant. Look at us. All grown up at last."

"I know, right? Sucks, doesn't it?"

"Don't make me laugh. I beg of you."

"Sorry."

Grant parked outside his parents' home just as Mac arrived in one of the marina trucks and Evan pulled up on Mac's old motorcycle. Another bike pulled into the driveway, which turned out to be Adam.

Standing beside the passenger door to help Dan, Grant called out to his brother. "Where'd you get that bike?"

"Rented it," Adam said. "What're you all doing here?"

"Mom sent a text asking us to come," Mac said. "No idea what's up."

"How come I wasn't invited?" Adam asked.

"I guess you're not one of her favorites," Evan said. "But I could've told you that ages ago. Let's go find out what she's up to. I was right in the middle of something at the studio."

The others filed in ahead of Grant, who waited for Dan.

"Hope I'm not intruding on a family moment," Dan said.

"Don't worry about it. There're no secrets in this family."

Inside, Grant's parents and Uncle Frank were talking to a woman Grant didn't recognize. He hadn't heard his uncle was on-island. Grant and his brothers greeted Frank with hugs.

"Here they all are," Linda said. "Our sons Mac, Evan, Grant and Adam. Oh, and Grant's friend Dan is here. He was on the boat, too."

When she said that last part, Grant took a step back. Who was that woman?

"Boys, this is Betsy Jacobson. Steve's mother."

"No," Grant said. "No." His feet moved seemingly of their own volition as he bolted from the house. The drumbeat of denial, *no, no, no*, echoed in his ears as he ran from the home where he'd been raised in a cocoon of love and understanding. They wouldn't understand what he couldn't reconcile himself.

"Grant! Stop! Wait."

"Grant!"

He heard his brothers calling his name, but still he ran, blinded by tears, stumbling and nearly falling over a crack in the sidewalk that had always been there. And then strong arms were around him, stopping his forward motion. Mac.

"Stop. Grant... Don't run. I've got you."

Something in him broke as his brother's formidable strength surrounded him, holding him, protecting him from the tsunami of overwhelming agony that forced gut-wrenching sobs through his body.

"It's okay." Mac held him so tightly that Grant could barely breathe. He wanted to beg his brother to not let go. If he did, Grant might drop off the cliff he'd been clinging to for days now. "Let it out." Mac's hand on the back of Grant's head kept his face pressed tight against his big brother's shoulder. "Let it go. No matter what it is, we love you, we'll always love you."

"No," Grant said between sobs. "No, you won't."

"Yes, we will. That could never change. Nothing you could do would make me not love you."

"He's right," Evan said from behind Grant. "He speaks for all of us."

"You don't understand," Grant said.

"Make us understand, buddy," Adam said. "Let us help."

He wanted to so badly. He wanted to unburden himself on the three brothers he loved more than almost anyone in the world. There was nothing they wouldn't do for him. He knew it and believed they'd stand by him no matter what. But he was so afraid to say the words, to confess what he'd done, especially with Steve's mother in their home.

"Let me in."

Grant heard his father's voice and stiffened.

Mac smoothly transitioned him into the arms of their father, who held him even more tightly than Mac had.

"Tell us what has you so upset," Big Mac said. "Put it out there, get it off your chest, let us share the load."

Surrounded by the unconditional love of his family, Grant could no longer hold back the words that poured forth. The boat, the crash, landing in the water with Dan and Steve, both grievously injured, not knowing where Mac or Evan were and faced with an unimaginable choice: save one of his best friends or save the man he'd met only that morning. He couldn't save them both and save himself, too.

"Oh God," Mac said. "God."

"I couldn't save him," Grant said, choking on sobs, "and now his mother is here, and I have to tell her that? I have to tell her that I let him go because I couldn't save him *and* Dan?"

"Grant..."

He pulled back from his dad and found Dan staring at him, stricken as realization set in.

"I chose you," Grant said. "I chose to save you, and now he's dead, and it's my fault."

The circle of men around him sniffled and wiped their eyes. He'd never seen any of them cry, let alone all of them at once.

Dan came over to him and hugged him as best he could. "It's not your fault. It's the fault of the ship that hit us, the fog, the bad luck of being in the wrong place at the wrong time. There was nothing you could've done but survive. You saved my life. It's thanks to you that Steve and I aren't both dead."

"That's right, son," Big Mac said. "Do you give yourself any credit for saving Dan?"

"I wanted to save them both," Grant said, depleted by the emotional firestorm.

"You couldn't," Adam said. "And no one will blame you for reaching for the one who's been your friend for so long."

"Not even Steve's mother?" Grant asked him. "Will she understand? I can't tell her this. She's come here for answers, and I can't tell her. I can't."

"We'll do it for you," Mac said. "We've got your back. We've always got your back."

Big Mac framed Grant's face with big hands, forcing him to meet his father's steely, determined gaze. "I'm proud of you, son. You saved Dan's life. You saved my life and your mother's and Stephanie's by saving your own. You faced an unimaginable dilemma, and you did the best you could. That's all anyone can ever do."

He choked back a sob. "Don't be proud of me for letting Steve die."

"You didn't let him die," Big Mac said. "That was God's will. Not yours."

Grant broke down anew at his father's absolution—absolution he didn't feel he deserved, but which brought a measure of peace anyway. Giving voice to the agony he'd borne alone had also helped.

"We're all behind you, Grant," Evan said. "It was a nightmare out there. Mac and I can attest to that. One minute we were on the front of the boat, and the next minute we're in the water, in the fog and we can't find each other. How you managed to save Dan—as well as yourself—is amazing to me, and I'm sure to Mac, too."

"It is," Mac agreed. "I had all I could do to keep my own head above water. I have no idea how you were able to save Dan, too."

Grant didn't know how he'd done it. A lot of the details were vague, but letting Dan go hadn't been an option. He remembered that much.

"Let's go in there and face Steve's mom together," Big Mac said. "She wants the truth. She *needs* the truth. Let's give that to her, and maybe it'll set you free, too."

Grant didn't know if anything could set him free from the nightmare he'd been living over the last week, but sharing his burden with his brothers, his father and his friend had helped. Exhausted and wrung out from the ordeal of confession, Grant let his dad guide him into the house.

ADAM LET the others go in ahead of him and remained on the porch for a minute, collecting himself. Seeing his brother so undone had upset him tremendously. To him, Grant had always been cool, sophisticated, incredibly talented and somewhat aloof, untouched by the troubles that plagued regular mortals. Seeing him brought low by the tragedy of Steve's death had shaken Adam.

He leaned against the rail on the front porch, staring down at his mother's rose garden and thinking about how arbitrary and capricious life could be. His brothers had left with two other men on a spring morning to participate in a sailboat race. By the day's end, one of them was dead, one was gravely injured, and three others were changed forever by the harrowing experience.

"Adam?"

At the sound of Evan's voice, Adam turned. "Yeah?"

"Are you coming in?"

"In a minute."

Evan joined him in leaning against the rail. "He was her only child."

"Christ," Adam uttered.

"I guess she raised him alone after the dad split. She taught him how to sail, got him interested in the sport. And now..."

"She's feeling guilty for encouraging him to do what he probably loved more than anything."

"Something like that."

"I can't believe what happened to Grant out there."

"The poor guy. No wonder why he's been so messed up."

"One of us should call Stephanie to clue her in to what's going on."

"Good idea. I'll do it."

Adam stood by Evan's side as he placed the call to Stephanie and told her what Grant had finally confessed to them. "She's on her way," Evan said when he ended the call.

"It'll take some time," Adam said, "but he'll get past this."

"You think so?"

"You don't?"

"I think it'll haunt him for a long time."

"We'll take care of him. Stephanie will, too. We'll get him past it. Somehow."

Evan put an arm around Adam and gave him an awkward hug. Growing up, Adam and his younger brother had spent more time punching each other than hugging. But now he leaned into his brother's embrace, thankful for the comfort.

"I'm glad you're home," Evan said. "I'm glad everyone is home."

"Me, too." There was, Adam thought, nowhere else he'd rather be.

. . .

LISTENING to Mac relay the tale of epic struggle to Steve Jacobson's mother was among the most excruciating things Grant had ever been through. The poor woman wept throughout the telling, during which Mac's voice never wavered from the soft, soothing tone he began with.

By the time he was finished, everyone in the room was in tears.

Uncle Frank slipped an arm around his brother, propping up Big Mac, who was taking the retelling of the story hard. It was equally hard for Grant to hear it again, but he was thankful to Mac for doing the talking for him. He didn't think he could've gotten through it himself. But now he felt the need to say something to Steve's mother.

"I'm sorry," Grant said. "I'm sorry I couldn't save them both."

Betsy took a new tissue from Linda. "After the crash... When you were in the water, was Steve conscious?"

"No."

"Is it possible he might've already been dead?"

"I don't know," Grant said. "I wish I could tell you what you need to know, but I wasn't able to get to him to confirm that."

"I ask because it would give me comfort to know he didn't suffer, that perhaps he was killed on impact."

"I suppose that's possible."

Betsy wiped her eyes and took in the group gathered before her. "Thank you all so much for seeing me. I know it was difficult for you to relive what was a terrible day for you, too, but I appreciate it more than you'll ever know. I won't take any more of your time."

"Don't go." Linda took the other woman's hand before she could rise. "You're welcome to stay for as long as you'd like. We've got plenty of room, and we'd love to have you." She glanced at her husband.

"Please do stay," Big Mac said. "The island is a wonderful place to recover your footing."

"I wouldn't want to inconvenience you," Betsy said.

"It would be no inconvenience," Linda said. "We'd love to have you."

"A change of scenery would be a welcome relief," Betsy said. "Since

Steve's memorial service, I've been rattling around in my house, feeling aimless and lost."

Linda smiled and squeezed Betsy's hand. "No need to be lost and alone when you can be among new friends."

"You're all very kind. I appreciate your offer, and I accept your hospitality."

The front door slammed shut, and Stephanie came rushing in, looking teary-eyed and dismayed. She found Grant in the group and came right over to him.

"Someone called you," he said, surprised to see her. He knew he shouldn't be surprised that one of his brothers would've thought to call his fiancée. Grant had never been so happy to see her.

She sat on his lap and wrapped her arms around him, telling him everything he needed to know without saying a word.

Relieved and a little less burdened than he'd been earlier, Grant held on to her for dear life.

AFTER GRANT LEFT WITH STEPHANIE, Dan asked Mac to take him down to the docks so he could see Kara. Reeling after what he'd learned about the accident, he needed to be with her.

"You should come to Luke's tonight," Mac said as he drove down the hill. "It'd do you good to be among friends."

"I'll see how I feel a little later."

"Can I say something?"

Dan liked Grant's brothers a lot, and had become closer to them since he'd lived on the island. "Can I stop you?"

Mac uttered a quick laugh. "I don't know you very well, but I can guess how I might feel after hearing what you just heard."

"And how's that?"

"Guilty, overwhelmed, questioning why you lived and he died, wondering how you possibly go forward from here knowing what you now know."

"Pretty accurate assessment."

"Here's the deal. He died. You lived. There's no changing that fact.

So it would seem to me that there isn't much point to beating yourself up over something you had no control over."

"You remind me a lot of my brother, Dylan."

"How's that?"

"Always the big brother."

"I'm sorry. I don't mean to overstep."

"You didn't. I miss him. It's been a long time since I've been big-brothered."

"He died?"

Dan nodded. "2005."

"I'm so sorry. I didn't know."

"Thanks, and thanks for the words of wisdom. I do appreciate them."

"Any time you need a big brother, it's one of the few things I've ever been truly good at."

Crooking a brow at Mac, Dan said, "By whose estimation?"

"My own, of course."

Despite the pain it caused his battered ribs, Dan laughed harder than he had in more than a week. "Thanks for the ride."

"Come to Luke's."

"I'll try."

Frustrated by how long it took him to do even the simplest things, Dan eased himself out of the truck and shut the door, waving at Mac as he drove off. Dan walked slowly down the main pier, scanning the pond in search of Kara's maroon launch, but didn't see any sign of her.

He took the ramp to the launch dock and eased himself onto the bench, which was empty of passengers. The throbbing pain in his ribs and arm indicated his pain pills were wearing off. He'd learned to stay on top of the meds, even though he'd rather forego them. However, not taking them wasn't an option. He'd never experienced pain quite like that of broken ribs.

Sitting alone, watching the action in the harbor, he had time to absorb what he'd learned that afternoon and to think about what Mac had said. Dan thought of his parents, who'd already lost one son tragically, and his two older sisters, who'd lost a brother. Dylan's death had been horrible for all of them, and Dan was grateful that his family had been spared another sudden loss.

Yet it was difficult to separate his own gratitude from the profound sense of grief he felt over Steve's death. He'd spent only a morning with Steve but had enjoyed his company, his sense of humor and his expertise with the boat. Steve had called himself the lucky one, the only member of his group who'd escaped the stomach bug.

Dan was pondering the deeper meaning of luck and fate when Kara's launch came into view, zipping between boats as she made her way back to the floating dock where she picked up and dropped off passengers. She was almost there when she noticed him waiting for her.

Her expression was full of consternation and questions as she competently brought the launch to a smooth stop against the dock, looped lines over cleats, conversed with disembarking passengers and offered a hand when necessary. After the last passenger had gone up the ramp to the main pier, she got off the boat and came over to him.

Hands on hips, ball cap perched on her head, she gave him a look of annoyance that any mother would respect. It occurred to him right in that moment that she would be a wonderful mother someday. "*What* are you doing here, Torrington?"

"I was missing you."

"How'd you get here?"

"Grant and Mac."

Kara sat next to him on the bench, taking a perusing inventory of his features. "Are you in pain?"

"A little."

"Did you take your pills?"

"Earlier."

"So they're wearing off."

"Maybe."

"*Dan!* What're you doing here when you should be home on the sofa?"

"It sort of happened like this..." Dan told her about Grant coming to visit, going with him to his parents' home and the emotional discovery of what had really happened after the accident. "I was right up the hill from you, and I wanted to see you. I needed to see you."

"I'm so sorry," she said, cupping his face with her hand as she contended with a flood of tears. "It must've been so shocking to hear all that."

"It was upsetting, to say the least, and then to have to face Steve's mom, knowing how it had gone down. Poor Grant was a mess. I knew it was bad for him out there, but I had no idea how bad."

She hugged him, and Dan sagged into her embrace. Her fingers curled around his nape, cradling him. Resting against her, any doubt that he'd fallen in love evaporated into the soft spring air. They stayed that way for a long time. All the while, Dan prayed for her customers to stay away.

"Kara?"

"Hmm?"

"I want to tell you something right here on the dock where you and I began."

"Is this where we began? Or was it in Luke Harris's kitchen when I took one look at you and knew you were going to be big trouble for me."

He pulled back from her, grinning like a loon. "Big trouble, huh?"

"Very big trouble."

"I love you."

Her eyes widened, and her lips parted ever so slightly, making him want to take full advantage of the invitation. "You do?"

On pins and needles waiting for her to say she loved him, too, he studied her expressive face, looking for a sign that she felt the same way he did. Any sign would do.

"Is that okay?" he finally asked after a very long pause.

"I think so."

"You *think* so? What does that mean?"

"You haven't met any of my sisters yet. There're still a few single ones—"

He kissed her as hard as he'd ever kissed her before, pouring every ounce of love he felt for her into the meeting of lips and tongues and teeth. He kissed her until he had to stop because of the screaming pain in his side. "I don't care if you have a hundred single, fetching sisters, you're the one I want. The only one I want."

"You say that now, but—"

Pinching her lips together, he said, "Kara, listen to me. Please listen. What your ex-boyfriend did with your sister was despicable. It was despicable on both their parts. But I'm not him. I've waited a long time to feel this way again, and there's nothing I wouldn't do to continue feeling this way for as long as I possibly can. I feel this way for *you*. I love *you*. Your single sisters can go straight to hell for all I care."

She was smiling when she leaned in to kiss him, taking the lead this time and blowing him away with the force of her desire. "I love you, too, you knucklehead. I was just testing you."

Her words filled him with overwhelming relief and satisfaction and a tad bit of annoyance. "That was not nice."

"I know, but it was funny listening to you send my poor sisters straight to hell when you haven't even met them yet."

"That wasn't my fault. You set me up."

"Has anyone ever told you that you talk way too much?" she asked, kissing him again.

"I've heard that a time or two in my life." Thrilled with her, he lost himself in the kiss, forgetting all about the pain in his ribs and the pain in his heart he'd carried for so long after his ex-fiancée cheated on him.

A throat was cleared behind him. "Ah, excuse me, Kara?"

She broke the kiss and pulled back from Dan.

He turned—carefully—to find one of her drivers standing behind him, looking embarrassed to have caught the boss making out on the dock. For her part, Kara didn't look the slightest bit embarrassed, which pleased Dan tremendously. Only a few weeks ago, she would've been mortified.

"Oh, hey, Tim, is it six already?"

"Yes, it is."

"Let me get my stuff off the boat, and then it's all yours."

Dan never took his eyes off her as she gathered her belongings and went over a few things with Tim. When she was done, she got off the boat and came over to him. "Ready to go?" She held out a hand to help him up.

He took hold of her hand and got up, grimacing at the pain in his ribs.

"We need to get some meds into you."

"I won't say no to that."

They went up the ramp to the main dock, where Dan dropped her hand and put his good arm around her, hugging her as close to him as he could get her. He kissed the top of her head and was delighted when he felt her arm curl around his waist, her fingers hooking into one of the belt loops on his jeans.

His body ached like a bastard, but his heart... His heart had never felt better.

CHAPTER 18

*a*bby dashed across the street to the Sand & Surf a little after seven. Inside Stephanie's Bistro, she spotted the table full of women across the big dining room and headed over to join them, relieved that Janey had saved a seat for her. She was the one Abby knew best and felt most comfortable with. Since she planned to stay put on the island from now on, she was looking forward to getting to know the other women better.

In addition to Janey, the group consisted of Maddie, Tiffany, Sydney, Grace and Laura, as well as a blonde woman Abby hadn't met before.

"Do you know everyone?" Janey asked after greeting Abby with a hug and kiss.

"Almost everyone," Abby said glancing at the blonde.

"Jenny, I don't think you've met my friend Abby Callahan. Abby, Jenny Wilks, our esteemed lighthouse keeper. We've got her to thank for organizing this girls' night out."

"Nice to meet you," Abby said as she shook Jenny's hand across the table. "Any excuse for a night out with the girls is fine by me." When the waitress approached the table, Abby ordered a glass of chardonnay. She was eager to see if she liked it better than the pinot grigio.

"It's nice to meet you, too, Abby. I've heard great things about the store you used to have."

"She's opening a new store right here in the Surf," Laura said proudly.

"That's great," Maddie said. "Thomas misses the Attic something awful. Will the new store be like the old one?"

"Laura and I are still working out the details."

"I told you to do whatever you want with the space," Laura said.

"In that case," Abby said, "it'll be Abby's Attic at The Surf, only a little smaller than its predecessor."

"I love that!" Laura said.

"Thomas won't care if it's smaller, as long as there're toys," Maddie.

"I'll be sure to consult with him before I place the order," Abby said.

"So there was a method to my madness in organizing a girls' night," Jenny said, "and I'm afraid if I don't put it out there right away, I'll chicken out. And I promised myself I wouldn't chicken out."

Jenny had the full attention of every woman at the table.

"What is it, Jenny?" Sydney asked. "Is everything all right?"

"Everything is better," Jenny said tentatively. To Abby, she said, "I lost my fiancé in the World Trade Center on 9-11."

"Oh my God. I'm so sorry." Abby felt like she'd been punched. And she thought she had problems?

"Thank you. It was a long time ago, but I've been kind of... stuck ever since. Then I came here last year, met some lovely new friends and began a wonderful new chapter in my life. And now... This is the part I don't want to chicken out of, so don't let me, okay?"

"You got it," Grace said. "We're all behind you one hundred percent."

Sydney slipped an arm around Jenny's shoulders and gave her a squeeze.

"I'm counting on that," Jenny continued as she leaned into Syd's embrace, "because I've decided I might be ready to date again. I'm not looking for anything serious, but I'm getting tired of my own company and... And, well, that's it. If you all know of anyone who might be fun to go out with, keep me in mind."

Laura whipped out a notebook and pen.

"Hold on a minute..." Jenny said, gazing at the notebook with trepidation.

"We've been waiting a long time for this moment," Sydney said. "If you think we won't take this job seriously, you don't know us at all."

Jenny moaned and dropped her head into her hands as the others laughed at her dismay.

"How about Mason, the fire chief?" Tiffany asked. "He's very cute if you like the big, burly type."

"Excellent," Laura said, making a note. "Who knows him well enough to feel him up?"

Maddie choked on a mouthful of wine. "I think you mean feel him *out.*"

"What did I say?" Laura asked.

They spoke as one, loudly, "Feel him *up.*"

Their hysterical laughter had heads turning in the dining room.

"Pipe down, you guys, or Stephanie will have us tossed out of here," Janey said.

"Where is she anyway?" Grace asked. "I thought we'd see her if we came here."

"Apparently," Maddie said, "Grant had a really rough day. I...I don't think it's my place to say what happened."

"Is he okay?" Janey asked the question that Abby was dying to ask, but she didn't dare.

"He will be. Eventually. Stephanie is with him."

Abby wanted to know more about what'd happened, but the question couldn't come from her. Maybe Adam would know. She'd have to think of some way to ask him without seeming too interested in Grant.

"So who knows Mason?"

"Blaine does," Tiffany said. "He's also friends with the Coast Guard officer who runs the Gansett Island installation. Linc Mercier."

"Putting him on the list," Laura said.

"You really think Blaine will be willing to play matchmaker on behalf of someone he barely knows?" Jenny asked.

Tiffany smiled sweetly. "He'll do it if I ask him to."

Maddie let out a low whistle that inspired cat calling among the other women.

Tiffany's smile only widened. "What can I say? I've got the power."

"And she knows how to use it," Maddie added.

"You said it, sis."

"What about your brother, Laura?" Sydney said. "He's not seeing anyone, is he?"

Laura chewed on the end of her pen. "No, but I'm not sure he wants to. I'll feel that situation *out* myself. Let's put him in the maybe column."

"We're all relieved that you're not planning to feel up your own brother," Janey said.

"Har-har," Laura replied. "Speaking of brothers, how about yours?"

"Which one?"

"The *single* one."

"Adam? Hmm." Janey seemed to think it over while Abby held back the urge to tell them he wasn't available. He was hers.

The instant she had the thought, she wanted to hit rewind and un-have it. He wasn't *hers*. They were hanging out, having fun. It would be foolish of her to put her eggs in his basket when things were so unsettled for both of them. He lived and worked in New York. While his business might be lost to him, all his contacts were there. Even though she knew his departure was probably inevitable, the thought of him leaving filled her with irrational sadness.

Laura looked directly at Abby. "I heard Adam might be seeing someone."

Abby squirmed as all eyes landed on her.

Janey's mouth dropped open. "Shut. The. Front. Door. You and *Adam?*"

"Maybe. A little."

"Oh my God! You said I might know the guy you've been seeing, but you never said it was my *brother!*"

"I'm sorry." The other women hung on her every word. "We've spent some time together. It's no big deal, so don't make it into one."

"So you'd be okay if we fixed him up with Jenny then, right?" Laura asked with a conniving smile.

"Well, um…"

"Don't answer that, Abby," Jenny said. "He's all yours."

"He's not *mine*. I never said he was."

"Mac said he's going back to the city," Maddie said. "Something to do with his business."

Maddie's words struck Abby like a punch to the belly. She'd been living a fantasy with him, picturing a life on the island with her running the shop and him working as the island's resident computer guru, solving everyone's problems. All along he'd been planning to go back to the city, while she'd been putting down new roots that she couldn't pull up a third time. Not even for him.

She'd come back to the island determined to move forward with her life, and that was what she was going to do. The interlude with Adam was never meant to be more than just that—an interlude. If she was determined to learn from her past mistakes, she needed to keep in mind that there was a world of difference between a pleasurable fling and a bona fide relationship.

"We'll strike Adam from the list for now since he seems to be otherwise occupied," Laura said. "Tiffany and I have our assignments. The rest of you keep your eyes open for other possibilities."

"What about David?" Janey said of her ex-fiancé.

"I hear he might be seeing someone, too," Maddie said with a mysterious smile.

"Who?" Janey asked.

"My friend Daisy from the hotel."

"That's an odd pairing," Tiffany said.

"Why?" Maddie asked, instantly on the defensive. "Because he's a doctor and she's a hotel maid?"

"I wasn't even thinking of their professions," Tiffany said.

"How did you find out they were seeing each other?" Grace asked.

"Daisy is babysitting for us tonight," Maddie said. "She asked if it was okay to have a friend over after the kids go to bed. I told her she's not fifteen. Of course it's fine. Then I had to know who..."

"Naturally," Tiffany said with a grin for her sister.

"She told me she and David have gotten to know each other since the latest episode with her nasty ex-boyfriend. Apparently, they came here for dinner last night, so they've gone public."

"I really like the idea of them together," Janey said. "She's so sweet and kind. He needs someone like that."

"I just hope..." Maddie shook her head, seeming to think twice about what she'd planned to say.

"What do you hope?" Janey asked.

"That he doesn't do to her what he did to you," Maddie said softly. "I don't think she's as strong as you are."

"I can't say for sure," Janey said, "but if I had to guess, I'd bet he's learned his lesson about fidelity. He's not a bad guy. He made a mistake." She shrugged. "Who among us hasn't?"

"You're awfully forgiving," Tiffany said.

"What's the point of holding a grudge? I'm happy with Joe, and what happened with David is ancient history. Besides, if David hadn't done what he did, I never would've ended up with Joe, and that would've been truly tragic."

"You won't hear me say a bad word about him after he saved my daughter's life," Maddie said. "Mac and I are eternally grateful to him."

"We all are," Janey said.

"So first there was a Mac and Maddie, then a Joe and Janey and now a David and Daisy," Tiffany said. "How cute are we?"

Very cute, Abby thought, not mentioning the possibility of an Adam and Abby.

"So I have some news," Grace said with a big smile.

All eyes turned to her.

She placed her left hand on the table to show off an engagement ring. The table erupted into squeals and congratulations and calls for champagne as they demanded Grace tell them the whole story about the engagement. When everyone had been served a flute of bubbly,

Janey raised her water glass in Grace's direction. "Welcome to the McCarthy family, Grace. We're so very happy to have you."

"Thank you. We're very excited, but I don't think Evan has told your parents yet, so try to keep a lid on the news until he gets a chance to tell them."

"He'd better hurry up," Janey said. "Voodoo Mama will be picking up a signal."

Maddie let out a snort of laughter that set off the others.

Abby happened to glance at Laura as she pushed away her glass of champagne and closed her eyes. "Is Laura okay?" Abby whispered to Janey.

"Laura?" Janey said. "What's wrong?"

Laura opened her eyes to meet her cousin's gaze. "Just a little nauseated. Sorry."

"Are you still feeling the effects of the stomach bug?" Grace asked. "It's been more than a week. You should be feeling better by now."

"Turns out," Laura said with a sheepish grin, "it wasn't the stomach bug after all, but rather a case of twins."

"Oh my God!" Tiffany said. "You're having *twins?*"

"Apparently."

The news was greeted with more happy noise from the others.

"It's a good thing we know the owner of this place," Sydney said. "Otherwise, we'd be so kicked out of here."

"No kidding," Maddie said.

"Is it my turn to share a bit of news?" Janey asked.

"The floor is all yours," Sydney said.

"Joe and I have made a decision..."

"Which is?" Maddie asked.

"We're staying here this year after the baby is born."

"Oh, wow," Maddie asked. "That's big news indeed! What about vet school?"

"I'm taking this year off to be a mom, and then we'll see."

"Was this your idea or his?" Tiffany asked.

"Mine. He took some convincing. He wants me to finish school."

"I want that for you, too," Maddie said, "but if I'm being entirely selfish, I'm thrilled you'll be here this year."

"So am I. The closer I come to delivering, the more anxious I was getting about balancing school and motherhood. When I finally told Joe how conflicted I was feeling, he said we'll take a year off from Ohio if that's what I want."

"Aww," Grace said. "He's so sweet."

"He really is, especially after he's gone to such lengths to make it possible for us to live in Ohio during the school year. So we'll be looking for a bigger place on the island ASAP since we don't have room for the baby at my house."

"Talk to Ned," Maddie said. "He's got the inside line on real estate around here."

"Joe was going to check with him about it at poker night."

"What'll you do with your place?" Abby asked.

"Rent it, I suppose."

"Sold," Abby said.

Janey's eyes lit up. "Really?"

"Yep. I need a place, and yours is absolutely perfect."

"Yay," Janey said, clapping her hands. "I love it when everything falls into place."

"My turn?" Sydney asked.

"I was wondering if you were going to spill your beans," Maddie said with a warm, encouraging smile for her friend.

"Blame the champagne," Syd said. "It's loosening our lips."

"Tell them," Maddie said. "It's very exciting news."

Sydney took a deep breath. "I wasn't going to say anything because it's such a long shot, but Luke and I are going to the mainland next week so I can have surgery to reverse the tubal ligation I had after my daughter was born."

"Oh, Syd," Jenny said. "That's wonderful."

"It's no guarantee that I'll be able to conceive again. I'm trying to keep my expectations realistic, but I'm a tiny bit excited to be taking the first step, except for the part about having surgery."

"We're excited for you," Grace said, reaching across the table to rest her hand on top of Syd's. "We all know what a big step it is for you."

The others nodded in agreement. Abby recalled hearing about the terrible accident that had taken the lives of Syd's husband and young children and admired her courage in trying to have another baby with her new husband.

"It seems we all have much to celebrate," Maddie said. "I propose a toast to good friends, good times and new beginnings."

Abby was more than happy to drink to that.

TWO HOURS LATER, the women were finishing their fourth bottle of champagne and the wide variety of appetizers they'd decided to share when the guys came ambling into the restaurant.

"Oh my God!" Maddie said when she caught sight of her husband and the other men. "They do this *every* time!"

"They crash girls' night out," Janey said to Abby. "Every. Single. Time. We can almost set our watches by them."

Abby smiled at Janey's obvious pleasure in her husband's arrival, but all she could see was Adam, grinning as he came toward her with Mac, Evan, Joe, Owen, Blaine and Luke in tow.

"What happened to poker night?" Maddie asked Mac.

"No one could beat Ned, so we started getting bored. It was either come here or go find trouble somewhere else. We figured you'd rather we came here."

Maddie raised a brow, her expression skeptical. "How long did it take you fools to come up with that story?"

"On behalf of all the fools, I'm offended," Mac said, stealing a kiss from his wife.

Adam leaned in to whisper in Abby's ear. "Having fun?"

She loved that his arm was resting on the back of her chair, just shy of touching her. "Lots of fun." The endless flow of champagne had made her a tad bit giddy. "I think I've found my drink."

He raised a brow as he took in the empty bottles on the table. "Is that so?"

"Uh-huh. It's my favorite so far."

"How much have you had?"

"Just enough," she said with a wink that made his eyes darken with what might've been desire.

Janey turned to them and gave her brother the death stare. "What did Grant have to say about this?" She waggled her finger between him and Abby.

"You told my sister?" he asked Abby.

"They were going to fix you up with Jenny. I couldn't let that happen."

He smiled at her and then turned his attention to Janey. "He, um, he told me not to screw it up the way he did."

"And how's he doing?" Janey asked Abby.

"So far, so good," Abby said, her inhibitions lessened by the champagne. "There's still time for him to mess up, though."

"True," Janey said. "He is a man."

"And he's fully equipped with ears, among other things," Adam muttered.

Abby giggled at their sibling banter.

"If you screw it up, I'll kill you myself," Janey said.

"I stand warned," Adam said.

In a matter of minutes, the guys had completely infiltrated their group. With the restaurant emptying of diners, Owen fetched a couple of guitars that he and Evan put to good use.

Abby couldn't recall an evening she'd enjoyed more than this one. Throughout the sing-along, Adam kept a warm hand on the inside of her thigh, reminding her of their plans for later. Maybe it was the champagne or perhaps it was the excellent company, but suddenly it didn't matter that he might be leaving or that she'd allowed herself to get more involved with him than she'd planned to. The only thing that mattered was right now. Tonight.

The rest would take care of itself. New Abby could handle a fling with a smart, sexy, sensitive man. If only Old Abby weren't so worried about her heart being broken once again when he left, everything would truly be perfect.

. . .

GRANT CAME AWAKE SLOWLY, disoriented by the dark and the deepest sleep he'd had in more than a week. As it occurred to him that he'd slept without the assistance of sleeping pills, he remembered what'd happened earlier. He'd totally lost it in front of his dad and brothers. Thinking of the scene he'd made and the way they'd come to his rescue brought new tears to his eyes.

Stephanie's hand landed on his chest. "You're awake."

"What time is it?"

"Almost midnight."

"Wow." The last he'd known, it had been around seven when Stephanie suggested he lie down for a while. "Have you been here the whole time?"

She kissed his shoulder. "Right here."

Wrapping his arm around her, he caressed her hair with his lips. "You missed girls' night out."

"There'll be others."

"You were looking forward to it."

"This was more important."

"I owe you an explanation for why I've been behaving so strangely since the accident."

"You don't owe me anything, Grant. If you want to talk to me, you know you always can. If you're talked out, that's fine, too."

"I should've told you before I told everyone else."

"There's no protocol for something like this. You talked about it when you were ready to. I'm glad your dad and your brothers were there for you."

"I lost it big-time. I think I scared the hell out of them."

"They were more scared when you were silent."

"How do you know? Have you all been talking about me?"

"Maybe a little." He could hear the smile in her voice as her hand moved in a soothing pattern on his chest and belly. "We've been very worried about you. How do you feel now that you've let it out?"

"A little better. It was hard to see Steve's mom and to hear he was her only child. I wish there was more I could've done for him."

"Do you realize that everyone considers you a hero for what you did for Dan?"

"I'm not a hero. Don't let them say that about me."

With her hand on his face, she turned him into her kiss. "Ask Dan if he thinks you're a hero. You did all you could, Grant. You did more than most people could've done. I try to imagine what it must've been like… To be separated from Mac and Evan, to not know what'd become of them while you're trying to keep yourself and Dan afloat in freezing cold water and dense fog for *hours*. You had to have been terrified and despondent and worried about me and your family and a million other things, yet you took care of Dan and saved his life as well as your own. If that's not the definition of a hero, I don't know what is."

Touched by her kind words, Grant deeply resented the tears that came despite his desperate desire to make them stop. "I couldn't help Steve."

"I know, but there's a very good chance that Steve was killed on impact."

"We'll never know that for sure."

"No, but you have to find a way to live with what happened. You did the best you could in unimaginable circumstances. No one blames you, not even Steve's mother. You have to find a way to forgive yourself."

"I'm trying." He used the back of his hand to brush the tears off his face.

Stephanie shifted onto his chest, pushed his hand away and finished the job, peppering his face and lips with soft, sweet kisses. "I love you, and I'm so proud of what you did out there. I'm choosing to focus on what you were able to do, not what you couldn't. I wish you'd try to do that, too."

"I will. I'll try." He tightened his arms around her, drawing strength from her love. "Thanks."

"For what, babe?"

"For staying home with me tonight, for standing by me this last week, for not giving up on me when I would've given up on myself."

"I'll never give up on you. I love you too much. Way too much."

"Not as much as I love you."

"Want to bet?"

"I'd bet on you any day, baby."

"I bet on us. There's nothing we can't handle."

He would do his best to get past what'd happened. He would try to stop thinking about the awful choice he'd been forced to make. He would focus on what he had rather than what had been lost. As long as he had Stephanie by his side and in his arms, he was confident he'd get there eventually.

It was after one the next morning when the party at the Surf finally broke up. Fortunately, Abby had traded champagne for water hours ago. Other than a few curious looks, no one had made much of her sitting close to Adam all night, which had been a relief. No one really seemed to care that they were spending time together.

With his hand on her lower back, he escorted her across the street to the Beachcomber.

"What's this about you renting my sister's place?" he asked.

"She's decided to take a year off from vet school after the baby comes."

"So I heard."

"They need a bigger place for the baby. When she said she'd be renting her place, I snapped it up."

"I love her house. It'd be perfect for you."

Her heart ached at the reminder that she'd be back to living alone, no closer to her one-time goal of being a wife and mother. That was okay, she told herself as they took the stairs to the third floor. She'd make a happy, productive life for herself, and if she fell in love again someday, it would be with someone who wanted her more than he wanted his next breath. Being with her friends tonight, she'd seen that kind of love in action and wanted nothing less than what she'd seen among the other happy couples.

"What're you thinking about?" Adam asked as he watched her withdraw her key card from her bra.

"You ask me that a lot, you know."

He leaned forward to kiss her forehead. "It's because I genuinely want to know what's going on in there."

She smiled at him, amazed once again at how attentive he was. "I was thinking about how happy everyone seems to be. Mac and Maddie, Luke and Syd, Tiffany and Blaine, Evan and Grace, Laura and Owen, Janey and Joe... Engagements and babies... They've all found the one they were meant to be with."

"I confess to feeling a twinge of envy over that tonight."

She opened the door and went in ahead of him. "Really?" she asked, turning to him.

"They've got it all figured out. They know who they're going to spend forever with. It must be nice to have all the questions answered so definitively."

"They're lucky to have that."

He put his arms around her. "I want that," he said. "I want the answers to the questions."

"Despite my statements to the contrary on the ferry the other day, I suppose I do, too."

"Have you considered that this, right here, might be the answer for both of us?"

Abby stared up at him, amazed again.

"I'm sorry," he said when she didn't reply. "I shouldn't have said that."

"No, I mean yes. Yes, I've considered it."

"You have. Really?"

She nodded. "I've let myself entertain a few fantasies in which you play the starring role."

He took her hand and sat on the bed, tugging lightly to bring her down next to him. "Tell me about them."

"I can't. You'll think I'm crazy. I left Cal only a few days ago. I've got no business having fantasies about you."

"Tell me anyway."

"It's embarrassing."

"After the stuff we've done together, you're still embarrassed around me?"

"This feels more intimate somehow."

He caressed her face, his touch setting off a riot of sensation that traveled to all her pleasure points. "Before you tell me, I have a confession that might make you never speak to me again."

She couldn't imagine never speaking to him again. "What's that?"

"When I found you on the beach last night? It was because I programmed your phone so I could find you. I felt guilty about it the minute I did it, and I felt worse when I actually used it."

"I don't understand why you would do that."

"Because I was worried about you. I didn't want some dickhead like that guy in the bar taking advantage of you. Selfishly, I wanted you all to myself. I'm sorry. Are you mad?"

"I want to be."

"My intentions were good even if I went about it the wrong way. I wanted to make sure you'd be safe. That's all. I promise."

She handed him her phone. "Turn off whatever you did."

Adam took the phone from her, clicked around in the settings and handed it back to her. "Sorry."

"Don't use your mad techno skills on me again. You got me?"

"Yes, ma'am."

"Could I ask you something that might make you mad?"

"What's that?"

"What happened with Grant today?"

"That doesn't make me mad." He relayed the story of what had happened to Grant after the accident.

By the time he was done, Abby had her hand over her mouth as she blinked back tears. "Poor Grant. What an awful thing. Is he okay?" She shook her head. "That's a stupid question. Of course he isn't okay."

"He will be. In time. We'll all see to that."

"Is it okay that I asked about him?"

"It's fine, honey." He kissed her cheek and then her lips. "Now, you mentioned some fantasies that involve me... I want to hear about them."

"I'd feel foolish to speak of things that'll never happen."

"Haven't I shown you that it's never foolish to ask for what you want?"

"That might work in bed. It's not as cut and dried in real life."

"It can be. There's nothing you could say that would make me think you were foolish." He corralled her hair into a ponytail that he held with one hand. With her hair out of his way, he bent to kiss her neck, leaving a trail of fire in his wake. "Tell me. I really want to know."

It was hard to form a reasonable thought with what he was doing to her neck. "I had this thought about running my new store while you served as the island's resident computer geek. See what I mean about it being foolish? Everyone knows you have to go back to New York at some point. You'll have to get back to your real life."

"What if that's not my real life. What if this is? What if you are?"

"Don't say those things. You don't mean that."

"How do you know? The last few days I've spent with you have been the best I've ever spent with anyone. Do you know what I adore about you?"

His use of the word "adore" killed her. "What?"

"That I can be totally myself with you. I don't feel the need to put on an act so I can be what you want. It seems you like me exactly the way I am."

"I do. How could I not like you? You're..."

"What am I?"

"You're amazing." Was there any other single word that could better describe him? Not that she could think of.

"Abby..." Their lips came together in sweet communion. His hands on her face made her feel safe, treasured, adored. The kiss turned hot and potent when he wrapped his arm around her, as if he needed to be closer to her.

Abby returned his embrace and let out a sigh of completion when he urged her to lie back on the bed. Wrapped up in his arms, Abby allowed herself to be swept away by the possibility that he might be the answer to all her questions. Wouldn't that be lovely? Wouldn't it be wonderful to feel this way all the time?

He drew back from her, gazing at her intently. "I want to make love to you. I want to show you what might be possible."

"I'm afraid."

"Of what, honey?"

"Of how you make me feel, of what will happen when you go, or what will happen if you stay..."

"Let's live the fantasy. For one night, let's pretend it's exactly the way you imagined it."

She looked up at him, so handsome and dear to her, and decided to take a gamble. "Okay."

CHAPTER 19

*A*t the look of utter trust she directed his way, Adam's chest tightened with emotions that hit him one after the other— protectiveness, tenderness and fierce longing. Even after what he'd recently been through with Sasha, he had no hesitation about giving himself over to Abby's keeping. Somehow he understood that he'd be safe with her in a way he'd never been with Sasha. He knew that now.

It had taken only a few days with Abby to show him there might be something far better waiting for him. And now he wanted to share everything with her, beginning with this one night steeped in a fantasy that was quickly becoming reality. During the hours he'd spent away from her, he'd thought of little else beyond getting back to her. Images of her had tormented his mind, making it impossible to concentrate on the poker game or the conversation or anything other than her.

After what they'd all been through with Grant earlier, his brothers had been more subdued than usual, too, which was probably the only thing that had saved him from being grilled by them about his obvious distraction.

He'd met a lot of women in his life, spent time with them, slept with more of them than he probably should have. Sasha had been his third significant relationship, but none of those three women had touched him in years together the way Abby had in the last few days.

One thing had become very clear to him—this was way more than a rebound.

She was different. She was *special.* She was everything he hadn't realized he wanted until he was holding her in his arms and she was looking up at him with those big trusting eyes that seemed to see all the way inside him. And she apparently liked what she saw, which made her that much more attractive to him.

All at once it was vitally important that he have a real chance with her. He wanted to find out what they might have together beyond the casual fling they'd begun with. He wanted to show her what she'd come to mean to him, and the best way he could do that was to focus all his attention on her. He needed to convince her that he could be what she needed, both in bed and out.

With that in mind, he helped her out of her clothes, taking his time to worship each bit of soft skin as it was revealed to him. When she was down to a lavender lace bra and panties, he said, "Keep your eyes closed. Don't think. Just feel."

"I'm trying."

As he removed his own clothes, he wondered if she realized she was trembling. "I want you totally relaxed." Adam let his hands do the talking for him, massaging the tension from her body as he moved from her shoulders down her arms, from her ribs to her hips, from thighs to feet.

Her small sighs and the loosening of muscles under his hands were the only indication he had that his efforts were having the desired effect.

"Turn over," he said.

She opened her eyes, gave him a wary look and then turned.

When she was settled, he started again with her shoulders, kneading her tense muscles until they were pliable before moving down. At the midpoint of her back, he unhooked her bra and let it fall open. It became a herculean effort to not fixate on the sight of the thong disappearing between supple cheeks. But he refused to rush this, so he took his time, working on her back until every muscle was relaxed.

He moved farther down on the bed, straddling her thighs as his hands coasted over her bottom, making her tense at first.

"Relax," he said. "No thinking. Just feeling."

"Adam…"

"Shhh. Feel." He squeezed for emphasis and smiled when she tensed up again before relaxing her muscles. "That's it." He slid his fingertips lightly over her bottom, letting one of them follow the line of the thong. That drew a sharp inhale from her. "Easy, honey. Relax. Let me touch you."

"Not *there*."

"Everywhere." He leaned forward to kiss her neck as his finger delved deeper, pressing against pleasure points until she wriggled under him, straining for more. Leaving her wanting, he withdrew and hooked his fingers into the waistband of the panties, dragging them halfway down, until the elastic was snug against the slope of her bottom. The sight was so erotic, he had to look away for a minute or risk embarrassing himself.

The guttural moan that came from her was even more erotic as was the scent of her arousal. Even though he knew it wouldn't help to relax her, he couldn't resist moving so he could kiss his way down her back, stopping at her panties. Touching his tongue to the tender skin just above the waistband, he drew a line right up the middle and then came down the other side, making her gasp.

"*Adam…*"

"Feel good?"

"So good. I didn't know…"

"You didn't know you liked to have your bottom kissed?"

She dropped her head to the pillow, groaning. "Do you have to say it like that?"

Laughing at her dismay, he said, "Yes, because it turns you on. Knowing what you like turns me on, too."

"It does?"

"Uh-huh." He tugged on her hips. "Lift up on your knees."

"I don't think—"

"You're not thinking, remember?"

Sighing, she did as he asked.

He arranged her so her bottom was raised and her chest pressed to the bed. She'd wrapped her arms around a pillow, almost as if she needed something to hang on to. "That's it," he whispered, blowing lightly on her bottom and watching as goose bumps formed on her skin. The reaction pleased him. Everything about her pleased him. He took advantage of her new position to kiss and lick and nibble on her cheeks until she was writhing and pressing back, looking for more.

Adam added his fingers to the mix, sliding them over the silky damp fabric between her legs, making teasing passes over her clit until she was nearly begging him.

That was his cue to move things along. He reached for the condom he'd left on the bedside table and put it on quickly before he eased her panties slowly down her trembling legs. When she wasn't expecting it, he leaned forward and dragged his tongue in a half circle, making her scream.

He loved making her scream, he realized as he did it again, leaving her teetering on the verge of release when he turned her onto her back. Adam pushed her hair out of her face as she reached for him, seeming almost desperate.

"Not quite yet, honey."

"Oh God, please. I can't take it."

"Yes, you can." He cupped her breasts and drew one nipple and then the other into his mouth, sucking and biting and teasing as her hips rose seeking him. Releasing one breast, he ran his hand down her belly to cup her, urging her legs apart as he found her slick and ready. He focused on the tight bead that throbbed under his fingers as he sucked hard on her nipple, watching her expressive face for the reactions he wanted.

"That's it," he whispered. "Come for me, Abby."

He kept up the dual assault until the orgasm overtook her. Adam kept his fingers pressed against her as he pushed into her a little at a time rather than all at once, which he would've preferred at this point.

Her muscles squeezed him intimately, but didn't try to force him out. Encouraged, he gave her more. He wanted so badly to know if it felt good, but he was afraid to ask, afraid to jar her out of the moment to remind her that this act had been a problem for her in the past. So he let his body speak for him and took his signals to proceed from her breathy sighs and throaty moans.

He'd given this a lot of thought since she told him about her past troubles, and he'd come to the conclusion that he had to keep her so aroused and engaged that there wouldn't be an opportunity for her fears to take hold and sabotage it for her. So he pressed against her core with his fingers and continued to tease and torment her breasts with his lips and teeth as he worked his way into her in slow steady increments.

Only when he was fully embedded did he nuzzle her neck and kiss her. "Hey," he whispered against her lips.

Her arms encircled his neck as she opened her mouth to admit his tongue.

Adam flexed his hips, and watched her eyes fly open in surprise. That was when he knew he'd succeeded in overwhelming her senses so completely she hadn't thought to be nervous about taking him in.

And she was just now realizing it.

"Good?"

"God, yes, very good."

"That's what I want to hear."

"Adam... How did you..."

"Let's talk about it later. I'm a little busy right now." He gathered her into his arms and held on tight as he took them both on an amazing ride. He kept her on the knife-edge of arousal the entire time so her brain wouldn't take over and ruin it for her. Because of their earlier encounters, he knew the signs of her impending climax and tried to be patient. He refused to let himself go until she'd gotten there first.

With his lips close to her ear, he whispered, "Don't think, just feel. It's so good. So hot." As he spoke, his fingers found her clit, caressing and coaxing. Her thighs began to quiver against his hips, so he picked up the pace, thrusting into her harder than he had before.

"Don't stop," she said, raising her hips to match the rhythm he set.

"I won't stop."

"Adam..."

"Let it happen, honey. I'm right here with you, and you feel so good. We've got all night. I'm not going anywhere. I'm all yours."

His words more than his actions seemed to break her. She lifted off, pressing against him urgently. Her nails scored his back, which nearly undid him.

"Yes," he whispered, giving her the hard, steady strokes she seemed to like best. "Just like that."

Afterward, she trembled in his arms as he pressed kisses to anywhere he could reach before reclaiming her mouth.

When he filled her again, she broke the kiss. "You didn't..."

"Not yet. I want another one from you first."

She whimpered as she looked up at him, her face flushed and her lips swollen from his kisses. "You have no idea how lucky you were to get that one."

"It wasn't luck," he said with a cocky grin. He hooked his arms under her legs and moved them farther apart, which sent him deeper.

Judging from her gasp, he'd found the spot he was looking for and kept up the deep strokes until she came again.

"So beautiful," he said, staring down into her eyes when he finally took his own pleasure, although pleasure wasn't a good enough word to describe it. It was bliss, ecstasy and, in many ways, deliverance from a past that hadn't included feelings like those she aroused in him.

He released her legs but couldn't bring himself to disengage from her, not as long as her internal muscles continued to ripple with after-shocks that had him hard again in record time. Still lodged deep within her, he worked a hand under her to squeeze her bottom. "How do you feel?" he asked, worried that he'd been too rough.

"I...I don't know."

He raised his head from her shoulder so he could see her face. "I didn't hurt you, did I?"

"No, God, no... It was... I don't understand."

"What don't you understand, honey?"

"I've had all these problems with sex, but with you... I didn't know it could be like that. I felt like I was someone else."

"You're the same beautiful, sexy woman you've always been—the same beautiful, sexy woman who knows what she needs in bed and finally told someone. You gave me the keys, baby." He kissed her once, twice and then a third time because the first two were so satisfying. "You told me what to do, and I did it. That's all it was."

"You say that like it was no big deal, when it was a huge deal for me."

"It was for me, too. I love the way you feel, so hot and so sweet at the same time. You make me crazy."

She curled her legs around his, drawing him deeper into her. "Will you do it again?"

Adam laughed, delighted by her. "As many times as you can handle."

"I've got a lot of fake orgasms to make up for."

"Good thing we've got all night."

"I think we're going to need it."

FEELING like she'd just been admitted to a secret club where all the answers to her most vexing questions were housed, Abby gorged on him. They did it with her on top, and then he took her from behind and blew her mind all over again. She was officially addicted to sex with Adam McCarthy.

"You're a fucking god," she declared at four a.m. when they finally collapsed on the bed, seven orgasms later.

"Excellent swearing." His chest heaved from the effort to draw air.

Abby should've been utterly exhausted, but she was exhilarated instead. She caressed his chest and belly, where his penis lay spent. "I think we broke it," she said, studying him with puckered lips that amused him.

"You'd better think of some way to fix it if you want more."

She had an idea of what fixing it might require, another act she'd never particularly cared for in the past. But after all he'd given her, she was willing to try for his sake.

Rising to her knees, Abby began with kisses to his belly, giving special attention to each of the well-defined muscles that rippled in response. She moved down to discover he was fully onboard with her mission. "That didn't take much effort on my part."

"He's not completely convinced, so you might want to make sure he's here to stay."

She smiled as she took him in hand, stroking him gently, trying to learn what he liked—and what he didn't. There seemed to be much more of the former than the latter. "I'm not very good at this."

"You're holding the evidence to the contrary."

"What do you like?"

"Anything you want to do. I promise I'll like it."

"Anything?"

"Use your imagination."

"How's this?" Abby bent down to run her tongue over the tip, which drew a sharp inhale from him.

"Very good. Do it again."

She did it a second time, adding a bit of suction.

When he fisted a handful of her hair, she let him guide her down, taking him into her mouth. "Use your tongue. Yes, *yes*, like that. Abby... How can you say you're not good at this?"

Encouraged by his response, she took him deeper the next time.

"Stop." He tugged gently on her hair. "Stop."

She looked up at him. "Did I do it wrong?"

"No." Adam sat up and reached for another condom and then for her. "You did it perfectly right. So right that I'm about to explode— again." He tucked her hair behind her ear. "Come here."

"I'm here."

"Closer."

Abby straddled his lap. "Is this close enough?"

"Almost." With his hands cupping her bottom, he raised her and brought her down on his length.

"Is this close enough?" she asked.

"Not quite." His lips hovered close to hers, and his chest hair tickled her breasts as she took him in. "Now wrap your arms and legs around me. That's it. Tighter. Mmm. Perfect. Finally close enough."

Abby took advantage of the opportunity to comb her fingers through his thick dark hair. "I love your hair."

"I love this spot on your neck," he said, placing a kiss that made her sigh. "You do that every time I kiss you there."

"Do what?"

"Sigh with pleasure—at least I hope it's pleasure."

"It is." She'd never known such pleasure. Sex without anxiety was all new to her, and she discovered she quite liked it. "So much pleasure, I'm drunk on it."

"So much better than tequila, huh?"

"Way better."

"Kiss me."

Happy to do as he asked, Abby brought her lips down on his and kept them there as he picked up the pace. When he reached down to coax another orgasm from her, she tore her lips free and held on tight to him. As she climbed toward release, she couldn't believe the way he seemed to always know what she needed. Lost in a sea of overwhelming pleasure, Abby was barely aware of him turning them so he was on top as he drove them to the finish line, which they reached together in a moment of utter harmony.

They remained locked together for a long time afterward. Abby had never felt closer or more in tune with another human being. Here was what she'd always wanted and had begun to fear she'd never find. Once again, however, she'd ended up with a man whose home and life were elsewhere. She wouldn't think about that until she had to, she decided as he lay heavy and warm on top of her. For now, for as long as they had together, she'd enjoy every minute and then let him go when the time came.

"I can feel you thinking again."

"How can you feel someone thinking?"

"You get all tense, and your lips get tight." He traced a finger over her mouth to make his point. "What're you thinking about?"

"Nothing, really."

"Don't start lying to me now, Abs. Not when you've been so honest about everything else."

His insight only made him more appealing, if that was possible. "I wish things were different. That's all."

"What things?"

"I wish you were planning to stay here, for one thing."

"How do you know I'm not?"

"Maddie said something tonight about you going back to New York to deal with your company. That was news to me."

"Sorry you had to hear it that way. Nothing has happened yet beyond asking my lawyer to get involved. I expect it to drag on for months, which is why I didn't say anything. There's nothing to say until something happens."

"What'll you do if you win?"

His hand moved in a soft caress on her back. "Hard to say until it happens. If it happens."

"What made you decide to fight?"

"I got past the shock of it all and finally got mad. When I called my lawyer, he was already mad on my behalf and had only been waiting for my call to press forward. He says we have a very strong case." Adam shrugged. "I'm trying not to think about it until I hear more from him." He raised his head from her chest and kissed her. "I'm sorry you heard it from someone other than me."

"It's okay. I understand why you wouldn't want to talk about it."

"In the meantime," he said, kissing her, "I'm right where I want to be."

"So am I."

When he started to withdraw from her, Abby stopped him. "Stay." She wanted him to stay forever but would never ask that of him. She told herself this was enough. If it was all they ever had, it would be enough. But even as she had the thought, she knew it wasn't true.

ADAM WOKE to sun streaming in the window and Abby warm and naked in his arms, her legs wrapped up in his. Since he couldn't move without disturbing her, he stayed still and enjoyed the peaceful quiet of the morning after a night he wouldn't soon forget. The sex had been incredible. But more incredible had been the emotion, the intimacy and the connection he'd experienced with her.

Now that he knew what he'd been missing with Sasha, he couldn't believe he'd stayed with her as long as he had. He was more convinced than ever that she'd done him a huge favor by screwing him over—in more ways than one.

If he were being honest, it was also a huge relief to no longer have the weight of responsibility for the company weighing on him every minute of every day. For many, many years, he'd loved the work, the rat race and the thrill of watching the company he'd built from nothing find success unlike anything he could've dreamed of at the beginning. But after nearly two weeks away, it was a major revelation to realize he didn't miss it—at all.

With his mind and body fully relaxed and sated from the best sex of his life, Adam dozed off again, waking to his ringing phone sometime later. After years of running for ringing phones, he ignored it because he could. When it rang again about five minutes later, he thought about getting up to find it but couldn't seem to work up the effort it would take. The third time it rang, Abby stirred.

"Is that your phone?"

"Yeah. Third time in fifteen minutes. I'd better get it." By the time he disentangled from her, he'd begun to worry about his family as he pulled the phone from the pocket of his jeans. He glanced at the caller ID and saw his lawyer's name. "Hey, Rick. What's up?"

"Glad you finally answered."

"Sorry, I was sleeping in."

"Must be nice."

He glanced at Abby in the bed, eyes closed, lips plump and swollen from passion and dark hair spread out on the pillow. "It's very nice."

"We've had a somewhat major development in your case."

Hoping Abby would go back to sleep, Adam took the phone into the bathroom and closed the door. "What's that?"

"Sasha resigned last night. The board has reached out to you with a letter of apology and an invitation for you to return as CEO. They've set a meeting for four o'clock today, and they'd like you to be there. This is moving very quickly, Adam. We've got them right where we want them, and this is your chance to return on your own terms. I got the sense that they're prepared to move forward with other management if you're not interested."

Adam listened to Rick and tried to absorb it all. Sasha had left. The company was his for the taking if he wanted it. Did he want it?

"If you don't wish to return, and part of me wouldn't blame you if you didn't, they still have to buy you out, and they know it. So the ball is totally in your court."

The events of the last two weeks raced through his mind like a movie on fast forward—Sasha's betrayal, the loss of his company, the accident that had nearly claimed the lives of his brothers, meeting up with Abby on the ferry and the time they'd spent together since then, culminating in a night of incredible passion.

He thought about how he'd started CSI in his living room with a friend who'd taken a better offer soon after. Adam had moved forward alone and turned the company into a multimillion-dollar enterprise through years of hard work and dedication. Then he recalled how it had been taken from him in the course of one unbelievable afternoon.

"Adam? How do you wish to proceed?"

Images from the night with Abby flashed through his mind like an erotic movie, muddling his brain and complicating what would've been an easy decision only a few days ago.

And then, in a moment of utter clarity, Adam knew exactly what he needed to do. It was so obvious it made him laugh to think of how foolish he'd been to think there was anything else he could do.

"Let them know I'll see them at four."

"I'll meet you there."

With his decision made, Adam took a shower and got dressed. When he was ready to go, he sat on the bed and ran a hand from Abby's shoulder, down her arm to grasp her hand. He leaned in to kiss her cheek and then her lips.

She came awake slowly, her eyes fluttering open. When she saw him looking down at her, she smiled. That warm, sweet smile confirmed that he was doing the right thing. "You're all dressed."

"I have to go to New York for a meeting about the company later today."

Her smile faded, and her brows furrowed. "Has something happened?"

"Apparently, Sasha has resigned and the board has invited me to return on whatever terms I set forth."

"That's amazing, Adam. I hope you plan to make them grovel a bit."

"Of course I will."

"I'm happy for you."

With his hands flat on either side of her, he gave her a lingering kiss. "Want to come with me?"

"I wish I could, but Laura is counting on me to get the store open. Janey and Joe are looking at one of Ned's places today, so I'll hopefully be moving into their current house soon. I've got to get my stuff out of my parents' basement. Lots to do here."

"I know." He kissed her again. "I'll call you."

"No," she said. "Don't call. Let's not make promises we can't keep. It was lovely. I enjoyed every minute we spent together, but let's not make it into something it's not. You've got your life in the city. My life is here, and I just can't do another long-distance relationship. Not even for you."

"Abby—"

She touched her fingers to his lips. "Please. Don't say it. Go back to your life. I'll be okay. I promise."

"Don't sleep with strangers," he said with a teasing grin that didn't match the dismay he felt at leaving her.

"I won't. You've ruined me for casual sex."

"That was my goal."

She reached for him, and he went willingly into her sweet embrace.

His lips brushed against her neck, making her tremble. "Don't let anyone ever try to convince you that you aren't perfect exactly the way you are."

"Adam," she said with a sigh.

He held her for a long time, longer than he'd intended to. "I'll be back."

She shook her head. "No promises."

He cupped her face and kissed her one last time. "Take care."

"You, too. Fight for what's yours."

"I fully intend to."

As THE DOOR clicked shut behind him, Abby put both hands over her mouth to muffle her sobs. She wanted to chase after him, to beg him not to go, to tell him she loved him. But she'd done all that before and couldn't do it again, even if she already loved him more than she'd ever loved Cal or Grant.

Everything was different with him. It had taken only a few days to know that for certain. From that very first encounter on the ferry, it had been different. *He* had been different.

"God, you're such an idiot," she whispered through her tears. "All your declarations that you're done with men, and you let *this* happen? How did you manage to make everything worse in only *three* days?"

If there were a prize for world-class losers in love, Abby would have to be a contender for first place.

Though her inclination was to stay in bed all day and lick her wounds, she dragged herself into the shower. Every inch of her body ached from the night of exquisite passion. As the hot water pounded down on her, she let the tears flow freely, determined to get them out now and then get on with it.

She'd done enough crying over men for one lifetime. She'd never forget the time she'd spent with Adam, but it was over now, and she would survive. Somehow, someway, she'd get through this the way she'd gotten through all the other setbacks. She spent extra time on her makeup to cover the damage left by a mostly sleepless night as well as the ravages of tears and had just finished drying her hair when a knock sounded at her door.

She resented the burst of excitement of wondering if he might've come back. When she opened the door, she found Janey rather than Adam in the hallway and tried to mask her disappointment.

"Come in."

Red-faced and breathing hard after hauling her pregnant self up the three flights to Abby's room, Janey sat on the edge of the rumpled bed. "We didn't get a chance last night to talk about you and Adam."

The words struck Abby like a shot to the heart. There was no her and Adam. Not anymore. "There's nothing to tell." Abby kept her tone light to hide the heaviness weighing on her heart. "We got tattoos, hung out, had some fun. He's on his way to the city today. Back to work where he belongs."

"*My* brother Adam got a *tattoo?*"

"A map of Gansett on his arm."

"Where's yours?"

Abby held out her leg for Janey to inspect.

"I love that. It's gorgeous."

Pleased by her friend's response, Abby said, "I love it, too."

"Did it hurt?"

"Like a mother-you-know-what." Swearing would never, ever come naturally to her, no matter how hard she tried.

"I hadn't heard he was leaving."

"Apparently, he didn't know either until he got a call this morning about a meeting this afternoon."

"You've been crying."

"Maybe a little, but I'm okay. Did you and Joe look at the house?"

Janey nodded. "Ned had us over there first thing. We loved it. It's perfect. It even has a fenced-in yard for the puppies."

Relieved that Janey hadn't pursued the subject of Adam any further, Abby said, "Where is it?"

"About a mile from Mac and Maddie's. That was definitely a selling point."

"So you're going to buy it?"

"I think we will. Why rent when we'll need a permanent residence here eventually?"

"True."

"My place is all yours at the end of the month."

"That soon?"

Janey rested her hand on the baby bump. "We don't have much time to waste if we want to be settled by the time Junior makes his or her debut."

"Can't blame you. I'll help you move."

"I won't say no to that." Janey held out a hand to her. "Why do I feel like there's something you're not telling me?"

Abby took her hand and sat next to Janey on the bed. "There's nothing to tell. Honest."

Janey gave her the best hug she could with the baby in the way. "I'm so happy to have you home again, but I'm sorry about the circumstances."

Abby closed her eyes and absorbed the comfort that only an old friend could offer. "I'm very happy to be here." That would be true if it was the last thing Abby ever did.

OVER THE NEXT FEW WEEKS, Abby threw herself into getting the store open in time for the start of the season. She helped Maddie and Laura plan a baby shower for Janey and Joe, and spent time with her parents, who had plenty to say about the tattoo.

Abby let them go on about the dangers of needles and the permanence of tattoos, but every time she looked at the pretty purple flower she felt proud of herself for trying something new. The tattoo served as a permanent reminder of a lovely few days when everything had felt possible again.

By the time she moved into Janey's house on the first of June, her parents had thankfully run out of things to say about the tattoo. They helped her move and unpack boxes she'd left at their house when she went to Texas. She'd expected to open those boxes again after she and Cal were married and she sent for her things at home.

Her parents seemed to recognize that Abby was going through a difficult time and took a break from asking questions about her plans. As far as they knew, she was mourning her breakup with Cal, and she said nothing to disabuse them of that notion. She was grateful for their help and their company, and left it at that.

On the first night in her new little house, she was in bed when her phone chimed with a text just after midnight.

You said I couldn't call. You never said I couldn't text. I want you to know I miss you, and there isn't any other way to tell you.

Abby smiled as she read the text, her heart racing with excitement. The phone chimed again.

I hope you're behaving and staying out of the bars.

Don't you dare write back to me, do you hear? If you do, that might mean we're having some sort of long-distance relationship...

...and you don't do those anymore. So I will say goodnight. Sleep tight. And did I mention I miss you?

By the time the flurry of texts stopped coming, Abby was laughing and crying and smiling—and absolutely dying to write back. She wanted to ask how things were going with his business. She wanted to know if he'd been reinstated or if he was still fighting. She wanted to know everything that had happened since she last saw him and to tell him everything that had happened to her.

But she didn't write back. She'd set the rules and she had to stick with them or risk losing more than her heart this time around. At times, it felt as if her very sanity was at stake. So she didn't write back. Rather, she read and reread the texts he'd sent at least a hundred times before she finally fell asleep.

. . .

317

ABBY WORKED long hours at the store getting ready for the opening and took on a part-time job helping Laura at the registration desk. She went out of her way to stay busy so she wouldn't have time to think about Adam, except for late at night when the day was done and she had nothing but time to think about every minute they'd spent together and indulge in yet another reread of the texts he'd sent more than a week ago now.

Laura came down the stairs to relieve Abby after a three-hour shift at the front desk. "Here I come. Sorry I'm late. Holden was fussy and didn't feel like eating on my schedule."

"No problem," Abby said. "I have nowhere to be tonight."

"Thanks for rolling with my crazy schedule."

"It's been fun helping out." Abby gathered up her purse and backpack full of paperwork related to the store. She was about to leave when the need to ask the burning question that kept her awake at night stopped her from moving forward.

"Is everything okay?" Laura asked, tuning into Abby's hesitation.

"Could I ask you something?"

"Sure. Anything you want."

"Have you heard whether Adam was able to regain control of his company?"

Laura's eyes went wide. "*You* haven't heard?"

Abby shook her head. "I haven't spoken to him since he left."

"I thought you two…"

"We were. Past tense. I can't do the long-distance thing again. I just can't."

"I can see why you feel that way. From what I heard from my Aunt Linda, the ex-girlfriend is out, and the board of directors reinstated Adam. He got the company back."

"That's wonderful," Abby said sincerely, even though her heart was breaking. He'd be staying in the city where he belonged. It was a good thing she'd ended things with him when he left. In light of this development, that had been the right thing to do.

"If you think it's wonderful, why do you look so sad?"

Abby forced a smile as she shrugged. "It was fun while it lasted."

"Aww, honey." Laura hugged her. "I'm sorry it didn't work out."

Abby returned the embrace. "You'd think I'd be used to things not working out by now." Nothing that came before had hurt as much as this did. "I'll see you in the morning."

"Will you be okay?" Laura asked.

"I'm like a cat. I always land on my feet."

The analogy made Laura laugh as she waved to Abby. Outside, the soft spring night seemed to almost mock her misery with its fragrance and beauty and the promise of lovely warm days to come.

She took her time walking home, grilled some salmon for dinner and ate in front of the TV. After dinner, she took a bath and was immersed in bubbles when her phone chimed with a text. As she lunged for it, water sloshed over the sides of the tub. She had the fore-thought to at least dry her hand before she grabbed the phone.

I'm thinking about how you looked floating naked in the moonlight, and I'm hard as a rock.

I dream about you every night. I can smell you and taste you and then I wake up alone, and I'm crushed. Devastated. Demolished.

Don't do it. Don't write back. Not unless you mean to never stop writing back. Do. Not. Do. It.

By the time Abby absorbed his words, a puddle had formed around her feet and it took every ounce of willpower she could muster not to write back. Maybe if she hadn't known he got back his company she could take the risk. But now that she knew he planned to stay in the city, she couldn't. She just couldn't get any more involved with him than she already was.

She grabbed a towel, her movements jerky as she wrapped it around herself. Torn by what she wanted more than the next breath and what she knew was best for her, Abby sat on her bed and stared at the phone for a long time, hoping to find the wherewithal to protect her battered heart from more agony.

And then it chimed again, making her startle with surprise and elation.

I forgot to tell you. In my dreams, your dark hair is spread out on the pillow and we're making love like we did that last night. I've relived that night over and over and over again.

I'll never forget that night. I'll never forget any of it. I have a tattoo to remind me of you every time I look at it. Mine is starting to heal. I hope yours are, too.

Don't write back. Unless, of course, you think about me as much as I think about you... Unless you might have the fortitude for one more long-distance relationship... I'll understand if you don't. But I'll always wish you did.

Abby never slept that night. As the hours wore on, her resolve began to weaken and the need to write back became nearly desperate. When her alarm went off at seven, she hit snooze four times before she dragged herself out of bed and into the bathroom where she was confronted with the mess she'd made the night before.

Her heart was heavy as she went through the motions of showering, telling herself over and over again that she was doing the right thing. Her life was here. His was there. And as much as she loved him, she couldn't do the long-distance dance again. Not even for him.

Emerging from the shower, she pushed through the hair drying and straightening ritual, even though exhaustion clung to her every movement. In the time it took to dry her hair, she decided that if he texted again, she'd either have to write back or change her phone number.

THE STORE OPENED with much fanfare the first Saturday in June. It had come together exactly as Abby had hoped, part practical, part whimsical and very much in keeping with the tradition of Abby's Attic. Practically everyone she'd ever known on the island came in that first day to welcome her back, including Grant and Stephanie.

They greeted her with warm hugs.

"Congratulations," he said while Stephanie poked around the store. "It's even better than the original."

Abby thought so, too, but he was the first to say it out loud, which she appreciated. "Thank you. It's nice to be back in business. How've you been?"

"Better."

"Glad to hear it."

"I'm sorry things didn't work out with Cal, but it's nice to have you back on the island."

"There's no place like home."

His smile reminded her of old times, many of them good times. "Ain't it the truth?"

A customer in need of assistance interrupted them. "Excuse me," Abby said. "Duty calls."

He left with Stephanie a few minutes later, giving her a wave and a thumbs-up on the way out. It had been nice to see him and to feel nothing more than warm friendship toward him.

Abby spent the rest of the day on her feet with no time to think of anything other than work and customers and inventory. It was just like old times, and it was exactly what she needed.

She hired a high school girl to work some weekend afternoons in the store, which was how she was able to break free for Janey and Joe's shower at Mac and Maddie's house two Saturdays after the store opened.

The guys had apparently done some significant grumbling about having to attend a baby shower, but Maddie had made the case that the baby was Joe's, too, so why should he be left out? And if he had to be there, he needed reinforcements.

Abby suspected Joe would've been happy to leave the shower to Janey and the women, but he knew better than to say so. As one of the hostesses, Abby helped Maddie and Laura with the food and drinks, and then sat next to Janey to record who each gift was from so Janey could write thank-you notes.

With the exception of Joe, who sat dutifully next to his wife as she opened their gifts, the guys retreated to the kitchen, where Mac had stashed a case of cold beer. They occasionally shouted ball-busting words of encouragement to Joe, who replied with a raised middle finger each time.

"Joseph," his mother said sternly after the third such incident sent the guys into hysterics, "you need to set a better example for your child."

The comment earned her a middle finger from her son, which made everyone laugh—no one more so than Carolina.

Abby's laughter died on her lips when Adam strolled in through the sliding door from the deck, wearing a sharp navy pinstripe suit with a light blue dress shirt that was open at his throat.

His mother jumped up to greet him with a hug. "Adam! I thought you weren't going to make it."

He returned his mother's hug, but over her shoulder, he sought out Abby. "I was able to get free sooner than expected. Slim flew me over."

"We're so happy you could make it," Janey said, waddling over to hug her brother.

He kissed her cheek. "Wouldn't have missed it, brat."

Since it was a complete surprise to her that he was due home, Abby's entire body felt like it was on fire as he trained his intense gaze on her. It was all she could do to keep track of the gifts as Janey opened them when she wanted to run to him and hug him and kiss him and tell him how much she'd missed him.

And she'd missed everything about him. The sound of his voice, the scent of his cologne, the brush of his whiskers against her cheek, the soft slide of his lips, the rippled muscles on his belly—

"Abby?" Maddie's voice jolted her out of her thoughts about Adam. "Did you get that one? The tub and bath products from Francine and Ned?"

"Yes, right." Her face flamed with embarrassment when she realized all eyes were on her, including Adam's. His small smile told her he knew he'd rattled her by showing up unexpectedly.

"Need a break?" Laura asked.

"Of course not. I've got this."

An hour had never passed more slowly. Janey oohed and aahed over every tiny article of clothing and each piece of equipment. How one baby could need so much stuff was beyond Abby. The whole time, she wanted to urge Janey to hurry up.

Adam was in the kitchen with his brothers and the other guys, laughing and talking and seeming completely at ease as he leaned against the counter with a beer in his hand and a smile on his face.

How could he be so calm when she was coming out of her skin?

"That's it," Laura said, relieving Abby of the notebook. "You're fired."

"Sorry. I'm distracted today."

"No kidding." Laura followed Abby's gaze directly to Adam. "And you said it was over... Doesn't look over to me."

"Hush. It *is* over." Abby's words rang hollow to her own ears. All her resolve to resist him had fled the second he walked through the door looking better than any man had a right to look.

Laura snorted in disbelief. "Whatever you say."

After what seemed like hours, Janey finally finished opening the mountain of presents. With Joe's help, she got up and made a beeline directly for the bathroom.

Abby knelt on the floor stuffing wrapping paper into a trash bag, wondering how to go about getting a minute alone with Adam with his family all around them. A shadow fell over her as black leather wing tips appeared before her eyes.

"Come outside with me."

Startled by his voice and his nearness, she looked up at his outstretched hand as a million thoughts spiraled through her mind, including all the reasons why she'd be better off declining his gruffly spoken invitation. But then she made the mistake of looking at his face and at the dazzling blue eyes that were gazing down at her with blatant affection and desire.

"Please?"

As if there'd ever been a choice. She took his hand and let him help her up. The conversation around them died out as they headed for the door, where Grant stopped them with a hand to Adam's chest.

Grant looked at Abby. "Everything okay?"

"Yes," she said, amused and touched by his protectiveness. "Everything's fine."

Grant gave his brother a long look before he lowered his hand and stepped out of their way.

"Sheesh," Adam said when they were outside. "My brothers are the biggest jack asses."

"You love them." Abby followed him down the stairs from the deck to the yard where Mac and Maddie had exchanged vows two summers ago.

"I thought Janey was never going to finish opening her presents," he said as they walked hand-in-hand away from the house toward the meadow that abutted the yard.

"Me, too. I was dying."

"How come?"

She bumped against him. "Like you don't know that you've been driving me crazy!"

"I did exactly what you told me to do."

"You did much more than that, and you're fully aware of what it did to me."

"What did it do? Tell me."

"It made me want things I said I was done with. It made me wish I hadn't already been through this same thing twice before so I could say to hell with it and do what I really wanted to do."

"Which was what?"

"Write back, to start with."

His smile unfolded slowly across his gorgeous face, making his eyes light up with mirth. He stopped walking and turned to her, the late afternoon sunlight bringing out red highlights in his hair that she hadn't noticed before. The light blue shirt made his eyes even more vivid than usual. She'd never been so happy to see anyone in her life. "What would you have said, if you'd written back?"

"That I'm happy you got your company back."

"Are you?"

"Of course I am. That company was yours, and what happened was wrong."

"Yes, it was."

"Did you see Sasha?"

"Once, briefly, when I was packing up my stuff in the apartment. She apologized, I said thank you, and that was the end of it. She knows she screwed up royally."

"Were you…happy to see her?"

He shook his head. "Not one bit. I couldn't be happy to see her when I was so busy thinking about you all the time."

Only with him standing right next to her, with his expensive cologne filling her senses, was she finally able to fully acknowledge how desperately she'd missed him. "You did?"

Nodding, he said, "Did you think about me?"

"*All* the time."

His smile warmed the places inside her that had gone cold when he left.

"I'm glad it worked out for you, Adam."

"It hasn't worked out for me. Not yet."

"What do you mean?"

"Do you know why I went back in the first place?"

"To get back the company that was rightfully yours?"

"Primarily, but it was also to take care of the employees who'd made the company successful. After I was restored as CEO, my first order of business was to recommend to the board that we entertain one of the many offers we received when word of the shakeup in our ranks hit the news. It took a while to find the right buyer. I wanted someone who'd retain my staff."

Abby was still trying to wrap her head around what he was saying when he added, "I sold the company. We signed the papers this morning. Thus the suit."

"You…you sold the company."

"I sold the company."

She looked up at him, daring to hope… "Why?"

"It's not what I want anymore. I want other things now."

"What other things?"

"For one thing, I thought it might be fun to be the island's resident computer geek. Things are a mess around here. They need me."

It wasn't lost on her that he'd used the same words she'd used to describe the fantasy she'd built around him.

He put his arms around her, drew her in close to him and pressed his lips to her forehead. "And then there's this girl I can't seem to stop thinking about. She looks a lot like you, actually. She's sweet and funny and thinks she needs to become someone else entirely before she'll be worthy of the kind of love she deserves. But, you see, she's managed to make this guy fall madly in love with her just by being her perfectly perfect self."

Abby had to be dreaming. Was he really saying these things to her? Was he really in love with her? Was his life in New York really over, and was he home to stay?

"Say something, will you? Please?"

"I love you, too."

And then he was kissing her, and it was all very real and very, *very* perfect.

A loud cheer erupted from Mac and Maddie's deck.

Adam laughed against her lips and held her tighter so she couldn't get away. Not that there was anywhere she'd rather be, even with his entire family watching them.

"I missed you so much," she said, her eyes closed as he held her against his chest.

"I wanted to call you every day, even though I promised I wouldn't. I finally couldn't take it anymore and had to send the texts, even though I was worried they'd make it worse for you."

"They didn't make it worse. They were like a lifeline. It meant so much to know you were suffering, too."

"I was suffering. Big-time. The only reason I went back was to get rid of the company so I could come home to you. I didn't think it would be fair to tell you what was going on until it was a done deal. I was afraid it would drag on for months, but then one of our rivals came forward and made an offer we couldn't refuse. Since they're retaining my entire staff, I didn't even have to stick around to deal with transition issues. I'm done as of ten o'clock this morning. I had Slim waiting for me at the airport, and here I am."

"Is this really happening, or is it just another fantasy?" It had never occurred to her that he'd sell the company and come home.

"Your fantasy was so much better than any reality I've ever known. When faced with running the company again or being here with you, it was a no-brainer."

All the time he'd been gone, he'd been laying the groundwork to come back to her. Abby wondered if a heart could burst from happiness.

"It's about time you finally got your happy ending, sweetheart."

"It's about time you got yours, too."

"You're my happy ending." He kissed her again, this time more intently as he fisted her hair and teased her with his tongue, tempting her with promises of much, much more. Many passionate minutes later, he seemed to remember where they were and who was watching. He glanced at the deck and then back at her. "I guess we've officially gone public."

"Looks that way."

He held out his hand, and Abby happily took it. "What do you say we get busy turning your fantasy into reality?"

"I say I'm all for it."

"And how do you *really* feel about six kids?"

"I think you're freaking crazy."

Laughing, he put his arm around her and kissed the top of her head as they strolled toward the house. "Crazy about you, but your swearing still needs work. We've got time to work on it. Lots and lots of time."

EPILOGUE

"*I* brought you a present," he said hours later when they were finally at her place, finally alone. His entire family, including Grant, had seemed thrilled for them, which had only added to Abby's joy at being with him again.

"What is it?"

He gestured toward the hallway. "Let me get it."

"It's in *my* room?"

"I dropped my stuff here on the way to Mac's."

"You were taking an awful lot for granted, mister."

"I was hopeful." He kissed her and seemed to forget all about her gift until she squiggled free.

"You said something about a present?"

"Ah, right. So I did. Be right back."

Abby watched him walk away, still wanting to pinch herself to believe this day had actually happened.

"Don't look."

She curled up on the sofa and covered her eyes. "I'm not looking."

When he sat next to her, the pervasive odor of leather filled her senses. "Okay, open your eyes."

On the coffee table, he'd laid out a black leather jacket with matching pants and gloves.

"If you want to learn to ride a motorcycle, you need the protective gear." From his side of the sofa, he produced a sleek silver helmet with a built-in face mask that he handed to her.

He understood her so well—better than anyone ever had. "This is awesome! I love it. Thank you."

Taking the helmet from her, he put it on the table. "I can't wait to see your ass in those pants."

Laughing, she hurled herself into his arms and held on tight. "It's the best present I've ever gotten."

"Some girls want diamonds and gold. My girl is happy with leather and tattoos. How did I ever get so lucky?"

Hearing him call her "his girl" was the frosting on the cake of a perfect day. "We both got lucky." With her hand on the back of his head, she dragged him into another kiss. After weeks without him, she couldn't get close enough fast enough.

Starting at the hem and working his way up, he pulled the dress she'd worn to Janey's shower over her head and tossed it aside, taking a minute to appreciate the lacy pink bra and panties she'd worn under it.

She yanked on his belt buckle and moaned with frustration when it refused to give way.

Laughing against her lips, Adam took care of it for her and groaned when she wrapped her hand around his erection. "Condom. Need one."

"No. I'm on the pill. Please...hurry."

"You don't like to hurry."

"I do now."

Still wearing the suit coat, dress shirt and pants, he pushed aside her panties and gave her what she needed in one thrust that made them both gasp from the sheer thrill of it.

She had no thoughts of the past when she took him in effortlessly, as if she'd been born to love this man and this man only. The powerful relief of being back in his arms and their swift, frantic coupling combined to leave her breathless.

"God, Abby... I love you so much. I can't even tell you how much."

"I love you, too," she said, her arms tight around him.

Knowing they had all the time in the world to give each other, she came, sobbing his name, clinging to him as he surged into her, lost in his own release.

Abby had traveled a long and winding road to get to where she belonged. It turned out the third time really was the charm. With her heart and soul filled to overflowing with his love, she'd finally gotten it just right.

Thanks so much for reading *Waiting for Love*! I hope you enjoyed it.

Check out *Time for Love*, David and Daisy's story, available now. Turn the page to read Chapter 1!

TIME FOR LOVE

CHAPTER ONE

Daisy scurried about the spacious living room, picking up toys, folding blankets, plumping pillows and generally doing anything she could to stay busy. It had taken forever to get her friend Maddie's three-year-old son Thomas into bed. He'd been excited to have Daisy babysit for him and his sister Hailey, and Daisy was praying she'd heard the last of both kids as she prepared for her special guest.

Thinking of him made her stomach flutter with nerves. Why in the world had she invited him to come over to keep her company after the kids went to bed? Why in the world was she running around Mac and Maddie's house, straightening up as if it were her own home? As if she'd ever live anywhere this nice.

Maddie sure had tumbled into a pot of gold when she met and married Mac McCarthy. Not that Daisy begrudged her friend's happiness. Quite the opposite, in fact. Maddie was one of the best friends Daisy had ever had, and no one deserved to be happy more than Maddie did.

It's just that sometimes Daisy wondered if she'd ever find the kind of happiness Maddie had with her devoted husband. Daisy's most recent relationship with Truck Henry had turned into a disaster when he got violent with her—more than once. That was over now, and for good this time.

She'd learned her lesson about giving second chances to people who didn't deserve them. Too bad she'd had to suffer badly bruised ribs and a host of other injuries before she wised up. She'd rather not think about those unhappy memories when her new friend David Lawrence was coming over to hang out with her.

Why had she invited him?

It had been a weak moment the night before. He'd taken her out for a lovely dinner at Stephanie's Bistro and had asked what she was doing the next night, which was how she'd ended up inviting him to her babysitting gig.

Now she felt like a foolish teenager waiting for the captain of the football team to show up. No doubt he had far better things to do than hang out with her on one of his rare nights off. He'd probably felt obligated to accept her invitation, and the whole thing would be painfully awkward.

When it came right down to it, they had absolutely nothing in common. She was a hard-working—if perpetually poor—housekeeper at the McCarthy's hotel, and he was the island's only doctor. She'd come from a family that invented the term dysfunctional, whereas he'd been raised with his sisters on the island and gone to a top college and medical school in Boston.

She'd dated one loser after another while he'd been engaged to Mac's sister, Janey McCarthy Cantrell. Janey was married now to Joe Cantrell and expecting their first child at the end of the summer.

Daisy had never heard what went wrong between David and Janey, but their long relationship had ended suddenly two summers ago. She could've asked Maddie and almost had a few times, but she'd been unable to bring herself to actually pose the question.

In the meantime, David had been so nice about coming by to check on her injuries and so gentle with her as she recovered. They'd fallen into an unlikely friendship that continued when she stopped by the clinic a couple of times to share the influx of food her friends had brought her. David worked so hard that he often missed meals, and it had seemed only fitting to share with him when he'd been so good to her.

It was foolish, she knew, to let her heart get all pitter-pattery over a guy who was just being nice to her because that was his job. It was doubly foolish, she also knew, to nurture the world-class crush that had come from his many kindnesses. Thus, it was triply foolish to be hoping that something might come of the time they'd been spending together.

Romance, Daisy thought, *is so fraught with peril.* At least it always had been for her. She simply chose the wrong men. The habit dated back to high school when she'd yearned for a boy who turned out to be a cheating pig. Next came a lovely guy who became a mean drunk and then another with a gambling addiction she'd failed to recognize until he'd wiped out her meager savings account.

Then came Truck and his meth addiction and meaty fists.

Daisy shuddered thinking of the awful night when Truck most likely would've raped and killed her if the island's police chief, Blaine Taylor, hadn't broken down her door and stopped him from finishing the job.

A knock on the sliding glass door made her startle. Had she really wasted all that precious time thinking about things that couldn't be changed? And now David was here and she probably looked like a wreck after wrangling babies all night. She combed her fingers through her long, blonde hair, hoping to restore order as she walked over to the door to unlock it.

"Hey," he said as he came in smelling of fresh air and a hint of cologne that made her want to snuggle in close to him. He wore a navy blue button-down Gansett Island shirt with khaki shorts.

Daisy had never seen him dressed so casually. "Hey."

"Are they asleep?"

"I think so. I'm told it's a minute-to-minute thing."

He smiled, revealing a flash of straight, white teeth that made her want to sigh with pleasure. She had a thing for a great smile, and David Lawrence's smile was one of the best she'd ever encountered. Coupled with thick, dark hair and serious brown eyes, that smile was downright potent. Even the slight bump in his otherwise perfect nose was appealing.

"Is that..." He brushed at something on her shoulder, making her nerve endings tingle. "Spit-up?"

"Oh crap," Daisy said, mortified. Heat singed her cheeks and made her scalp itch. "I forgot that Hailey nailed me at bedtime. I'll just run up and borrow something of Maddie's. She won't mind."

"Don't bother." He took her hand and led her to the kitchen, where he wet a paper towel and went to work on the spot on her shoulder.

Daisy had never been more acutely aware of her own intake of oxygen than she was in that moment with his face about six inches from hers as he worked with single-minded purpose to clean the spot off her thin top. While focusing on the shine of his dark hair, she concentrated on drawing in enough air to remain conscious without gulping in the deep breaths she desperately needed.

"There," he said after an interminable few minutes. As he backed away from her, his fingers brushed against her neck, and damn if she didn't gasp. "Sorry."

"Oh no, don't be sorry. I...um..."

"What's wrong, Daisy?" He studied her in that deep, dark, serious way he did so well.

"Nothing," she said in a cheerful tone that sounded forced, even to her. "Want a beer or some wine or something?"

"I'd rather know why you seem so uncomfortable. I thought we had a nice time last night. I was looking forward to seeing you tonight, but if this isn't a good time, I can go."

"No, I don't want you to go." Daisy covered her face with her hands. "I'm making a total mess of things."

"Tell me what's wrong." He covered her hands with his and gave a very gentle tug that revealed her eyes.

"I'm nervous, and that makes me feel stupid."

"Why are you nervous?"

"Because you're here. Because I invited you, and I wasn't sure if you really wanted to come or you just said you would because I asked you to and you didn't really want to—"

And then he was kissing her, and Daisy's brain cells positively fried the second his lips landed on hers.

He was a really good kisser, as if that was any big surprise. His lips were firm but soft and moved over hers in a light caress that was neither too much nor too little. It was just right, and quite simply one of the best kisses she'd ever received. Just as she began to relax and kiss him back, he withdrew.

"Sorry," he said, his forehead leaning against hers. "I didn't mean to do that."

"I'm glad you did that."

"You are?"

She smiled, because really, how could she not? He was so cute. "Maybe you'll do it again sometime?"

"We might be able to arrange that."

Daisy discovered she was no longer nervous about having him there. Now she was nervous for a whole other reason, a much better reason. "Do you want to watch a movie?"

He took a step back from her. "Sure."

"Maddie left some on the coffee table if you want to see if any of them interest you. Popcorn?"

"I won't say no to that."

"How about a beer?"

"Will you have one, too?"

"I'm going to stick with Coke."

"Then I will, too."

While she made the popcorn in an oil popper that Maddie had once told her dated back to her high school years but still worked perfectly, he went into the living room to check out the movies. Reliving the kiss, Daisy was acutely aware of him in the next room.

What did it mean? What was he thinking? Was he looking for a summer fling or something more lasting? What was she looking for?

335

Nothing serious. That was for sure. After what had happened with Truck, she'd been prepared to swear off all men permanently. But then David kept showing up, chipping away at her defenses one visit at a time.

"These are all chick flicks," he said.

"In case you haven't noticed, I am a chick."

"Oh, I've definitely noticed."

Daisy nearly swallowed her tongue.

"Have you seen *Love & Other Drugs?*" he asked, as if he hadn't just totally rocked her with that comment. "Looks kind of good. A girl with Parkinson's falls in love with a drug rep."

"Leave it to the doctor to pick a medical movie."

"Um, I believe it's a chick-flick romance that happens to include a disease. There's got to be something in it for me."

"Who is in it?"

"Jake Gyllenhaal and Anne Hathaway."

"I should probably mention at the outset that I have a huge crush on Jake Gyllenhaal. I'd hate for you to be threatened by my ogling."

"I believe I'm man enough to handle your crush."

As she carried the bowl of popcorn and two Cokes into the living room, she tried to remember the last time she'd enjoyed a conversation with a man as much as she enjoyed every conversation with him. He never talked down to her or made her feel like she wasn't as smart as him, even though she was nowhere near as smart as him.

After she put the bowl and sodas on the coffee table, he handed her the movie and she popped it into the DVD player. She sat on the sofa, careful to leave at least a foot between them, and reached for the popcorn bowl.

David opened both sodas and put them on coasters.

As she dipped into the bowl, his hand brushed against hers. Daisy pulled hers back and then felt like an idiot. So his hand had touched hers. Why did she have to react like a teenage girl on a first date?

The movie's opening credits had just begun when Daisy heard a noise at the top of the stairs. She handed the bowl to David, got up to

336

go investigate and found Thomas sitting behind the baby gate, his blanket and teddy bear with him.

"What're you doing up, honey?"

"I want Mommy."

"Mommy and Daddy are out with their friends, but they'll be home soon."

"Who were you talking to?" Thomas looked around her to see who was visiting.

"You know Dr. David, right?"

"He gave me a shot," Thomas said, his feathery brows knitting into an adorable scowl. "It hurted."

"Come here, sweetie." Daisy extended her arms, lifted him over the gate with the blanket and bear and carried him downstairs. "We have a visitor," she said to David.

"Hi there, Thomas," David said.

Thomas burrowed his face into her neck.

"I believe Thomas is annoyed with you. Something about a shot?"

"Ah, yes. Sorry about that, pal. Just trying to keep you healthy."

"It hurted," Daisy said, earning a smile from David.

"Do you know what else is really important to staying healthy?" David asked.

Thomas turned toward David.

"What's that?" Daisy asked.

"Sleep. We need lots and lots of sleep, especially when we're three years old and our bodies are using so much energy to grow."

"I growed," Thomas said. "Mommy measured me on the wall."

"If you want to keep growing and someday be big and strong like Daddy," Daisy said, "you have to go to sleep." She drew the blanket up to his shoulders and rubbed his back. He popped his thumb into his mouth and cuddled up to his bear.

As Daisy brushed her lips over Thomas's hair, her own hair slid over her face.

Before she could tend to it, David had it secured behind her ear. The brush of his fingertips against her cheek and ear gave her goose bumps. She ventured a glance at him and saw that he was watching her with sexy eyes attuned to her every move.

Oh my.

Time for Love is available in print from *Amazon.com* and other online retailers, or you can purchase a signed copy from Marie's store at *shop.marieforce.com.*

OTHER BOOKS BY MARIE FORCE

Contemporary Romances

The Gansett Island Series

Book 1: Maid for Love *(Mac & Maddie)*

Book 2: Fool for Love *(Joe & Janey)*

Book 3: Ready for Love *(Luke & Sydney)*

Book 4: Falling for Love *(Grant & Stephanie)*

Book 5: Hoping for Love *(Evan & Grace)*

Book 6: Season for Love *(Owen & Laura)*

Book 7: Longing for Love *(Blaine & Tiffany)*

Book 8: Waiting for Love *(Adam & Abby)*

Book 9: Time for Love *(David & Daisy)*

Book 10: Meant for Love *(Jenny & Alex)*

Book 10.5: Chance for Love, *A Gansett Island Novella (Jared & Lizzie)*

Book 11: Gansett After Dark *(Owen & Laura)*

Book 12: Kisses After Dark *(Shane & Katie)*

Book 13: Love After Dark *(Paul & Hope)*

Book 14: Celebration After Dark *(Big Mac & Linda)*

Book 15: Desire After Dark *(Slim & Erin)*

Book 16: Light After Dark *(Mallory & Quinn)*

Book 17: Victoria & Shannon (Episode 1)

Book 18: Kevin & Chelsea (Episode 2)

A Gansett Island Christmas Novella

Book 19: Mine After Dark *(Riley & Nikki)*

Book 20: Yours After Dark *(Finn & Chloe)*

Book 21: Trouble After Dark *(Deacon & Julia)*

The Green Mountain Series

Book 1: All You Need Is Love *(Will & Cameron)*

Book 2: I Want to Hold Your Hand *(Nolan & Hannah)*

Book 3: I Saw Her Standing There *(Colton & Lucy)*

Book 4: And I Love Her *(Hunter & Megan)*

Novella: You'll Be Mine *(Will & Cam's Wedding)*

Book 5: It's Only Love *(Gavin & Ella)*

Book 6: Ain't She Sweet *(Tyler & Charlotte)*

The Butler Vermont Series

(Continuation of the Green Mountain Series)

Book 1: Every Little Thing *(Grayson & Emma)*

Book 2: Can't Buy Me Love *(Mary & Patrick)*

Book 3: Here Comes the Sun *(Wade & Mia)*

Book 4: Till There Was You *(Lucas)*

The Treading Water Series

Book 1: Treading Water

Book 2: Marking Time

Book 3: Starting Over

Book 4: Coming Home

Historical Romances

The Gilded Series

Book 1: Duchess by Deception

Book 2: Deceived by Desire

Single Titles

Five Years Gone

One Year Home

Sex Machine

Sex God

Georgia on My Mind

True North

The Fall

Everyone Loves a Hero

Love at First Flight

Line of Scrimmage

Erotic Romance

The Erotic Quantum Series

Book 1: Virtuous *(Flynn & Natalie)*

Book 2: Valorous *(Flynn & Natalie)*

Book 3: Victorious *(Flynn & Natalie)*

Book 4: Rapturous *(Addie & Hayden)*

Book 5: Ravenous *(Jasper & Ellie)*

Book 6: Delirious *(Kristian & Aileen)*

Book 7: Outrageous *(Emmett & Leah)*

Book 8: Famous *(Marlowe)*

Romantic Suspense

The Fatal Series

One Night With You, *A Fatal Series Prequel Novella*

Book 1: Fatal Affair

Book 2: Fatal Justice

Book 3: Fatal Consequences

Book 3.5: Fatal Destiny, *the Wedding Novella*

Book 4: Fatal Flaw

Book 5: Fatal Deception

Book 6: Fatal Mistake

Book 7: Fatal Jeopardy

Book 8: Fatal Scandal

Book 9: Fatal Frenzy

Book 10: Fatal Identity

Book 11: Fatal Threat

Book 12: Fatal Chaos

Book 13: Fatal Invasion

Book 14: Fatal Reckoning

Book 15: Fatal Accusation

Single Title

The Wreck

ABOUT THE AUTHOR

Marie Force is the *New York Times* bestselling author of contemporary romance, romantic suspense, historical romance and erotic romance. Her series include the indie-published Gansett Island, Treading Water, Butler, Vermont and Quantum Series as well as the Fatal Series from Harlequin Books.

Her books have sold more than 9 million copies worldwide, have been translated into more than a dozen languages and have appeared on the *New York Times* bestseller list 30 times. She is also a *USA Today* and *Wall Street Journal* bestseller, a Speigel bestseller in Germany, a frequent speaker and publishing workshop presenter.

Her goals in life are simple—to finish raising two happy, healthy, productive young adults, to keep writing books for as long as she possibly can and to never be on a flight that makes the news.

Join Marie's mailing list on her website at marieforce.com for news about new books and upcoming appearances in your area. Follow her on Facebook at www.Facebook.com/MarieForceAuthor and on Instagram at www.instagram.com/marieforceauthor/. Contact Marie at marie@marieforce.com.

Lightning Source UK Ltd.
Milton Keynes UK
UKHW020718091220
374848UK00009B/2240